RISE OF THE DAWNBRINGER

THE BORNBANE SERIES
BOOK ONE

I.A. TAKERIAN

AN ANCIENT DARKNESS. A LAND UNRAVELED.
THE THREADS OF FATE TORN ASUNDER.

RISE
OF THE
DAWNBRINGER

THE BORNBANE SERIES

I.A. TAKERIAN

This is a work of fiction. The characters, incidents, and dialogues are products of the author's imagination and are not to be construed as real. Any resemblance to actual events or persons, living or dead, is entirely coincidental.

Copyright © 2022 by Isabeau A. Takerian

All rights reserved. No part of this book may be reproduced in any form or by any electronic or mechanical means, including information storage and retrieval systems, without written permission from the author, except for the use of brief quotations in a book review.

Cover Art by Moonpress.com

Map drawn by Rachael Ward

Chapter headings drawn by Etheric Tales

ISBN: 9798352229811

ACKNOWLEDGMENTS

To Mama and Dada, whose love is bound by the threads of destiny eternal.

To Amber, who waded the vast seas of chaos to find Zenafrost.

To Mina and Garrick, for their constant, unwavering loyalty.

To Charlotte, the first to stand beside me and take up arms.

To Kris, for giving his voice to my world.

To Teppi, for reminding me that there is strength in gentle sweetness.

And to all those who have stood as the shield against impossible darkness.
This is for you.

PROLOGUE

Excerpt from The Book of Delinvalian Histories:

*I*n the beginning of all things, the Zenoths came from the Far Beyond, well past the sun and moon and stars. Each being, made of pure energy, harnessed wondrous magicks. Some manipulated the earth on which they strode, some the mighty waters, and some harnessed pure sunlight. All could create entire worlds, lush with green trees and crystal blue waters, yet none could create ever-changing sentient life. Dissatisfied by their lonely existence, the Zenoths met to join their powers as one. From this brief but harmonious union rose a new world, a world unlike any that had ever come before; mighty enough to host the Zenoths and their powerful magicks.

This place, with its rolling hills, sapphire waters, and ample forests, was to be called Zenafrost: their namesake. From their magicks stepped forth the first breaths of sentient life; new beings, created in the Zenoths image. So overwhelming was this union that the even earth of Zenafrost developed a soul of its own. It began to create new magicks, that soaked through the whole of the world.

The Zenoths, overjoyed with their beautiful new home, stayed to watch as these lives grew. As a sign of their devotion to the children of

Zenafrost, these creators bestowed a gift. A gift that would grant all who took it magick of their own.

But with these new powers came grave consequence. Alongside the people of Zenafrost, the mysterious magicks of the earth grew mightier with each passing day. And this wondrous surge of new power drew the attention of one whose soul was already teetering on the edge of the abyss: Mezilmoth.

Mezilmoth was a Zenoth obsessed with power. He saw Zenafrost not as a unique thing of beauty, but as an empire waiting to be seized. With this dark goal encompassing his every thought, the magick within him began to change. What was once pure and bright became foul and blackened. His need for power warped him, driving him beyond the brink of madness.

Mezilmoth became consumed with becoming the one, all-powerful being to rule not only Zenafrost, but all the cosmos. Thus, he demanded that the Zenoths, and the people they so adored, bow down before him as their one true God. This defilement of Mezilmoth birthed a new, dark magick.

Using his blighted powers, Mezilmoth corrupted thousands of souls in Zenafrost. All he touched fell before him, twisted and bent to his bidding. War between Mezilmoth's forces and the people of Zenafrost broke out across the land. The Zenoths, vastly weakened by the darkening of magick, devised a desperate plan. They would seal him and his madness away.

Forever.

The Zenoths travelled to the very edge of Zenafrost and raised a massive expanse of land into the sky, well beyond the reach of those far below. Together, they tore a door through the very fabric of the universe that opened into a place within nothingness, a realm at the End of All Things. Here is where they sealed Mezilmoth away, trapped behind the Dark Gate forever more.

But the damage caused by Mezilmoth's conquest was irreversible. Now fragmented and impure, magick had been forever changed in Zenafrost.

In the muck of the swamps to the North, Mezilmoth's first followers raised the kingdom of Ylastra. The powers of these magick users, driven mad when deprived of their master's energy, mutated into Chaos Magick. The Ylastrian people were left doomed to a life of murderous rage.

Far to the East, in the shadow of the great mountains, rose a race of people who came to be known as the Dreads. Unlike the Ylastrians, the Dreads had survived the change in energy, and become true beings of darkness. Their powers were that of the rawest evil.

To the West, amidst plentiful crops and flower flecked meadows, lived those born without the Zenoth's gift of magick. Humans, for the most part just and strong, built their homes there in the Kingdom of Delinval: a monument of hope and prosperity.

But Mezilmoth the Deceiver had not been silenced. His corruption began to weaken the Dark Gate, allowing his blight to seep into the land and whisper darkness into the world.

Like a dagger from the shadows, swift and unexpected, the Dread Queen swept forth with a terrible army. Driven by the whispers of the Deceiver, she rained fire and brimstone upon Zenafrost. Forests, villages, and fortified cities fell before the Dreads. She gave no quarter, granted no mercy, spared no life.

She burned the city of Delinval to the ground and gathered the children at the gates. And with her dark magick, she set each innocent ablaze as a final declaration of war.

From the ashes of this great battle, King Grathiel rose as hero of not only Delinval, but of all Zenafrost. Striking an accord, he joined forces with the Ylastrians and set out to stop the Dread Queen for the sake of all humanity. Using military might combined with chaos magick, King Grathiel turned the tide of the Great War. The Dread forces were bested, and their bloodied, beaten Queen was brought before the Kingdom of Delinval to pay for her crimes.

The people demanded her head.

Filled with insatiable greed as the dust of war barely settled, the Ylastrians rose against Delinval in attempts to take the throne and land for themselves. Even with the Delinvalian forces dwindled, wise and cunning King Grathiel predicted their plot and struck them down in one swift battle. This final act of betrayal made magick seem beyond salvation; a thing twisted and torn into the darkness it now wrought.

In pursuit of peace, Grathiel struck one last pact with the Ylastrians. He would cease the bloodshed, but the Ylastrians would never again be allowed to roam outside the borders of their black kingdom. The Great Truce was struck, and the cloud of death finally vanished.

And so began the Age of Purity. Though the Dread's darkness had ravaged the lands beyond, within the shining kingdom of Delinval, magick and war became a thing of the past. Under the care and protection of their savior, King Grathiel, they flourished in their peace.

CHAPTER 1
IN THE BEGINNING

The kingdom of Delinval lay in stark contrast to the mysterious, war-torn lands of Zenafrost beyond. High walls of white stone surrounded its forested borders, glittering with murals made of sun-bright crystals depicting great battles, monumental wealth, and the joy of the Delinvalian people. Soldiers lounged and paced along the parapets above the gates, though not for security or a show of strength; the kingdom had not known hardship or enemy for nearly twenty-one years.

Inside the walls, the inner city bustled with life and the sounds of prosperity. City-folk, of high and low birth, roamed the crowded cobblestone streets in the warmth of the day. Barkers called from their shops, shouting out wares and foodstuffs, and blacksmiths, serenaded by the sound of their clanging hammers, pounded out their latest works of art.

The center of the city lay dressed in streamers and flowery wreaths in preparation for a grand celebration, while the streets themselves were dotted with small carts loaded down with wooden swords and hobby horses. A growing, chattering crowd had already begun to gather around open booths and tables to laugh, drink, and enjoy the evening's festivities.

Atop the hill at the very back of the city, facing down the steep mountainside to the ocean below, lay Castle Delinval. Its mighty, glimmering towers could be seen for miles in every direction, its glory a testament to the love King Grathiel had for his people. It had been the king and his armies that led that final march, against all odds, to end the war over two decades ago. He who had lain waste to the Dread forces and brought their Queen to kneel in her death.

It was said the Dreads began the war in the name of their "great and almighty one." The Deceiver: Mezilmoth.

"And that is why, twenty-one years later, we celebrate our victory in the Great War with the Festival of End. To honor our brave knights, and to give thanks to our savior, King Grathiel who, with the stroke of his mighty sword, ended the threat to our bountiful lands and—And are you *listening*, Mara, for Beyond's sake!"

Lady Lenorei slammed her book down onto the desk, startling Mara. She had been staring out the window again, lost in fancy, wishing she were anywhere else in the world but here.

Eyes still glazed, she turned to stare into Lady Lenorei's annoyed face. "I'm sorry, what?"

The woman's gaunt face pinched tighter. Mara had come to know that expression well over the years; a lecture usually followed.

Mara groaned loudly, threw back her head, and raked an agitated hand through her mess of tight curls. "Every year," she grumbled. "Every single year before the festival we go over this, Lady Len. I could recite this part of our history in my sleep."

Lady Lenorei bristled at the shortening of her name, just as she'd done every time Mara had said it since childhood. The woman folded her arms and clicked her tongue. "Yes, every year. And every year, you seem to find a way to completely ignore everything I tell you." She raised an appraising eyebrow. "You know your duties and responsibilities, Mara. You must know all your histories before you take your seat in the court."

Mara grimaced at this. Her parents, like so many others, had died during the Great War. Her father, the crown prince and captain of the castle guard, had fallen during one of the many blood-fueled battles. Her mother had then died in childbirth, due, rumor had it, to the heartbreak of her losing her one true love. This tragedy had left Mara in the care of her uncle, King Grathiel of Delinval. And since the king had no children of his own, it meant that she, Mara, stood as next in line to the crown; a fact that she'd been reminded of every single day since before she could remember.

Though she knew it was a profound honor, Mara's right to the crown had caused her nothing but hardship throughout her life. The ladies of the court threw her cold looks and whispered venomous insults behind her back. Their daughters used to steal her toys and tear them into pieces; they once took Mara into the woods for a game and, when she was lost, abandoned her there for the night. Now in their adulthood, they joined their mothers in their quiet damnation of her existence.

The boys who lived in the castle presented an entirely different problem. Cackling, they taunted her, burnt her already night-black curls with candles, and pushed her in the mud before High Tea. But the older Mara got, the less the boys bullied and the more they tried to grope. It was a change their fathers all encouraged, knowing Mara could be their family's ticket to the crown. She found she much preferred the malice of the women.

At least Adrian didn't put his hands on her, even if she could see his romantic ideas in his weighted gaze. She hoped he wouldn't get too serious about it; she would be lost without her best friend, the only one who spoke to her like a real person. At least his interest kept the other lords somewhat at bay. But at almost twenty-one, Mara was running out of time to hide. With her birthday quickly approaching, she needed to learn everything required to take her seat beside her uncle in their court. She would be given more responsibility not just within the castle, but also with the kingdom and their people. And though she adored her city and knew what her future eventually held, she could think of nothing less thrilling than studying the ins-and-outs of Delinvalian politics. Particularly on a day like today.

"Please, Len!" Mara begged. She clasped her hands together in a prayerful pose and stuck out her bottom lip. "I will do anything you ask of me! I will go over every book and every scroll. I will listen to you go on for *hours* about your dissections of the early religious tomes. But let me do it *tomorrow*. The festival's today! And we're wasting it away up here learning new depths to the word 'boring'!"

Lady Lenorei took off her too-large glasses to rub the bridge of her hooked nose. Frustration etched its way across her aged forehead. Finally, she sighed, closing the thick book—*The Book of Delinvalian Histories*—with a snap. "Nothing changes with you, Mara. Whether you're ten, fifteen or twenty. I've never met a less patient lady of the court in all my years of service to this kingdom. One would think you'd have a modicum of decorum, considering your station."

Excitement dancing in her eyes, Mara let the jab slide

past her. "So…does that mean we're done?" She was already halfway out of her seat, bouncing with anticipation.

Lady Lenorei turned from Mara, waving her hand dismissively, and Mara rushed for the door.

"Be here tomorrow—*before* lunch, Mara!" Lady Lenorei called after her. "An excess of drinking at tonight's ceremony will not excuse you!"

Mara rushed through the castle hallways, barreling past bowing lords and ladies along the way. She paid them little mind. They feigned respect solely because she would be their queen one day. Before she'd even started up the twisting staircase to the tower, she could hear their whispers hissing up behind her.

"*Deformed,*" one voice said.

"*Absolutely grotesque,*" another said, bursting into laughter.

They were talking about her ears again. The tops had been fused to her head when she was born, and the midwife had been forced to slice through skin and cartilage to separate them. Left with deep, angry scars across the tops of her ears and up the sides of her head, she'd developed a habit of tugging on her curls to hide them when she was nervous. Both children and adults could be cruel, and their hateful slurs used to make Mara sob till all hours of the night, alone and destroyed in her bed. But as she grew, and as she discovered a deep friendship with Adrian, she'd begun to lean into things she loved and ignore the things she didn't. Now, insults tended to slide off her back like water.

The hateful words grew fainter as she climbed, soon becoming too distant to hear.

Arriving at her chambers, at the end of the tower hallway, she bowed her head to the pacing guard, and slipped in through her door.

The curtains to her windows were drawn, and crystals hanging from the ceiling twinkled in dim candlelight, most likely lit by servants who were constantly trying to clean her room. Based on the remaining clutter, it looked as if they had given up before they'd even begun, only bothering to straighten her bed.

The floor was still covered in drawings she'd made of the city the day before. Broken bits of hard paint were scattered throughout the debris strewn all over the stained marble floor. Dried herbs and flowers hung from the white walls surrounding her, covering every inch not already taken up by poems and pictures.

Mara crossed the room, the train of her skirt pulling paint and paper behind her. She flung open the curtains, threw the shutters wide. A gust of wind swept past her, twisting through her hair. Smiling, she closed her eyes, breathing in the smell of sweets and flowers from the city far below. Music had already started up in the square, combining with the joyous sound of celebrating voices.

She hurried out of her dark green dress and stood before the open window. The cool air nipped at her bare skin, and her smile widened. This was going to be a momentous day.

Tugging her hair up into a ponytail, she grabbed her leathers and began dressing enthusiastically. In Delinval, the Celebration of the End brought Mara's favorite thing in the whole world: the Tournaments. Every year since she could remember, she'd sat beside her uncle in the stands, watching the men of the kingdom test their mettle in contests of jousting, archery, and hand-to-hand combat; the Tournaments gave them all a chance to win glory without the bloodshed of battle.

Many of the higher born ladies found the Tournaments too rough for their tender sensibilities. Mara loved them all. But the sword-fighting really made her heart raced.

She would never forget the first time she had watched a real fight, the sound of metal racketing through the air. Lord Lingrain had caught one of the King's knights in his wife's bedchambers, resulting in his immediate challenge, a duel for honor and what remained of his dignity. Mara had stared in awe and wonderment, watching what looked like an angry dance, full of fury, passion, and focus.

Afterward, she had begged her uncle to let her take lessons. The members of the court had scoffed at this, every lady turning up their nose at the notion. "*A lady, learning the swords—let alone the princess?!*" they had proclaimed. "*Utter lunacy!*"

But King Grathiel had laughed at them. "Let the girl learn the sword," he had said, waving them off. "If it keeps her from running amuck through the castle all day, let her learn whatever she wishes."

Mara stood before the mirror in her bedroom, evaluating herself. Her body wasn't built like other ladies her age. Hers was full, with rounded curves and firm muscle sliding beneath subtle softness—difficult to conceal beneath leather armor. She had gathered supplies to stuff her armor—a bit of woolen batting collected from the castle seamstress, and shredded straw from the knight's stables. Now, breasts bound in a wrap and padded in all the right places, her usual curvy figure looked straight and blocked with no signs of womanhood.

She beamed at her reflection. "Yes," she said. She grabbed her metal helmet from her dresser and pushed it down over her ponytail. "Yes, this will absolutely work."

No one at the festival would ever suspect she was a

woman, never mind their princess. There wasn't even a single black curl poking out from beneath her full-coverage helmet that hid the wide smile on her face. Her grand scheme was going to work. It *would*.

With her twenty-first birthday came the impending reality of an arranged marriage. Her uncle was already in talks with many of the nobles about whose heir would take her hand. It was simply expected of her to comply. Just another part of her pre-planned life as future queen of Delinval. This left Mara with only one choice. She had to prove to her uncle that she was strong enough to rule on her own; that she didn't need a man sitting beside her on the throne to run the kingdom with a fair but iron fist.

She would do something wild, something totally unexpected, something she had only dreamt of since she was a little girl: She would win the swords at the Tournament and prove her worth beyond all doubt, in front of the King *and* her people.

With her longsword slung high on her back, Mara slipped out of her chambers. This time, no lords or ladies stopped to bow as she passed. On the contrary, no one spared her a passing glance as she made her way through the castle and out into the sunlit courtyard. Knowing she could slip through them all unseen gave her a thrill of excitement. It was refreshing to walk the halls of her home without worrying about forced smiles and hateful whispers.

When she reached the courtyard, Mara stared in awe at the decorations; the castle steward and his staff had outdone themselves this year. Reality set in as a crowd of smiling, laughing people walked past her waving tournament flags. Nervous butterflies flitted through her stomach, and she suddenly felt slightly nauseated. *This will work*, she reminded herself. *And then what?* her brain prodded back.

She shook her head clear of those thoughts before they

could sit heavy on her chest. *Not today*, she thought. She would not let that darkness bring her low today.

Mara loved her people. And, one day, after her uncle had passed on to the Beyond, she would rule them with the same firm care and understanding that he had. But she'd always felt off about that, like a riddle with no true answer; there was no better way to describe the feeling. It was as if she'd been born in the wrong place, at the wrong time, to the wrong people. If she could have flown away on her daydreams of battles and sword fighting, she would have done so long ago.

She sometimes wondered if the lords and ladies were right about her. Perhaps a more devoted education would silence that nagging voice begging to escape. Perhaps what she needed *was* to mature, to settle and bow before a husband. The mere notion alone sickened her, squeezing around her heart, and leaving her breathless.

Gulping down her nerves, she rounded the corner and emerged into the Grand Arena. The already large crowd piled into the stands around the dais that her uncle and the court would soon fill.. The flutters in her stomach began anew, but she forced them down again, lowered her head and headed towards the combatants' tents.

A beady-eyed man sat at a small table near the entrance, smelling like he hadn't showered in days. He scowled up at her approach. "Aye?" he snarled, holding out his hand.

Mara had prepared for this. She pulled ten gold pieces from her breast pocket to pay the entry fee.

The man bit each of the coins, testing to see that they were genuine, and she cringed at his yellowed teeth and greying gums. He pocketed the coins, picked up a quill, and looked down at a long piece of parchment. "Name?"

Mara froze. She had so carefully set everything up, but

it hadn't occurred to her think up a name?! Mentally kicking herself, she cleared her throat. "Errrm..." She stared out over his head, her eyes landing on the pigpen across the river, and the words tumbled out before she could stop them. "My name is Pigsmy," she blurted. She cleared her throat, remembering to make her voice sound rough and masculine. "Pigsmy Rivertrough."

She looked down at the beady-eyed man, her eyes wide beneath her helmet visor, hoping she'd sounded convincing. The man nodded, scribbling down the name she'd given, and then motioned behind him toward to the opening of the tent.

Mara straightened, feeling more confident that her plan seemed to be working.

The inside of the tent smelled enough to make her gag.

Every type of man was there—tall, small, pudgy, slight —all packed together in the stifling heat; sweating, swearing, drinking. A few of them were throwing punches on one end of the tent, sending the bulk of the crowd back towards the other side.

Mara found herself squeezed in amongst them all, but not a one of them looked at her twice. She was by far the shortest in attendance, even in her padded armor, the smallest.

She poked her head up through a gap in the crowd and looked around until her eyes fell on the other swordsmen, gathered towards the back of the tent, awaiting their call. There was only a handful of them, five in all. Most men preferred the glory to be gained from the joust, the more celebrated contest amongst the nobles.

Her eyes fell on a tall, handsome man with a bored expression on his face. His honey-colored eyes were staring coldly across the room, eyeing the fight on the other side of the tent with mild disgust.

Smiling beneath her visor, she elbowed her way through the crowd until she stood directly in front of him.

He gazed down at her, raising one eyebrow lazily. "What's your problem?" he asked in a tone much huskier than any Mara had heard her friend use before. "Never seen a lord this close before?"

Mara rolled her eyes and replied just loud enough for him to hear. "Try not to sound so full of yourself, Adrian. Your ego will suffocate us all in here."

His jaw dropped, the color draining from his face.

She grinned beneath her visor. "Surprise!"

Regaining himself, Adrian wrapped his hand around her arm and yanked her away from the other four combatants. He pressed her back against the canvas tent and leaned in, effectively wedging his body between her and the crowd.

"Have you completely lost your bloody mind?!" he hissed at her. He looked around them, eyes wide with panic.

Mara puffed out her chest, pushing him back from her.

"You know I've been training for this!" she hissed back. Pride made her stand a little taller. "I've been telling you my plans for months now. What did you think I was talking about?!"

"I didn't think you were actually *serious*!" He groaned, dropping his head into his hands. "I thought it was just your motivation for practice! Everyone has dreams, no matter how *foolhardy* they may be!" He shook his head. "I can't let you do this. Absolutely not. What if you get hurt—

"You will not *let* me do it?! I am not a dog, or a child to be scolded. I *am* doing this. I have to prove to him—"

"Prove *what*?!" Adrian looked ready to cry. "Mar, your

uncle isn't going to let you out of your commitments just because you entered some stupid sword fight!"

"Win," she corrected firmly.

Adrian pulled his eyes up to gaze into hers through the visor of her helmet. "Pardon?"

"He will listen to my wishes because I am going to *win* this stupid sword fight. And if you try to stop me, I'll tell that mousey man at the entrance that I caught you trying to steal his coin pouch. And then what will you do, your lordship?"

Mara's tone dripped with cruel promise.

Adrian stared at her, mouth agape and eyes flashing with anger and worry. Finally, he shook his head and heaved an exaggerated sighed. "You're a real thorn in my side, Mara. Do as you wish, I know better than to try and stop you," he said, much to Mara's relief. "But if the King asks, I knew *nothing* about this. I already regret that I do, Zenoths bless me."

CHAPTER 2
EXPECTING THE EXPECTED

In the first round, Mara faced Tristan Revalin, who, though twice her age, competed in the sword contest every year. Incredibly fit, Revalin awaited each challenge shirtless, showing off his rippling muscles until the last minute, when he would finally don his quilted shirt and chest plate. His helmet visor left the lower half of his face exposed, and Mara cringed inwardly at his dark, arrogant smirk. She hunkered low and prepared for his initial onslaught.

The moment the bell rang, Revalin lunged for her. Mara pivoted out of the way with ease. Revalin tumble past as if in slow motion. Her years of training with the captain of Grathiel's guard, not to mention her frequent sparring sessions with Adrian—who was one of Delinval's finest knights—had more than readied her for close combat. It was going to take a great deal more than brute strength to best her.

As Revalin stumbled past, she took the opening and slammed the butt of her sword into the middle of his back.

He went sprawling into the dirt. The crowd rose to their feet, cheering and roaring with laughter.

Mara had no time to celebrate.

Revalin bounced back to his feet, his smirk changed to a snarl. Like an injured bear, he took after her. She met his blade head-on. The force of the impact drove her heels a full foot back through the soft dirt. Thinking he had her, he disengaged, moving away to ready his next attack.

Mara knew better than to give him the chance to regroup.

Arcing her sword wide, she slashed out at him again and again, always moving forward, always keeping a constant, even distance between their two bodies. Revalin's snarl faded into a deep frown of concentration. Before he dealt a single blow, Mara knew the match was over. The man's footing slipped. She pressed her advantage. His sword flew from his hand and dropped into the dirt. Bested, Revalin fell to his knees before her.

The crowd erupted in uproarious cheers, filling her heart with pleasure and pride. Reaching out, she offered a hand to help Revalin to his feet. He smacked away her offer and staggered up on his own. Then, giving a quick bow to the throne, he rushed from the arena in a huff.

Round one over, Mara thought. *The worst is yet to come.*

MARA WATCHED Adrian fight two consecutive matches from the mouth of the combatant's tent. And though she had trained with him for years, she still found herself amazed at his abilities. He moved with such swift, deliberate action, flowing like water as he danced around his opponents. She rarely got the chance to see him from an outside perspective; typically, she was the one going toe-to-toe with his unforgiving blade.

He looked like art in motion, a marvel and wonder to behold. She cheered along with the crowd at both of his quick victories, despite the dark pall was beginning to fall over her. If she won her next match, and she fully intended to do so, only Adrian would stand in her way.

She had bested him a few times before in training, but those victories had been few and very hard won. And, despite her dire motives for entering the Tournament, Adrian was not the type of person to simply let her win, most especially not when he disapproved so vehemently to what she was doing. No, he would show her no quarter. And Mara would have it no other way. It had been drilled into her head throughout her swords training to always follow the code of the Knights. They were simple rules, dealing mostly with honor and courage. There was no honor in winning a battle half-fought.

Mara stepped up as her next match was called, determined to give it her all no matter what came next. She recognized Matthew Cramer, only son of Lord Cramer instantly, thanks to his flashy bronze-plated armor. Lord Wilhelm Cramer would do anything to put his kin on the throne, but his son was, incredibly, even worse. A large man, he loved to corner her at official events and grope her while no one could see around his massive bulk.

Mara approached him now, noting his cocky smile beneath his helmet's visor. She was going to enjoy laying this one low.

A sudden shout pulled Mara's gaze to the combatant's tent. "Yeah! Go Pigsmy! Whoop!" Adrian stood at the mouth, cheering wildly. The crowd joined in, stomping their feet, and chanting her name—well, Pigsmy's name. Adrian's flashing eyes were centered on Matthew, and she wondered if he was remembering the most recent masque ball when Matthew had caught her in a corridor alone and pinned her to the wall. Luckily, Adrian had spotted them and pulled the groping swine off of her. Despite Matthew's large size, the event had resulted in a fist fight between the two men, and Matthew being carried off, bloody and half-conscious, from the ballroom.

Bolstered by Adrian's vociferous support, Mara turned her full focus on her opponent. The bell rang, beginning the match..

Though undeniably a bastard, Matthew was not weak by any stretch of the imagination. His blows shook her to her core and left her arms trembling. Unlike her previous match with Revalin where she'd focused on keeping their bodies close, she found herself forced to keep a steady distance from Matthew as he lunged and parried. His sword dwarfed hers in size, much like his towering body, cutting through the air with such brutal force that it whistled the wind with every slash. He drove her round and round the arena, granting her no reprieve, no moment to switch to any offensive positions. Still, she managed to hold her own while searching for a way to best him.

Noticing a slight hitch to his gait, her eyes flitted toward his feet, evaluating his movement; he was, indeed, favoring his right leg, as if he had a prior injury. The slight limp was not enough to throw off his strategic assault, but Mara hoped it might be enough for her to exploit.

When next Matthew brought his sword up to swing towards her torso, she dove beneath his arm and spun behind him before he had a chance to react. Her shorter stature was now her advantage. He stumbled slightly, and Mara smiled to herself. He pivoted, unwittingly offering her the advantage, and she took it without hesitation.

She lunged, her sword sliding across his bronze chest piece to lock beneath his arm. This had a two-fold effect; it threw his hand high and loosened his grip on the hilt of his sword.

Mara leapt into the air, reached out, and wrenched the sword from his grasp. By the time Matthew had fully turned to face her, she already had both his blade and hers pointed firmly at his throat.

The crowd roared. Mara felt overwhelming glee in watching Matthew Cramer kneel before her in the dirt.

She glanced up across the arena towards the dais and the court's high-backed chairs. She didn't dare look at her uncle, fearful he might somehow recognize her in that instant, but she did steal a glance at Matthew's father seated off to the side. Wilhelm looked disgusted by his son having to kneel on the ground before such a tiny soldier, bested for all to see. Mara might have felt pity for Matthew had he been anyone else. As it was, she had to fight back a laugh as Matthew slouched his way from the arena.

At last, the final match-up; the one Mara had been dreading since coming up with her grand scheme. As she stood before Adrian, admiring the look of him clad in his one-of-a-kind black metal armor, the younger women in the crowd squealed in delight. The wind sifted and rustled through his brown hair, and she wondered at her immunity to his charms. He really was quite impressive, holding his sword out in front of him like the royal knight he was; the very picture of nobility and strength.

Eyes twinkling beneath his visor, he bowed low to her. "I was praying you would be beaten before it came to this," he murmured. "Such a shame I'll have to leave you with a bruised ass. I'm told Matthew Cramer values it above all your many charming assets."

Mara rolled her eyes. "Again, with that ego. Adrian. It's a wonder we've not all been crushed under its immense weight."

His lips twisted into a playful smirk. "Your tongue is quick, princess, I give you that. But what about your sword?"

With the ring of the bell, he engaged.

It was a dance they had performed a thousand times before. They matched one another, hit for hit, and the crowd oohed and awed around them. Every step Mara took, Adrian mirrored. Every lunge she made, he expertly parried. He knew her fighting style better than anyone. But she also knew his.

Unbeknownst to Adrian, Mara had been practicing more advanced fighting styles on her own. She had worked dead into the night for months now, hidden away in her chambers and using the bedpost as her target. Knowing how Adrian fought, and coming up with a strategy against it, filled her with indescribable guilt. Though she knew it was the only way she would have hope of emerging victorious.

Focusing her eyes on his center, she watched and waited for the perfect moment. This was no easy feat; Adrian kept himself carefully guarded even as he opened to slash at her. But all she needed was one single moment, one lucky misstep on his part to gain her advantage.

She soon lost herself in the match, and the world around her disappeared. Mara cut from above and he parried. She cut from below, and he deflected. Every lunge she performed, he evaded or swatted away with ease.

Heart hammering in her chest, she noted his honey-colored eyes dancing with delight beneath his visor. He was grinning like a fool, having the time of his life.

They circled round and round, and she struggled to maintain her focus. Her arms, already exhausted from her previous matches, were beginning to shake with fatigue—something, to her dismay, Adrian had already taken note of. His jaw locked in a cool look of victory; she could see him setting himself up for the winning strike. His arrogance stabbed at the wrathful monster inside her, adding insult to her freshly bruised confidence. Desperate, she searched for the split-second she needed.

There.

It happened in an instant. Adrian lunged forward, overextending by a fraction of a hair in his sureness, and she employed the move she'd been practicing in secret for weeks. She stepped to the side, let his sword slice into empty space, and launched her own attack. As he spun to face her, sword extended in attack, she grabbed on to his free arm. Yanking it hard across his body, she slammed the butt of her sword into his chest. She heard the breath leave him as she gave another pull on his arm. He spun around in place; eyes wide in surprise as Mara launched herself onto his back. Her forearm locked into place against his throat, Adrian unable to dislodge her as he thrashed. Hooking her sword beneath his, she drove upwards with a mighty thrust. The strike took all her remaining strength and forced a strangled battle-cry from her chest.

There was a terrifying moment where it seemed that he might keep his grip, but then he released, and his sword went flying through the air and clattered to the ground behind them.

She had done it.

The crowd thundered their feet, roaring with ear-splitting pleasure. Mara released Adrian and he turned to stare down at her, his eyes beneath his visor now registering shock along with a tinge of embarrassment. Then, just as quickly, he was smirking again. He dropped to one knee and yielded to her with all the humility and grace of his training.

Mara beamed down at him, letting the crowd's cheers fill her with courage. Then she turned to face her uncle on the dais.

He sat on his tall throne, flanked on either side by lords and ladies of his court who were swept up in the enthusiasm of the crowd. He was dressed in his customary deep-purple velvet robes, his neck dripping in gemstones. His reddish beard was neatly trimmed, his hair slicked back, and the golden royal crown winked on his head in the afternoon sunlight.

"Come!" he called to her. He threw his arms wide and welcomed her forward. "Let me gaze upon the face of our kingdom's best swordsman!"

Keeping her stride confident and strong, she stepped forward to stand before him and dropped to a knee, bowing low. This was the moment, her moment. Her uncle was finally going to see her for who she really was: powerful, intelligent, capable. She was a Queen in her own right, not someone in need of a man's lead.

Filled with resolve, Mara stood and removed her helmet. Her ringleted ponytail tumbled out across her shoulders, and the crowd let out a loud gasp. The court slowly recognized the dirt and sweat splattered face of their princess, and every jaw on the dais drop in open-mouthed horror. The crowd began buzzing with whispers.

Finally, her uncle raised his hand. A heavy silence fell over the arena. He stared down at Mara, his face unreadable. She squared her shoulders and gave him a proud smile. Of course he would be irritated by her deception, but surely he could see the great accomplishment she'd achieved here today. Surely, he could see—

He let go with a deep belly laugh that struck at Mara's heart. She cringed as the entire crowd joined in.

"I believe a thank you is in order!" King Grathiel shouted over the laughter echoing through the arena. "To our fair men who humored my beautiful niece today with their swordplay! I applaud you all for holding back and allowing her this opportunity to shine!"

Mara's confidence faltered. This was not at all what she had expected. Far from being congratulatory, beyond getting angry, her uncle was instead acting as if this had all been some sort of pre-feast entertainment, something to keep the silly little princess preoccupied for a time.

Anger heating her cheeks, she opened her mouth to retort, but King Grathiel waved one bejeweled hand to quiet her. The crowd fell silent as well. "It was an absolute pleasure, my pet," he cooed at her. "I could think of no better way to show off this hobby that occupies so much of your time." He finished this condescending statement with a wink.

Mara opened her mouth again, but the flash in her uncle's eyes made her bite her tongue. *Hobby?* she thought. The word cut through her like a hot knife. Adrian had been right. How stupid of her to think that anything she might do could make a difference. She was a princess and would never be allowed to do anything other than that which was expected of her.

She felt gutted, only dimly aware of Adrian standing behind her. Her uncle motioned for Lady Lenorei to step forward from her place off to the side of the stands. "Would you be so kind, my Lady Lenorei, to assist Princess

Mara in getting ready for tonight's ceremony? It may take steel cloth to remove those layers of mud from her skin." King Grathiel laughed again, and the crowd echoed the sound.

Lady Lenorei hurried toward Mara, looking as if she'd been slapped across the face. Mara fought with the urge to defend herself, to make it clear to her uncle and everybody in attendance that *she* had done this, that she had won the day with her own skill and ingenuity. But her uncle and the crowd had already turned their attention to the jousting match being set up across the arena.

Numb, Mara allowed herself to be led away, her confidence melting into cold resignation.

LADY LENOREI CURSED her for a full hour after they returned to her room. Phrases like "Zenafrost's biggest moron" and "unmanageable swine of a girl" were still stinging Mara's ears nearly an hour later. She had been dressed in a gossamer purple dress to match her uncle's robes, and the strips of flowing fabric clinging to her body were a far cry from the muddy leathers she'd been wearing earlier. Her hair was pinned in an uncomfortably tight crown around her head; Lady Lenorei had used the hairstyle to punish Mara for her foolishness. Instead of a helm, a silver tiara now perched atop Mara's pile of raven curls.

She was seated at the high table placed at the foot of the castle. It was filled with lords and ladies of the court, all facing down onto the city square where villagers now made merry. Adrian sat beside her, his body stiff as he sweltered beneath her silent fuming. Her friend had long ago learned not to interrupt her brooding, particularly when it came to conflicts with her uncle.

King Grathiel sat on a throne beside her, chatting in muffled tones with Adrian's father.

In the center of the square stood a large figure of a woman, made entirely from hay. This was something the villagers built every year—the queen of the Dreads in effigy. Though Mara understood why it was burned during the otherwise cheerful festival, it never got any less disturbing to watch.

She stared at it now, wishing she could be anywhere else in the world.

Mere hours ago, she had been sure that her plan would work, so sure that her uncle would at least hear her out after she'd proved herself. But all her plotting and practicing had been for not.

As if in response to this thought, her uncle leaned towards her. "Mara," he crooned. He placed his large hand over hers and patted it gently. "Don't be cross with me, darling. You put me in such a bad spot today."

Mara turned to meet his eyes and bristled at his sad expression. Anger rose up inside of her once again. "A bad spot?" she said through her teeth. "I fell *three* of your finest men, without any assistance whatsoever, and you made it seem like I was some...some *child* they were entertaining. None of those men 'went easy on me', uncle, and you know it. You didn't even give me a chance to speak."

He patted her hand again, nodding knowingly. "This is true, pet. But I couldn't very well sit there in front of my entire kingdom and celebrate our princess rolling around in the dirt, besting all my mightiest men. It would've gone over so poorly, Mara dear, what with you so close to your twenty-first birthday."

Mara felt Adrian stiffen next to her and knew he was

listening. "Ever so close to being married off, you mean," she retorted.

Her words, spat out without thinking, pulled a sharp breath from Adrian.

But her uncle simply nodded. "There are things expected of you, Mara. Of every person privileged enough to wear a crown. And it is seldom easy to do what we must. You know this."

Cold silence sat between them. Mara stared down at her hands, the hole in her heart growing bigger. Though friendly, there was a firm command to her uncle's voice that left no room for her to further engage him on the matter. He did this every time she brought the subject up; silenced her before she had a chance to speak.

Sighing, the king reached into his billowing robes, pulled a long ornate box from within its folds, and placed it on Mara's empty plate. "This was to be a birthday gift." He sat back with his goblet of wine, watching her closely over the rim. "But I know how upset you were after today's…events. So, I thought you could open it early."

Mara lifted the lid from the box and gasped. Laid inside atop a pillow of satin was a stunning dagger, encrusted in jewels that sparkled like stars on a moonless night. Its blade was of the darkest metal, with branches of ivy etched across its surface. And the largest gem she'd ever seen, a dark green that seemed to go on forever within its facets, adorned the middle of the hilt.

She picked it up. It was perfectly weighted. "It's beautiful," she breathed. Spellbound, she studied every curve and every detail.

"It's very old," her uncle murmured. "But it reminded me of you: breathtaking and lethal when wielded correctly. I felt it only fitting that you be the one to have it." His eyes grew suddenly misty, and he let out a soft sigh. "Zenoths bless, you remind me so much of your dear mother, may her soul live on forever in the stars. Your smile is the very ghost of her." He winked at Mara, then took a sip of his wine, turning his attention to the crowds beyond.

Mara rolled the dagger across her palm, watching the gems glint in the lantern light. Its beauty was beyond words, its exotic metal making it clear that it had been forged outside the city walls. She had never seen this sort of workmanship before, so delicately intricate. Not even the castle forge, whose blacksmith made pure works of art, stood as its rival. But she also saw the dagger for what it really was: a bribe. Though it was a thoughtful and dazzling gift, it would not deter her from her original mission. She *would* speak to her uncle about her future… whether he wanted her to or not.

His gift changed nothing.

Her uncle stood and raised his hands, silencing the huge crowd gathered in the square below. He lifted his goblet in the air and began to speak, his voice booming out for all to hear. "Twenty-one years ago today, I stood here amongst you good peoples and raised up a great victory cry!"

The crowd applauded and cheered, howling up at him.

"Twenty-one years ago today, we stood victorious against the Dread armies. I brought their Queen to kneel before you and washed the streets red with our justice on this very spot!"

More uproarious cheers at this. The sound was almost deafening.

King Grathiel's expression darkened as he continued. "And though our mighty kingdom has stood, protected and proud, for these twenty years…we must never forget. We must never forget those we have lost, and how close we came to *ruin*…" He trailed off for a moment, lost in the memories of the time before. It pained Mara to see his eyes glazed by whatever he was seeing in his mind.

"And in that memory," he went on, forcing a smile once more. "We choose to *celebrate*. Not only for the lives no longer with us, but for the hard-fought victory we laid claim to that day."

Torches were brought towards the statue made of hay, the statue that symbolized the Dread Queen whom King Grathiel had beheaded in the square. The sight of the fire worked the crowd into a frenzy, and they roared with approval.

"Let us drink!" her uncle shouted. "Let us sing! Let us be merry till dawn in honor of the End!" He downed the rest of his goblet in one gulp, gave the signal, and the torches were tossed onto the effigy.

The Dread Queen was ablaze in moments, and the Delinvalian people began singing and dancing around its base.

From her seat at the table, Mara heard Adrian tut his disapproval. He murmured something, words she only barely caught over the jubilant crowd. She could have sworn she'd heard him murmur, "Savages."

As the moon rose over the kingdom, the evening's festivities neared a fevered pitch. The king, drunk, danced with a group of female courtiers. His hearty laughter, mixed with their tipsy giggling, echoed through the castle's courtyard.

In contrast, Mara was throwing herself a pity-party. Having given up on glassware hours ago, she'd grabbed a full bottle of mead and was now making her way back towards the castle. She wanted no more of the carefully spoken words of nobles, the harsh looks, and cold whispers of ladies, or the hungry, disgusting leers from drunken lords. All she wanted now was her room and warm bed, to be away from the merriment and noise after such a heartbreaking day.

Adrian appeared beside her, his long legs easily keeping up with her stumbling feet. He eyed the mead in her hand. "So. We've decided to drown our sorrows at the bottom of a bottle then?"

His tone was light, his way of trying to break her from her brooding mood.

Mara grimaced and took another swig. "Yes, well. Better to drown than have my life contracted off to another."

Adrian frowned at her. "You fought well today, Mara. Probably the best I've ever seen."

That was high praise coming from Adrian, Mara's biggest critic. She gave him a half smile. "Best in the kingdom," she slurred.

They dodged a group of young ladies who were giggling and stumbling over themselves. Mara noted that a few of them blushed at Adrian then glared daggers at her as they shuffled past. "You were right," she went on. "All that work…and *none* of it mattered." She pulled off her heeled shoes one at a time and then tossed back another massive swig of mead. "I'm still to be given away at the king's leisure."

She threw the shoes aside. Adrian caught them both, and then followed along beside her as she continued to walk and rant.

"I am to be a perfect, doting wife. A piece of art for a Lord's son to show off before I hand him my throne. It's barbaric!" she spat at him. "And I'm just expected to take it!" She swigged some more mead. "I am supposed to just sit back and let them buy me, bed me, and bump me aside to take what should rightfully be *mine.*"

Another swig and she started ascending the tower, grimacing as her bare feet hit the cold, marble steps.

"You are only expected to do as every other princess before you has done," Adrian replied. "And not every hopeful in your pool of potentials is a pig. There are some that would give you the tenderest of attentions. *Cherish* you, even. Would that be so bad?"

There was a softness in his voice and a hopefulness in his eyes that made Mara wince. His newfound attraction to her was something they both worked hard to ignore, but the unspoken tension between them seemed to be growing.

There were times she wished she could feel the same as he did, she'd even considered forcing herself to try, but she loved him too much to tease his heart that way. Truthfully, if she really was to fail at convincing her uncle to break with tradition and simply give her the throne, Adrian would be her first choice in a husband. Her loyal friend would make a great king, true and just, and she was certain he would indeed treat her with the tenderest of attentions.

At times she considered giving up on her quest and giving in to her uncle's plans, but her heart craved so much more. She wanted passion and adventure, not the boring mundanities of a marriage bed.

She took another swig of mead. "You wouldn't understand, Adrian. You're given none of the same restrictions as a woman. You can come as you like, go as you like, marry or not marry as you like. Your worth isn't determined by how desirable you are."

"Mmm," Adrian responded. He leaned closer to whisper, "Then I suppose it's a good thing that you are incredibly desirable."

Their eyes locked for a moment…a moment too long for Mara's comfort. To ease the tension, she punched him hard in the arm and continued down the corridor toward her room.

Adrian winced, rubbing his wound. "I take that back," he called, following after her. "You're a wicked minx that should be paddled daily."

At her door, he handed her her shoes, cocked his head, and stared down at her. "Honestly, Mara, you're much more than some object to be bought or won."

She felt a small blush warm her cheeks and took another deep drink of her mead. "If only my uncle were as sensible as you, Adrian." She shoved open her door and staggered into her room.

"Try talking to him tomorrow. You know how it is at these festivals, all pomp and circumstance. The king is a reasonable man. Perhaps there's a solution that appeases everyone." He had stepped closer as he said this, toe to toe with Mara. She froze, watching his eyes flicker momentarily to her lips. Then the moment passed, Adrian patting a hand on her head, making Mara feel instantly like a child. She batted him away as he turned to walk back up the corridor.

"Happy End Day, Mara," he tossed over his shoulder at her. "Things will look brighter in the morning."

Mara closed her door and crossed the room to her window. Unlatching the panes and pushing them open, she let the soft wind billow through the curtains behind her. The moon hung low over the distant mountains, and a soft fog was rolling in through the forest beyond the wall. The music from the festival floated up toward her on the warm breeze, and, despite her sour mood, she smiled.

Remembering her uncle's gift, she pulled the long box out of the pocket in her skirt. Its metal, so dazzling and exotic, glinted in the moonlight. The hilt felt oddly warm in her hand, seeming to radiate with a heat of its own. She turned it around in her palm, admiring its matchless beauty, until her eyes, heavy with drink, could have sworn the green gem winked at her.

CHAPTER 3
THE DARK OF THE NIGHT

The kingdom lay sleeping in the early hours of the morning, well before the sun had even begun to rise. Bathed in moonlight from the open window, Mara sprawled facedown on her bed, drooling, still in her dress from the festival. She'd pulled the pins from her hair, and black curls now sprang in a tangled mess around her face, while the dagger from her uncle rested on the nightstand beside her bedpost, inches away from her outstretched fingers. Her tiara had been tossed onto the padded bench by her feet, her legs dangling half off the bed.

She was having the most vivid, peculiar dream. She stood in a great wood, the likes of which she had only ever seen in paintings. The trees around her swayed in unison, shifted by the constant breeze. She heard something on the flows of wind, distant and all-together too near. Whispering voices tickled the back of her neck, but Mara remained unmoving. Someone walked towards her from the shadows of the strange forest. She could discern no features through its smokey appearance, but it exuded an incredible energy that made Mara feel intoxicated. Far from wanting to turn and flee the shadow figure, she found herself drawn to it by an irresistible pull.

It drew level with her, and something sparked deep in her core, a longing like none she'd ever known. The figure raised a hand to reach for her, and Mara extended hers in return, pulse quickening, her breathing hitched…

Noise somewhere in the castle stirred Mara from her slumber. Cracking open one eye, she groaned, her room spinning around her and her head throbbing angrily. Still feeling uncomfortably laden with mead, she grabbed a pillow and covered her eyes.

Mara assumed the shouts and running feet came from celebratory courtiers returning from a drunken night in the city. It was tradition during the Festival of End to see who could drink the most before the sun rose on the next day. The kingdom usually needed the entire next fortnight to recoup. Most years, it was the King himself who won that victory, but it sounded like this year someone else was going for the gold.

The noises increased in volume. Stomach lurching, head pounding feverishly, Mara squeezed the pillow tighter around her skull. *If only they would keep it down—*

BANG!

An explosion shook through the castle, jolting Mara out of bed. Now on all fours on the cold marble floor, she shook the remaining dregs of mead from her head and listened carefully.

With dawning understanding, she realized that the sounds were actually the frantic, clanging of swords colliding.

Heart in her throat, Mara jumped to her feet. Ignoring the room as it rotated around her, she dashed to the door. Cracking it open, she stole a quick peak down the corridor.

Shouts and screams echoed up at her from every corner of the castle. More bangs shook the stone walls around her. She heard a clamor of footsteps coming up the spiraling tower steps. The breath froze in her chest.

A group of her uncle's guards rounded the corner. They rushed towards her. Mara breathed a sigh of relief.

"What's happening?!" she shouted. The men looked pale, cold sweat dripping down their faces.

"My lady!" the one closest to her gasped. "You must lock yourself in your room! They're coming!"

The guards surrounded her in her doorway, swords drawn, eyes fixed back up the corridor from which they'd come. The noises from below were growing louder. Mara could hear the shrieks of the lords and ladies in the rooms below hers.

"Who?!" Mara demanded. "Who is coming?!" Seeing fully grown men cowering was rising panic in her like a tidal wave.

The guard gulped as he answered. "Invaders, m'lady. Invaders have infiltrated our back lines. They're already in the castle."

Mara stared at him in horror for a moment before he finally shoved her backwards and slammed the door closed, shutting her up in her room. She quickly locked the door and then slowly backed away as if it might bite her.

Invaders? she thought. It wasn't possible. Delinval was an impenetrable fortress with nothing but unforgiving ocean at its back. Their closest neighbors lay to the east, in the dark, fallen kingdom of Ylastra— *Zenoths save us if they're the ones attacking!* Though they had once worked with Delinval to end the Dread threat during the war, Ylastra had quickly turned on their allies once victory was assured. Proving as greedy as the Dreads, they'd tried to take Delinval's crown and lands for themselves, even threatening to start a new war when the last had barely been won.

King Grathiel, forced to act, had snuffed out the Ylastrian threat in an instant. Since then, Delinval had lived under a fragile truce with the Ylastrian people, a gracious mercy by all accounts.

Shouts and a scuffle sounded outside her door. Mind racing, Mara darted to her nightstand and snatched up the jeweled dagger.

The guards on the other side of her heavy oaken door began to yell. There was a crackling boom like a tree falling, and their yells turned to blood-curdling screams.

She heard swords clamoring, spears and arrows being loosed. Then, another *bang*—this one made Mara squeak in surprise.

And then all noise ceased, all, save for the sound of Mara's labored breathing.

Her ears rang with the silence. The hairs on her arms stood on end. The air felt electrified, like the precursor to a lightning strike.

The handle on her door gave a shudder...then a soft *click* as it unlocked itself.

The door slid open, bleeding in lantern light from the corridor, and Mara dove behind it, tucking herself away in its shadow. A tall, muscular figure stepped soundlessly into the room clad in black leather armor from head to toe. She held her breath, her eyes widening at the broadness of his shoulders, and found herself disappointed that a thick hood hid his face.

She searched her mind for who this invader might be, noting the intricate scroll work carved into his armor. Ylastrian armor smiths were known for their craftmanship, but his seemed beyond even their capabilities.

Dual blades lay across a thick, broad back. Mara could

see spots in the folds of his cloak that looked heavy, weighted down by what she was sure were hidden weapons. He looked around slowly, tracing a path from the open window, across the littered floor, and to the empty bed. Mara's stomach dropped; he was looking for her.

A familiar feeling rose within her, a beast with fire for eyes. Righteous fury shot through her veins, threatening to burn her from the inside out. *How dare they!* she thought. *How dare they enter my home and attack my people! And for what? To kidnap a princess for ransom or slaughter? Not this princess. Not today! Not ever!*

She tightened her grip on her dagger and rushed forward.

The invader, his back to her, was still surveying the room. But he turned in an instant, and Mara's flashing blade was met with metal; he wielded a knife in each leather-clad hand and had locked her dagger between them. She leapt back but wasted no time before lunging again. He blocked her once more, but this time Mara was ready.

She jerked upwards as he brought his knives together to lock her in. The hilt of her dagger smashed into his square jaw. She heard a low grunt of pain as the force slammed her opponent's head back and knocked the hood clear of his face.

Mara gasped at the look of the man. He had a long thick scar that divided his face down the middle from forehead to chin. A row of black dots lined each cheekbone, with tiny intricate runes tattooed beneath each one. His hair was shock-white, disheveled, and sticking out all over his head. But it was his eyes that drew Mara in. In the dim glow of lantern-light, she could see they were a startling shade of blue, like water beneath a river of ice, and at that moment they were brazenly appraising her.

Mara faltered, staring up at him, open-mouthed. She'd never seen anyone quite so perfectly, ruggedly made. He looked carved from crystalline marble by an artist who'd poured their whole heart and soul into making this one dazzling creation. None of the men in her uncle's court, not even the ones with their share of beauty, had ever made her stomach flip like this. She found herself incapable of looking away as he held her gaze.

He whispered words she did not recognize. The tattoos on his face burned white hot, like fresh brands. His eyes glowed, like pulsing moonlight in the snow. Mara, captivated, could not move. Sudden pressure on her arms made her look down where thick, rootlike vines twisted around her body, binding her wrists together. The dagger dropped from her hand, and the impressive man swooped low, catching it before it hit the marble floor to slip it into a pouch at his waist.

Mara, dazzled by his appearance, had failed to put the pieces together. The glowing eyes, the characteristic point to his ears, the way he seemed to have single-handedly infiltrated the castle....

This man was a Dread.

She pulled in a breath to scream, but the vines had already wound their way up to her neck and face to gag her into silence. Unable to move, she stared in wide-eyed terror at the Dread. He was looking down at her, studying her with a strange intensity that made her feel stripped bare. Shouts and the sound of running feet echoed towards them from down the corridor. Help was on the way.

Reining in her fear, Mara tapped into her outrage and began struggling against her bonds. The Dread swore under his breath, wrapped a steely arm around her waist, and hauled her to the open window.

The sounds of her rescue grew closer; the guards were clambering up the spiral stairwell.

The Dread glanced down at the ground below, then flashed a smirk at Mara that revealed two perfect dimples set in carved cheeks. He whisked her up into his arms, pressing her into a cradle against his chest, just as the Delinvalian soldiers rushed into her room.

But the soldiers were too late.

The Dread threw them a glinting look over his shoulder and launched from the window with Mara in his arms.

She tumbled, down, down, down, her stomach threatening to expel all of its contents. Accepting her inevitable death, she squeezed her eyes shut, said a quick prayer to the Zenoths, and waited for the impact.

But no impact came.

A loud and relentless wind whipped up, blustering all around her and the Dread. Mara felt her momentum toward the ground slow and opened her eyes. They were hovering mere inches above the earth, the Dread's feet barely brushing the dew-soaked grass. The wind stopped, and his boots touched down. Mara was released into a standing position, and she swayed, blinking at what stood before her.

Was this a man or a woman? The pretty, petite features, set in pale skin that shone in the moonlight, were indistinguishable as either. Their build was tall but slight, dressed in the same dark leathers as Mara's attacker, but their ears were much longer and pointer than the Dread's. There was a long sword hanging from their hip, and their eyes seemed to look right through her.

There were two others standing there in the moonlight. One was a towering man who looked built of solid rock. His hair was cropped short at the sides, gathered in a small bun at the back and caked in something that looked suspiciously like blood. He wore a massive great sword strapped to his back and had all manner of throwing axes and knives hanging from a thick belt around his immense waist. Bones, blood-stained bits of cloth, and weather-worn jewelry hung from straps across his person. Despite the circumstances, he was looking down at Mara with an amused expression that made her seethe.

The other companion with them was a girl. She was curvy beneath shimmering armor that looked to be made of thick scales. Bottles of varying shapes and sizes adorned three separate bandoleers hanging across her full chest, and she wore a strip of fabric tied around her head to keep her short hair from falling into her eyes. She was staring down her nose at Mara as if she were a living Zenoth. "Silent as a mouse, you said," the girl hissed. Her eyes darted to the white-haired Dread. "No one will be awake after that party, you said. Does this *look* like no one is awake?!" She motioned to the guards shouting down at them from Mara's window, and then to the distant torches flicking in the courtyard as guards rushed towards their position.

Mara's kidnapper grunted. "You're just upset that I didn't follow your carefully laid plan, Eleanora." His voice was like silken darkness, dangerous and deep. "My plan left a far clearer impression."

"Ah, come on, El!" the massive man threw in, his booming bass of a voice laced with humor. "You can't tell me you didn't enjoy tearing down his men just a *little*. How long's it been since we've had a fight like this? Four? Five years?"

The Dread pushed Mara toward the big man. "You'll need to carry her for this first bit, Kain," he said, speaking as if Mara wasn't even there—as if she was just some piece of furniture he'd stolen from the castle.

The one called Kain reached out and flung her over one of his massive his shoulder. Mara screamed against her vine gag, flailing and thrashing, like a wild animal caught in a trap. Her efforts were useless against her bonds and Kain's remarkable strength. The big man sniffed her, making her cringe, and then barked a laugh. "Zenoths blood, she smells like she drank a whole tavern!" He patted her backside reassuringly. "Never fear, princess, I've spent many a moon smelling like that. Maybe not quite so pungently…"

Mara saw the torches of her rescuers moving closer and her hopes soared.

"They're coooming," El warned, in a sing-song voice.

The Dread in charge turned toward their pale friend. "Milios, let's give us a head start, yeah?"

Their tall companion nodded in reply and stretched out slender hands, fingers waving, and a strong rush of wind hit Mara full in the face. She gasped, suddenly realizing that it was this creature who had controlled the wind and caught her fall from the window.

The three of them, Mara in tow, moved quickly toward a hole blasted through the glistening stone walls that surrounded the kingdom of Delinval. From her uncomfortable perch atop Kane's hard-as-stone shoulder, Mara watched Milios work. Graceful hands raised. A great rumbling began, and a giant glowing wall of wind suddenly appeared behind them. Mara watched, shocked, as the energy from the wind-wall ripped up the ground beneath it, effectively cutting off the soldiers who were racing to save her. They passed through the wall, and she realized at once the direction in which they were heading…towards the Marred Lands on the other side of the kingdom.

Once the bustling outer city of Delinval before the Great War, the Marred Lands had been the capitol of illustrious trade all people across Zenafrost. And it was here the Dread Queen had laid her first strike. It now sat in ruins, devastated by the endless tide of battle. Worse yet, the land itself was said to be cursed, haunted by the innocent blood spilled upon it. To the Delinvalians, the Marred Lands was a forbidden place, visited only by dark things and foolish children who were dared by their friends to enter.

Mara had never been beyond the walls, let alone to the Marred Lands. She'd once dared Adrian to go when they were teenagers, and then begged him not to when he'd stubbornly committed to doing so.

Heart hammering in her throat, bones aching from Kain's bounding sprint, Mara closed her eyes and prayed for rescue. As the sound of the castle bells grew more and more distant, she tried not to imagine what dangers lay ahead.

CHAPTER 4
CURSED LANDS AND ANCIENT STONE

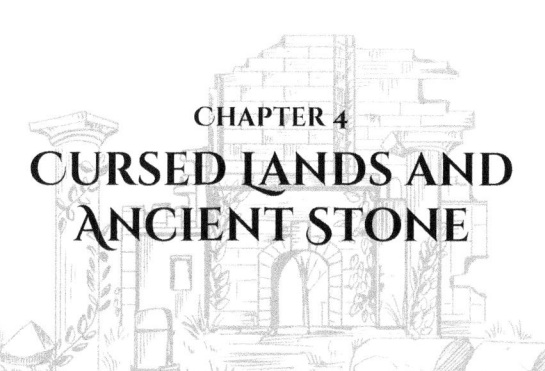

The sun was starting to rise as they ran across battle-worn earth. They were nearing the ruins of the Marred Lands, moving in silence while Mara continued to squirm on Kain's shoulder. The constant thrashing against his uncompromising grip was becoming exhausting, draining her of all strength. She heard Adrian's voice in her head, something he had said to her once in training. *"If you're in an impossible situation, save your energy and wait for the right time to strike."*

She stopped moving at this, letting her body be dead weight on Kain's shoulder. She knew in her heart they were coming for her. Her uncle's military force had always exceeded all others in Zenafrost, and he would never let them get away so easily. Most especially not with Mara as their victim.

She kept her eyes pinned to the horizon, waiting for the inevitable forces to ride towards them.

The group came up over a hill and Mara felt a thrill of energy run through her. Even without the cracked, ruined stone buildings, she would have known they had arrived.

Of all the times she had imagined leaving the kingdom's safety, all the times she had wondered what sort of old secrets and mysteries this place held, she had never in her wildest daydreams imagined she'd be seeing it like this.

The cobbled streets looked as if they had been beautiful once, indistinguishable carvings still visible in the stone. But all its previous splendor had been destroyed by battle and bloodshed, now overrun by the blackened earth. The very air smelled of death and darkness.

The terrain whizzed past her as they spurred forward with renewed haste. The sound of shouts and hoofbeats echoed over the hillside towards them. "Cyfrin," Kain called out as they moved faster through the abandoned streets.

Her original kidnapper responded to the name. "I can hear them. We're almost there. I can feel it."

As he said this, she felt a sharp jolt of something foreign throb in her head. Mara had barely enough time to wonder where "there" was when they shuddered to a sudden halt. Kain gave a mighty shrug and slid her to the ground. Vine appeared instantly and bound her legs.

They were in a large stone circle. Symbols like the ones under Cyfrin's eyes surrounded them, etched into the faces of the tall rocks. El rushed forward, kneeling beside Mara with her head bowed as Milios, Cyfrin and Kain whirled about.

Her uncle's soldiers, the ones fastest to arrive at least, came into view up the ruined stone street. The men raced towards them, shouting, and drawing their weapons. As they approached, the Dread's steadiness in the face of onslaught unnerved Mara. Milios' eyes glowed stormy grey, hands raised before them waiting to strike. Kain smiled, a terrifying fire in his gaze as he unsheathed the great sword from his back. Mara studied the weapon that glinted in the early dawn light. The blade, made of the same dark metal as her dagger, had tally lines etched in it, too many for her to count. She shuddered to think what they tracked.

Cyfrin, in contrast to his burly companion, had sheathed his knives. He stood with his head tilted slightly to the side, staring at the opposing forces barreling towards them. The runes across his flesh blazed white-hot, just as they had done in the tower. His eyes began to glow bright, ice-blue, and he raised one hand.

It happened faster than she could comprehend. Rocks rose from the ground and into the air, branches shooting up from the soil and angling themselves towards the men on horseback. Those too slow to react were tossed into the air as the limbs collided with them. Milios' wind caught them, whipping them higher and higher before slamming their bodies to the earth with resounding thuds.

The rest of her uncle's men surged forward, and Kain let out a battle cry as he ran headlong to meet them his weapon held high. Blood followed every slash of the man's great sword; he moved startingly fast for such a burly figure with a heavy blade. Milios looked almost bored as they moved their hands like an orchestral conductor, whipping the wind this way and that, tossing more and more soldiers skyward.

Mara's eyes fixed on Cyfrin. He moved with expert precision; his stare unfaltering as his hands sliced through the air with deadly accuracy. Crackling magick, a shade of blue deep as the Brisenbane Ocean, engulfed his fists in bolts of lightning. It let out sizzling *cracks* with every impact, cutting through metal, leather, flesh.

Mara tore her gaze from him and looked at El. Staring ahead, unblinking, her hazel eyes glowed bright like her companion's. Her hands on the stone in front of her, she was muttering something under her breath in the same language Cyfrin had used earlier. El's voice grew in volume, trumpeting around them with unnatural clarity in the chaos.

The ground below them began to quake, and Mara's stomach lurched. She watched Cyfrin, Kain, Milios wield magic and sword to block her uncle's knights, not defeat them. They guarded the entrance to the stone circle, so El could complete the terrifying magics that seemed to have the power to shake the earth. As Mara watched, horrorstruck, there was a great tremor, and the ground beneath her feet disappeared. The five of them dropped instantly. Mara let out a muffled scream as the ground above their heads snapped closed.

They were plunged into darkness, falling into the unknown. *I'm dead,* she thought for the second time that day. *I've been swallowed whole by the earth, and I am dead.*

But no impact came. Wind whipped around her. She opened her eyes to find herself hovering just above the ground, just as she had outside her bedroom window when Cyfrin had kidnapped her. She landed softly and let out a whimper despite herself, the contents of her stomach threatening once more to make a grand appearance.

Bright green orbs of light appeared around them, emerging from El's hands, lighting the space in a dim glow. As Mara struggled to catch her breath, the group dusted themselves off—as if falling through a hole in the world was an everyday occurrence.

She took a moment to look around. They had fallen into what seemed to be an underground tunnel system, that branched out in three directions under the Marred Lands. Thinking back through all the maps of Zenafrost that Lady Len had made her study over the years, she was positive none of them had shown this.

Milios crossed the stone floor and crouched in front of

Mara as she tried to writhe away. Curiosity lacing their expression, they cocked their head, and spoke to the others over their shoulder. "We should let her have water before we continue." Their soft voice held some sort of twinkling quality that reminded Mara of the brass chimes outside her bedroom window. "Better we sober her up as quick as we can. She's looking a bit green."

"I'll give her some of mine!" El said quickly, batting Kain's hand away as he plucked pieces of debris from her hair. She crossed over to Mara and shot Cyfrin a scalding look. "She can't do anything with your little nasties gagging her mouth."

Mara ceased thrashing as Cyfrin, who had been busy brushing the dust off his armor, set his blazing eyes on her. In the soft light cast by El's magick orbs, the deep scar across his face was nearly invisible. *How could everything about his imposing figure be so impossibly perfect?!* she raged to herself.

He raised his eyebrows. "And will you behave for us if I remove my little nasties?" he asked her, his tone mocking.

Mara remained silent, motionless. There was a moment's pause before Cyfrin sighed and waved his hand through the air in a dismissing motion. The vines around her mouth vanished, and Mara instantly began to shout at the ceiling above. "*Down here!*" she screamed. "*They've taken me down here!*"

Cyfrin rolled his eyes and turned away with his arms wide as if to say he knew she would react this way. Kain chortled at Mara's outburst, but El offered her a sad smile. "I'd save your breath, if I were you," she said, unstrapping a bottle from her side. "These tunnels were used during the wars and are protected by magicked wards. No one will be able to hear you out there, and they wouldn't be able to get in even if they did. Only our kind can open the entrance."

Milios was staring so hard at the side of Mara's face that she felt their eyes might bore a hole right through her.

"My uncle will not bargain with you for my life," Mara hissed at them, venom lacing every word. "He bows before no man."

Head angling like an animal fixated on their prey, Milios' eyes darted up to Mara's, glinting like the edge of a dagger. "I am no man," they replied, their tone infuriatingly calm. "And I have made many, of all kinds, bow."

Mara said nothing to this, drowned in the depths of their inhuman grey eyes.

El leaned forward. "Here." She brought the water bottle to Mara's lips and allowed her to take a gulp. But the girl had no sooner pulled the mouth of the bottle away when Mara spat it back in her face. Gasping in surprise, El fell backwards in the dirt.

"My uncle will have your heads for this!" Mara roared, thrashing against her bonds. Kain pulled the shocked El to her feet, snarling at Mara like a dog protecting its master. "He'll give you no ransom for me!" Mara screeched at him.

"*Ransom?*" Cyfrin spoke, his voice like ice splintering her bones. "And how much do you think your life is worth, Princess?" he asked, glowering down at her. "What price would you have us put on your head?"

Mara was taken aback by the question and his tone. He sounded almost offended at the notion of bartering her life for coin. He crossed his arms, his eyes narrowed in annoyance. She held his stare, pouring every bit of her fury into her gaze. "I wouldn't think the concept of what a life might be worth would even cross the minds of a bunch of foolish, Zenoths-forsaken Dreads."

The room grew dark, even as El's orbs burned brightly around them. Mara didn't see him move, didn't know how

Cyfrin had gone from standing feet away from her to so close they were sharing breath. But as he stood nose to nose with her, his face a mask of cold fury, she could feel the angry heat pouring off him. His jaw clenching with forced control, something flickered in his unfaltering stare. He put a finger under her chin, the leather of his glove rough against her skin as he angled her face to stare directly in to his. When he spoke, his voice was a muted rumble that somehow still echoed around them.

"I cannot decide if you are very brave, or very foolish," he said through his teeth. "But I must insist that you watch your tongue, highness." His ice-blue stare drilled into hers. "It would be unwise of you to act like a shrew our entire trip."

Mara blinked at the insult. She yanked her chin from his hand and took a breath to let him have it with her notoriously sharp tongue. But, with a wave of his hand, the vines reappeared over her mouth before she could get another word out. With a victorious smirk, Cyfrin turned back to his companions.

Mara strained to listen as the four of them stood a distance away, pointing down to a map Milios had pulled from a pouch and speaking in hushed tones.

"—was supposed to take them longer to realize she was missing," El was saying through her teeth, glaring at Cyfrin. "If you hadn't shot in and blasted through half of the castle guard—"

"The tunnels will lead us to the forest," Cyfrin cut in. "If we can get behind the tree line before they arrive, we'll have a clear shot—"

"And if we die in the forest…" Kain interjected, a look of alarm in his eyes. "Drake will reach into the Beyond and pull our souls back just to punish us himself. Not even death will save us from him."

"If we fail," Cyfrin replied, his expression grim. "Then it's not Drake's fury we'll need to worry about. It's the general's." They fell silent, exchanging fearful glances.

Kain clapped his hands, breaking through the sudden tension. "Well, I suppose it's a good thing we won't be failing then!"

"We need to get moving," Milios said, folding the map back into the pouch. "We're behind schedule as it is and standing here contemplating our agonizing demises if we should *not* succeed will only lead us to that very outcome."

The other three nodded in agreement.

Cyfrin threw a side-eye over his shoulder at the place Mara sat, jabbing his thumb back at her as he addressed Kain. "See if you can motivate our guest of honor, aye?"

Kain turned from the group as they gathered themselves and strode over to Mara. "Listen up, princess." He knelt in front of her, sighing. "We've got two options here. Option one." He held up one finger for emphasis. "I have Cyf unbind your ankles and you walk with us the rest of the way like civilized folk."

"Option two." A second finger joined the first. "I hoist you back onto my shoulder and you spend the next month forced to smell the sweat coming off my ass from hauling your wrathful carcass." He smiled mischievously at her. "I personally don't mind option two. It's been a long time since I've felt the touch of a woman—"

He yelped dramatically as El threw a rock at his back, hissing, "*Pig.*" Laughing, Kain winked at Mara, who recoiled slightly at the familiarity he seemed so comfortable taking with her. "Looks like she'll be walking, Cyf," he said over his shoulder.

The vines binding Mara's ankles vanished. She stood quickly, legs wobbling, and watched her four abductors move toward the tunnel on the right, not even pausing to see if she'd follow. She weighed her options. If she stayed where she was, Kain would come back and simply manhandle her the rest of the way to their destination. She had no idea where they were going, or how long it would take to get there. Kain had said "the rest of the month," but surely this was an exaggeration. They'd spoken of a forest, but the only forest she knew that was close by was the Forest of the Fallen. Certainly, they didn't intend to travel through there? She shuddered at the thought. Knowing the sort of monsters that were rumored to lurk just out of view in the tree's shadows, she knew her uncle's soldiers would be hesitant to enter—and for good reason.

She considered running as fast as she could down the tunnel to the left, but then looked down at her bare feet beneath the hem of her gossamer festival dress. She wouldn't make it far without shoes. How she longed to be back in her leathers and boots, shielded by thick hide from the elements and the probing eyes of the Dreads. In the end, she decided not to chance an escape and risk being carried around like a sack of potatoes again.

And so it was that, with a groan of resigned dismay, Mara started off down the orb-lit tunnel after her abductors.

CHAPTER 5
THE GHOSTS OF THINE ENEMIES

They walked for hours and finally emerged from the other side of the tunnel and out into the misty afternoon air. Mara, following a short distance behind the group, stopped in her tracks, a chill racing through her body. The edge of the Forest of Fallen lay directly ahead of them, treetops looming ominously overhead with fog rolling out from the deep shadows. Every story she'd ever been told about this dark place spun through her head all at once. It was said that the Dread's corrupted magicks had destroyed this once beautiful wood, twisting its splendor into the foreboding forest it was now. The Dread Queen had used it as a base for her forces during the Great War, and Delinvalian history books depicted it as the very epicenter of evil. She'd heard harrowing tales about the fiends that lived within the forest; of creatures with six eyes and four tongues who could suck the marrow from bones and wear your skin as a trophy, of monsters who could taste your heartbeat on the air, who knew every deep fear held in the farthest recesses of your soul and could wield it like a weapon against you.

Her four abductors had stopped as well, all of them eyeing the forest with trepidation. Their wariness angered Mara. They were the one's who'd corrupted the place to begin with.

She opened her mouth to tell them as much when a chorus of hoofbeats sounded in the distance.

Cyfrin's back stiffened. "Let's get on with it then." Not looking back, he led the way into the foreboding gloom of the Forest of Fallen.

Gulping, Mara planted her feet, refusing to follow. They were all insane to march willingly into that misty darkness.

Kain appeared beside her and looped his arm through hers. Eyes wide, she looked up at him and he gave her a wink. "Not to worry!" he said, pulling her forward with him. "I don't think we're in much danger. From what I've heard, the beasties in there much prefer the tender flesh of small children to the tough likes of us..."

If Kain thought his words would help, he was wildly mistaken. Whimpering, Mara dragged her heels and looked back toward the hillside where a cloud of dust rose up from the hurried approach of her uncle's mounted knights. She could see her uncle's soldiers now, silhouetted by sunlight. Rather than charge ahead, the horses, sensing the evil spilling out of the forest in front of them, reared up on hind legs, snorting, and pawing at the ground in terror. Some of the soldiers tried to force their mounts onward, knowing the grave urgency, while others just stared ahead with cold fear on their faces.

Arm locked with hers, Kain marched Mara forward, walking her right through the tree line and onto the narrow path where his companions stood waiting. Cyfrin waved a hand and massive thorned branches rose from the ground, crisscrossing over one another to form a deadly, spiked gate that blocked the entrance. Scowling, he drew the knives from his belt and starting forward at the head of their pack. His companions followed with their weapons ready, moving almost noiselessly through the wood.

Mara fought to breathe as she was compelled deeper into the bleak forest. The air was unnaturally still, void of the sounds of nature. Though leaves filled the trees above, forming a dense canopy, there was something off about the foliage. It was as if the trees had all been set ablaze, but never fallen to ash on the forest floor. They refused to move in the wind's wake, frozen for Zenoths only knew how long. The bark clung to them in strips that oozed black and brown sap like rancid blood. Tendrils of grey steam floated up from the forest and into the contrasting sunlight high above the canopy.

"Keep moving," Cyfrin said in a low voice, his eyes darting from twisted tree to gnarled bush.

"Yes, we don't want to be in here long," Milios whispered.

"I don't want to be in here at *all*," El mumbled with a visible shudder.

They walked in complete silence for hours, their pace hastening with every snapping twig and rustling in the underbrush. Mara's heart seemed to beat faster with every step, her anxiety peaking as the ominous energy of the forest pressed against her skin in a sickening caress. Finally, she could no longer suppress the nagging shudder.

Kain gave her a sideways look. "Try to stay calm," he whispered and gave her arm a little squeeze. "Your pulse is going to be like a beacon to anything out there listening. And rest assured, *everything* is listening." Mara gulped at this, her eyes glazing over in panic, and he flashed her a reassuring grin. "Stop worrying so much. We're not going to let anything happen to you."

She blinked up at him, dumbfounded. *Wouldn't let anything happen to her?* They had kidnapped her from her bed and were now dragging her through a monster-infested forest to whatever end they had in store for her on the other side She was completely within her right to fear whatever might be coming next.

As if in response to this thought, Milios held up a hand. "*Shh,*" they hissed softly. The group stopped instantly, and Cyfrin turned to look at Milios with a wary expression. A strange wind rose up, dancing around them franticly. The sound of faint whispers tickled Mara's ears, too quiet to make out the words, and she froze. No one spoke, all staring at Milios who gazed into the distance and listened. "*Coming. It's coming.*" Mara gasped against her gag, shocked by the soft voice that had sifted through her hair like a gentle wind.

Milios' eyes darted to Mara's, surprise flashing across their pretty face. Then they turned to Cyfrin. "We need to get off this path," they said. "But it will only scent us out if we run." They looked up into the trees and pointed skyward. "Going up could help cover our trail. Maybe even trick the beast back in the direction we came."

Cyfrin nodded, needing no further explanation. The four of them stepped from the path, grabbed on to the nearest trees, and began to climb. With a quick flourish of his hand, Cyfrin sent vines racing down towards Mara. They wrapped around her, hoisting her into the air. For the first time, Mara didn't struggle against her bonds. She was too afraid of being dislodged from the vine's grip and left on the ground to face, alone, whatever horror was hiding in the mist.

The four of them climbed quickly, with the speed and agility of those trained in the wilds. Cyfrin's vines lifted Mara up alongside them as they went. Finally, they all stopped, their heads just beneath the canopy, and turned to look down at the path far below where they'd stood just moments before. Black smoke had billowed out of the underbrush, its tendrils stroking the ground, licking at the tree roots, almost as if it were searching for something...

Searching for us, Mara realized. A cold sweat beaded on her forehead. The wind had stopped blowing, leaving them in an oppressive silence.

The smoke grew thicker, filling the path. And then something stepped out from within the swirling blackness. Materializing, as if from thin air, was something not human. It moved with an oozing gait as if its feet didn't quite touch the ground. It slid forward, its limbs long and gangly, seeming to grow and retract from its body in an erratic pulsing motion. Disjointed, strange noises emanated from it, like bubbling sludge and high-pitched screams. This was a thing of nightmares.

Remembering Kain's warning to her—*"Everything is listening"*— Mara bit down on her lip and forced herself to slow her breathing.

The creature seemed to be looking around. Mara squinted down at the spot where a face should have been, but hard as she strained her eyes she could see nothing but a black void. The longer she stared, the more her head began to ache, as if her body knew this was not something that should be gazed upon by human eyes. The beast's head spun around on its axis, turning in a complete circle as it surveyed its surroundings. A third arm, ending in pointed talons at the fingertips, shot from its chest and caressed the dirt where Mara had been standing. And then its tendrils laced around the base of the tree Cyfrin had just climbed, the one leading directly up to Mara.

She felt a scream well in her chest. This creature filled her with a terror unlike any she'd ever felt before. The dark energy billowing from the beast seemed to fill the entire forest and cast a pall over her heart.

The scream threatening to overtake her, a hand reached out and clamped down over her mouth. Mara's eyes flickered to Cyfrin, hanging half off the tree as he reached to silence her. He must have seen the fear in her face, known that she was about to reveal their position. The woodsy smell of pine and honey filled her nose, she tasted the dirty leather of his glove. He shook his head slowly, mouthing the word, *"Don't."* For a moment, she was wildly tempted to scream through his hand regardless, to show him she wasn't a woman to be commanded. Thankfully good sense got the better of her, and she nodded once in acquiescence.

He withdrew his hand, keeping his eyes on her face, as he pulled back into his tree. Suddenly, the creature below them shifted, cocking its head to the side. It drew in a long, shuddering breath, and Mara was sickened to realize that it was smelling the air in search of them—*tasting* it, just as the stories had said. She squeezed her eyes shut and willed herself to think of anything else but the oozing creature below her.

She thought through the footwork of her latest sword training, tracing frontwards and backwards through the steps, one-by-one. She willed herself to be there in the training arena of the castle, wishing she could cover her ears and spare herself from the monster's horrifying sounds.

After the longest minute of Mara's life, the horrid sounds stopped. She opened her eyes to find that the creature vanishing noiselessly back into the underbrush. Mara prayed that no Delinvalian soldiers had braved their way into the woods to save her. She couldn't bear to think that any of them might find death in this monstrous creature's grip because of her.

Her four kidnappers remained in the trees for several more minutes. Mara hung silently beside Cyfrin, listening for any sound of its return. She didn't mind the wait; she was in no hurry to return to the ground. The monster had brought up a childish terror in her that still clung to her heart, leaving her shaken and drenched in cold sweat.

Finally satisfied, Cyfrin led the silent descent back down to the forest floor, Mara in tow. The vines released her, and she noted that the dirt under her bare feet where the monster had tread felt unnaturally cold to the touch. She looked around at the others.

Milios was whispering to themselves, eyes closed, the breeze that seemed to affect only them swirling through their green hair. Kain's face was dark, all the kind humor gone from his expression, and El was fidgeting nervously with a bag at her hip.

"They're not supposed to be out this far..." El said, breaking the silence that had rested between them. "What's a Reflector Beast doing this far from the Outer Plains?" She stared at Cyfrin, clearly expecting an answer.

Cyfrin just shook his head, staring with brooding eyes at the place the creature had disappeared. His gaze flicked to Mara before settling on El. "We don't have the luxury of time to debate that question. If there's one dark beast in the area, then there's likely more." He gave Mara a once over while she stood shaking in front of him. His expression was unreadable. "You walk in the middle of us this time. Let's move."

Kain was standing off to the side, just over Cyfrin's shoulder. He was sniffing at the oozing black sap that still clung to his leather glove, eyeing the steam ascending from the tree before him with a scowl. "Never seen a tree do *that* before. They haven't all keeled over like the rest of the trees out there either." He stepped closer, inches from the blackened bark with his sword in hand. "How are they all still standing?"

Milios spun around, hand extended towards Kain and eyes wide. "No, *don't—*" But Kain had already raised his blade, slicing off a thick piece of bark to examine it more closely.

A scream ripped through the forest, originating from somewhere high in the canopy above. Black liquid bled like a river from the gaping hole left by Kain's sword. He leapt back toward the group, the bark he had extracted falling to the forest floor as the scream began to echo from everywhere at once. Mara cried out, both in shock and pain as the volume only grew.

Cyfrin swore loudly, drawing his swords from his back and standing before Mara like a shield. "You great, daft bastard!" he yelled at Kain over the screaming. "Not everything is a trophy for your damned collection!"

"They're Barkens!" Milios yelled. "Wandering Barkens! They've been corrupted! Don't let them touch you!"

Branches were snapping all around, the limbs of trees descending towards them as the creatures unfroze from their dark slumbers. The screams were deafening now, Mara certain that her ears would bleed from the power behind it. The trees were bending, reaching as far they could with dagger-like branches dripping in the black ooze. Mara watched a limb from the tree nearest her suddenly extend, shooting towards her face. Her muffled cry of terror was drowned out by the screaming trees.

Someone grabbed her arm and pulled her roughly to the side. Cyfrin appeared where Mara had just stood as El spun her out of harm's way. Like a lightning flash, he struck through the poisoned branch, rending it from the limb. "*RUN!*" His voice boomed through the blinding noise. The screams were shaking the earth beneath them, and Mara was being pulled once more by El.

They ran. Mara ignored the rough terrain beneath her bare feet, letting terror set her pace. Milios whipped the wind in a vortex, striking the deadly Barkens back as they moved. Their trunks seemed to be fused with the ground, rooting them to the spot. It was a small miracle, but only just. Branches came inches from Mara, poised to pierce her heart, her stomach, her head. Each was struck from the air by Cyfrin, who had positioned himself like an impenetrable shield beside her.

As they flew through the screaming forest, Mara felt tears flooding from her eyes. Her blood had grown cold in her veins. *I'll never make it home,* her thoughts cried, frantic. *That was the last I'll ever see of my uncle, and I gave him nothing but grief. And Adrian, oh Adrian. I'll never make it home. I'll never make it home.* She sobbed, the sound once again muffled and lost between the gag and the screaming.

When she finally *did* make it back to Delinval, she reassured herself forcefully, she would never again complain of its constricting borders or laws against traveling outside the kingdom. She would ask her uncle's forgiveness for all her complaining, and all her begging to explore and adventure. The only thing left in this world outside of Delinval was decay and rot.

CHAPTER 6
OF KINGS, CONS, AND BETRAYAL

An eternal, breathless sprint carried them clear of the forest. Mara had never moved so fast in her life or felt such utter terror. Her many stumbles might have been the end for her, but Cyfrin, never more than a breath away, caught her each time. The last time, he had swept her over his shoulder, still running with unnatural grace. Without her to slow them, they had shot through the last of the Barkens.

The group of them emerged from the forest onto a flattened hilltop, its rolling terrain as withered as the now eerily silent forest stretching miles behind them. Cyfrin slid Mara from his shoulder with controlled ease, panting as he left her on the ground to catch his breath. All four of them were winded, but no worse for wear. Mara, though not physically injured, felt like she was going in to shock. She stared unblinkingly into the dense fog beyond the hills, the smell of stagnant water filling her nose as she took shallow, trembling breaths.

The Dreads had sat themselves on the ground, pulling rations from their packs and beginning to eat. El crouched in front of Mara, her expression hesitant. "I'm going to have Cyfrin undo those vines. You need to eat before we start moving again. I'd advise you refrain from screaming this time…I don't think I need to tell you it's extremely dangerous out here." El nodded to Cyfrin.

Cyfrin rose from the ground with a sigh, coming to stand above her with arms folded across his chest. He met Mara's murderous gaze with a look of mild amusement, the ghost of dimples in his cheeks.

You'll be the first to feel my blade, she thought, imagining her sword racing towards his thick neck.

El sighed, rolling her eyes. "Whenever you're done looking *brooding and inquisitive*, Cyfrin," she said, earning a sneer from him.

He knelt down beside El. "You'd do well to mind your manners this time, *your highness*." He said the last part with so much sarcasm, Mara could almost see the words oozing from him. His eyes flashed, the runes on his skin gleaming white, and with a wave of his hand, the vines binding her vanished.

El placed a chunk of bread, three cheese slices and a handful of berries on a piece of cloth before her then sat down by the others to eat and look over their map.

Mara sat in silence, rubbing her wrists, and staring up at the darkening sky. She knew of "Wandering Barkens" from the tomes in the castle library. They were sentient trees, the first born directly of Zenafrost's magick. The lost texts described them as healers, storytellers; kind-folk.

The sickness plaguing the land had stripped them of any remenant of their past selves. Fleeing from them had nearly driven all thought of the first monster they came across from her mind. But as the adrenaline wore off, and the cold reality set back in, she found it impossible to keep silent. "That monster, the one before the Barkens attacked. What was it?"

They all stiffened, exchanging knowing, uncomfortable looks.

"That," Cyfrin spoke as the other three continued to look unnerved, "was a Reflector Beast. They're used as trackers and hunters by their creator, Mezilmoth." The silence following his words was heavy. It seemed as if the very air grew cold in response.

Mara gulped, too curious to stop now. "What's a Reflector Beast?"

Cyfrin's icy eyes bored into hers, but she did not flinch away from their power. "A Reflector Beast uses dark magic to prey on your deepest fears, that which you know could end you. It shows you things designed to break your soul, destroy every bit of hope and good in you. Then, when you're devastated, hopeless and defeated, it'll drag you back to the Dark Gate and toss you in. An eternity serving their maker in the End." His voice was thick with disdain.

"Disgusting buggers, they are," Kain added, nudging a rock across the ground with his foot.

"Cruel, cruel things," El said in a small voice, eyes wavering as she nodded in agreement.

Their reactions confused Mara. The Dreads served Mezilmoth, used his dark magicks to fuel their armies in the war. Why would they be so filled with fear and hatred of their own God?

Rubbing his jaw, Cyfrin turned back to his friends. "We're running out of time. Our best chance now is to cut through the mountains by way of Bardro's Gash."

Kain groaned at this. "Not Krakenbär, Cyf. That's asking for trouble. Nothing good has ever come from taking that path—"

"If there was another choice, we'd take it," Cyfrin cut

him off, his deep tone ominous. "But the longer we're out here, the more dire all of our situations become. You heard the General before we left: If we don't have her back by the time the moon's next full, we'll miss the ritual. Then it will be all our heads."

His words shot a chill of dread through Mara, reminding her of the gravity of her situation. *Ritual?* she thought, her eyes widening as the Dreads perused their map. These people were killers. They had ravaged their own lands, slaughtered countless numbers of her people, stolen her from her home. *Do they mean to sacrifice me?!* If they thought she was going to go along with them quietly, they were sorely mistaken.

Adrian had often told her she "lacked the capacity" to hold her tongue, even in the most dire of circumstances. Her uncle had insinuated for years that this, among other things, would make her a "difficult bride." Mara mustered every bit of the stern, uncompromising tone she had learned from Lady Len and leapt to her feet "Who is your general?" she demanded. "What does he want with me? Why have you kidnapped me if you do not intend to seek a ransom for my safe return? Where is it you're taking me? What is this 'ritual' you speak of?"

Unblinking, they all stared at her as she threw out her barrage of questions. Then, they turned in unison and continued eating and perusing the map as if she hadn't spoken at all.

Mara's fiery rage grew hotter in her chest. She glowered down at them, balling her hands into fists at her sides and puffing out her chest. "I am of the royal and honorable Delinvalian bloodline. The crown princess of Delinval. You *will* tell me who has sent you to capture me, and why—I *command* it!"

Cyfrin gave a stifled snort of laughter, and then they all

burst out laughing. "You hear that?" Kain chortled, shaking his head and smacking Cyfrin on the arm. "She's *the* crowned princess of Delinval! How foolish of us not to know that!"

Mara was fuming now as they continued laughing. The mocking sound reminded her of the tournament when the entire kingdom jeered at her as the King pretended she'd not just won on her own. Her vision went red, her entire body shaking. "I will not stand here and be mocked by you…you *mongrels*…you *Dreads*!"

Their laughter ceased instantly.

Mara cried out as thick roots sprung upward, entangling her, rooting her to the spot and binding her there. Vines twisted up the roots, wrapping around her mouth and gagging her once more. Cyfrin stalked toward her, expression dark, his tattoos glowing. "You speak without knowledge," he growled. "Your *honorable* people forced that name upon us as part of your King's great narrative. We are not *Dreads*, we are *Odelians*. And I will not allow you to stand and shoot slurs upon me and my friends, regardless of your misguidance. Remove that word from your vernacular, or you can walk the rest of the way gagged."

Though his voice was weighted with anger, there was something odd in his tone, something that sounded strangely like sadness. The scent of pine and honey, the same she had smelled when he had covered her mouth from screaming in the forest, surrounded her. Mara realized that the woodsy aroma originated from him, and not from the trees themselves as she had first thought. He returned to where his friends were sitting. El gave Mara an apologetic look as Kain stared at Cyfrin with a strained expression.

Mara struggled against her bonds, her face burning with anger. She didn't care what they called themselves, didn't care if they took offense to her calling them "Dreads". Even if her uncle *had* given them the name, it was for very good reasons. They were power hungry, selfish, and renowned for their evil deeds. They couldn't help themselves, so poisonous was the dark magicks they wielded.

The war may have been won by her uncle and their people, but it did not change the price they all were now forced to pay. She let out a muffled cry of frustration and continued to struggle against her bonds.

"What's the plan, then?" Milios said, breaking the silence with their musical voice. "Most paths to get to the Krakenbär Mountains are either eroded away, or too sick with the darkness to walk across safely without the risk of being infected."

Cyfrin pointed down at the map, dragging his long finger across its surface in an arching line. "We'll need to hug as close to Ylastra as we can. The swamps aren't ideal terrain, but it's better than wasting days picking our way across rubble and hiding from darklings."

They all stopped moving at Cyfrin's reply, exchanging weary looks. El thumbed the top of a potion bottle attached to her chest anxiously. "Are you sure there's not a different route we could take?" she asked. "Us, getting that close to Ylastra after what happened…"

"Yeah, I can't see King Normigone throwing us a party after what happened last time we entered the Underkingdom." Kain was rubbing the back of his head as he spoke, a grim smile on his face. "His exact words were 'I'll have your balls sent back to your village in a box if you ever set foot here again, you bastard savages', if memory serves."

"No, you're right. That's exactly what he said, right before he unleashed his chaos beast to chase us out," Milios added with a dull smile.

Cyfrin stood to his full, considerable height and looked down at the three of them with hardened resolve. "Caerani expects us back immediately, and time is not on our side. Have you not been paying attention? The darkness has been worsening by the day, far quicker than before. We cannot afford to take the longer path when the danger doubles by the second. Our mission is too precious."

He'd spoken the last sentence in a much softer tone, all four sharing a grave, meaningful look. They nodded slowly in agreement.

"Right then," Cyfrin continued. He stared down the hill but waved a hand behind him. Mara was released from the roots holding her to the ground, but vines still bound her mouth and wrists. "We need to put some more distance between us and Grathiel's legion. The forest won't keep them at bay long. They'll burn it down before they let us get too far ahead."

He didn't even look at Mara as he said this.

Kain fell into step beside her puffing himself up as he marched her down the hillside. "You heard the man," he said in a voice of mock superiority. "Right this way, your royal pain-in-the-arse!"

CHAPTER 7
IN THE BOG'S WAKE

Walking down the steep hillside into the foggy landscape below made Mara painfully aware of just how exhausted she was. She had only eaten a few bites of the food El had offered her before she had been bound once again, and her empty stomach growled. Glowering at Cyfrin's back, she rested the full weight of the blame on him.

Her hangover was one for the books. It gripped her head and body, making every step a concerted effort. Even her sweat smelled of mead, and she felt woozier with every gust of stale breeze. The five of them reached the bottom of the rolling hills and stopped, surveying their next steps with great care. The fog made visibility limited, but Mara was able to make out the area below.

Marshy wetlands stretched out around them as far as she could see, which explained the stagnant water she'd smelled earlier. In the distance, through the heavy fog, loomed massive walls made of blackened stone. They struck a ghostly presence in the thick, drifting air. Chains adorned the exteriors, wrapping back and around, stretching well above where the eye could follow. This was the dark city: the chaos kingdom of Ylastra.

Mara noted how similar the entrance looked to that of the kingdom of Delinval, almost as if it were the white city's dark counterpart. But no visible gate lay in sight against the towering barricade. Instead, giant wooden stakes, tall as trees and nearly as wide, shot out all around the perimeter. The message they struck was very clear: *Keep Out.*

They started off through the swampy grounds, their feet squelching uncomfortably through the muck, and Mara fought not to squeal or gag as the ankle-high mud squeezed up between her toes. The smell of old, rancid water constricted her breathing as she struggled to keep an even pace through the swampy earth clinging to her feet.

"Glad to see this place is just as cheery as ever," El said through her teeth.

It felt like a thousand eyes were watching them as they marched down the hill. Mara could hear noises coming from within the mist pressing around her, the sounds of beasts and monsters hiding just out of sight. She shivered, holding her bound wrists against her chest. There was something foul about the cries; something desperately unnatural. Cringing, she tried not to think about whatever could be making them.

Cyfrin dropped back to walk beside her. She stiffened, keeping her nose upturned and her steely gaze straight ahead. She was surprised when he shrugged the heavy cloak from his back and moved to drape it over her shoulders. His scent engulfed her in their closeness, the pine and honey she now associated with her hatred of him. Moving quickly, she stepped out of the way, dodging the gesture without even looking at him. Cyfrin sighed, clearly annoyed, slung the cloak back over his own shoulders, and hurried forward to walk just ahead of her. She wouldn't be accepting any gesture from him—now or ever.

Mara was now the furthest away from her kingdom that anyone her age had ever traveled. Her uncle had closed the gates to their pure, untouched inner city right after the massacre of the Marred Lands at the very beginning of the Great War. Even after they'd emerged victorious, he'd had the foresight to know what sort of darkness would stem from the aftermath. He had protected them from all the nightmarish horrors now roaming Zenafrost. It used to drive Mara mad, the feeling of being trapped; the knowledge that she, like everyone else in Delinval, would never set foot outside its walls.

That feeling had changed the instant she had been kidnapped.

Everything she had seen thus far was either dead, dying, or corrupted by the forces of dark magick poisoning the earth—a far cry from the stories of lush forests and rolling meadows of flora that Lady Lenorei had told her stories of at bedtime. The land was sick, and Mara felt another surge of anger which she settled, once again, on the lean back and broad shoulders of the man walking in front of her. Cyfrin and all the Dreads like him were to blame for this. She longed to put a blade to his throat and draw it back slowly across his flesh, to make him atone for all the evil his people had done.

Mara wondered if, given the opportunity, she'd have the courage to do such a thing. She was doing her best to put on a brave face, but with every step she took, leading her farther and farther from Delinval, her fear mounted. She wondered about the ritual they'd mentioned, at the implications behind needing her there, and her blood ran cold with the possibilities.

Eyes on the wet ground, Mara was lost in dismal

thought when she suddenly walked right into what felt like a brick wall. Startled, she looked up into Cyfrin's stony stare. The four of them had inexplicably stopped, and she walked directly into him. His hand shot out to steady her as he and his companions stared into the dense fog that lay ahead. There were shapes forming in the mists. Odd, long shapes with round bobbles perched on the top.

The mist cleared a bit and Mara's eyes went wide. No. No not bobbles.

"Heads," El groaned.

They all took another step forward, Mara with them, and the objects came into sharp relief. Dozens of heads, in various degrees of decay, sat perched on the ends of tall stakes jutting up from the marsh. The gruesome parade lined the outside of the high walls, assuring they were impossible to miss from any angle.

Mara recognized Delinvalian jewelry hanging from the gory necks of several of the severed heads, and she couldn't help the whimper that escaped her.

Milios moved inches away from one, its mouth twisted into a frozen final scream. They stared into its vacant eyes. "The heads appear to have been ripped from the torsos quite vigorously." They tilted their head to look underneath its gaping neck.

"Well," Kain said with a wry twist of his lips. "Normigone and his men seem to be coming along nicely locked away in their kingdom of sludge. Posting heads on sticks at their doorstep is clearly not an obvious sign of them going *completely* mad and feral."

El was grimacing at the row of slaughter. "What kind of creature could tear them clean from their bodies?"

Mara closed her eyes and tried to dismiss the vivid images of monsters ripping her head off she was bringing to life in her mind.

"If we stand here much longer, Eleanora, we're bound to find out," Cyfrin replied in a sarcastic tone. He was still holding on to Mara's arm and she hadn't thought to pull away. She'd been too transfixed by the sight before her.

She stepped away from him, and he finally let go to lead them all forward once more.

The group, including Mara, closed ranks, drawing close to one another to protect themselves from what might lay ahead. Mara thought back to their conversation on the hilltop, how they had discussed being kicked out of Ylastra once before. Through her haze of growing fear, she wondered what sort of crime someone would have to commit to be banished from such a malevolent place.

They crept into the shadows of the great stone wall, weapons drawn. With her hands bound impenetrably together, Mara had never felt more vulnerable. If her captors should fall to some beast, like the one they had nearly run afoul of in the Forest of Fallen, and she was this defenseless... She shivered at the thought.

"Just out of curiosity, Cyf," El whispered. "What's the plan if we draw the Ylastrian's attention?" Cyfrin's shoulders tightened, and El clenched her teeth. "You don't have a plan?"

"Of course, there's a plan," he whispered back, not meeting her livid stare. "The plan is don't get caught. Thus, eliminating the need for a second plan."

"That's how we work best," Kain breathed, giving Cyfrin a hard slap on the shoulder that sunk him deeper into the muck.

El groaned. "Play it by ear, and pray to the Zenoths that we don't have our assess handed to—"

A scream stopped them all in their tracks.

Without a word, the four of them circled Mara with

weapons ready. El's eyes glowed green and orb-lights shot from her hands to illuminate the foggy path before them.

There, her body halfway submerged in a pool of deep muck, was a girl who looked just a little younger than Mara. She was entirely covered in mud, and her eyes were darting around in a panic as she clawed hopelessly at the sludge. Her stare fell on them as the area lit up. "Please!" she gasped, reaching a hand towards them. From the way she was panting, it sounded as though she had been struggling there for hours. "Please, help me!"

El took a step forward, visibly concerned, but Milios put out a hand to stop her. "Wait," they said. "Something's not right," Gray eyes cold with inquisition, they stared down at the pathetic, crying creature in the mud.

Cyfrin took a cautious step towards the girl, his wary eyes beginning to glow bright blue as vines rose from the bog towards the girl. "Grab on to this," he said carefully as the vine reached for the girl's clawing grasp.

"Please!" she repeated. "Help me!"

But Milios was right. Even Mara sensed something was desperately wrong here.

The vine touched the girl's outstretched hand, and her eyes went dim, as if all the life had been suddenly sapped from her. "Help me," she said again. Her voice was thick now, as if she were speaking from underneath the muck.

"Back!" Cyfrin commanded. The group retreated up the path and he positioned himself between them and the girl.

Mara watched in horror as the girl's features began to melt before her eyes. Her face, like dark wax down a candlestick, began to droop, and Mara heard El whimper in horror.

"Help me," the girl said once more.

She began to haul herself from the muck pit. Her

movements were jarring, as if her joints weren't connected or simply not there at all. Mara backed away, the others following suit, as all defining features fell from the girl's form.

Standing there now was some sort of malformed mud creature, looking as if someone with only the vaguest understanding of human anatomy had sculpted it. There were several eyes sliding down its front, and a gaping maw slicing clean through the place where its neck had been. Great, wet sputtering noises emitted from it, expelling droplets of black sludge with every breath. "Please," the distorted voice wheezed again, filling Mara with a cold dread. "Help me."

Then it lunged.

It rocketed forward with frightening dexterity, and shards of different colored magicks shot towards it from Milios, Cyfrin and El's outstretched hands. All three magicks collided with the monster, bubbling menacingly as it absorbed each with a little *pop*.

There was a moment's pause as it stood, swaying in place. Then there came a loud sizzling sound, and the creature split itself in two. Its twin flopped out of the muck of its companion, coming to stand directly beside it with a gurgling groan.

Cyfrin and Kain swore in unison. Cyfrin had backed all the way up to Mara, standing at an angle to keep her shielded.

"Help me," both creatures now said in unison using the same innocent voice. The sizzling noises hit a crescendo, and there was a loud *crack!*

"Watch out!" El yelled. She grabbed Mara by the arm and pulled her to the side. The rest of them dove out of the way as shards of the magick they had fired at the creature shot back at them from inside the sludgy bodies.

"It's chaos magick!" Milios called out. They all got back to the feet, covered in mud. "We must stop firing at it, or it will turn our own powers back on us tenfold!"

"To the Ends with that!" Kain hollered, letting out a battle cry as he lunged forward with his giant sword. His blade drove into the first mud creature, cleaving it clean in half. The top portion of it slid to the ground with a sickening squish. Its companion let out a terrifying shriek and lunged at Kain with a dozen flailing limbs, forcing him to the defensive.

The parts of the creature cut down began to shudder in the muck. Mara froze with panic as the pieces began to pull towards one another of their own accord. And then the creature rose from the muck as two brand new monsters.

Milios, Cyfrin and El drew their weapons and joined Kain in the fight. Mara stood watching, eyes wide, wishing more than anything that she had something to defend herself with. Hands still bound together, and as distracted by the fight as the rest of them, she startled when something grabbed her ankle. Her eyes shot down to a hand, black as night, jutting out from the mud pit. Before she could even think, it gave a mighty yank, and she stumbled into the dark pool.

Being dragged irresistibly down below the surface of the bog, she let out a yell that was muffled by the vines that had her muzzled and overshadowed by the sounds of battle. The muck trembled as she struggled to break free, but the thing slowly pulling her under was too strong. Her bound hands served as nothing more than a weight as she thrashed. She could feel whatever held her ankle tightening its grip as it pulled her down. The sludge was up to her neck now, cold and slimy against her skin.

Her muffled sounds of panic reached a fever pitch, and

finally Cyfrin heard them. He whipped around, disengaging the multiplying army of enemies. The swamp was now past her gagged lips, only the top of her head and her bound hands, held up over her head, were visible. With a sound like cracking thunder, Cyfrin shot towards her, his eyes glowing bright as the blazing runes on his skin. The vines around her wrists and mouth vanished. Desperate, she stretched her hand toward him as far as she could, but it wasn't enough.

The last thing Mara saw was the wide-eyed panic on Cyfrin's face as he reached for her and missed.

CHAPTER 8
CREATURES OF CHAOS AND MUCK

Mara groaned, stirring from sleep. She had dreamt of the strangest things, of monsters and magick, of ancient ruins and heads on spikes. Her head was throbbing. The world seemed to spin round and round. She cursed to herself, putting a hand over her closed eyes as she swore to the Zenoths never to drink again. Lady Lenorei would be livid. There was no way Mara would be able to focus properly today after such a fitful night. Her entire body ached—she felt as if she had barely slept at all.

A smell filled Mara's nose, the scent of stale water and dirt, and her eyes flew open. She lay on a stone slab, a heavy blanket draped beneath her. Torches hung from the walls of blackened rock, providing dim light. Chains draped across the stone, ending in shackles, made of a strange metal that vibrated ever so slightly.

Mara leapt to her feet, swearing as they responded with a throb of pain that shot up into her ankles and calves. It had not been a dream at all, but a waking nightmare. One that seemed to only be getting worse. She spotted a heavy door, the only entrance to the room, and rushed for it. She shook the handle, but it was locked from the other side. Mara threw herself against the door, slamming her shoulder into the wood. It didn't move an inch.

She drew back, her heart rising to her throat, shoulder aching. She was a prisoner, and she had no idea where she was or how long she had been there, asleep, vulnerable. An image flashed through her mind, the last thing she could remember before waking up. Heads on stakes. Mud up to her neck. Multiplying monsters made of chaos. And Cyfrin, eyes wild as he dove to save her.

The sound of dripping water echoed off the rock, and Mara looked up. It was too dark to make out the ceiling, but the wetness of the room seemed to stem from up above.

She drew her eyes back to the room, looking for any possible escape, but the unforgiving door seemed the only way out. She looked around, her eyes falling on pieces of what looked eerily like human bones. She forced herself to ignore them, refusing to succumb to the overwhelming panic that threatened to consume her whole.

Footsteps sounded on the other side of the door, hurrying towards her. Mara spun around, looking for something to use to defend herself. But save for the stone slab, the blanket, and the chains secured to the wall, the cell was empty. The lock clicked, and the door swung wide.

A man stepped into the cell. He was slightly shorter than Mara, and stocky. Beneath his thick armor, his skin was pitch black, and he had white symbols burned into his arms and face. His eyes were a feral shade of red, and tiny trinkets and dangerous-looking blades adorned his leather clad body. He was smiling at Mara, and she flinched away from the pointed yellow teeth exposed beneath his curling lip. He gave a grand bow that sent his long grey ponytail sweeping the dusty rock beneath him. "Welcome to the Underkingdom of Ylastra, your highness."

His deep, rasping voice grated on Mara's ears. Her heart sank. Thanks to her studies, she knew a lot about Ylastrians, and none of it was good. Aside from their betrayal during the war, the chaos magick users in Ylastra were said to be even more unpredictable than Dreads. Chaos magick was unstable, by its very nature, driving all who used it to madness.

Mara remembered the staked heads of the fallen outside the kingdom's walls, and bit back on a scream of fear. Standing taller, feigning more courage than she had, she looked down her nose at the dark wedge of a man and spoke. "Why have you brought me here, shadowling?"

He looked up from his bow, prolonged to the point of parody, still smiling in a way that made her stomach sick. "Apologies, my good lady." he replied. "I'm sure this must all be very confusing for you. I put you in here to keep you safe till you awakened. You're currently in the heart of our kingdom, built under the bog to keep out unwanted guests."

He extended a hand towards her that she refused to take. Still, his smile did not falter. "We had received word from King Grathiel's legion that his most beautiful princess had been plucked right out of her bed in the dark of the night. There's a reward to bring you back to your kingdom. *Alive.*"

Mara felt a thrill of terror run through her as his smile widened at the word "alive." But she held her ground. "I'm sure my uncle will be more than grateful to you for freeing me from those…*people.*" She'd stopped short of saying the word Dread, fearing Cyfrin might appear at the utterance of it. "And for saving me from that monster out there in the bogs."

The man shook his head and tutted at her. "That was no monster," he said, taking a step forward. "That was Esmeralda. Didn't you like her? I find her to be quite the amusing companion. I crafted her from my own magick, you know. Sent her to the overearth to retrieve you."

He looked pleased with himself and paused as if waiting for praise. But Mara stayed silent.

He stepped closer, now only a few feet away and eyeing her as if she were a pig on a spit. "I didn't realize the ones that had taken you were of magick themselves. Few and far between we are since the War. Will have to renegotiate our reward with your dear Uncle. Could have been a lot more difficult, capturing you. Lucky thing you came right to me."

The way he'd said it—with relish, like a hunter who had finally trapped his prey—made Mara squirm.

"Oh, you are such a pretty thing. Such a pretty, pretty thing." He reached out and grabbed her hand before she could step back. His lips grazed the top of her knuckles, and she snatched her arm back. He giggled in response, sounding unhinged, and then clapped his hands together in excitement. "Yes, he'll have to pay me quite handsomely to part with you. Come, my sweet princess. We shall present you before our dark King Normigone. He'll be so pleased with me, gathering you up so quickly. Such a pretty, pretty thing."

Mara had almost decided the man was quite mad when he threw back his head, cackling and murmuring unintelligibly. Now she was sure: he was mad. Her stomach flipped in on itself, and she straightened her shoulders, determined to force aside the fear clutching her heart. "King Grathiel will not take kindly to my being treated like your prisoner," she spat.

"Oh but, deary, you *are* my prisoner. Or my plaything

if you continue to be naughty. I haven't decided which I like you more as of yet." His words shot cold fear through Mara, and his eyes flashed with glee at her obvious horror. "Enough of this babble!" he exclaimed. "The King has been waiting patiently for you to awaken! Come! Come!"

He eyed her, his lecherous gaze doing a slow once over of her body as he drew his tongue across his lips. "First, we shall dine on fine wine and food. You look positively exhausted!" He bowed low again, murmuring as he backed out of the cell.

Mara stared at him, wishing she could do anything but following him out. Before this dark man had shown up, she'd been praying to be let out; now all she wanted was to slam her cell door in his face and lock it soundly between them.

Resigned, she stepped out into a rounded rock tunnel, similar in appearance to her cell. Torches hung every few feet, casting long shadows up the walls that stretched into the ceiling above. But now that she was getting a proper look at it, she found it wasn't a ceiling at all. It looked like the ground of the bog above, though without the sparse and blackened reeds. Mara's eyes narrowed as she watched waves of iridescence roll across its surface. *More magick*, she thought with a grimace. *Will I never be free of it?* The smell of stagnant water was overwhelming in the cramped tunnel, and spikes of rocks shot out of the ground here and there.

Dozens of guards stood at attention outside her cell, all with the same dark features as the man who'd kissed her hand, though their faces were void of the strange glowing runes that adorned his flesh. The stout man snapped his fingers, and two guards stepped from the pack. They came to stand at attention on either side of Mara, their spears tipped in a glowing golden metal that pulsed with vibrant energy. Her host was humming a cheery tune, looking ecstatic as he turned on his heel and started leading her down the tunnel. The guards followed in formation around him, the two by Mara leading her in step.

She had never felt so helpless. All her life, she had been capable and strong, even able to overpower men twice her age and size at times. But that was when she had her sword in her hand. Not when she was barefoot, unarmed and wearing nothing but flowing strips of mud-soaked fabric. Angry tears welled in her eyes. She swallowed them back, refusing to give up hope.

Noticing hollowed out windows in the rock wall, she began looking for an escape. She peered through one of the windows as she passed and gasped. Beyond the sprawling tunnels, she could see glimpses of a massive, glowing city, built into the cavern walls. Bright lights winked at her from building windows as they passed. She could hear voices echoing through the cavernous space from the carved city as the people within went about their lives. An odd, low hum was coming from somewhere below the city, emanating from a giant chasm that separated the kingdom and her tunnel. Mara's eyes were met by nothing but darkness as she peered into the empty spans. Something about it made her skin crawl, but she had no time to wonder why as they marched her onward.

She now realized that the great, blackened stone walls in the bogs were a ruse. A false entrance, leading any potential invaders to assume the city lay just beyond. The Underkingdom of Ylastra was just that: a kingdom built in the shadowy underbelly of Zenafrost.

Mara's mind raced as she tried to sort out a plan. Waiting here for these people to decide her fate seemed the worst possible strategy, especially if the insane man now half skipping up the hall in front of her had any say in it.

But she was underground, in a kingdom she did not recognize full of people who would sooner sell her to the highest bidder than help her. She had no money, nothing she could use to bargain. Should the Ylastrians decide she was more use to keep than to return to her uncle, escape looked hopeless.

And what if he decides I'm to be kept as his plaything?! Mara thought with a grimace, repeating his previous words in her head. *Surely my uncle will come to save me,* she reassured herself. Even so, the images of the Delinvalian heads lining the outer walls in the bog haunted her. Now, in a burst of fear, she could picture Adrian among them. She shook her head, willing herself to stay calm. This was neither the time nor place for panic.

The crazy man led her towards a tall doorway, its frame disappearing into the dark wetness above. Softly glowing candlelight illuminated the room beyond. He stepped through the threshold and Mara followed, her guards remaining by her side while the rest of the soldiers stayed in the tunnel.

The ceilings here, unlike the murky sludge of the tunnel, were actually made of the same black rock, and intricate carvings of dark men in glorious battle adorned the surface, lit by candles floating above Mara's head that were held aloft by magick. A long table made from black marble sat in the center of the room, and there was a sprawling fireplace against one wall that cast shadows over a pair of tufted, wing-backed chairs. Mara noted that the flames within the hearth smoldered purple, and they seemed to crackle with new life as she and her host entered.

The stout man stopped and turned to face her, gasping in exaggerated shock. "Ah, but I've completely forgotten myself in the excitement! I should have given you a name to go with my face. Forgive me, Princess, and please allow me to introduce myself. My name is Demiel, Keeper of Ylastra, Blade of the Black Crown, and right hand to our wonderous dark King, Normigone." He straightened with an air of great grandeur and met Mara's eyes once more. She glared down her nose at him, refusing to speak till she was certain of her own safety. He motioned dramatically to the table, where she heard the soft tinkling of glass being set down. Plates had appeared at opposite ends of the table; strange meat slices, all with sauces of various colors, had materialized. Large crystal goblets sat next to bottles of darkly swirling liquid in front of each plate, and Demiel pulled out the chair at the end nearest to them.

She remained unmoving. She wasn't interested in his feigned niceties. She wanted to go home.

With a nod of Demiel's scarred head, the guards flanking Mara grabbed her under the elbows and forced her roughly into the seat, then stood at attention on either side of her. Demiel sat at the other end of the table, a good twenty feet away, and poured a dark purple liquid into the goblet in front him. He lifted the glass, his eyes narrowing as he stared at Mara over the brim. "You know," he started, pausing to take a sip. "It's the strangest thing. I feel as if I've met you before. Is this your first time in our lovely kingdom, princess?"

Mara couldn't stop the sneer that contorted her face let alone the words that tumbled out with it. "*Lovely* is hardly the word I'd use to describe this foul place."

Demiel froze, the guards on either side of her stiffening. She bit her lip, cursing her careless tongue. There had never been a time in Mara's life where she was able to keep herself quiet, and that had caused many issues over the years.

Watching her carefully, Demiel lifted his fork and

began to eat. Determined to convince him to surrender her to her uncle, Mara searched back through her memory, looking for anything that could help her. She remembered Lady Lenorei talking about the truce that Delinval and Ylastra had come to after the war, the promise to cease all harm and live as peaceably as they could. The heads of her people torn from their bodies, coupled with Demiel's suggestive threat to simply keep her as his toy…neither could be deemed "peaceful". *Do not show fear,* she scolded herself. *Give him nothing but your strength, Mara. It's just like the negotiations that take place at court. What would Uncle do?*

Mara raised her head high at the thought. She glared down the long table at Demiel. "There is no honor in bartering for my safety, in placing a coin amount on my life. You have saved me from my captors, and for this I am quite grateful. You will be rewarded for your efforts. But my uncle will not take kindly to what you speak of. The Great Truce states—"

Demiel cut her off with a shrill laugh, throwing his head back for emphasis. "*The Great Truce?*" he mocked, and Mara's face went red. "When marched up to the city walls, child, did you not see my wonderful decor? Did it go—" He flashed her a wicked smile. "—over your head?"

The images of dead eyes and soundless screams locked for all eternity on decaying faces flashed through Mara's mind.

Demiel laughed again, a maniacal sound, his eyes glinting with delight at her horror. "And you *must* have seen the fantastic jewelry I left on the ones foolish enough to try and enter our borders? Of course, you did! I can see it all over your pretty, pretty face. Did that give you the impression that I cared for any *truce* your people tried to force upon us, girl?"

Mara felt an angry retort rising in her throat, but she

forced herself to keep quiet. She was in way over her head. She had no weapons, no allies, and no means of escape. An impossible situation by all counts, and one she was in danger of making much worse with her willful tongue.

Demiel took another gulp from his goblet. "Your uncle, for his part, will do as I wish. If, that is, he wants our great and noble king Normigone to return you back whole." He eyed her across the table, his tongue licking the stain of wine from his lips. "There are many pieces you could lose and still be considered *alive*."

He pulled a mocking pouty face at her before his eyes turned inquisitive again. He leaned forward, squinting to focus. "You must tell me. We've met somewhere before, have we not? We *must* have. Your face is so familiar…such stunning ivory flesh. I would never forget." Mara shook her head, but Demiel continued to stare. "Are you the last of the direct Delinvalian bloodline, girl? Do your parents yet live?"

Mara's nostril flared with suppressed emotion as he continued eating the strange meat on his plate. No one ever spoke of her mother, or her father for that matter. He had been a mighty general in the Great War and had given his life protecting her kingdom and its people. Her mother, frail and sickly, had passed away giving birth to her not long after. The ladies of the court had never let Mara forget that it had been her coming into this world that had cut her mother's life short. There were few portraits of either parent in the castle; it hurt her uncle to remember his younger brother and the life he'd lost while fighting that Zenoths forsaken war. The life he could have had with not only his brother, but with Mara, were it not for the Dread's greed.

She scowled as Demiel dabbed the corner of his mouth with a napkin. He motioned down to the plate before her.

"Will you not eat? I promise I haven't poisoned it." His shifty smile returned. "Our great king will want to see you fed and rested when we arrive before him. He wants to give you a full examination to ensure you are indeed Grathiel's lost princess, and you'll need all your strength for that." He shook his head, his red eyes gleaming. "It truly is a shame. I would so love to know how your flesh feels beneath my blade. But he did make me promise not to harm you. *Yet*."

The cold indifference in these words sent a shiver down Mara's spine, pulling another shrill laugh out of Demiel. *A full examination*, his words echoed around her mind. It took the breath from her body, leaving her too stunned to reply.

She didn't move the rest of the meal, determined not to give him any reason to sate his blood lust on her. Demiel ate and went on about how familiar she looked to him. Finally, when he had finished eating, he slammed both fists down on the table. Mara jumped at the suddenness of the motion. "To feel this strongly about my knowing you…" he said. "Perhaps it is destiny, blood of Delinval. Perhaps we knew each other in a life past, eh? A world beyond this one?"

He stood from his seat and crossed over to her, leaning in uncomfortably close, forcing her to push back into her chair. He flashed his sharp teeth. "Let us see if we'll know each other much longer in this one. Come!" He clapped at the guards. They pulled Mara's seat out from under her, forcing her to her feet.

Demiel strode from the dining hall, licking his fingers clean, speaking over his shoulder to her. "We mustn't keep the dark king waiting any longer. He gets *so* unmanageable when he's impatient. Tedious." He led them out into the torch-lit tunnel, the crowd of guards gathering around them once more.

Mara's eyes returned to their searching for escape. There had to be some sort of exit, some way to reach the surface from this miserable underground mire. But her frantic gaze only saw solid rock and the Underkingdom beyond the windows as they drew nearer to it. Heart thundering in her chest, pulse growing more erratic with every step, she finally emerged into a cavernous chamber with tunnels leading off in all directions. Her eyes returned to the muck-covered ceiling, held in place by the shimmering, constant magick. Mara had the sudden suspicion that this muck didn't just *look* like the bog above, but that it *was* the bog above. She recalled being dragged down through the mud, that Demiel had come for her from within its depths. *If that's the only way in or out of here, then I'm doomed*, she thought with a whimper.

She was still staring at the ceiling when Demiel stopped short, the guards all following suit. She heard his breath catch, and then he began to spin around in a circle, eyes wild as he scanned the cavern.

"Shame." The voice that cut through the room seemed to reverberate from everywhere at once. Mara felt it in her soul, the air falling deathly cold and quiet as it swept through. "I thought there would be much more of a fight getting in here. I'm disappointed in you, Demiel. You're becoming careless."

From behind her, Mara felt a hand grip her shoulder. She recognized the smell of pine and honey at once.

Cyfrin.

He stood a full head taller than either of her guards who jolted in surprise as he seemed to appear out of nothingness beside them. She felt instant relief followed by gut-wrenching shame that she'd felt it all.

Cyfrin was staring at the stunned man before him with a mischievous smirk on his dimpled face. Demiel was no longer smiling. His expression had twisted into rage and his red eyes burned at Cyfrin. "You," he breathed, starting to shake.

Cyfrin smiled, a vision of relaxation, and ruffled the top of Mara's head in an annoyingly possessive way. "Me!" he chirped, his voice full of cocky pride. It was unlike the dark, brooding air he had shown her thus far, though his voice still held the same bite of authority that made Mara's blood boil. He turned and snarled at the guard beside him who retreated into the group at once. The guard at Mara's shoulder fell back without Cyfrin even needing to growl at him.

Demiel looked livid. "You were commanded to never set foot here again, Lightcleaver!" he screeched. "Were told what would happen to you and your people if you ever dared!"

Cyfrin let out a dry laugh and stepped casually in front of Mara, positioning himself between her and Demiel. "Are you truly still angry after all these years?" Cyfrin tutted at Demiel, shaking his head. "It was a few scrolls and some ancient bottles of musty wine, Demiel. Get over it already."

"*They were documents from the Temple of Moons Past!*" Demiel shrieked at Cyfrin. The guards surrounding them drew their weapons as one. "Thousands of years of history —of irreplaceable artifacts! And your gang of miscreants used them to roll and smoke your herbs! You drank from the consecrated wines of our ancestors, you half-breed whore!"

Cyfrin shrugged, looking unfazed. "We came to help mend our broken alliance. *You* were the one who started serving us deep wine all through our meeting. If anyone's to take blame here, I feel a large portion of it should fall on your shoulders. You were our host that evening, after all.

Tell me, what did your idol, the king, have to say about your failure that day?"

Demiel roared at this, and Mara felt a ripple of angry, dark energy circle the room. "You will answer for your insolent tongue, you wretch!" he shouted as the guards collectively took a step towards them. "You will give me the princess, or I will cut off your limbs one by one and pry her from you *myself!*"

Cyfrin's fists clenched at his sides. Mara peeked around his broad form to see Demiel smiling again, but it was an evil expression, dripping with malevolence. "And you *boy*," he added with contempt, brandishing his finger towards Cyfrin. "You're so painfully idiotic that you walked right into enemy territory *alone*. Oh, mighty Lightcleaver, Caerani's obedient little pet. You are nothing but a bastard *child*."

Mara felt the crackle of electricity coming off Cyfrin; it prickled her skin, and she imagined his ice-blue eyes burning bright as she the runes on his exposed skin between his leather bracers and chest-piece begin to glow. He let out a bark of a laugh. "Ah, see, that's where you've wildly miscalculated, Dem." His voice was light, but Mara could hear the underlying threat beneath the words. "I am never alone. I'm simply much *faster* than my war party."

Sound erupted all around them. Explosions, screams, the clang of metal on metal. Mara spun around in time to see El, Milios, and Kain come barreling into the cavern from the tunnel behind her. Magick shot from El and Milios, Kain's sword no more than a blackened blur as he dashed forward. Demiel roared again, and Cyfrin pulled Mara out of the way as the man shot an arrow of purple chaos magick towards them.

Cyfrin positioned Mara behind him as Demiel, roaring still, raised his hands high above his head, then dropped to his knees and brought his fists down onto the ground, slamming them into the rock. There was a mighty *boom* and the earth below Mara's feet trembled.

"Don't think I missed that little comment, Cyf!" Kain roared over the throws of combat. "*Faster*, my ass! You just blew past the guards and left us to deal with the rubble!"

"Not the time, Kain!" El shot back, ripping potion bottles from her belt and tossing them into the torrents of wind Milios conjured before her.

"Hope you're ready for reinforcements!" Cyfrin called back to Kain over the clatter of their fighting. "It looks like we're about to entertain the whole kingdom!"

Kain smiled broadly at him, felling another Ylastrian with one arcing slash. "Bring them all!" he laughed, resuming his combat as Cyfrin's crackling magick joined the fray.

CHAPTER 9
BANISHMENT AND ACCEPTANCE

The cavern echoed with the shouts of the Ylastrians. Mara gasped as enemies began to pour in from the front and the back of the tunnel. The Dreads were taking on five to six men each, and making it look easy. El threw potion bottles from her bandoleer onto the ground. The glass shattered and sprayed the Ylastrian forces with something diabolical that sizzled and bubbled as it melted through armor, flesh, and bone, rending screams from the men as they fell to their knees in anguish.

Milios, looking wholly unbothered, used their control over the wind to whip one of the guard's bodies around like a battering ram, slamming him, headfirst, into his comrades, sending them flying into the rock walls with satisfying thuds.

Kain was absolutely beaming. He moved with such unnatural grace that it looked as if he were floating off the earth. His great sword seemed an extension of his mighty arms, flying in a dance of death as he brought down five, then ten, then twenty men.

Cyfrin seemed to be enjoying himself just as much. Bright blue lightning shot from his hands as he kept Mara shielded behind his body. Her eyes fell on Demiel as she peered underneath Cyfrin's outstretched arms. Panting, the man stood stock still in the middle of the chaos. He had his hand over his face, and an eerie, dark purple smoke was drifting out from between his fingers.

Cyfrin seemed to note Demiel's condition and swore loudly. Dropping the three men in front of him in a brilliant burst of electric blue magic, he yelled to his companions, "We've overstayed our welcome, all!" Another enemy charged, and he put the Ylastrian on the ground. "Shall we see ourselves out?"

Kain, Milios, and El closed ranks. There came a noise like thunder, dwarfing the sounds of combat. Demiel screamed an inhuman cry that vibrated and echoed off the damp stone walls of the tunnel. He threw his head back, and Mara gasped, drawing closer to Cyfrin's broad back on instinct.

She watched as Demiel's face warped and elongated. Long, purple thorns sprang from the surface of his skin and his eyes became circles of bright, white light. Screaming like an animal, he dropped down onto all fours. Talons burst from his fingertips. His skin stretched beyond its limits and the gut-wrenching crunch of breaking bones cut through the crisp air. His flesh bubbled, the veins beneath becoming black as he grew.

Cyfrin fired lightning from his hands in a great arc around himself, Mara, and his companions, creating a temporary barrier against the Ylastrian onslaught. Milios grabbed hold of Kain and El and sent a blast of air at the ground, shooting the three of them straight up and out of the oozing ceiling high above. Cyfrin reached out to Mara. She took his hand without hesitation. He wrapped an arm around her waist and pulled her close to him. His sweet, woodsy smell filled her nose. She felt his powerful muscles flex beneath his leathers as he gripped her tight. "Hold on to me," he said.

Demiel let out a dragon-like roar. He looked like nothing Mara had ever seen before, save perhaps within a nightmare. He had grown to five times his size and gave no signs of stopping as his skin continued to stretch. His body had begun sprouting scales across his exterior, fangs dripping in black ooze now descending from his mouth. Like a dragon from the legends of old, but one stripped of wings and deeply corrupted. Purple smoke huffed in great clouds from his mouth as he roared. *This is Chaos Magick*, she thought. *Zenoths save me.* His legs, now twice the size of tree trunks each, ended in taloned hooves. His skin was pulsating like a heartbeat, grey and transparent enough to see the black veins writhing beneath through the scales. The Ylastrians beneath him seemed torn by this transformation. Some screamed and fled to the tunnels in terror, others fell resolutely behind him like an army of mice below his terrifying frame. He turned his monstrous gaze on the two of them.

Eyes wide and staring at Demiel, Mara wrapped her arms around Cyfrin's neck and tightened her hold. He squeezed her close against his body, pointed his free hand at the ground, and the runes on his skin flashed bright white. A burst of power shot from his palm, the stone trembling under foot. Then the rock beneath them cracked in a perfect circle and began to rise in a pillar with them aloft. It jettisoned them upwards towards the ceiling, and Mara, terrified, squeezed her eyes tight, but not before seeing a dimpled grin appear on Cyfrin's face.

She felt the sludge of the mud ceiling close in around her. She was pressed from all sides and tried not to panic.

The entire world had become the weight of the muck and Cyfrin's arm wrapped around her, securing her to him with unwavering strength. Just as Mara felt she might suffocate, they rocketed out into dense fog above ground. She gasped for air, forcing deep breaths into her lungs, and she opened her eyes.

They were back in the bog, the sky bright through the mists above them. She realized with a shudder that she had spent an entire night down in the underkingdom. Luckily, El, Kain, and Milios waited for them at the surface now. The instant she and Cyfrin stepped off the rock pillar he had conjured, the sludge around them all began to bubble.

"We have to move!" El said. She was staring at the muck puddles now frothing as they boiled. Heads began rising from their centers.

Cyfrin turned to Mara, his blue eyes alight with urgency. "Don't complain," he said and hoisted her up and into his arms. He cradled her against his chest as if she weighed nothing, and the four of them started running.

Mara had never seen people move so quickly, sprinting over the hilly terrain as if the muck didn't cling to their legs with every step. Begrudgingly, she wrapped her arms around Cyfrin's neck once more and stared past his shoulder as they escaped. Ylastrians, men and mud monsters alike, were rising from the pits, roaring, brandishing weapons and taking chase.

"El!" Cyfrin shouted.

El stopped and spun about with a look of stony determination on her face. Kain and Milios kept moving, Cyfrin, Mara in his arms, flew past. El stood her ground, eyes aglow. She threw her arms open wide in the direction of the perusing Ylastrian forces.

A dense, green mist flowed out of her body, sizzling viciously as it mixed with the air. It surged forth with unnatural swiftness, twisting to surround the Ylastrians who began grabbing their throats, gasping and sputtering. Their faces turned purple. Their eyeballs swelled and burst from their skulls. With bodies dropping to the ground in front of her, El turned away, looking grim, and sped to catch up with her companions.

They continued running well after they had crossed out of the bog and away from the shadowed walls of Ylastra. The ground they now raced across was blackened as though fire had recently ravaged the land. Their footsteps crunched against the dead earth, and all signs of plant or animal life had vanished.

The group finally slowed to a halt at the edge of what looked like a small cliff face. The terrain here was hollowed out, marking where water had once flowed—a great scar of what Mara was sure had been a thing of great beauty. Cyfrin set her down as the four of them panted, working to catch their breath.

And then Kain began to laugh, the joyous sound out of place in the barren wastes around them. "Zenoths bless me, I had forgotten about Demiel's little temper tantrums!" he chuckled.

Cyfrin let out a breathless laugh. "Can't seem to ever leave that place without swords at our backs, or a chaos beast at our throats."

Wiping sweat from his brow, Kain sat down and pulled his great sword from his back to wipe the blood off it. El let out a hearty sigh and collapsed to the ground beside him, her eyes closed, her chest heaving. Milios, looking unfazed by the battle, sat down next to El and stroked her hair.

Mara's attention fell on Cyfrin where she found his sharp eyes tracing up her body. His gaze finally met hers, and she felt the heat of a blush rise up her neck. "Did they hurt you?" he asked gruffly, his eyes lingering on the blood spatter across the front of her filthy, torn gown.

She shook her head, still dazed from what she just witnessed. "None of this blood is mine." She pulled at her bodice to look down at the gore fusing with the gauzy material. "I got too close to one of your friend's killing blows." She angled a look at Kain, who beamed back at her.

Cyfrin looked unconvinced. His uncompromising stare drifted to her ears, and his eyes flashed. Extending his hand towards her, he rubbed his thumb in a feathery touch up her cheek to the tip of her right ear.

Mara felt a surge of electricity rush through her and pulled away.

Cyfrin's expression went dark. "Strange place to hold such heavy scarring." His tone was strained as he said it.

Mara pulled her tangle of curls over her ears, affronted. "That's none of your business," she hissed.

Sighing, Cyfrin turned his attention to El. "El, did you bring any spare armor with you?"

Eyes still closed as Milios pet her head, El waved vaguely at the pack she had tossed a few feet away. Cyfrin walked over and crouched next to it, dug through its contents, and then returned to Mara holding a bundle of clothes.

He handed her a set of worn leather armor, complete with a bodice, pants, bracers, and boots. "It'll be a while before we get the chance to rinse the muck off us. But you should change now that we have a moment to catch our breath." He smirked. "Unless you prefer running half-naked through the countryside."

Baring her teeth, Mara snatched the armor from his hands. "I wouldn't be half naked in the middle of the damned countryside if you lot hadn't stolen me from my bedroom! This is my dress from the festival, and I don't recall you offering me the chance to change before you threw me from an open window!"

The smirk fell from Cyfrin's face. "The festival?" he asked.

She lifted her chin, indigent. "Yes. The one that celebrates the end of the Great War, and our victory over the Dre—"

Cyfrin bristled, but she caught herself before she finished saying the name he so loathed.

He waved a hand and turned his back to her. "Feel free to change into those leathers." He sat down next to Kain. "We promise not to look."

"We do?" Kain joked.

El, still lying with her eyes closed, kicked Kain in the back, hard. He yelped when her heel made direct contact with his spine. Cyfrin seemed true to his word, keeping his eyes on Kain, who used a dagger to etch tally marks into his blade.

Mara continued to stare at them all, expressionless. It was clear they needed her alive for whatever they had planned, why else would they have risked their own lives to save her from the Underkingdom. But still why give her clothes and common courtesies? Surely her comfort was not something that took priority.

"Thank you." The words came out at a volume barely above a whisper. "For not letting the Ylastrians keep me, I mean. Thank you."

Milios appraised her for a moment, then bowed their head in acknowledgment.

El opened one eye and gave Mara a small smile. "What? You didn't want to stay and watch Demiel's rampage cause a cave-in?" she asked.

Kain laughed, his back still turned. "Yeah," he said.

"You could've stayed in a nice cozy cell, and Dem would've fed you little scraps of rat meat... Much better than taking your chances with us, right?" He elbowed Cyfrin and gestured back towards Mara.

Cyfrin waved a hand behind his back to let Mara know he'd heard her apology, earning him a sharp look from El and a harder jab from Kain's elbow. Finally, Cyfrin cleared his throat and looked up at the bright sky. "It was my duty to rescue you," he said softly. "It was the least I could do after you so eagerly allowed yourself to be captured—for the second time in as many days, I might add."

Mara sneered at his jest, heat rising again in her face. His words held an extra stinging weight, as she had thought them to herself only hours before. *He's right, the arrogant bastard. You've allowed yourself to be bested not once, but twice*, she thought, peeling the mud-caked dress from her body. It was beyond dishonor, beyond shame. Developing her strength and skill for combat was all that had kept her sane during her lonely upbringing, the knight's code of "honor or death" acting as her compass. Yet when faced with true, *real* danger...she had done nothing but falter. She glared at the back of Cyfrin's head, furious at him for spurring this train of thought once again. How much longer would she have to put up with Cyfrin's commanding demeanor, or his rude remarks?

It felt like a lifetime ago that she had stood before her uncle at the tournament, claiming before all that she was strong enough to lead a kingdom on her own. She scoffed at her own arrogance, pulling the leathers roughly over her mud-caked skin. She was not given a shirt, granted only a bodice and bracers for her torso. Her scowl deepened at the useless tatters left of her skirt, ripping them off completely and yanking the pants up to her waist.

Her thoughts continue to gather in speed, and panic. A

blade would stand no chance against their ancient magicks, Cyfrin had already proved that. *The only hope is uncle's forces coming to my rescue,* she thought, disgusted that she needed to be saved in the first place. But as she forced herself to believe this, she wondered what sort of might would be needed to best her captors. As the carnage that had just unfolded in the tunnels of Ylastra played through her mind, her heart sputtered with the possibility that, perhaps, none could.

CHAPTER 10
IN THE STONE AND STARLIGHT

The borrowed leathers Mara now wore fit her well enough, though they were much heavier than she had expected. The material was rough against her skin, the hide barely enough to buffer the sharp edges of the thick scales covering it. Mara marched in unrelenting discomfort, fidgeting constantly, until an exasperated sigh burst out of her. All four of the others turned to look at her.

"I am truly grateful for the armor, but why in the name of all Zenoths do you wear this stuff?!" Mara demanded, her voice thick with agitation. "Surely plain leathers are much more practical?"

Kain, Cyfrin and Milios averted their eyes as she said this. But El gave her a sad smile. "My magick is extremely volatile," she said in a soft voice. "It eats right through leather, most metals too…which would make for an awkward battlefield experience, you can imagine. These scales come straight from a dragon's hide. The only thing that doesn't disintegrate against my power."

Mara startled at this. Dragons were a thing of legend to her. A myth of old, passed down in storybooks from one generation to the next. She turned her eyes skyward, wary, as if one would swoop down at that very moment to snatch her up. The strange shine to the scales made sense now, as did El's constant cautious use of her abilities.

Understanding El's reasoning did not make the armor any lighter or the boots any looser; Mara's feet throbbed angrily with every step. She reminded herself repeatedly to be grateful that she did not have to cross the increasingly rough terrain barefoot.

They had arrived in an area of flatlands that was probably once lush with stunning life. Mara tried to imagine how it might have looked, but it was impossible. Not even a shade of that former glory remained on the earth, now laid barren by war and sickness.

On the second day of their journey, Mara had been awestruck as a massive mountain range loomed into view on the horizon. The snowcapped tops disappeared into the heavy cloud-cover, merging as one in the distance. It drew closer and closer as time passed by, and she took to straining her eyes every so often trying to see where it ended to the east and west. But it looked like the range went on forever, only expanding further as they advanced upon it.

They travelled for days on end across the deadened landscape, only stopping for a few hours every night to make camp. Mara could see no landmarks out here, though the Dreads seemed very clear on where they were going. Mara grew exhausted and sore from sleeping on the cold, hard ground. The constant anger inside of her burned hot. She spent every waking hour waiting to bolt, looking for a spot where she could gain an advantage. But it was hopeless. There was nowhere to run, nothing for miles in every direction.

The four warriors spoke in brief intervals along the way, their eyes never once staying still as they watched all directions for possible assault. Mara found herself drawn to El's warm demeanor as the time passed, though she refused to let anyone see it. El tried speaking to her multiple times a day to no avail, but Mara couldn't help but be grateful for the small interaction. It was enough to remind her she still existed, and that this was, sadly, not a nightmare from which she might soon wake.

Kain and Milios spent most of their time too fixated on their surroundings to pay her any mind. Milios would often throw her a curious look as the wind trailed across her face, but no more than that. Mara had noted within their first few days together that Kain only had eyes for El, glancing between her to their path and back again for hours on end. On the occasion that Kain was focused elsewhere, Mara had often caught El stealing her own looks at him. Clearly, they were attracted to each other—and wistfully oblivious to each other's feelings.

Unlike his comrades who spared Mara of most interactions, Cyfrin only grew more enraging by the hour. He had, much to her dismay, become more relaxed with their increasing distance from Delinval. His sullen brooding had become less and less, replaced by an innate curiosity that left Mara feeling wrathful at his every breath. Mara had never met anyone whose very existence made her so furious. He had taken to walking alongside her every day, his matching his gait to hers, regardless of how fast she walked. When he wasn't chiming in to Kain's vivid reenactments of battles long past, Cyfrin was whipping out disarming questions at her around his wicked smirk.

This morning, he had settled on her skills with the blade. "I have to admit, you caught me off guard in your tower," he was saying. "Here I was, expecting a squealing damsel, and instead I was met with a blade from the shadows. I'm curious who was tasked with teaching the crown princess the ways of the sword."

He was walking close enough that their bodies were nearly touching, and Mara felt the familiar buzz of electricity against her skin as it radiated off his. Annoyed, she drew away from him by several feet and kept her silence.

He let out a small laugh, and Mara saw the smirk rise of his rugged face from the corner of her eye. "You were trained well, that much is clear. Though, your approach was flawed; your technique, years outdated. A reflection of your teacher, not your talent. But with the right guidance…" He shrugged. "I think you could have real promise, your highness."

Mara scowled as he said this, and he laughed at her look. It was such a relaxed sound, his face almost glowing as he beamed. It made his scar less harsh somehow, and the runes tattooed across his skin pulsed with momentary light. She felt her cheeks grow hot as she stared and dropped her gaze to the earth before he could see. He called her *"your highness"* frequently, and with such sarcasm that it made Mara want to rip out his tongue. It made her stomach flip in a way that she hated, associating the feeling with the very smell of him. If she walked too slow or fell too far behind, Cyfrin would blame it on her "delicate, royal sensibilities." His eyes would glow with mischief, narrowing as he sneered at her. She would try to not give him a reaction, knowing it was exactly what he wanted, but she was often unsuccessful—much to Cyfrin's satisfaction.

This morning had been the same as the last in most

aspects. The bright sun bearing down was not quite powerful enough to break through the clouds and warm the unnatural chill in the air. Mara walked in silence behind El, arms crossed, throwing mutinous looks at Cyfrin. He hadn't bothered binding her at all today, a gesture that did nothing but offend Mara. It was like a slap in the face. *Not even worth tying up. How pathetic can you be, Mara?* she thought, letting out a frustrated sigh.

Kain was regaling El with how many Ylastrian chaos wielders he had downed in the Underkingdom countless days ago, and El was laughing at his theatrical reenactment. "There I was, surrounded. There had to have been fifty on me, no! Sixty! There must have been *sixty*!" He shadowboxed before him, and El doubled over with laughter.

Cyfrin shook his head, eyes glinting. "Right. If you had sixty on you, Kain, then there must've been a hundred on me."

Kain guffawed at him. "A *hundred?!*" he said, dodging as Cyfrin tossed a small rock at him. "You know, I think you must have hit your head in that battle, Cyf. Caused long term damage, it did; your brain is clearly scrambled. How many fingers am I holding up?"

He waved his hand an inch from Cyfrin's face who raised one finger and pointed at Kain's shoulder. A small spark of lightning shot out and into Kain's body. He yelped and stumbled back. El howled with laughter.

Milios smiled at the now squabbling pair. "Well, if we thought relations with the Ylastrian court were strained before…" They side-stepped as Kain made to trip Cyfrin but missed. "I wouldn't be surprised if this was the final straw for King Normigone. It never did take much to set him off, and I can't imagine Demiel unleashing his chaos form and rampaging through the tunnels went over well. We should be on the watch for retaliation."

"We wouldn't have had to make things more *strained* if Demiel hadn't come and snatched up our princess," Kain replied, pointing his thumb back at where Mara was walking.

Mara's fury flared white hot. "Things wouldn't be strained for *any*one if you hadn't snatched me up in the *first place!*" she snarled, speaking for the first time in days. Her voice was raspy, almost a bark as she spat the words at them.

They continued walking up the path, but El threw her tender smile back at her. "It was unavoidable," she said, facing forward. "It's not as if you would have left willingly. There was no other way to get you to come with us."

Milios cleared their throat and El fell silent. There were many things they spoke of in hushed tones each day, and Mara had gotten the distinct impression that there was something specific they weren't meant to say around her. The frequent, strange looks and whispered conversations; the long winded, heavy silences whenever she would speak. She bit her tongue, aching with curiosity, but too dedicated to her silence to attempt to satisfy it.

"We're nearly to the gash," Cyfrin said, all his momentary lightheartedness with Kain gone. The other three stiffened, and Mara felt their energy slip back into one of watchful eyes and bated breathes. Cyfrin slouched a little, squaring his shoulders and drawing his blades as his steps became more precise. This was the Cyfrin she had met in the tower, the one whose eyes were haunted with whatever horrors they had seen and done. It was the darkness that shadowed whatever light had been exuding from him these last few days of their journey, and one that appeared with every threat of danger.

Mara saw his bright blue magick envelop his blades, and her eyes went wide. Even in her present situation, she could appreciate a thing of beauty, and *this* was most certainly a thing of beauty. The way the magic crackled and swirled around the sharpness of the dark metal was mesmerizing. The bolts seemed to elongate the edges, driving them into whip-like tendrils off the tip. They laced up the hilt, engulfing his hands and forearms. Mara, lost in the swirling dance of the lightning, could not take her eyes off it.

As they approached the mountains, the sun overhead began to disappear behind the peaks. They were coming towards a narrow opening in the rock that Mara hadn't even noticed before, too small to see till this exact moment. Only wide enough to fit two through at a time, it sat between two of the mountains and stretched farther than she could see. It was wild, unnatural, and the longer she looked at it, the stranger it became. Her mouth fell open. It wasn't *two* mountains that hosted this pass at all. This had been one single, great mountain at some point in the distant past.

Something had sliced it clean in two.

There were bones laid across the mouth of the passage, of beasts and monsters that dwarfed even Kain and Cyfrin in size. The group stopped, and all of them turned as one to stare in silence at Cyfrin. His eyes were on the ground, his disheveled hair shadowing them with a faraway look on his face. Kain clapped a massive hand on his shoulder. Mara recognized it as a gesture of comfort.

"We can find another way through," El said softly, her eyes pained as she exchanged a knowing look with Kain.

Milios nodded in response. "We can always try going up and over," they suggested. "It would take time, but we could manage it if Kain carried Mara."

Hearing her name spoken by one of them filled her with renewed irritation, but she kept silent as she continued to stare at Cyfrin. Something about the way he stood there told her it would be unwise to start in on him now. His hands were balled into fists at his side, his eyes still locked on the deadened earth. His tattoos flickered with white light as the veins flared beneath his skin.

Milios frowned a little at Cyfrin's lack of response, looking concerned. "Or we could always try the passage through the other side of the mountain—"

"Stop." Cyfrin's voice, though ragged, was commanding. He shrugged off Kain's hand and took a step forward, looking off into the pass. "This way is the fastest, and the safest by comparison. It'll only take us two weeks to the other side if we move quickly enough. It's the best option, and I'll hear nothing more of it. We cut through this way." He held a hand behind him and didn't turn around as he spoke the next words. "Princess. You'll walk with me."

Kain, El, and Milios exchanged looks combining surprise and deep understanding. When Mara did not move, Cyfrin slowly turned to face her.

His eyes were misty, his expression pained. His new air of humorous mischief was gone, the first she had seen it falter in days. He motioned to the space beside him. "Please."

Mara blinked. Perhaps it was his breathy, fragile tone. Or maybe she felt curious about what lay beyond the pass. No matter the reason, Mara took two steps forward and came to stand beside Cyfrin. His hand flexed at his side, the tendons straining against his tanned skin.

Milios took up the lead, murmuring something as the breeze that always surrounded them whipped through their hair. Kain cleared his throat and bowed theatrically at El. "Allow me to escort you then, my lady!" he said, eyes full of boisterous humor to lighten the tense energy. Milios chuckled, and color rose on El's cheeks. She furrowed her brows and flicked the top of Kain's head as she crinkled her nose. They fell into formation behind Mara and Cyfrin.

The air in the pass was frosty, as if even the sun, burning brightly above, did not dare warm it. Mara walked as far off to the side of Cyfrin as the path would allow, which was not much by any means. They were traveling in stony silence once more, so Mara studied the back of Milios as they moved. She watched as their hair floated idly in the mystical breeze that surrounded just them. Every now and then, the sound of whispers drifted back to her. Sometimes from Milios, but other times seemingly from the wind itself. Her mind wandered as they walked, flinching at every sound echoing off the towering rocks. The cracked stone drew her memory back to her time in Ylastra, and she felt the hairs on her neck stand on end.

Her captors had moved as one, not even needing to speak as they erupted with their unstoppable force. It was a sort of magick all its own, the way they worked in tandem. She thought about how many men each of them had taken down. Not a hundred, as Cyfrin had so pridefully proclaimed. But damn near close.

Mara bit her lip, wondering how many soldiers and knights her uncle would send to rescue her. Even with their mightiest men, she couldn't think of anyone more powerful than just Kain alone. But perhaps if they could come at them with a big enough force…surely not even *they* stood a chance against an entire army.

Did they?

Mara had never been uncomfortable with small spaces but walking Bardro's Gash for the following two weeks broke something within her. With each day, it seemed to get harder and harder to breathe, the sunlight barely reaching them this far below the mountain's shadow. Her only respite were the spots along the path that would open wide, casting sun and moonlight upon them as they made camp in the cavernous spaces. But these were few and far between, as the path always narrowed again immediately.

They sat around the campfire one evening, eating their dwindling rations, when Mara forced herself to speak. She felt she would go mad soon if she didn't. "Is it much longer till we've left this place?"

They all looked up at her in mild surprise upon hearing her voice, but it was El who spoke. "Zenoths bless, I was just about to ask the same thing. Milios?"

Milios drew the same ragged map from their pouch that Mara had seen them peruse so many times before. They laid it close enough for Mara to see in the fire light, pointing at a spot somewhere towards the back end of the mountains. "We are somewhere around here, at the moment. I suspect we'll be to the other side in only a few days' time."

"Starting to wear on you, eh?" Kain asked, raising his flask with a knowing look, and nodding at Mara. "I've seen grown men five times your age reduced to sniveling sods in this pass. The walls feel like they're pressing in on you yet? Or have the echoes made you feel like you might be going mad?" His eyes became distant, his expression vacant as if remembering something horrible. "The echoes are always what get to me…"

Cyfrin kicked Kain in the shin. "Not sure the voices in your head count as an echo, Kain." As Kain rubbed his shin, glaring, Cyfrin snatched the map from its spot next to Milios. He rose from his place by the fire and came to sit beside Mara, who had begun to hyperventilate a little at Kain's words. Cyfrin's nearness electrified the air around her; she didn't want to admit it, but she welcomed the grounding that gave her.

Cyfrin placed the map onto her legs, careful not to touch her as he did so. "I'd reckon you've travelled farther than any Delinvalian your age ever has. Never mind this Zenoth's damned pass. Look at all the land you've covered so far."

Mara watched as he placed his finger atop a small drawing to the westernmost side of the map. A castle, with the word "Delinval" below it. Her gaze followed as he drew a line through the Marred Lands, across the Forest of the Fallen, through the bogs of Ylastra and onward. He stopped exactly where Milios had, finger poised on a spot halfway through the Krakenbär Mountains.

"This is not forever. You'll be back to the great vastness of our journey again in no time." Cyfrin said, in a soft tone that made Mara's face feel warm. She turned her head away, gazing intently at the opposite wall to hide the rising flush in her cheeks.

The anxiety welling in her chest had loosened, despite her feelings of animosity towards Cyfrin. Though the circumstances were awful, he was right: she *had* travelled further than any her age had even thought possible. Further than she herself had imagined in her wildest daydreams. *You wanted adventure, Mara,* she thought as Cyfrin pulled the map away and resumed his dinner. *What a foolish thing to have ever wished for.*

With each passing day, Mara's captors grew wearier. Their banter had ceased, all air of relaxation gone. Mara, grim, wondered what sort of things could possibly be lurking in the dark to keep them so constantly alert. She had frequent nightmares of the Reflector Beast, cursed Barkens, monsters made of muck and the Ylastrian overtaken by his own chaos magick. All these kept her from ever inquiring as to what else could be on the prowl.

The sun was hanging high overhead as they walked this morning, a rare occurrence these days.

"Sunlight means we're close to the exit," El mused, enthusiastic.

"Zenoths be blessed," Mara breathed, more relieved than she had ever been before. Cyfrin had insisted they use some of the drinking water to clean themselves before they packed up camp that morning. Using torn pieces of fabric Milios had pulled from their pack, the five of them had been able to scrub the layers of dirt and grime from their faces and hands. It wasn't much, and it did nothing for the groups collective smell, but it had made Mara feel a fraction more relaxed.

They had been walking into the late afternoon when Milios shuddered to a sudden halt. The rest of them followed suit, all four growing still, even Mara, who strained her ears to listen.

The wind whispered against them as they came to a stop. The four threw nervous looks around, Kain fully spinning to face their rear. And in the soft blowing sounds of the breeze that she felt were speaking to Milios, Mara heard one word: *Above*.

Milios and Mara's eyes shot to the sky at the same time, and Mara could not stop the cry of fright that escaped her. Poised on the wall of the mountain above them was a monster wrought of terror itself. Four massive, long limbs, the size of tree trunks and jointed like broken knees, stuck out from all sides of it. There were a dozen tiny arms extending from its torso, picking away at the rock before it with their many sharp claws. Two horrifying, stretched legs descended over its head from its back, ending in long, ivory fingers. On its face, it wore the front portion of a humanoid skull, bits of dried flesh still attached to the surface. Spikes of broken bones, all from different races and beasts, had been driven into the monster's head, a crown from a nightmare.

It clung to the rock like a spider, its head cracked at an unnatural angle as it stared down at them all. Mara could see a sludge-like black ooze dripping from a gaping maw underneath the human skull. Even at this distance, she was able to make out the many rows of sharp fangs within it. It leapt from the wall with great power and landed with a boom, blocking the path before them as the earth around it cracked in every direction. The broken ground turned black beneath its feet. Mara drew her hand to her mouth to keep from making another noise, feeling the blood drain from her face.

It towered above them all, its body wrapped in tendrils of smokey darkness. Slits of eerie green light radiated out from the place in the skull where eyes should have been. It raised one of its hands and pointed a finger at them. The finger was impossibly long, jointed in sickening ways. Mara realized with a thrill of panic that it was made of many human finger bones, all fused together. The last one was sharpened into a needle-like point, quivering in the air before them. It cocked its head once more. Then it spoke in a voice that made Mara clap her hands over her ears.

She did not understand its garbling, thrashing sounds, but they drove every thought from her head except for one word. It was shouting from every corner of her mind, echoing through her every fiber.

Run. Run. Run.

CHAPTER 11
BLOOD, SOUL, AND STONE

The others drew their weapons faster than Mara's eyes could follow, positioning themselves as best they could in the narrow pass. She was pushed into the middle of the group, shoulder to shoulder with El and Milios while Kain and Cyfrin stood before them. The ground below was rolling like waves, rock and dirt pushing in then out in an odd sifting motion. It was making Mara sick. El cursed through her teeth as she ripped a large, purple bottle from her waist and chucked it hard at the beast.

It connected with a long tendril of smoke that appeared like a shield before the beast, exploding in a fountain of sparks. Something was beginning to rise from the frothing ground all around them. And as Mara stared in horror, she realized they were bones. Root and rock were rising together to piece them into misshapen skeletons of all sorts. Some had the heads of men, some of monsters. Cyfrin swore as more skeletal ghouls rose behind them.

Milios' face, usually so unperturbed, had fallen grim as they spoke. "It's Mezilmoth's Necromancer."

Kain laughed in response to this, a cold, humorless sound. "Of course it is. We've gone much too long without something trying to kill us." He extended his sword toward the creature and prepared to lunge.

Cyfrin held out a hand, stopping him. "He's one of the Prime Corruptions. If we let him touch us with that magick, we'll be blighted, Kain. Use your head. We'll need to get you a safe opening."

The Necromancer's black magick had surrounded his minions, lacing through their joints and the earth that held them together. It gave the sockets of their eyes a dark, pulsing void-like quality. Mara felt a mass of energy ripple through the air, and Milios pulled her out of the way just in time. There was a crackle of magick, a sting at her neck as something grazed her. Mara cried out.

Cyfrin roared as he watched it happen, felling a group of the undead in one mighty burst of his magick. The ghouls began to dive at the group, more bolts of white-hot power shooting around Mara. They were met with Kain in front of her, who swung his weapon high and brought it down in an arc across them with almost no effort. The bones would disconnect from each other for only a moment after each impact. Then, the swirling black magick of the Necromancer would reconnect them all together as if nothing had even happened.

Cyfrin's blades were a blur of blue lightning as he slashed through bone and stone and pulsing darkness. Milios was throwing the ghouls high, slamming them to the ground with such ferocity that it shattered them apart in an instant. But with every fallen skeleton, five more would take its place, using the discarded bones of their allies to fortify themselves.

Another bolt of magick whizzed above Mara's head as El pulled her in to a ducked position. As she moved, pushing her down behind Cyfrin and Kain, the necromancer lifted its head high. It reminded Mara of her uncle's hunting hound, trying to lock in on its prey. A tongue, forked like a snake and dripping with dark green ooze, flicked in and out of his mouth.

Mara felt cold as she realized he wasn't just smelling the air. He was *tasting it*. He dropped his head suddenly, his ominous, glowing eyes fixated directly on her. It pointed towards her through the small gap in Cyfrin and Kain's shoulders. The finger extended like a whip, quick as a viper as its tip raced towards Mara. She gasped as it collided with some invisible force mere inches from her face.

Milios' hand was extended towards her, creating a shield of air that guarded her as they continued to toss ghouls high. The Necromancer let out an ear-splitting shriek that made Mara's blood freeze. The skeletons that had been downed were rebuilding on the ground around them, joining the fight as an unending force. The Necromancer was scurrying towards the wall, mouth wide and glowing eyes still set on Mara.

Cyfrin yelled back to Milios over the din of chaos. "Get her as high as you can!"

Milios nodded and Mara was instantly swept off her feet. She yelped as the wind whipped her into the air above the fight, the Necromancer's unflinching gaze following her as she ascended. Bolts of white magick shot towards her from the ghouls on the ground, but the wind stopped them in their tracks long before they reached her. The Necromancer roared as its minions failed again and again. It couldn't reach her by climbing, couldn't reach her with magick from the ground. She watched something dawn in its pulsing eyes, and it turned to raise two hands at Milios.

Black smoke erupted towards them, surrounding Milios in an orb of darkness in less than a second. It completely engulfed them, tossing them careening backwards through the narrow pass. The wind whipping around Mara, keeping her airborne, ceased. And she began to plummet towards the ground.

She screamed, her eyes wild and arms flailing as the ground rocketed towards her. She heard a great roar as she dropped, and something slammed into her. It knocked her sideways out of the air as the breath left her chest. Arms were wrapping themselves around her, dragging her into a roll as they struck the ground. Mara opened her eyes when the movement had ceased, wincing.

She was on top of Cyfrin, straddling him as she stared down into his scarred face. His arms were still around her from the roll, holding her against him. He was staring up at her with the strangest look, his eyes distant and his mouth slightly ajar. The look vanished as he turned his attention up at the ghouls now racing towards them.

His eyes filled with a rage unlike anything Mara had ever seen. The blue glow leaked out from his pupils and threw the whites of his eyes into its blaze. The glowing runes on his skin, usually burning white, had been lost to this same blue hue. Without looking at Mara, he moved his hands to the back of her head and the arch of her lower back.

Moving fast, he rolled her off him and crouched above her like a wild animal, eyes on the enemy. The ghouls dove towards them in one huge wave. Cyfrin waved a hand above his head, and a stunning blue dome of crackling magick sprang to life around him and Mara. She stared up at it, awestruck.

He had bloody cuts across his face and neck, the picture of a warrior in battle. His glowing eyes dropped down to her. It looked to Mara like he was scanning her for damage, momentarily ignoring the droves of ghouls slamming into the dome. Dimly through the shield of magick, Mara heard the shriek of the Necromancer. There was a distant *boom*, and the dome of blue light was suddenly bathed in darkness. Mara could see the Necromancer's cursed magick eating away at the outside of the shield, scratching to get in at them.

She whimpered, shutting her eyes. It was worse than any of her nightmares, worse than anything her anxiety could imagine. They were going to die here, torn apart by the claws of the undead or else consumed whole by whatever darkness the Necromancer possessed. Mara heard a growl echoing up from deep inside of Cyfrin, could feel it reverberating into her body from his. She opened her eyes a fraction of an inch, mouth agape.

His eyes were balls of blue lightning, tiny bolts cracking out from them as he growled through his teeth at the darkness. He let out a ground-shaking roar, throwing his arms wide, and the dome burst into an explosion of blue lightning.

The dark magick vanished in an instant. Cyfrin's bolts shot into each ghoul, cracking, and rupturing every bone from the inside before they fell pulverized to the dirt. He let out a noise, somewhere between a grunt and a whimper. His face was screwed up in pain, as if the great burst of magick had drained him. His eyes dimmed back to their normal glow as he stood, turning back to face the Necromancer and his friends.

Milios had broken free of the dark bubble of magick, though Mara could see a spike of bright silver hair now present in their dark green tresses. Kain was angled in front of El, teeth barred at the Necromancer and bleeding heavily from a cut on his head. El appeared to have pieces of bone shards sticking out of her face and armor. Milios was in some sort of standoff with the Necromancer as Kain and El waited for an opening through its whipping tendrils of smoke. It was roaring like a wounded animal, Milios' magick pulling hard on its whip like finger to hold it suspended in the air.

El tossed a bulbous bottle high, white sparkling sand falling on to the monster from above as it shattered. Steam began to billow out from its body, its skin melting away in the places it struck. Its screams reached a new pitch at this. Cyfrin's hands were now aglow with the beautiful blue lightning from his blades. He moved so quickly that the air pulled forward behind him as he lunged. It took Mara's breath away once more as she watched from the ground.

Reaching the place where the Necromancer fought so desperately to escape Milios' grasp, Cyfrin raised his crackling hands high. He brought them down with such vigor that Mara heard a *crack* like thunder. There was a flash of glowing white light, and the Necromancer was shrieking in tongues. The light overtook the passageway, blinding them all in its brilliance. There was a deafening ring resounding, like standing inside a massive bell. Mara blinked hard to regain focus as the light vanished a full thirty seconds later.

The Necromancer's finger had shattered all the way up to its boney hand. Agonized, the creature cradled the finger in one of its tiny arms. The sound echoed off the stone around them and rumbled towards the sky. The smoke that surrounded it had disappeared. Kain moved forward in a flash at the same time the light extinguished. His great sword drove through the air and collided with the top of the Necromancer's head. It made a sound like an axe through a tree trunk as it sunk into it.

Screams ripped the air and sounded like a hundred different beings at once. They bounced off the walls and through them, dropping Mara to her knees where she stood by the sheer force of it. There was a *boom* and all light momentarily disappeared from around them, plunging them in to pure darkness.

The sun shone once again. Black ooze soaked into the ground, racing into the cracks in the stone. Many different bones lay piled where the Necromancer had once stood. Panting, the travelers stared at the ashen bones for a moment before Cyfrin shot a bolt of magick at it. The pile erupted in blue flame, crackling as they burned to black dust before their eyes. There was a long silence.

Kain laughed. The sound, so unnatural after their experience, made Mara stare at him, aghast. He plopped on the ground next to the pile of dust, wiping blood from his great sword and pulling the knife he used to carve tally marks from his hip. "That's one for me then, Cyfrin," he said as he began to etch on one side of the blade. "You might have hurt him and did, well, *that*." He brandished the craving knife, which Mara could now see was glowing white hot at the tip of its own accord, towards the pile of dust. "But I gave him the killing blow. And we all know that's all that *really* matters."

"It seems his essence managed to escape," Milios said, knelt on the ground and studying the cracks where the ooze had vanished. "You killed his shell, but rest assured he's on his way to acquire a new one as we speak."

Kain guffawed, shaking his head. "As good as dead, then! Did you get a look at that thing?! It'll be *years* before he's able to build himself a vessel as strong as that one." He raised the carving dagger, squinting as he pointed it towards the smoldering pile of bone ash. "I count that as a kill."

Cyfrin was rolling his eyes, shaking his head as he approached where Mara knelt on the ground. She was trembling, her palms clammy and face wet with sweat as she stared open-mouthed at the dust. Cyfrin reached out his hand and she looked up at him with wide, glassy eyes. "That's not even the worst of them," he said with a small smirk as he helped her to her feet.

Mara felt like the walls were pressing in on her in earnest. Her breath came in hurried gasps, the blood cold in her veins. Cyfrin stepped closer to her, and she hated how calm she felt at the nearness. "We should be at the exit soon," he said softly, as if he knew how panicked the tight pass made her. "Hard to fight in these close of quarters, but we'll always manage. We'll hurry as fast as we can to leave here, alright?"

The gentle, caressing tone of his voice stopped Mara's anxiety cold in its tracks, and she could only nod in response. He motioned to the place beside him, waiting patiently for her to step forward into it. She allowed him to walk closely at her side, not trying to step away as she usually did. It was reassuring having him there, and she cursed herself for thinking it. They marched with renewed speed, exhausted by combat, but anxious to avoid any other monsters hanging about. The hours passed without them speaking, save for the five minutes Kain spent bragging about his killing the Necromancer.

"I wish you had let me keep a bone before you burnt it all to shit, Cyf," he said in a disgruntled tone from behind Cyfrin and Mara. "I could've used a new trophy." He thumbed some of the trinkets at his belt fondly, many of them bits of bone, fangs, and tanned hide.

El elbowed him in the side. "They'd been tainted, you idiot," she sneered at him, and Mara could practically hear her eyes rolling.

"Ah, well. There is that."

The way these people interacted with each other made

her deeply jealous, though she could barely admit it to herself. She had never had a close relationship with anyone, save for Adrian. And even then, it was nothing like this playful merriment they all shared. No one at her uncle's court had ever wanted anything to do with her; of the adults, only Lady Lenorei had treated her with any kindness when her uncle wasn't looking. Though she never showed it and pretended to be unbothered by what they all thought of her, it pained her to be so alone. It had her entire life.

"Oh." It was a soft, sad proclamation and it pulled Mara instantly from her musings. Milios had stopped in front of them, staring at what looked to be the exit to the pass a few yards ahead. Mara glanced around their shoulder and gasped.

The rock face all around the exit was stained in black and red blood, baked to the stone by the unrelenting sun. There were piles and piles of bones gathered against the walls, pushed to the sides over years of wind whipping down the breezeway. There was a space on the ground a few feet away from them that looked like a perfect, symmetrical crater, the ground indented and scarred all around it. She could see the earth on the other side of the exit, and it looked like the night sky had laid itself to rest there. Jet black crystal jutted out from the rocks, towering above the entrance, and jettisoning up towards the clouds beyond. The crystallized ground exploded out from one central spot at the very mouth of the pass, looking like a frozen river of darkness. El let out a muffled sob.

"By the Beyonds…" Kain whispered from behind.

"What happened here?" Mara breathed, and she felt the air get sucked out from around them at her words.

"Failure." It was Cyfrin who had answered, and Milios turned to give him a reproachful look. "Utter, complete failure happened here. Keep moving." His voice was muffled, and he kept his face tilted up and out of Mara's inquisitive gaze. She could hear El still crying gently behind her, heard Kain whisper a soft "*shh*" to her as they continued forward out of the pass. They emerged into the setting sun and Mara shivered despite its glow.

It was much colder here in the dark marshy lands they had arrived in. She turned around to look back at the mouth of the mountain pass as they exited. The crystal pillars were massive, shooting out around the rock face and towards the space where they stood. It looked like the formations were reaching for them, poised in frozen attack. The ground underneath them, and for a few yards beyond, looked like solid lava as it sparkled in the setting sun.

"Are you alright?" Milios was standing next to Cyfrin, head cocked to one side and looking concerned as they inquired. Mara couldn't see Cyfrin's eyes through his mess of white hair, and he was deathly silent. She opened her mouth to speak as her curiosity got the better of her once again, but El flashed her a look through the tears clinging to her lashes. Mara closed her mouth.

Whatever had happened here was clearly unspeakable to them. Mara could see and feel their pain tearing through the air, hitting her square in the chest with its power. And even though these people were her mortal enemies, even with their many crimes…Mara couldn't help the empathetic heartbreak that ripped through her.

Cyfrin finally lifted his head to look at Milios. His eyes looked hollow, void of the blue light that always danced just below the surface. There was no sign of the boisterous energy from their journey to the mountains; no shadow of the brooding that contrasted it in times of threat. There was simply nothing. "There's a patch of good earth not far from here. If we move quickly, we can make it there and set up camp before nightfall." His voice was emotionless, ignoring Milios' question completely. He turned to begin walking away from the mountains without as much as a glance back.

They all stood staring after him for a moment. Then Kain let out a heavy sigh. "Come on," he said, motioning for them all to follow him. "He's got horrible directional sense. Poor thing will be completely lost if we're not there to guide him."

El pinched his arm at the joking tone and he looked at her with indignation. Mara gave a final glance at the black crystal in the stone mountain before following the group of them into the marsh behind Cyfrin's stalking form.

CHAPTER 12
A STAIRWAY TO OBLIVION

When Cyfrin had said "patch of earth," he hadn't been exaggerating. It was no more than fifteen feet in every direction, but it was a soft spot of moss that lacked the spikey rocks all around them. It was the first bit of life Mara had seen in weeks, and she felt like she would weep at the sight of it. The group had set up a small fire, cooking a skinned rodent that Milios had killed for their dinner. Cyfrin was downing an entire bottle of mead, sitting a little away from them. She recognized the drink at once from the smell and her stomach lurched still at the thought of consuming any. Mara noted the look of concern that exchanged between Kain, Milios and El as he drank.

Kain was rotating the rodent over the fire, speaking to El and Milios of what he would be eating when they got back to their home.

"Ends be damned, I'd even take Drake's batwing soup over another shadow rat," Kain had grumbled. "But just think of it: fresh, warm bread from Yilord's tavern, great fillets of boar, hot off the fire at the Halls, berries plucked just that day from the grove…"

El listened intently, eyes blazing as she thought of all the hearty foods he vividly described. Milios played on a tiny flute they had pulled from their sack, its sounds whispering like bird song around them in the night. Mara ate the bits of rodent Kain sliced off greedily, not realizing how famished she had been till the food was presented to her. She ignored the raised eyebrows and condescending look from Kain as she scarfed her portion.

When she finished, she set the cleaned stick aside and cleared her throat loudly. Kain and El, who had been toasting each other as they shared a second bottle of mead, turned to look at her. Milios continued with the flute. "Where exactly are you taking me?" she asked for what felt like the hundredth time, folding her arms across her chest. "You keep saying we're close to the village—what village are you talking about? I've studied all the maps of Zenafrost, and there's only the Forgotten Woods and the Brisenbane Ocean in this direction. All the books I've read state that the Woods are long cursed, and thus impossible to enter. So, I ask again… Where are you taking me?"

Kain smirked, motioning for El to pass the bottle. "Maps and books, eh? Perhaps Delinval's accounts are mistaken then? Have you ever considered that?" he asked, and El nodded solemnly.

"Perhaps you've been lied to." Cyfrin spoke for the first time since arriving at camp. He was staring up at the moon, the neck of half his bottle of mead grasped in his hand.

Mara gave him an aggravated look. "Then enlighten me, oh one of infinite wisdom. Where are you taking me?" She emphasized each word following the jab, holding

Cyfrin's gaze as he dropped his eyes to hers. The light was still gone from them, their surface glossy with drink. She had seen that look in her own reflection during one of the many sleepless nights of drinking alone in her room. He raised an eyebrow as his eyes traced across her face. There was a flicker of something burning deep within his gaze, but he turned his head to look back at the moon without responding.

Milios stopped playing their melodic tune and spoke. "Delinval's histories are only half correct. The Forgotten Woods are not cursed, but they *are* impossible to enter for most."

Mara's confusion must have flashed across her face. Milios grinned. "I suppose there's more that you're unaware of than you previously thought. The woods are the home of my people, the birthplace of the Forest Dwellers. We were born, not of the Zenoths magicks, but directly of Zenafrost herself as she evolved.

"The woods are where my people take their first breaths. And they are protected by ancient magicks, the likes of which even Grathiel's forces cannot penetrate. The Odelians, allies of our people and the lands, were granted permission long ago to live amongst us. That homestead is where the remainder of them fled from the war."

Mara bit back the retort she had thought up in response to the mention of her uncle, not wanting to shut down the conversation when she had so many questions still. "That monster in the pass, the Necromancer. You called it a Prime Corruption."

Milios' expression grew serious. "Yes. One of the first Fae to be imparted with Mezilmoth's corruption. He was once a great healer among his people, a miracle worker, of sorts. When his magick was tainted, that power of life was twisted into what we all just witnessed, Necromancy.

Forbidden, soul-altering and the polar opposite of the life-giving magick he once held. We should all be thankful there weren't more powerful beasts laid to rest in that pass for him to utilize."

Mara shuddered at the thought, frowning at this newest bit of knowledge. "That magick you lot use…it didn't look like the dark magicks the Necromancer wielded."

Milios nodded and El grumbled something that sounded like "dark magicks my ass" before they continued. "No, only Mezilmoth and his disciples wield the dark magicks. Which, contrary to your belief, none of us are." Milios' eyes glinted at the words, and Mara flushed with embarrassment under their accusatory stare. The look vanished in an instant, and they continued calmly. "Our magicks descend from the Zenoths. The Odelian's come from the magick cores gifted unto them by the Zenoths of old. Forest Dweller magick is typically of the earth, given to us by the All Mother that is Zenafrost herself. Personally, the winds and I have a deep understanding of one another. The bond between us has been forged over many hundreds of years, and they allow me to utilize them because of this respect."

They nodded at El who winked over the brim of her glass. "Eleanora's magick is poison-based, a branch of evolved powers from the old cores. She can create and shoot acid from her body, as I'm sure you've deduced on your own by now. But her real talent comes from using it to make those pretty little potions she's got there."

El shook her bandoleers covered in jars as response, the neon, glowing liquids within them swirling around as they clunked together. Mara remembered the cloud of unmanageable acid that burst forth from El during their escape from Ylastra. The image of what it could do flashed through her mind. She shuddered.

"Cyfrin's what you'd call a special case," Milios went on. "His mother was one of my people, a Forest Dweller. She had a nigh untouchable talent for bending the earth to her whim. Forest Dwellers are bound to Zenafrost by the old magicks. Sworn to protect her, at all costs. We don't breed, as you do. There's no need, as we spring forth from the world herself." Milios paused, and Mara felt an odd chill ripple across their group. Their eyes darted to Cyfrin, leaned back, and staring at the sky. He had grown very still. Mara noted how carefully Milios chose their next words. "Cyfrin's mother, though…she was never one for tradition. And when she came to be with child, there was no talking her out of it. Not even at the very end."

Milios didn't need to say the words for Mara to know what they meant. Cyfrin's mother, much like her own, had died during childbirth. She felt a wave of empathetic pain wash over her, keeping her eyes fixed on Milios. It took monumental effort to stop herself from turning with sympathy to look at Cyfrin. They sat in thoughtful silence for a moment.

Mara understood their slight differences in appearance now. This was a race of people she had never even heard of before, somehow given life from the earth which they called "All Mother." Milios words shot through her head. *"I suppose there's more that you're unaware of than you previously thought."* And they were right. Not a single day had passed that Mara wasn't reminded of how very little she knew of her world. How very little they had been allowed to know in Delinval.

"His father is a descendant of the Lightcleaver bloodline," Milios was saying, breaking through Mara's dark musings. "They have a unique core magick that can be directly traced back to the Zenoth's first gift to us. It never changed, never evolved, or branched off into the more common magicks we see today. It passed down solely from father to son. Cyfrin's ability to create and control lightning is something that does not exist outside of his family."

Cyfrin was staring up the stars, but his eyes were unfocused as he listened to Milios speak. His cold expression remained unmoving.

"When Cyfrin was born, he was the first of his kind." Milios continued, pulling Mara's attention back to them. "It doesn't typically happen, but he was born with both types of magick within him. It's how he's able to conjure earth and stone to his bidding. It has always been quite fascinating to me—"

"And I!" Kain cut in, his words slurring a bit. He squinted at Mara through his one open eye, brandishing his fist into the air. "I have no magick at all!"

Mara blinked. She saw him in her mind's eye, his sword gutting through those Ylastrians, through the Necromancer. "None at all?" she repeated in utter disbelief.

Kain beamed at her, looking proud. "Not a lick! It's all pure brawn here!" He flexed his massive arms as example and El rolled her eyes dramatically. "My ancestors, Beyonds rest their souls, chose not to take the bloody gift. Took the path less burdened and became tradesmen instead. Fat good it did us in the long run though, eh?"

Mara was still staring at him, fear rolling fresh through her. He wasn't using magick when she'd seen him fight? He had kept up easily with his comrades, had even *laughed* while in combat. She shuddered to think of the damage he could do against her uncle's men—against Adrian. She shook her head, aggravated, forcing the intrusive thoughts from her mind as she hurriedly changed the subject. "How old are you all?"

She remembered Milios referring to hundreds of years of training and she knew that Dreads—*Odelians*, she corrected herself—were supposed to be immortal. And though the four seated around her looked to be her age, she knew better than to take it at face value.

Milios looked contemplative, rubbing their chin as they thought. "Hmm. That's a tough question. We don't keep track of age as well as mortals do, I suppose," they said, looking around at their friends. "I know for certain that I passed the three thousand-year mark some time ago. Not sure I can pinpoint exactly when, though. Let's see here… Eleanora is six hundred and seventy if I'm not mistaken. Kain's somewhere in his fourth century, bless his young soul. And Cyfrin… Cyfrin's seven hundred and nineteen years of age."

"Seven hundred and twenty," Cyfrin grumbled, now laying on the cool dirt ground with an arm over his eyes.

Milios nodded. "Yes, yes. Seven-hundred-and-twenty. Has it truly been so long?" They laid back on the ground now as well, El and Kain flopping backwards too with small, hiccupped giggles. Mara stayed seated, staring down at them all with her mouth slightly agape. Her mind was reeling, and she wanted to know more. Hundreds, *thousands* of years these people had been alive, walked the lands and seen this place when it was a thing of pure beauty. In comparison, her twenty-one years seemed like nothing more than a moment. A blink of an eye, in the grand scheme of an Odelian's life.

"You all look so young," Mara said, finding it hard to grasp the concept of eternal life.

Milios chuckled. "When we come of age, usually around our twenty-fifth birthday, our bodies slow the process of normal decay to almost a stand-still. It'll be thousands of more years before you see a wrinkle grace my face."

"Eternal good looks do nothing against a blade, mind

you," El chimed in from her seat slouched against at Kain. She was drawing a finger lazily across a deep scar on his forearm, Kain's gaze skyward and the vein in his neck throbbing fast at her touch. "We live forever, barring the heat of battle doesn't snuff us out."

Mara's gaze narrowed. "You were all in the war then?" Her voice was cold as she asked, Kain and El falling silent across from her as they cuddled against each other. Milios looked unphased.

"Yes. We were in many, many wars over the years across Zenafrost. Battles for pride, or honor, Zenoths bless them. But the one twenty years ago...that one was by far the worst I think any of us had seen." A cold breeze kicked past them, and Mara shivered against it as Milios continued. "The four of us fought together, side by side, as we have always done. And sacrificed a great deal in the same fashion. It was not only Delinval that lost much in that battle for conquest."

They sighed, closing their eyes and laying back onto the mossy ground. A soft smile rose on their pretty face. "The days since the end of the war have felt all but hopeless. But destiny always has a funny way of working things out, in the end. Don't you think?" They went silent, their breathing slowing. Kain was already snoring, the sound echoing around them as he clung to El.

Mara laid down reluctantly, goosebumps raising on her flesh from the cold air. Her thoughts drifted to what it must feel like to be faced with the prospect of eternity. It was an overwhelming notion, almost daunting in its sureness. She had never pondered what "forever" truly meant, and her head ached the more she tried to grasp hold of it.

She floated off into the dark of sleep, mind clouded with these existential thoughts as she fell into fitful slumber.

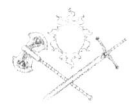

Mara awoke the next morning with the sun rise. An icy wind licked her face, but she realized she wasn't cold. The smell of earth, of pine and honey filled her senses and she forced her eyes open. The early rays of dawn nearly blinded her as she looked around.

The other four were already up, Kain and El looking distinctly disheveled from their night before as they ate their breakfast. Mara felt a weight on her body and looked down to see a long black cloak laid over her like a blanket. It was Cyfrin's.

He must have seen me shivering in the night. Given it to me for warmth, she thought as she stared down at it. Mara shot to her feet, holding it in front of her like it was burning to the touch. She walked over to Cyfrin, dropping it on the ground beside him with a hurried "Thanks" before she took her spot by the dying fire.

"It's about an hour's walk from here," Milios was saying, staring off into the distance while Kain tried not to gag over his portion of rodent.

"What is?" Mara asked at once. She had decided as she laid there last night that if she was to be with the enemy, she would glean as much knowledge as she could from them. It gave Mara a purpose, keeping her from despair with her self-given mission. Any small detail could be useful upon her return, nothing too small for her report to her uncle. That included, in part, their chosen path from Delinval to the Forgotten Woods.

"The stairway straight to a big old 'fuck you' canyon, is what. Steep. So very steep," Kain groaned, rubbing his eyes. El leaned back with sweat already beading her brow. Both looked vaguely green.

"There's a river basin that cuts through this side of Zenafrost," Cyfrin said, looking more alive this morning. "It runs from the Outer Plains down through Krakenbär and out towards the Brisenbane. Used to have a bridge across it before the darklings burned the damned thing down." He cringed, his eyes faraway with whatever memory those words triggered.

He shook his head, reminding Mara irresistibly of herself, as he tried to rid himself of the thoughts. "So, it'll be the Stairway of Oblivion instead for us. Runs straight down the cliff face to the bottom, leads across a narrower part of the river. Then it snakes back up the cliff to the other side."

El let out a small cry. "I'll be sick before we ever reach the top," she moaned.

"I'll be sick before we even reach the *stairs*," Kain whimpered in return, holding his head in his hands. They collected their things slowly, Kain and El wincing every time they bent down. They extinguished the fire and started back on their journey before the sun had fully cleared the mountains behind them.

Mara, though still shivering violently in the cold, firmly declined when Cyfrin offered his cloak. She was staring up to the marsh land to the west where the chilled wind came from.

"It's all ice up that way," Cyfrin said, following her gaze. "Freezing, unforgiving ice." He gave her a side-eye, the ghost of a smirk on his face. "If you're thinking of running out that way, I'm willing to give you a head-start. But you should take the cloak before you set off."

Mara straightened her back, her strides growing longer as she held her head high. He was teasing her, egging her on to elicit a reaction she would not gratify him with. She simply glared at him as he kept pace with her.

Hours later, they arrived at the edge of a cliff face that cut the countryside in two. Mara had seen more grandeur in the last few weeks then she had in her whole life, and this canyon was no exception. She could see, hear, and smell the river snaking far below them on the valley floor. Her eyes fell on the top of a winding wooden staircase haphazardly constructed into the rock. It led down to the bottom, steeper than should have ever been allowed, and she could see its twin spiraling up the opposite cliffside far across from them.

Mara tried to imagine, as she had every bit of land they had come across thus far, what this place would have looked like when it was alive. It was easy to picture the rolling green pastures and vibrant wildlife here over the sound of the rushing water. "We'll have to take it one at a time," Cyfrin was saying. His eyes shifted between the staircase and Kain, who was swaying in place. "Remember if you fall, we won't be able to use magick to save you."

Mara stared at him, startled. "Why not?" she asked, her heart skipping a beat. She thought of her feet catching beneath her, of tumbling down, down, down, no wind to stop her endless fall into death.

Cyfrin turned to her, eyes appraising. "The canyon is steeped in the powers that Zenafrost created long ago. Some believe this is where the heart of the world is, deep below the river and rock. It absorbs all magick for itself and leaves us with only our weapons while down in the basin. It's a heavy toll to pay, should you lose your step. So do try to keep up carefully, princess."

Mara gulped, ignoring the way he had said "princess." El shuddered and Kain let out another groan, but they followed in step behind Milios as they approached the stairway. Cyfrin stayed behind Mara, holding out an arm to indicate that she should follow. She scowled at him, falling in step behind El anyway, while Cyfrin took up the rear. He followed inches behind, and Mara could see his flexed hands hovering just out of her field of vision. He waited to catch her, should the need arise.

CHAPTER 13
AN EXCHANGE OF MAGICK

Mara had never been this high in the air, and she knew at once that she had no desire to ever be again. Every slanting step, she had to fight the wild urge to topple forward and off into the river below. Kain kept letting out slow, deep breaths, and El had paused a hundred steps down to expel her breakfast over the side of the thin railing. Milios was taking the stairs with ease, almost floating from one step to the next as they descended.

The closer they got to the river, the more deafening it became. A dull, constant roar filled Mara's ears, and she could see angry rapids frothing white against the dark stone. Cyfrin was following close behind her, no more than two steps away at any time. When they finally reached the riverbank, Kain collapsed to his knees. He kissed the ground passionately, groaning with relief. El leaned against the rock wall behind her, her face pale and lifeless.

Mara eyed the rapids with apprehension. "How are we supposed to get across, if you can't use your magicks?" she called out over the roar of the water. Milios pointed at

Cyfrin, who was walking away from them up the bank. Mara's eyes followed up the path he was taking and landed on a small makeshift bridge wrought of vines and branches. It hovered mere feet above the river, the water's boiling surface lashing it from side to side. It joined the two banks well enough, but Mara's stomach gave a lurch at how it moved in the rapids' wake. Kain and El seemed to share the sentiment.

"Zenoths' blood, could this day get any worse?" El groaned as they approached the bridge behind Cyfrin. Milios stepped on to the thick roots without hesitation, sliding with the same grace as they had taken the stairs, across the surface and on to the other side of the river in seconds. Cyfrin turned to look at Kain, who whimpered in response and grabbed his stomach.

Cyfrin raised an eyebrow, his eyes glinting. "Perhaps next time, you'll take it a little easier on the mead?" he said in a mock sweetness that had Kain shooting daggers from his eyes.

"Oh, you're one to talk!" he grumbled in response. "Sorry not all of us have drunk our way to an iron liver like you."

Cyfrin chuckled, rolling his eyes and stepping to the side. Kain shambled around him and on to the vines, looking murderous. They bowed under his massive frame, dipping into the rapids with each step. It took him much longer to pass across to the other side than it had Milios. His tanned face looked stark and green by the time he reached the opposite bank, falling to his knees in the dirt.

El stepped forward without a word, her translucent face set in a mask of solemn determination. She marched up on to the roots and paused, swaying on the spot. Mara saw her gulp.

"If you fall off and I have to dive in after you," Cyfrin

called over the roar of the rapids. "I won't let you live it down for a thousand years! 'Remember that time I had to save your sorry ass from the rapids', I'll say. I'll spend our every moment together reminding you again and again and again…"

El stiffened at his taunt, eyes flashing. But it seemed to be the fire she needed to start moving forward. She barely lifted her feet, gliding and sliding across the slippery surface. She touched down on the other side and crouched at the edge of the river, vomiting into its depths.

Cyfrin's gaze rested on Mara now, a hesitant look on his face. She didn't move. *If none of them can use magick, and the only one on this side of the river is Cyfrin…* Mara weighed her chances in her head, wondering if she could make a sudden dash for the stairs. Cyfrin seemed to see the thought pass across her face.

He cocked his head, an evil smirk curving his lips. "You can try to run, but I warn you: my lack of magick down here will do nothing to hinder my speed. And I am a *very* good hunter."

Mara glared at him, cheeks flushing with sudden heat at the thought of him chasing her across the vast countryside. Balling her hands into fists, she started on to the bridge with angry determination. She was moving fast, fuming at how pompous, how otherworldly arrogant he was. *How dare he speak to me that way? Aside from my being a princess, I am a lady. Did his father not teach him basic manners? Do magick users even believe in manners…?*

The vine bridge was swaying, the water underneath slicking its surface with an icy spray. Mara couldn't wait to get back to Delinval, couldn't wait to tell her uncle about the path to the remainder of the Odelian people and how to get there. They were foolish to let her see every step of their journey. A careless oversight on their part. Unless…

Unless they intend to kill me before I have the chance to escape. The thought filled her with such cold panic, her attention diverted from her path. The waves washed up underneath her, slicking the surface anew as she took her next step. Mara's foot slipped from underneath her, and she let out a yelp of surprise. Her eyes went wide as the world tipped sideways. Every muscle in her body tightened, bracing for the cold collision of the rapids.

But hands had reached out the instant she stumbled, grabbing her by the waist and holding her steady to the bridge. Cyfrin swore behind her, his breath brushing across her neck as his hands gripped her waist so tight it hurt. "Is that your escape plan then?" he said to her in a raised voice, his tone rumbling with anger. "Launch into the damned river and let it smash you to bits against the rocks?"

Mara drew herself up, tensing every single muscle to pull away from his touch by a precious fraction of an inch. Now she could think. She shot a nasty look over her shoulder. "I'd rather be flattened against that rock than spend another minute breathing the same air as you!" He sneered, then nudged her forward.

Her feet touched ground on the other side, and she felt a wave of relief pass over her. Mara glanced back at the sharp, speeding surface of the river and cringed. Despite Cyfrin's threat to dive in after El, Mara doubted very much if even the strongest of swimmers could have saved her from the rapids' wrath had she fallen in.

Cyfrin stared at Mara, his eyes stormy as if he imagined the same thing.

El glanced up, past Mara's shoulder. Her soft voice frightened, she said, "I lied before. Today hasn't really been that bad—not until now."

RISE OF THE DAWNBRINGER

A bloodcurdling scream sounded behind Mara, inhuman and as high-pitched as silver on glass.

Cyfrin swore once more, his face draining of all color as he pushed Mara back behind him. The four of them moved as one, drawing their weapons and turning to face whatever was now blocking their path to the stairs. Mara peered from under Cyfrin's arms and felt cold fear rush through her body.

Whatever this thing was, it was radiating a dark energy that felt more raw than anything they had yet to encounter. It rolled out in swirling tendrils to the ground around it, concentrated corruption spewing from its reach and into the earth below it. The places this darkness touched absorbed the corruption, drawing it into the ground like a sponge. This creature of shadow and death should not exist, should not share the light of day with them. It was hunched over, still standing at a solid ten feet regardless. There were no discernible features, save for the circular, glowing white eyes and gash of a mouth now opening and closing in the middle of its torso.

Black sludge dripped from its eyes like tears, sizzling as it dropped to the creature's heaving chest. It extended one long, stretched finger at them.

"Move!" Cyfrin called, as the creature let out another scream that scratched at the edges of Mara's insides. He reached behind him, grabbing Mara's wrist, and pulling her about. They all four dived in different directions, moving out of the way just in time to avoid the spear of black, pulsating magick that erupted towards them from the creature.

Cyfrin slammed into the stone wall, pushing Mara in between his chest and the rock. He pulled the two thin swords from off his back, his eyes burning down into hers. "Do not move from this spot," he commanded and turned to join the fight. Kain had already engaged the beast, slamming his sword into it again and again. The black tendrils shot out from its chest, intercepting each blow as it sliced at Kain's thick armor hide. Milios, El and Cyfrin joined the fray, and Mara found herself transfixed by the deadly dance of their combat.

They took turns circling the monster, dancing around each other from one spot to the next. It was magnificent, swordsmanship at its very best. Their blades moved in a furious whirlwind of attacks, not a one missing its intended target. The creature screamed again, and she could see energy building at its fingertips. At the same time, Kain took aim at the creature's head.

El and Milios drove their swords into the beast's torso and Cyfrin roared as his dual blades came down on its hand. Every weapon struck in perfect unison, and the earth below Mara's feet trembled. There was another ear-splitting scream and then a loud *bang*. And the monster erupted into a cloud of black smoke.

It hung in the air where the beast had just stood, and Mara could have sworn she heard a faint whispering coming from its swirling depths. It shot straight into the sky above them, disappearing out of sight in seconds over the cliff edge. The four of them stood, blades still extended and breathing ragged. The river's steady roar became the only sound for a long moment.

Mara broke the stillness, shaking herself free from the shock. "What in the End's great gate was that?!" she yelled in a panic, staring at the blackened spot where the creature had fallen.

"Darkling," El replied, hand on her side and wheezing as she sheathed her needle-sharp rapier. "Another beast from the Outer Plains. One of Mezilmoth's."

"I thought you couldn't use magick down here?!" Mara

demanded, standing above the black patch of ground, and eyeing it. The dirt had been burnt to a fine, sandy powder that was starting to float away on the wind.

"Right, *we* can't." El motioned around at the four of them. "Our magicks were born of Zenafrost, and they operate under her rules alone. Darklings, Reflector Beasts, the Prime Corruptions, all Mezilmoth's disciples…their power isn't the same as ours. Dark magick was born of the Deceiver and doesn't follow the laws that bind ours."

"Let's hold off on the history lesson," Cyfrin said, staring up at the place where the black smoke had disappeared. "I want to be off the staircase and able to use my magick before that thing finds a new host."

Mara wanted to ask what he meant by "new host" but feared what the answer would be. They took off up the stairwell to the surface, moving as fast as they could with their still-wet feet on the steep wooden steps.

CHAPTER 14
RESCUE

They reached the top of the second staircase in record time. Mara kept imagining the darkling descending upon them from the top of the narrow steps, and it spurred her to move as quickly as her body would allow. She never once looked down, fearful of somehow toppling off the edge with the motion. But the fading sounds of the river were enough to tell her how high they had climbed.

All five of them sank to the ground as they reached solid earth, winded and exhausted from the trek. As they panted and fought to catch their breath, Mara had the chance to take in their surroundings. They were sitting atop a vast shelf of flat lands, as far as the eye could see. As with all the places they had crossed thus far, the earth lay dead in every direction. But Mara could feel something off about where they now stood. It pricked at her skin, the hairs on the back of her neck standing on end in warning. The corruption here was far more concentrated than the lands across the canyon.

A dull rumbling was coming from a towering, sheer

cliff far in the distance to the north. It reached impossibly high, vanishing into the dark sky above it and blocking every bit of the landscape beyond. Mara stared with wide eyes, and Milios followed her gaze. "The Outer Plains," they said in response to her unspoken question, nodding towards the cliffs. There was a dark storm gathering in the skies above it, and thunder gave a threatening rumble from overhead.

"Outer Plains…" Mara repeated, distracted, eyes still fixed on the strange cliffs. The clouds above it were swirling with black and purple energy, white lightning lacing in veins across the cover.

"Aye. The Zenoths shot the plains far into the sky to help keep the Dark Gate safely out of reach, away from any that might be foolish enough to try and open it," Milios continued in a soft voice. "It was their final act before leaving Zenafrost forever. Or so legend says."

Mara whipped around to face them, eyes wild. "You're telling me that the Dark Gate, the doorway to all things evil, is *real?* And we're just going to take a casual stroll through its domain?" she asked, exasperated. If the ancient texts were to be taken at face value, the Zenoths had sealed Mezilmoth away up there eons ago. They'd locked him in the End of All Things, a place he drew all dark souls to when they passed on. There he remained still, damned for all time in payment for his crimes against Zenafrost.

The corruption was so focused here because *this* was where the darkness called home.

But Mara had thought most of these tales were just that, stories her maids and Lady Lenorei had told her to make her behave as a child. "*Eat your dinner, lest the dark ones come and snatch you from your bed for misbehaving!*" "*Listen and pay attention, or we shall call upon the darklings to steal you away for your carelessness!*" Standing here after everything they'd been through, all the things she had seen on their way across the whole of Zenafrost, Mara was finding it difficult to see the difference between fact and fairytale.

Kain spat in the direction of the Outer Plains, eyes narrowed. "Never gets any less ominous, does it?"

"Better than whatever the Dark Gate looks like, I'm sure," El replied with a shiver.

Mara sputtered, still dumbstruck. "Every single thing that's been sent to kill us has come from *right there*, and you lot aren't the *least* bit concerned? What's to stop a Reflector Beast from coming for us? Or a whole *army* of them!"

Cyfrin laughed, drawing Mara's panicked eyes to his. "Ah, there's the squealing damsel I expected to find in Delinval."

"Reflector Beasts don't travel in packs, actually," Milios said in their most matter-of-fact tone. "We'd be much more likely to run afoul of a pack of Darklings."

Mara fumed, too enraged to spare Milios more than a passing thought. Her lip curled into a snarl at Cyfrin as anger replaced her fear. "You have marched me, unarmed, to stand at pissing distance from the End of All Things, and you have the gall to *mock* me?"

Cyfrin cocked his head at her. His three companions suddenly busied themselves with preparing camp. He took several steps towards Mara, who held her ground and raised her chin in indignation. "Tell me, princess. If I gave you a blade to arm yourself, would you not use it to gut me and my friends without hesitation?" He bent forward a fraction, leveling himself with her murderous stare. "Be honest, now."

Mara clenched her fists at her sides, her teeth gritting. *I would run you through the second my hand met the hilt, cocky bastard*, she thought. But she forced herself to straighten her back, flashing him the simpering smile she so often used with the nobles in her uncle's court. "Weren't *you* the one to tell me my training left much to be desired? What threat could I possibly be to you?" She batted her eyelashes as she spoke with false sweetness, steadying her breath to keep herself from shaking.

Cyfrin blinked, the runes on his skin pulsing white for a moment. Then he breathed a laugh, standing up straight and turning from Mara. "I'd just as soon walk myself naked into the Dark Gate than put myself between you and a weapon, your highness," he said over his shoulder.

The fake smiled dropped from Mara's face. A deep scowl replaced it.

"You're lucky looks can't be weaponized, Cyf," Kain said, eyeing Mara with an amused expression. "She would've dropped you dead where you stand just now, with that stare."

THEY MADE camp at the edge of the cliff, facing the great rock that led up to the Outer Plains. All five of them lay with their backs to the cliffside, eyes fixed on the horizon for possible attack. Thunder rumbled in the distance, a seeming constant storm swirling over the Dark Gates. As Mara tried to drift off, lightning flashed in sharp relief around the campsite. She knew the others lay awake as well; four pairs of eyes reflected each flash of lightning. She could not remember falling asleep, but she had restless, shifting dreams, haunted by dark, evil monsters.

When she began to stir the following morning, she felt herself being pressed firmly from all sides. Sluggish, Mara peeled an eye open to look around. During the night, the four warriors had moved in around her. El lay cuddled into her side, her arm wrapped around Kain whose head lay in the crook of El's shoulder. Milios lay above Mara, the tops of their heads touching each other. That left only one person.

Mara's breath caught in her throat as she looked down her body. He lay with his head on her stomach, eyes closed, scarred face tilted up in her direction. Cyfrin. His white hair was spread across her scaled armor; his lips parted slightly as he took in slow, easy breaths. Mara went still, her eyes wide as she stared down at him. A distinct heat simmered in her belly, and not the usual fury she associated with Cyfrin. This was something different, something smoldering and aching. Laying her head back on the ground to center herself, she closed her eyes and waited until every one of her companions had awoken before stirring again.

They started back on their journey as the first beams of sunlight poked up over the horizon. A fog had rolled in overnight, blurring the distance in every direction. They set a much slower pace than they had before, as all five of them had been drained by the month-long journey. *A walking nightmare where I've nearly died three…four times?* Mara thought to herself with a grimace.

She couldn't remember what it felt like to be well-fed, well-rested. She was driven now by nothing but spite and anger. And the knowledge that her uncle's soldiers could not possibly be far behind them. Though, with every passing day Mara had become less and less sure of this. The fog was thinning ahead of them as they walked, and something was becoming visible through the mists. Mara froze in place.

Yards away from them, she could make out a great, deep trench that gutted the flatlands. It stretched as far as her eye could see, harsh in its abruptness. It stood a good thirty feet deep, a steep slope dropping down the width of it. But what pulled the breath from Mara's chest was what lay just on the other side.

Perfectly outlined by the trenched earth, the first she'd seen since they left Delinval, were trees—*living* trees—the likes of which she had never encountered. A massive, lush green forest stood mighty over the otherwise barren landscape of Zenafrost. Tiny, multicolored orb lights floated through the wood, the dense foliage flowing in the wind. It looked unreal after the nothingness she'd grown used to seeing. Its beauty was the kind poetry was made for, though she could think of no words strong enough to match the feeling this place sparked in her.

Milios smiled at her as Mara closed her gaping mouth. "Welcome to the Forgotten Wood, they said, and Mara saw how relieved they all looked. Every one of their bodies had relaxed, a feeling of sudden calm passing over the group.

Kain gave a huge stretch, a smile breaking across his face. "Zenoths bless, I cannot *wait* to sleep in an actual bed. I didn't think it was possible for bones to ache this much. I'm getting old."

"Mmm, talk to me when you've had your thousandth birthday," Milios replied with a wink as they started towards the trench. Mara swallowed hard, still frozen to the spot.

There had been no sign at all of her uncle's men for the better part of a month. Not since they had vanished into the Forest of the Fallen. *That feels like a hundred lifetimes ago*, Mara thought with mounting despair. And if what Milios had said before was true, none would be able to pass through the borders of these woods once they entered. She looked around, frantic for a moment, but realized she was well beyond the hope of escape. Trying to stall for time, she stepped forward and spoke. "The trench…what made it?"

Kain and El exchanged angry looks, Milios' eyes growing sad. It was Cyfrin who answered as they walked. "We call it the Deep Walk. Twenty years ago, Grathiel's army chased the Odelians back to the farthest reaches of Zenafrost. Back to this place. Grathiel was intent on finishing us all off, but their army could not pass the wards of the Forgotten Wood. Not even with their immense force. So, we made our last stand here."

He motioned broadly around him, face dark. "His men stood for days, releasing an unending torrent of attacks on the tree line. But none could break her barrier or pass through her shield. The onslaught scarred the earth and gouged deep into her depths, marking her forever."

Mara's brow furrowed at this. Every history book she had ever read stated that the Marred Lands were where the Odelians made their final stand against her uncle's forces. That was where his soldiers had captured the Odelian Queen and brought her to the kingdom to meet her fate. But she was beginning to question everything she knew, hating herself for how much the Odelians had gotten under her skin. *It's a lie*, she thought, angry. *These are the same people who convinced the whole of Zenafrost that they were our allies for centuries. They are masters of illusion and fabrication. This is no exception*. And yet, here she stood across from what seemed to be proof of Cyfrin's tale.

Mara was lost in thought when they arrived at the edge of the Deep Walk. The sight before her brought her crashing back to reality. The walk down the slant of the trench was painfully steep, the bottom of its wide depths still marred by the signs of battle. Bones were scattered everywhere, skeletons sticking out of the ground impaled on thick, twisted roots. There were shields and weapons half-buried under rock and time, and pieces of armor were hanging from the bones still held together. Cyfrin and Kain swore in unison.

Riding on horseback towards them along the edge of the trench was a large squad of her uncle's soldiers. The flag of Delinval flew amongst them, a great battle cry erupting as they spotted their group. Mara felt her heart leap from her chest. They had come at last, and not a moment too soon.

Arrows loosed from their bows and flew towards them. Milios raised a hand, wind shooting in an arc outward to meet their deadly tips. It knocked every bolt clean from the air, tossing them to the side. A group of the soldiers were almost upon them, driving down the trench side while the rest jeered at the top. "Get her into the woods!" Cyfrin called to El, his eyes and runes beginning to glow.

Kain was laughing, his great sword already in hand. "You Delinvalians are always so quick to offer your blood to my blade!" he boomed. He shot forward as the men at the bottom leapt from their horses. They did not move as Kain threw his sword high, charging right into the first man. The knight stared with a bored expression, unmoving. Kain brought the blade down upon him and there was a sound like wet cloth tearing.

Kain let out a cry of pain. He was thrown careening back from the troops, coming to rest with a loud *crack* yards away at the bottom of the trench. El cried out. Abandoning Mara, she ran in after Kain. He wasn't moving, his arms and legs fallen in odd angles about him. Mara felt a sudden pang of sadness as she watched El throw herself to her knees beside him, eyes frantic. The Delinvalians in the trench advanced upon them, weapons drawn as the knights above continued to jeer.

"They've been tainted, Cyfrin!" Milios called out, the

wind whipping about them. "They must have taken the cursed pass through the mountains to cut us off. Their souls have been corrupted by dark magicks."

"I can see that, Milios," Cyfrin replied, his voice low and deathly calm. He was holding both blades in his hands, their edges tipped in bright blue, crackling lightning as he glowered towards the soldiers. "El! Get Kain past the border!"

Kain stirred, so El managed to pull him to a sitting position as he groaned. Mara was betrayed by the relief she felt at seeing him alive, and by the regret that filled her as she watched blood pool beneath his body. She forced herself to look away as they retreated, taking in the battle that had begun.

No one was looking at her. No one stood guard as her uncle's soldiers surged forward in to combat with Milios and Cyfrin's magicks. She could see ominous black smoke surrounding many of the knights, reminding her of the darkness that seemed to emit from all Mezilmoth's creatures. *Milios said they had been tainted*, she thought as her heart pounded faster and faster. *But they're our kingdom's army. I know these men, sickness or not. And they've come to rescue me.* Mara broke into a run, eyes half shut as she sprinted straight in to the Delinvalian forces. She felt magick whizzing past her as she moved blindly and collided hard with someone's metal chest plate.

Stumbling back a little, she opened her eyes to face whoever she had run in to. Standing, armor gleaming in the early evening sun, was one of the knight captains: Lord Lingrain. He was smiling down at Mara but there was a strange sort of hunger there that made her stomach unsettled. But she grabbed his arm, almost tearful as she spoke. "Thank the Zenoths you came for me! Please, I can help you! You've seen me in combat! Just give me a sword and I can—"

Something was wrong. Black steam was leaking out from the joints of Lingrain's armor in earnest, his eyes dull. Mara had known him her whole life, seen the sort of distaste he had when he looked her way. It was the same distaste everyone in her uncle's court had for her and her claim to the throne.

But the way he was looking at her now was nothing like that. He had the eyes of a predator, full of pride that he had caught such a large meal. Unnerved, Mara moved to step back from him. She inched towards the chaos of battle, where Milios and Cyfrin fought the mass of soldiers alone. Lingrain let out a wild laugh and reached out faster than Mara's eyes could follow, faster than she'd ever seen the man move before. He grabbed hold of her wind-swept hair, weaving his fingers into the mess of curls and forcing her down to her knees. She cried out in pain and surprise, slamming into the ground as her hands flew up to her scalp.

"And here your uncle told me your capture would be difficult." Lingrain leered down at her and began dragging her from the trench by her hair.

CHAPTER 15
A MAN CORRUPT

Mara screamed in agony. Lingrain had her hair wrapped around his hand and was yanking it out by the root. He was laughing in triumph, waving at the small group still on horseback at the edge of the trench above them. They cheered in response. She kicked and struggled, trying desperately to pull out of his grip as he continued to drag her upwards. She felt like a prize deer, caught in the hunt.

"I want you to know, princess," Lingrain said over her screams. "Your uncle told his troops not to grant you special treatment upon your retrieval. So disappointed he was that you had abandoned us, dearest. When the Ylastrians told us of your escape, of how you *fled hand-in-hand* with the Dreads...Well, the King didn't take kindly to that one bit. He commanded that you be treated as a prisoner. An enemy to the crown! I was *stunned*. Downright *thrilled*. You know what we do to prisoners back in the kingdom, don't you, Mara?" He ripped her hair upwards, and she screamed louder. She was unable to get her footing beneath her on the steep slope, Lingrain shaking her with unhinged vigor. "It's a long journey back to Delinval, and we've been gone from our womenfolk many, many moons, chasing you and your friends across the continent. The men deserve a nice reward, and I look forward to stripping that armor off you piece by—"

There was movement above her, quick as a lightning strike. A blur of blue and white shot past Mara's face and Cyfrin's magick-laced hand sliced clean through her long, black curls. The smell of burnt hair surrounded them, her locks smoking at the tips as his magick acted like a blade against them. Lingrain stumbled forward with the discarded length still wrapped in his fist, catching himself before he fell face first. Mara scrambled backwards. Cyfrin hoisted her to her feet, and she clung to him, staring at Lingrain in horror and disbelief.

Cyfrin shook her. "Mara, you need to move!" he said, pulling her focus from the spot where Lingrain was dusting himself off. Cyfrin's eyes rushed across her face, a flicker of pain sparking behind the wrath in his stare. "Follow Kain and El into the wood. Milios and I will handle this." He pivoted to face Lingrain, positioning Mara behind him. The image of his back standing resolutely between her and danger, shoulders squared and head high, was all but burned into her brain.

Dark black smoke seeped from Lingrain's nose, and he smiled maliciously at them.

"*Go!*" Cyfrin commanded over the sound of Lingrain's renewed laughter and the clatter of battle surrounding them. The order overrode Mara's shock. She turned on her heel and ran back through the trench, over the old bones and fresh bodies now laying bloodied in the dirt. Magick whizzed past her, missing by inches as Milios' winds whipped by to shield her escape. She dashed into the woods, barely registering its immense beauty as she crossed the tree line.

A few feet in, propped against a massive tree and only semi-conscious, was Kain. El knelt beside him, her hands hovering over a gaping wound in his side. The injury was bleeding profusely, and a soft green glow was emitting from El's palms and seeping into Kain's ravaged flesh. She glanced up as Mara approached, her expression strained and sweat beading down her face.

Mara dropped to her knees on the other side of Kain. She felt cold, and she could tell from the steady shaking of her hands that she was in shock. There was a long moment in which the only sound was Kain's heavy breathing and El's softly humming magick as she traced across his wound. Mara's head was spinning, trying to disassociate her brain from her body as her pulse thundered. She brought a hand up and ran it through her hair, tears welling in her eyes as she felt all the length she'd lost. She couldn't believe it, didn't understand it. Her mind tried and failed to grasp at reality through the fog of disillusion.

There was a mighty *boom* that shook leaves and birds loose from the surrounding trees. Then the sounds of battle in the distance ceased. El glanced at Mara, her jaw clenched. "That man, the one who grabbed you...was he someone you knew well?"

Mara nodded slowly, tears falling down her face. "He...he's the captain of one of my uncle's troops. I've known him since we were children..." She was crying in earnest now, the last few words coming out a whisper. She was feeling every bruise and cut on her body as the adrenaline wore off. Every injury she had taken over the last month, every sleepless cold night, every monstrous encounter, it all came crashing down on her at once. The aching feeling covered her entire body, even her insides feeling the battered thrum of pain. She spoke without thinking, feeling dazed. "He said...he said it didn't matter how I was brought back. He said my uncle didn't care, that he thought I was an enemy to our crown, that he had ordered..."

"I know," was El's only reply. She looked livid. The woman refocused her attention back to where Kain lay fighting for his life, her face screwed up in a mixture of rage and concentration.

Mara couldn't wrap her head around what had just happened. She'd waited for an entire month for this moment, praying to the Zenoths that her uncle's forces would find her in time. The notion that her uncle would, for even a moment, believe that she had betrayed them... She shook her head, begging her tears to cease.

El did not look up from Kain as she spoke. "He was a friend of yours, then?"

Mara's thoughts ran wild, all shouting at once to be heard. She shook her head, remembering all the times Lingrain had mocked and bullied her throughout her life. "None of the royal court ever liked me." Mara said, trying to reassure her trembling heart. "They all thought me too different. That I didn't deserve the throne, or my title. They would've loved nothing more than to see me dead if it would clear a path to the crown. Even when I was safe within the castle, it never stopped their disdain. And that darkness that had overtaken Lingrain...it obviously made him mad. He must have been lying about my uncle issuing that order. Must have been trying to inflict as much pain as he could, as he always did..."

"Must have been," El repeated, but her voice was distant and hollow. The silence fell once more, and Mara stared down at Kain's wound. It was sealing itself shut, the bleeding slowing before their eyes.

"How are you doing that?" she asked, distracted from her twisting grief as Kain's breathing steadied.

El closed her hands, the glowing dissipating as she began dabbing the dried blood from around the wound. "Years ago, I left the Hidden Village to study amongst the Forest Dwellers, in this very wood. It helped keep me sane after the Great War," she replied, poking the skin around Kain's gash. There were black veins beginning to etch around the outside of it, and El's frown deepened. "The healing power comes by pulling life from the earth itself, which isn't much help when everything's already dead out there. This is the only place it'll work anymore."

She waved a hand around them at the woods, and Mara finally took a moment to absorb her surroundings. The ground was covered in soft green moss and clovers, the sound of bird song whistling overhead. There were strange, glowing flowers poking up in patches all around them, and Mara had never seen such thick, tall trees in all her life. Flitting about lazily through the canopy were tiny balls of light like the green orbs El had once conjured in the tunnels beneath the Marred Lands. They glowed in every color imaginable, and Mara felt that she would have found them worthy of being painted, had she not been in such a bad state.

There was movement and the sounds of footfalls approaching them. Wincing, Mara shrank back against the tree closest. But it was Cyfrin and Milios who emerged from the shadows to greet them. Milios looked unscathed, though blood was caked up to the knee of their boots. They were picking pieces of what looked like human flesh from their armor with a mild expression on their face.

Cyfrin, on the other hand, was dripping in dark red. The long bracers he had been wearing were ashen, reduced to strips of charred leather dangling from his wrists. His exposed arms were covered in angry, lightning shaped burn marks, barely visible beneath the tattooed runes and considerable amount of gore clinging to him. Mara saw no cuts on him to indicate the blood was his. He stepped forward and kicked the bottom of Kain's boot.

Kain opened one eye, looking up at Cyfrin's blood spattered face. "How much did I miss?" he grumbled; his voice groggy. He coughed and blood flecked forth from his mouth. El wiped it away with the rag she had been using to clean his wound, looking grim.

"Everything," Cyfrin replied, frowning down at his companion. "But it wasn't the brunt of the forces I'm sure Grathiel's sent. Just the most foolish. There will be more, and you'll have your moment to redeem yourself."

Kain gave him a weak smile, wincing and grabbing his side.

"We have to get him back quickly." El's voice was soft and stoic. "This wound is tainted. He needs treatment beyond what I can give."

"What have I told you about attacking before we assess, Kain?" Milios asked, kneeling beside him to examine the wound. "One would think you'd have learned your lesson, these past centuries."

"Swing first," Kain groaned as Milios measured the black veins extending from his wound. "Assess the bastards once they're good and dead."

Mara turned from them, looking at the forest line beyond without really seeing it as tears threatened to spill forth once more. She saw Cyfrin move out of the corner of her eye, walking towards the place where she sat. He crouched down, eyes softening as he watched her. "Are you alright?" he asked, his gaze passing over the new cuts brought by Lingrain dragging her up the slope. His earlier wrath still flashed in his eyes as Mara turned to face him.

Words failed her. Her hand raised to her head of its own accord. She dragged it through her chopped hair. Tears welled in her eyes.

Cyfrin reached out and tugged at a loose curl hanging in the middle of her face. "I like it this way," he said, his voice gentle. The runes on his skin pulsed with color as he drew the strand behind her scarred ear, electricity buzzing against her cheek. "I can see your face now."

Mara's lips parted as she stared at him. He offered a soft, crooked smile, raising just one of the dimples in his cheek. He pulled his ice-colored stare from her, standing to address Milios. "Send word ahead of us. Let them know we've made it to the woods." He turned to Kain who was poking his wound while El batted at his hand to stop him. "And you, oh lord of not looking before you leap, can you walk?"

Kain looked up at him, offended. "Of course, I can walk, you insufferable ass!" he replied, pushing himself to his feet with unsteady legs. El hovered beside him, her face gaunt. "I've had my guts hanging out of me before, and I still walked myself back to our camp on my bloody own while holding them in with my *bare hands*!"

He twisted his face into a dramatic expression of woe as he pantomimed the experience. El rolled her eyes as Kain chuckled and she her arm around his waist to steady him. Milios stood and offered a hand to Mara, who took it without thinking. She felt like a shell, too lost in thought and despair to fight these people any longer. Cyfrin's steely gaze passed over her again as he came to stand at her side.

Battered and worn, the five of them turned together and began walking into the dense wood beyond.

CHAPTER 16
OF THINGS LOST AND FORGOTTEN

They had been walking for only a few hours before Kain's heavy wound needed tending. Mara had caught glimpses of it, and even she could tell that the spiraling black veins stretching around it were a bad sign. The group stopped in a small clearing, the sun dropping low overhead. Mara felt like her stomach had been left somewhere in the Deep Trench, and her heart had filled the pit left by its absence.

The four Odelians spoke in muted tones while Mara tried not to think, tried not to listen or to feel. The stunning woods only deepened her feeling of disconnection; she could not bring herself to enjoy the beauty. A distant, quiet voice in her head noticed how incredible it would be to draw this place, but she had no energy for the fleeting thought.

El peeled back Kain's blood-soaked undershirt. It clung to the drying gash, re-opening the wound in places as she pulled. He winced as she handed him a small potion bottle from her belt, popping the top into the bushes before he downed its contents. From her seat on the mossy ground,

Mara could see the black streaking veins stretching from the wound, worse than just an hour before. She had never seen anything like it.

Kain's companions were worried, and Mara sensed this was the corruption they had been so afraid of. The things it could do to a being were something she wished she could erase from her memory. Lingrain's dead eyes flashed through her mind and she shivered. "What happened to those men? The ones that came for me?" she asked, her voice hoarse.

Milios stood at the edge of the clearing, whispering to the wind, so Cyfrin turned to answer. "There's a pass not far from the borders to Grathiel's kingdom. It's a quicker way to the Deep Walk from the Krakenbär, but it's not without its risks." The forest around them seemed to chill at his words, and his eyes grew darker as he went on. "The earth there is particularly steeped in dark magick. Legend has it that the pass is where Mezilmoth's magick first became tainted. And I believe it. I've seen some of the most pure and powerful souls I ever knew be consumed by the darkness there."

He was eyeing Kain's wound, and his face grew angry. "We opted for Bardro's Gash for that very reason. It does bad enough things to mortal men, as we were just unfortunate enough to witness firsthand. The effect that sort of corruption has on magick users…" He shuddered. Brow furrowing, he turned his attention to Milios. "You're muttering, Milios. What's going on?"

The air around them stopped moving as Milios stepped back towards them, still staring off into the woods with a look of apprehension. "Something's coming. Something of old that smelled us out as soon as we set foot in the woods."

Cyfrin was at Mara's side in an instant. With El's assistance, Kain managed to stand, though on weak legs.

"I thought we were safe here!" Mara hissed. The prospect of encountering yet another nightmarish beast was something she wasn't sure her heart could withstand.

Milios was standing still as stone. "Mostly, usually safe. There are magicks here that even the Forest Dwellers do not speak of. Magicks from the time of the Zenoths. Ancient forces, and not all of them safe." The wind returned, swirling around Milios in a furious gale. They whipped around, eyes wide. "She's found us."

Cyfrin reached out and grabbed Mara's arm, pulling her behind him, his runes glowing white. "Who has?" he breathed, but there was a cold fear in his voice that made Mara believe he already knew the answer.

Milios stared. "The One who Sees."

El gave a loud whimper.

Kain looked like he might be sick. "We already gave her our damned gifts on the way *out* of here. We've nothing else to give!"

"She'll flay us alive," El whispered, eyes darting about the clearing. "I told you we should have brought more with us! We have to hide!"

But Milios shook their head, grim. "There's no time. She's here."

Mara knew at once that something big was upon them. She could no longer hear the forest, so musical around them mere seconds before. There was a strange twinkling noise coming towards them from the shadow of the trees, like the ringing of distant bells.

Cyfrin whipped around to Mara, grabbing her shoulders, getting close enough to her face that she could see tiny freckles dotted across his nose. His runes pulsed with white light, casting an ethereal glow onto his eyes. Her body went still at his touch, her breath ceasing with his sudden closeness. His voice was set in a tone of cool command as he spoke. "I know I'm the last person you want to take orders from, believe me. I hear you. But you need to listen to me: Keep quiet; keep your eyes down. Do not look at her face, under any circumstance. No matter what she says to you, no matter how badly you may want to look."

The twinkling seemed to be surrounding their clearing, and the rest of the group had dropped their gazes to the ground. El's eyes were shut tight, and Kain had angled his unsteady body in front of her.

Mara could feel their heavy fear as it sucked the air from around her. Cyfrin shook her gently and she looked back into his terrified eyes. "I need you to do as I say. Do you understand me, Mara?"

Her name chased the fog from her brain. Without a word of protest, she dropped her head to stare at the ground. Cyfrin walked her backwards till she was up against the tree next to Kain and El. He turned around, putting his back to her, and presenting the image that had been burned into her brain over the past month: Cyfrin protecting her.

The twinkling noise came to a sudden stop. The smell of dust and something sickly-sweet overwhelmed Mara, and a strange energy shot an electric thrill through her body.

"Well, well," a voice drawled towards them from everywhere at once. "What beautiful surprises I've been blessed with this night."

It was a woman's voice tickling the back of Mara's neck, as if whoever this being was stood right behind her. Her tone was like honey and butter, warm and inviting as it caressed her every nerve. Mara found it extra telling, therefore, that every inch of her had been filled with dread at the sound of it. Like a beautiful spider, deadly and poised to strike at the first sign of weakness.

"Please, oh One Who Sees all." Mara felt Cyfrin, his head lowered, bend his back to deepen his bow. "We've meant no harm in entering your wood without your rightful gifts. We did not expect to be graced with your presence."

There was a threatening hissing noise and a loud *crack*, then someone was standing before Cyfrin. Mara saw his back tighten as she stared at the creature's feet. Or where feet should have been. Instead, there was what looked like gnarled tree roots jutting out from under a glimmering, golden cloak. Each branch moved individually from one another, pulsing as if they each drew breath. Mara could see large, pointed thorns that were dripping in dark green liquid covering the bark, and she gulped.

"You will be silent, Lightcleaver." Her soft tone shot through Mara like an ice spike. "Or your gift to me for passage shall come from your *flesh.*" There was a wet slurping noise, and Mara pushed back harder into the tree, willing herself to disappear within it.

This isn't happening, this isn't happening, Mara's mind reeled in a panic. *Please, please just let me wake up. Please, please, please.* She heard a sharp intake of breath. "Ah," the voice continued. "But you *did* bring me a gift, soldiers of Caerani."

Cyfrin was pushed roughly to the side and slammed into the tree beside Mara. The smell of dusty sweetness was all-encompassing, and Mara squeezed her eyes shut as the One Who Sees tilted her chin upwards.

Mara heard her soft laugh. Another sharp intake of breath followed by what felt like a barbed tongue grazing the side of her cheek. She shuddered, shying as far back into the tree as she could go but keeping her eyes firmly shut. She felt Cyfrin move next to her, felt his fingertips graze her hand as if reassuring her.

The One Who Sees hissed low, batting their hands apart. "I knew I smelled you, spawn of old. Won't you look at me, chosen one? Won't you show me what you've locked away so deep in your soul?"

A cold finger drew across her sweat covered forehead, pushing her hair out if her face. The creature laughed again, the sound coming from the very recesses of Mara's brain. "This face… This is a face I have seen before. So many lifetimes ago, and again some decades past. But she was not you. Nearly, almost you. Could have fooled all, but not I. You are not what you are supposed to be, girl. Yet, it is close. So very close"

"Please," Cyfrin spoke again. Mara felt him drop to a knee beside her. "Please, we meant no disrespect, oh great one. Our friend is injured. We wish only for safe passage back to the village. It is of dire importance, which I am sure you know."

After another long moment, the One Who Sees stepped back from Mara and she let out a steadying breath. Cold sweat beaded her neck, and her skin felt electrified across its surface.

"Lightcleaver," The One Who Sees addressed Cyfrin. "I will expect *two* gifts on your next voyage through my wood. Or I will wear you and your friends as my next cloak. Mark me, for you know I am true to my words. And you, one who bears not their name." Mara kept her eyes to the ground, trying not to shake as the gnarled root legs stepped closer to her. "When you were sundered from your intended path, the threads of fate nearly became lost. I grant you safe and swift passage through these woods, and with it my regret. Time is running out."

There was a mighty noise, like a thousand wind chimes

in a storm. Mara felt herself moving, whirling at a dizzying pace though her feet remained rooted to the ground. They slowed to an abrupt halt, and the One Who Sees was gone. The sound of birdsong chorused around them once more, and Mara fell to her knees on the mossy ground. She felt winded, her body trembling uncontrollably. Kain slumped down beside her, panting and trying to sheathe his great sword.

Milios' brow was furrowed, studying the trees around the clearing. "She's travelled us to right outside the village borders," they said, voice full of earnest surprise. "We're nearly home."

"Zenoths bless, whose idea was it to bring her only one gift each?" Kain moaned, gripping his chest above his heart as he shook.

"Ah, that would be you, if my memory is correct," Milios said, raising an eyebrow. "You were quite adamant that she'd never stop us twice in one journey, and that bringing more items would only *slow us down* in the long run." Kain looked bashful at this.

"When does the One Who Sees ever appear that close to the border?" El asked, her eyes wild.

"I told you." Milios replied, frowning. "She smelled us on the winds. Smelled *her*." They nodded to Mara who gaped at them all.

"Me?" she cried, incredulous, exasperation overthrowing the panic still ripping through her. "Not a word she said made any sense! What was that thing? What in the damned End of All was she talking about?"

Milios blinked at her, taken aback by her outburst of anxious questioning. "Ancient magicks dwell in ancient beings," they replied. "The One Who Sees was one of the first creatures born of old. She possesses the power of the

All Sight; it shows her threads in time, fate, and destiny. As for what she spoke of…"

They paused a beat and Mara watched as Cyfrin threw them a sharp look. Milios caught it, the energy shifting suddenly, and they smiled at Mara. "She is very old and has seen much. Perhaps too much. I think it's driven her quite mad over the years. Take the gifts, for example. She demands one gift, one that truly means something to you, from every creature she encounters in this forest. And if you fail to bestow one upon her, then she will take one from you that she deems worthy. Rarely to your benefit. Today, we are extremely lucky."

"Speak for yourself," Kain grumbled. He stood propped between Cyfrin and El, the color gone from his face.

Milios gave him an apologetic look. They turned and led the way from the clearing. The trees in this place were different than the ones Mara had previously seen—thicker and full of pine needles down their trunks. The One Who Sees really had sent them someplace new by magick the likes of which Mara had never seen. *Magick that can take you miles away in the blink of an eye*, she thought as her stomach lurched. *That creature could have whisked me to the Dark Gate in an instant.* She wrapped her arms around herself, imagining being tossed into a bottomless black pit by the One Who Sees.

The deeper onto this new forest path they drew, the more wildly fantastic the plant and animals became. Berries seemed to twinkle with starlight; small, fuzzy creatures whistled happy trills at them before somersaulting into the underbrush. Mara caught a glimpse of a bird through the foliage whose tailfeathers looked to be made of actual rainbows. Kain was breathing in shuddering, shallow gulps, but Mara could barely hear him over the sound of birdsong and the cool night breeze through the leaves. Even in her near-shock and desperation, she couldn't help but be mystified.

"Your home..." she said to Milios, unable to contain her awe any longer. "I've never been somewhere so beautiful, in all my years." And it was true. Nothing could ever hope to compare to this splendor, not even the glimmering high streets of Delinval.

Milios stopped, turning to face her. A wide smile had broken out on their face. "Thank you. Wait till you see theirs."

"Finally," El gasped from behind her, out of breath from helping to drag Kain through the woods. Mara looked over Milios' shoulder, her body freezing in place.

Sprawling out behind them through an opening in the trees was a village silhouetted, sparkling in the moonlight. It stretched into the woods, completely hidden save for the twinkling lights and sounds of life.

The hidden village of the Odelians.

CHAPTER 17
A VILLAGE OF SEA AND SKY

Growing up within the glittering kingdom of Delinval, Mara was accustomed to things of beauty. From its flora, painstakingly kept by the farmers, to the hand-picked gemstones that lined the marble streets, she was comfortable with grandeur. But *this*. This village in the forest, standing poised on the edge of the Brisënbane Ocean, took her breath away.

Built into the stone and trees, seeming to grow out of the ground as far back as Mara could see through the dense wood, were buildings of all shapes and sizes. They were laced in delicately trailing vines and ivy, blending them into the landscape. Flickering candlelight burst forth from the windows, and the multi-colored orbs that lit the forest danced through their cobblestone streets.

A river bubbled along in the distance, flowing straight across the edge of the village, disappearing into the trees beyond. She could see a masterfully carved stone building, too small to be a castle but too large to be a normal homestead, peeking out through the trees on the other side of the canal. The smell of cinnamon and citrus clung to the already pine-soaked air, and she could hear boisterous voices drifting to them on the sea breeze.

Mara stood thunderstruck at the start of the cobblestone path that led into their village. Crickets trilled around her, the sound of frogs and soft, humming night creatures in the trees creating a chorus of epic proportion. It made her feel almost relaxed. The waves of the Brisënbane crashed against rocks somewhere beyond the wood across, but Mara could only catch glimpses of it through the trees. The clatter of it was so dimmed by the surrounding plant life that she could hardly believe how furious the waters looked.

There were people running towards them up the path as the group emerged into the village's warm glow. Mara stood behind Milios, trying to make herself as small as possible. Five people charged down the cobblestone street. The first, a plump Odelian woman with jet black hair and blue eyes brimmed with worry. She was wearing a flowing white shirt tucked into a pair of leather pants, her face covered in black soot save for two circles around her eyes where she had apparently been wearing goggles. The second was a man equal in size to a bear. His face was heavily scarred, leading up to deep burn marks on his hairless head. He wore similar attire to the woman, his sleeves rolled up to reveal massive forearms. His eyes too were fraught with worry, his clothes dusted in the same black soot.

On his other side strode a woman of such incredible presence that Mara stood up straighter by instinct. Even in the dim glow around them, Mara could see how devastating her beauty was. Sharp features were placed to perfection on a face that could have been carved straight from marble, it was so smooth. Her eyes flicked upwards at the corners, their color glinting like jade stone set ablaze.

Her full lips were pulled into a tight line, her face a mask of grim determination. Her white-blonde hair had been tied atop her head, flowing down to her waist. Mara could see the intricately crafted hilt of a great sword strapped to her back. She wore armor like Cyfrin's, though the leathers cut perfectly across her body looked thinner than his. They were a deep shade of red, and Mara could see scales like the ones lacing El's armor woven throughout it.

Two men flanked her from behind, wearing black leather and looking weary. Having grown up in the world of nobility, Mara recognized them at once as bodyguards. She tried to silence the battle between fear and anger inside her as they approached. Even in the heart of the enemy's lands, surrounded by their people, she could not help but wish she had a sword in hand to exact vengeance for her kingdom. Her heart gave a strange flutter at this thought.

What if, by some final blow of my own sour luck, uncle really did issue that order? What if he truly believes me to be a traitor to the crown? Is Delinval still my home then? Mara could not recall a time where she hadn't been hated by her uncle's court purely for who she was. They hated her reckless tongue, and forward thinking. Her prowess with a sword was nothing but a shameful mark on her family name, and her foolhardy dreams of adventure were a point of great mockery to the nobles. *The lot of them would be more than happy to believe I had abandoned my station.* Her mind felt broken, the wind rustling her jagged, cropped hair serving as a constant reminder of what had just occurred.

Cyfrin, still covered in the dried blood of the Delinvalian knights, stood before her. Mara felt the familiar pang of anger rise in her throat. *He killed the only ones that came to bring me home,* her thoughts roared. But a growing voice was probing from somewhere deep within her.

Whether it was by command from the king, or by the darkness that had taken them, those knights meant me harm. And regardless of his reasons for doing so, Cyfrin prevented it. He saved me.

The large man and woman reached them first, moving at a jog with panicked faces. They grabbed Kain from El and Cyfrin's arms. "Oh, my boy!" the woman cried as Kain groaned, stumbling a little as they pulled him upright. "What in Zenoth's name did you do?!"

"The usual," El answered. "Ran himself in headfirst without waiting to understand the situation."

The bear-like man put his hands on his hips, tutting at Kain with a disapproving look as the woman held him up. Mara could see the resemblance now. These were his parents. "Ends be, boy. You've got such a big brain in that hard head of yours. Can't you at least *try* to use it?"

Kain looked up at him, sweat dripping down his face. "I did use it, Father!" he wheezed through clenched teeth as his father looped a great arm underneath his other side. "And it told me to kill *them* before they had a chance to kill *us!*"

"And look how that worked out for you," El scolded. "We need to get him to the healer. I've done the best I could, but it's nowhere near good enough." She took the lead before Kain and his parents, and they half-dragged him up the path into the village. Cyfrin came to stand before the stunning woman, bowing his head a fraction to her.

"General," he said in a low voice as the woman glowered at him.

Mara gaped. *This is the general? This stunning, slight woman is the one they've all been so afraid of?!* Her eyes passed across the massive hilt strapped high on General Caerani's back, gulping as she took in its incredible size.

"Sorry we're late. Ran in to some troubles on the road. The corruption…it's much worse than we expected. We didn't come across a single patch of green on the way here. And every animal we happened to encounter was already tainted with the darkness, or close to death." Cyfrin gave her their findings in a clear, even tone. A soldier delivering his report. It was the first time Mara had ever seen him be so diplomatic, and she was struck by how well it suited him.

But Caerani was no longer looking at Cyfrin. She took two mighty strides forward, and Milios stepped out of the way to reveal Mara behind them. Her gaze was unflinching as her eyes bored into Mara's. Mara felt heat rise in her cheeks but returned the stare with just as much vigor.

"Caerani," Cyfrin was saying carefully behind her. "This is the princess. The one they call Mara."

Caerani's lip curled up slightly, reminding Mara of a cat. "Mara," she repeated, and the air seemed to heat as she spoke with a voice like rolling flame. She was studying her face, and Mara worked to keep her eyes from showing her discomfort. "You know that name means martyr, do you not?" she asked in a drawling tone.

Mara blinked. *She mocks me? This was the name given to me by my mother with her dying breaths. It is all I have of her.* She bit her tongue to keep these angry thoughts silent, glowering up at the woman.

Caerani's eyes flashed at the challenge in her stare, but she slid her gaze from Mara's face and spoke now to

Milios. "Go with Kain and Eleanora. If he's blighted as badly as he looks to be, they'll need your assistance."

She gave Mara another once over before next addressing Cyfrin. "You two, come with me." Caerani turned and started up the path towards the village without another word. She waved a hand at her bodyguards, who bowed their heads in silent understanding before taking their leave. Cyfrin came to stand beside Mara, motioning gently for her to follow the General.

If Mara had thought the view from outside the village was magnificent, it was nothing compared to how it looked walking its winding streets. Nightlife bustled all around them. Clinking glasses from open taverns, laughter spilling from the wide windows of houses. Mara smelled something warm and savory on the breeze and her stomach growled loudly in response. If it weren't for the life and lights shining all around, Mara might have never guessed this place was a village at all. The beauty was so blended into the wood and earth; she wondered how long it had stood for it to be joined together as such. Buildings were hewn straight into the rock faces, roofs curving around trees that grew straight from the middle of their homesteads. It was like something out of a fantastic dream.

The three of them turned down a side street and on to a mossy path through undisrupted wood. The sound of rushing waves was growing louder, the orb lights flitting around casting long shadows as they walked. After several tense minutes of silence, the group emerged into a large clearing on the other side of the path. Mara felt her jaw drop.

The wide clearing dipped into a steep cliff, which shot straight down into the ocean beyond. The moon, full and shrouded in a ring of furious golden light, peeked up over the water. It was larger than Mara had thought possible, and the ocean seemed to disappear into where they met at the horizon.

All the records claimed the waves of the Brisenbane were lethal, capable of destroying even the most stalwart of vessels. It made sea travel impossible; not a soul who had tried had ever returned alive from her hungry depths. This knowledge only served to further Mara's shock when her eyes fell on a dock at the very bottom of the cliffs. But not just a dock. *A ship?! This cannot be possible*, she thought through her reverence. Mara took in the water below it, noting how it was unnaturally calm in the area surrounding the ship. Its wood was matte black, flecked in the same kind of red as Caerani's armor. Magnificent masts rose from its decks and into the darkened skies, the incredible sails draping across them flashing in the starlight. A flag rose high above the top mast, a black ornate skull embroidered into the dark red surface.

Mara squinted down at it as they approached a grouping of large tents off to the side of the clearing. There were figures moving across the deck below, the sound of tinkling glass, quick fiddles and uproarious laughter carrying to her on the sea breeze. Carved on the front of the ship in red wood, mouth open and wings spread wide around it, was a fearsome dragon. The moonlight glared off its talons, revealing each to be tipped in real gold. It looked so real, she felt it might take flight at any moment.

Mara pulled her eyes from the tamed waters below the ship and took in the clearing as they neared the largest of the tents. There were spears and training swords on racks in the middle of huge dirt fields. The ground looked scorched in places, completely torn away in others. There were footprints tracking through the dirt, many of them barefooted. This was unmistakably a training ground.

Mara had spent countless hours in one of her own back in Delinval. Hers had been tidier, more ornate, but the basics of it were the same, as was the intention behind it. She shuddered to think of more warriors like the four she had just spent a month with, loose on the unsuspecting world.

Cyfrin stood at the mouth of the tent, holding the flap open for Mara to enter behind Caerani. She paused, eyeing the strange symbols painted above the entrance. The first was a sun, a rudimentary depiction of one at best. The second seemed to be a small flame, reaching up towards the tip of the tent. The last, drawn by what could have been a child, was a skull. Two distinct horns sat on either side of its head, and Mara shivered as she stared at it. *What sort of strange warning is this?*

Her musings were cut short as Cyfrin cleared his throat, motioning impatiently for her to step forward. "One can only serve as a doorstop so long, your highness." He held the tent flap a little higher for emphasis as he said this. Mara sneered at him but stepped inside the tent none the less.

A large round table took up much of the space, high-backed chairs tucked in all around it. Orb lights floated about above their heads, flitting between the dried herbs and meats hanging from the canvas ceiling. The table was cluttered with all manners of things. Potion bottles, pieces of carved bones, unusually glowing stones that were vibrating softly as Mara stared down at them. A dagger stuck out of the wooden tabletop, pinning down a massive map that took up most of the surface. She glanced over it and saw many landmarks that weren't drawn on the maps in Delinval. Her stomach gave another lurch of upset at this.

Caerani took a seat facing Mara and nodded to the chair across from hers. Mara took it, grateful to at least be off her feet and on a soft surface, and Cyfrin slid into a seat beside her. There was silence for a moment, Caerani observing Mara over the tips of her fingers as she drummed them against one another. She turned to look at Cyfrin. "So. You four, my best and brightest of the bunch." Her voice was tinged with sarcasm. "I thought I had stressed how vital it was for you to be here *before* tonight's full moon, so that preparations could be made. And you, in turn, assured me that I had nothing to fear. And yet..." She motioned towards the mouth of the tent, where the light from the full moon peeked through. "Did the time somehow elude you on your travels?"

Cyfrin grimaced at the bite in her tone. "We were well aware of the moon phase, General."

"Then you must also be aware of my disappointment. That time would have been more than well spent, and now we must proceed forward with a near cruel abruptness. Tell me, as the head of my most powerful War Party, what in the damned End of All kept you?" Her expression was stony, raising one sculpted eyebrow as she set her burning gaze on him.

Mara saw Cyfrin stiffen beneath her stare. "Milios' theory prior to our setting out was correct. The magick flows that power Zenafrost, most markedly the ones beneath the earth to the west, are tainted beyond use. It was impossible to harness enough energy to simply travel us across the countryside. As I said, the lands are far worse than we ever imagined. Even the places that had been alive a year ago are now drained and dead. It's allowed his beasts to travel more freely."

Caerani's eyes flashed. "You're telling me you were so detained by a few darklings coming to sniff about? These past twenty years have been difficult, Cyfrin, but have they truly made you lose your touch?"

His eyes narrowed, but his tone stayed even as he replied. "It's not merely darklings traveling across the mountains now, Caerani. We almost ran afoul with a Reflector Beast in the forest past Delinval." Caerani's expression darkened at this. Cyfrin looked exhausted, pinching the bridge of his nose and sighing. "Then there were the blasted Barkens, the Corruption in the Pass…Not to mention the entire day we lost having to rescue her from the Ylastrians."

"Normigone's people? You allowed her to be taken from you by chaos wielders?" She looked livid, and Cyfrin bowed his head. Mara saw shame flicker across his face before he evened his expression and met her glare.

"Demiel used his magick to distract us and…and I let it. No harm came to her, though we did lay waste to a good many of his men before our goodbye." The ghost of a smirk played on his lips at the memory, but immediately fell away at the look on Caerani's face.

She glared at him a moment longer before giving a heavy sigh, shaking her head. "You'll need to give me a full report after the ritual. Bloody underkingdom…I'm sure that will come back to bite us in the ass. Not that Normigone was overly fond of us to begin with—"

Mara slammed a fist down on the table and they both looked at her in surprised. *Enough. It is enough,* she seethed in her head. *They have dragged me through unspeakable, harrowing dangers, with threat of being corrupted by whatever darkness blights our lands with every passing step. My own people may have forsaken me, due to that mishap in the damned Underkingdom.* Mara was tired of remaining silent while they all carried on about her. As if she was just coin to be gambled, or a lamb to be slain.

The fire ignited in her stomach, and she rose from her chair, glowering down at them both. Caerani's eyes widened a little and Cyfrin's eyebrows raised high. "I demand answers." Mara was surprised at how steady her voice was given how hard her heart was pounding, how sweaty her palms had become. "You have taken me from my home, stolen me from my people, forced me to walk with *him*," She threw a venomous glance at Cyfrin who sneered at her in return. "For weeks on end, putting my life in the gravest of peril with *no* explanation and I demand to know why." She raised her head a little higher as she stared down at Caerani. "What do you people want with me?"

Caerani gazed at Mara, her gaze fierce but with a suspicious shine in the corners of her eyes. The tent was silent, the sounds of the forest and ocean filling the space. The General opened her mouth to speak, and the flaps of the tent flew open. Mara spun around, jumping at the sudden break in the silence. A man stood there, and Mara knew at once that he was an Ylastrian. She took a step away in panic, the back of her thighs colliding with the tabletop and stopping her in her tracks.

He was tall, though not quite as tall as Cyfrin or Kain. His skin was dark as the night sky behind him and etched with brightly glowing tattoos. His hair was white as Cyfrin's, damp and wild about his strong face. His eyes were a shocking shade of red, and they stared at Mara with unbridled intensity. He wore dark black armor that glinted with a deep purple hue in the orb lights around them. There were blades too numerous to count adorning his body. Daggers in each of his boots, knives across his bandolier, twin blades crossing his back, and a long sword hanging from his hip.

Tiny potion bottles, swirling with all different colored liquids and gases, swung from his bracers and belts. He wore a necklace that dropped low on his chest, made up of what looked to be rat skulls. A black, weather-beaten box hung at the hip opposite to his sword, held to his body by a thick golden chain that laced through his armor and around. He wrapped his knuckles hard against the lid of the box once, a huge smile breaking across his face as he stepped into the tent. "By the great gate's end," he said. "You look *just* like her, don't you?"

CHAPTER 18
THE PAST UNDONE

His words clung in the air, spinning around Mara as she stared blankly at his exuberant face. Caerani gave an exasperated sigh, dropping her head into her hands as the man's smile faltered. "Excellent. So glad you could join us, Drake."

Her tone was dripping in sarcasm and the man strode past Mara, coming to kneel dramatically beside Caerani's seat. He kissed the top of her hand and up her arm. She yanked it away and flicked him on the forehead. "Oh, how I've missed your delicate ways, my darling!" he said, beaming down at her as he stood.

Caerani glared at him, but a slight flush rose in her face as she grimaced. His eyes fell on Cyfrin. "Zenoth's blood, man, you look like walking death. And you smell even worse. Was the trek really that bad?"

Cyfrin gave him a look of disdain, making a rude gesture with his blood covered hand. Drake chuckled, dropping his attention back to Mara. "So! What have I missed?"

Caerani locked eyes with Mara, who stared back,

confused. "What does he mean?" Mara asked, and Drake's face fell as he looked between them slowly. "I look just like who?"

He looked dumbfounded and stared at Caerani, open mouthed. She glared up at him with renewed intensity. "You haven't told her?! I just assumed someone would have by now! Don't be angry, love, I was just shocked! I didn't expect...well, Caer, she does look *just* like—"

"*Just like who?*" Mara said through her teeth. She was losing all sense of worry for her well-being. The frustration at being kept so in the dark about her own fate had reached a fever pitch.

Drake looked uncomfortable under Caerani's glowering stare. The general rose from the table, Cyfrin following suit. "It'll be no use just telling you," she said to Mara. "All our words will be twisted at once by your hatred. You'll need to see it for yourself." And she led them all out of the tent and into the warm night air.

The four of them walked back up the mossy path through the trees, emerging on to the cobblestone streets of their village. Cyfrin kept throwing Mara nervous looks out of the corner of his eye, and her anxiety began to grow. She had to fight the wild urge to turn and run with every step, knowing it would achieve nothing but her potential early demise. They were moving towards a small, ornate bridge which led over the crystal blue river and off around the towered building beyond. There were Odelians walking past, many of whom were singing, laughing, and speaking jubilantly with one another. Some turned to smile at them as they passed, welcoming Cyfrin back with joyous cries and pats on the back.

A few people startled as they looked at her, gasping and stumbling away as if she had struck them. Mara glared back, holding her head high. They had every reason to fear her, every right to tremble before the Delinvalian princess now in their midst. She wondered if they suspected how afraid she was to be there, wondered if her face betrayed it.

They passed a building that heated the street outside with its orange glow. El and Milios stepped out from inside as they approached, looking tired. Caerani glanced at them. "Is he dead?" she asked, nodding towards the building.

Mara looked inside and could see Kain laid on a soft bed within. His parents sat on either side of him, speaking softly to one another, and thousands of potion bottles glowed on the walls around them. A small man sat at the head of the bed, his hands placed on either side of Kain's face. An iridescent red glow emitted from his palms as Mara watched.

El shook her head, and Mara could see she looked much brighter than she had earlier. "You know Kain. Harder than rock, and tougher too. He'll heal up fine."

"Might we accompany you, General?" Milios asked, the breeze that only affected them drifting softly through their hair. "We'd like to be there when it happens."

Mara's stomach gave a lurch. *This is it. They're taking me to the ritual*, she thought as she suppressed a whimper. *I'm about to be sacrificed, and they're all speaking as if it's a casual stroll through the wood. No wonder my uncle called them Dreads. This cold, cruelty...it's barbaric.*

Caerani had given a curt nod to Milios before continuing forward on the path. El fell in step beside Mara, giving her a nervous smile that made her feel somehow more terrified. *Like a farmer saying goodbye to their prized pig, before sending them to slaughter*, she thought, frantic.

They crossed over the bridge and up the path hugging the towered building. Mara was distracted from her panic by how artfully made the exterior was, studying the deep carvings wrought into the wood. Caerani must have caught her staring at its splendor, for she waved a hand towards it as they passed. "That's the Grand Halls. It's hosted every Odelian royal to ever walk these lands, plus their court."

"Empty now then, isn't it?" Mara pushed as much malice into the words as she could, determined to fight till the bitter end.

Cyfrin made a low growl of warning, lip curling in a snarl at Mara.

Drake scoffed, not bothering to turn as he addressed her. "My, what cruel malice. Though I'm not sure what I expected from one raised in a place like Delinval."

Caerani had stiffened at Mara's retort, but she shrugged. "True, tis but a shell of what once was. But it's merely been waiting for its heir to come home."

They stepped off the cobblestones and onto a mossy path into the woods. Unlike the trail to the training grounds, this one had been adorned with glowing gemstones all along its ground. They pulsed like a heartbeat, leading them deeper into the woods with their many-colored lights.

They rounded a bend and found themselves standing before a great stone temple all but hidden in the trees. It was carved out of the high, mountainous rocks behind it, and stood with almost no walls to allow for the open air. Mara could see the inside lit dimly by the orb lights and caught glimpses of glittering tapestries and beautiful statues within as they passed. She began to hear moving water, and the soft humming of the night creatures grew quieter as they approached the sound. The river that they followed stopped at the top of a steep cliff face, and Mara could see something glittering away below it. Approaching the edge, she felt herself overwhelmed once more by the beauty before her.

The river flowed in a steady waterfall off the edge of the cliff and into a magnificent gleaming lake of water in the basin below. The reflection of the sky on its smooth surface made it look like liquid moonlight, but it was what surrounded it that dazzled Mara. Thick crystals protruded from the ground and walls of the waterfall's basin, standing eight, nine, ten feet tall. They each twinkled of their own accord, mimicking the starlight above. Mara saw they matched the softly glowing rocks in the moss-covered path that led them here, pulsing with the same unified power.

A staircase made of wood and vine wrapped down the rock beside the waterfall, and Caerani led them slowly down into the valley below. All noise vanished as they reached the bottom, replaced by the musical sound of the waterfall on the crystals. Walking towards the water's edge, Mara could see swirls of light and darkness dancing just below the surface. It looked alive, and the earth under her feet felt energized in a way that set her teeth on edge. She was so mesmerized by its depths that at first she did not see the woman sitting on the lake side, who stood as they approached.

She looked like Milios, with her long ears and braids of emerald-green hair. But the similarities stopped there. This woman wore long, flowing robes made of flower petals that whispered about her bare feet and draped low over her long fingers. A circlet of dark black metal sat spiraling across her forehead, blending into her rich brown skin, and a veil was tucked up underneath a band on her head. Fragments of crystals, like the ones emerging from the earth around them, had been attached in scrolling patterns across her cheekbones.

She bowed her head low to Caerani, her impossibly purple eyes not leaving Mara's face. "The princess." It was a statement, not a question, as she continued to stare deep into Mara's eyes. The intensity of the gaze made Mara uncomfortable, almost like the woman was somehow stripping her soul bare.

Caerani nodded in response to her words. "We hadn't the time to prepare her, Tiamo. They've only just arrived."

Tiamo freed Mara from her stare and nodded up at the full moon above. "And not a second too soon. The ritual is tricky and will only work under the highest light of the fourth moon. We're cutting it very close."

Caerani put a hand on the middle of Mara's back and led her forward to the water's edge beside Tiamo. "Then we shall allow you to work." She stepped back to join the rest of the group, all with looks of worry and apprehension on their faces. Cyfrin's expression was still and steady as he watched. Mara looked at the surface of the water then back to the woman beside her, eyes wide. *Am I to be drowned beneath this moon?*

Tiamo was pulling the veil down over her eyes, shadowing the mischievous glint that flashed through them. "You look as if you're about to be hung. Have you ever been ancestral travelled before?"

Mara stared blankly at her, admiring the vinelike lace of the veil now covering her face. "I don't know what that means," she replied, frustrated.

The woman smiled at her; a twisting grin that made Mara instantly unsettled. "I expected as much. Oh, I do love a first timer. Just remember to keep a tight grip on my hand, and try not vomit when we arrive, will you? I can't stand the smell." She reached out to Mara and grabbed her hand before she could draw it away.

There was a sound like water rushing all around them,

and an overpowering feeling of being pulled backwards. She felt weightless as they tumbled through blurring colors, though she and Tiamo remained firmly planted on the lakeside. Mara's body was growing hot, like she had been sprinting across a great distance. Just when she thought she would surely burn in this unending free-fall, they slammed to a stop. The world came into sharp relief around them.

They were standing in the exact same spot by the lake, but it was daytime now. The sunlight reflected the sky down onto the crystals, giving the illusion that they were standing amongst the clouds. The waterfall babbled away happily as the birds sang their mesmerizing songs. Mara glanced to the group standing behind them, but they all looked like shades of themselves. Shadows with vague features hovering in the air. She looked down to see that she too was oddly see-through. Tiamo smiled at her look of panic, gripping her hand tighter as Mara twitched to pull away.

On the lakeside before them stood a large gathering of Odelians, hushed and listening to the woman who stood speaking before the crowd. She had her back to Mara, dark auburn curls unfurling down over a stunning green dress. Mara's eyes fell on a crown, perched perfectly upon her head. "What…what is this?" she breathed, trying, and failing to grasp what was happening.

Tiamo nodded towards the crowned woman. "I have taken us one and twenty years into the past. This is the last time Queen Alora addressed the Odelians before setting off to aid in the war."

Mara stared at her in disbelief. It was too fantastic to be real, far more impossible than anything she had yet encounter in her dealings with magick. But she thought back to the One Who Sees, to her ability to send them somewhere else in an instant. *It cannot be*, she thought. *And yet...* Something inside of Mara was telling her Tiamo spoke truth. Clearly, magick was at play. Who was she to say what it could or could not do? "Can...can they see us?" she asked, her voice coming out as a whisper as she stared at the crowd facing them.

"No. We are merely observers of what once was; shades of soul I've sent in to the beyond of before. The ritual only allows us a few moments here. I advise you to watch carefully."

Alora was speaking again, and a hush fell over them all. Her arms were wide as she addressed her people in a voice that sounded like the warmth of sunshine. "...stand here together now. And we need not fear, for our great home will keep us all safe from the darkness at our borders."

There were soldiers standing around Alora, and Mara recognized the backs of Drake and Caerani flanking her on either side. Neither were wearing their armor, both clad in loose fitted shirts and dark leather pants. Drake had only the two blades crossed over his back, and Caerani held a staff aloft as she surveyed the crowd. The Queen went on. "I ask only that you love one another with all you are. This evil is not forever, and it is woefully weaker than any soul we have here. It is your light that keeps the darkness at bay."

A chilling silence followed her words. Mara felt a small sadness in heart as watched the people's eyes, filled with adoration as they gazed at their queen. No one suspected she would soon die. It pained her to witness.

"Queen Alora pivoted slightly, adjusting her feet, and Mara caught the glimpse of a round belly from where she stood watching. She stared, eyes widening. *The Queen was with child?*

Her mind raced, wracking her brain for any mention of this in their history books. She felt sick. Her uncle had beheaded this woman in the middle of Delinval. If this was real, if this truly was a glimpse into the past, then he had done so with no regard at all for that child growing within her. That wasn't the behavior of heroes.

That was the behavior of monsters.

But Mara bit back on this thought as Alora continued. "Though we have suffered greatly, though our beautiful lands have suffered as well…my friends, I have nothing but hope in my heart. Hope for us all to one day feel the love we once had for this land. For *all* its peoples. Hope that from the ashes of this despair, we will rise as one to be greater and more beautiful than we ever were before. I hope this for you all, and for my daughter. My beauty. My life. My everything. My darling Yvaine." And she turned straight around, looking directly at Mara.

It was like gazing into a distorted mirror. The woman had her same features, the same nose, large eyes, and dimpled cheeks. Her curls were even the same, the exact strip that hung loose in Mara's face hanging in the middle of hers. But this woman was a beauty far surpassing what Mara could ever see in herself; a truly ethereal being with her gentle smile and softly pointed ears. And she was staring as if she could see Mara standing there, an obtrusive presence in awe of her magnificence.

Tiamo looked, mouth slightly agape, between the two of them. She exclaimed softly in a language foreign to Mara. "Zenoths bless. It's like she can see you, isn't it? Like she knows you're here."

As if in response, the Queen rubbed her swollen stomach and smiled at her. Her face was so beautiful, so radiant, Mara felt she might weep. There was a small sound from the shadowed group sitting a few feet away, but Mara did not break eye contact. She didn't think she could if she wanted to, spellbound in the Queen's gaze. Then, the world around her began to blur. They were falling, falling, falling. It was forward this time, or at least it felt that way as they flew through the colored world once more. They slammed to a halt in the dark lake of the now, so hard that Mara swayed dangerously on the spot.

She felt sick and numb all at once. She wanted to scream, to close her eyes and shake away what she just saw. It was a trick—magick made to fool her. It had to be. But it felt so real, so unquestionable, as she had stared at the woman who looked exactly like her. The Queen of the Odelians. The Queen pregnant right around the time Mara had been born. The world was spinning again, but not from magick. Her head whirled, her pulse thundering loud enough that she felt all could hear. She turned to look at the group, staggering, and her eyes went wide.

The five of them were kneeling on the ground before her, heads bowed low. El had tears falling freely from her face, Milios smiling up at her with misty eyes. Caerani's head was bowed lowest of all, her hair falling in a curtain around her, and Drake looked like he could have cheered. Cyfrin was staring at her with an odd expression on his face, and Mara's vision began to tunnel on him. Everything around him fell away, and he was already moving before it even happened.

The last thing she saw as her knees gave way beneath her was Cyfrin shooting up from the ground, his hand at her waist a full two seconds before she buckled. And then her world went black.

CHAPTER 19
A QUEEN UNHINGED

Colors, bright and beautiful, swirled around her. Mara was floating in the crystal lake, drifting in weightlessness between the light above and darkness below. The Odelian Queen hovered in the air before her, casting glimmering starlight upon her face and singing a song in foreign tongue. Calm, the likes of which she had never felt, washed over Mara. She was beginning to stir.

Dreaming. She had only been dreaming. They must still be on the road leading them in to the Odelian village, exhausted and fatigued so badly that her dreams were hyper-vivid. But as she lay there with eyes shut, she realized her body was partially sunken into a cushioned, soft bed. There were pillows all around her that felt like silk against Mara's face, and a fur-lined blanket lay heavy across her body. Her eyes flew open, and she shot upright.

She was in a large four poster bed, blue velvet curtains draped around her. The room was built from dark, polished wood, and colorful tapestries hung from every wall. There were twinkling orb lights casting a glow on the many crystals swaying from the ceiling.

A balcony stood to her left, its doors thrown wide to let in the air from the village. Sunlight poured into the room, and the smell of cinnamon and sea floated in on the gentle breeze. Mara threw off the blanket, regretting the motion as her muscles cried out in agony. Yelping, she moved to stand.

"I would give yourself a moment before trying that. Your legs won't be quite ready yet." El was sitting cross-legged on a plush dark blue poof next to the bed, and Mara jumped as she spoke. El gave her an apologetic smile. "Sorry. None of us wanted to leave you to wake up alone in here. Cyfrin sat with you most of the night, but he and Milios have been in talks with Caerani and Drake all afternoon. Kain's been waiting to be dismissed by the healer, so I've just been waiting." She looked suddenly embarrassed. "Oh, please don't misunderstand! I wasn't *watching* you. I was watching *over* you."

Mara stayed silent, staring at her. El grimaced and stretched high, as if she'd been sat there for quite some time. "I didn't want you waking up alone in a strange place. I wouldn't want to, were I in your shoes. I can't imagine what this must be like for you."

"Must be like...?" Mara repeated back, and everything from the past night crashed in on her at once. She grabbed the sides of her head, gasping. El hurried over to the bedside table and poured a cup of water from a pitcher. She tried to hand it to Mara who smacked her hand away, leaping off the bed and wobbling as she stared at El, eyes wild. She felt like she was going to be sick. "What sort of trick is this?! Do you take me for a fool?!" she cried eyes darting around for anything she could use as a weapon.

The ornately carved oak doors opened as she spoke,

and Caerani, Kain and Milios stepped inside. "Ah, glad to see you're awake and processing," Kain said, smiling through his uncomfortable expression. They were all eyeing her with unease and apprehension. It only stood to further Mara's fury.

She spun around to face Caerani, pointing at her. "*You.* How *dare* you? What sort of game are you people playing at, trying to convince me that I'm one of you? What is there to gain from this?!" Her voice was shrill.

Caerani frowned at her, a sad look in her otherwise dazzling eyes. She folded her arms across her chest and raised an eyebrow. "I've never been one for games. And we have nothing to gain here but the return of our princess."

Mara let out a cold laugh. "*Your* princess? Is that what this is? You're trying to make me turn on my own people?" Her words were ice, seeking to harm. She stood a little taller, her chin tilting upwards as she glared at them all. "Hear me now: I will *never* abandon my kingdom. Your time and efforts in this ruse, which I'm sure were considerable given that performance, have been utterly wasted. I am loyal to none but my king and people."

She saw Kain wince at the tone in her voice. But Caerani did not falter, her eyes boring into Mara's as she replied. "I would have taken you for an idiot if you'd believed us, those you've only known as your enemy, without proof." She tilted her head, studying Mara's face. "We are to have dinner in the dining hall for the first time in twenty years this evening. If you join us, we will explain everything to you…answer any questions you may have."

She nodded to the tall, ornate dresser on the opposite wall. "Alora's old clothes are in there, and you look roughly the same size. El will come to escort you when food is ready." Caerani sniffed at the air and wrinkled her nose. "Make sure you bathe first. The lot of you smell like rancid bog water." And with that, she turned and led the still uncomfortable group silently from the room.

Mara remained rooted to the spot, breathing heavily. This had been the Queen's chambers. It explained the beautiful art on the walls, and the many dazzling crystals hanging above her. They caught the afternoon sun and cast small rainbows all around, clinking as they bumped softly against one another. She could hear a windchime on the balcony over the noises floating up from the village. Under different circumstance, it would have been stunning to her.

But not now.

The thought of dinner made her stomach ache, but she could not bring herself to pass up a good meal. *But to sit at a table full of them…what a cruel torture that will be,* she thought. And though she hated herself for it, cursed her endless curiosity, Mara couldn't help but wonder what they might tell her. She played back the memory in her mind of the crystal waterfall and the lake below; thought of the Queen's face as it turned to stare at her. She had looked exactly like Mara, undeniably so. She bit her lip as her mind continue to race. *I have seen magick change men, have seen the elements bent in their favor and to their whim. I have been sent through the very fabric of what should be, travelled miles in a second. This, all of this… It's just more damned magick.*

But she couldn't see what they had to gain. True, she was the crown princess of Delinval. She thought there were perhaps political motives at play, unforeseen to Mara somehow. Her title made her a worthy pawn, but she held no real power in Delinval. Turning her would earn them no reward on that front. The faces of the Odelians in the village flashed in her mind, staring at her as if they knew her. The words of not only Demiel, but also the One Who Sees echoed forth from her memory.

"Have we met before?"

"I've seen this face before."

Mara shook her head at these thoughts, grunting in pain at the motion on her stiff neck. Her uncle had told her how crafty Dreads were, how good they were at illusions and enchantments. She would not allow herself to fall prey to their tricks. No matter how convincing they might appear. Turning on her heel, she marched herself through the washroom doors to her right. The thought of a hot bath, of being clean and out of these Zenoths forsaken, ill-fitting leathers, was enough to drive all other panic from her head for the moment.

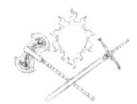

Mara couldn't remember the last time she had been this clean. They had made stops on their journey here to take turns pouring water on damp pieces of fabric to wash themselves with, but it was of little use. It did nothing for the layers of muck and dust that laid thick on her skin. It took her a full hour before she was satisfied with her work, looking down at her pristine body for the first time in a month.

She was standing in the bedroom once more, wrapped in a towel and watching the sun starting to set across the balcony. There was a portrait to the left of the open doors that pulled her gaze, dragging her almost hypnotically towards it. It was of Queen Alora, her dark green gown matching the bejeweled crown atop her head of auburn curls. She was giving a broad smile, the burning intensity in her eyes clear even with paint.

A gorgeous man sat beside her in stunning leather

armor, a brilliant golden crown on his head. He looked like he was mid-laugh, his chin pivoted upwards in frozen glance to the Queen. Mara stared at him, at his jet-black hair and boisterous green eyes. Eyes the same shade as hers, narrowed by a smile she had seen in her own reflection many times. She took a step back, yanking herself from the portrait and squeezing her eyes shut.

It isn't real. You're seeing things, Mara. Whether by magick, or by your own damned imagination. Not anywhere near satisfied with this answer to herself, she groaned and turned to the dresser. The clothes inside smelled of herbs used to deter insects—and roses. They varied between gauzy dresses befitting a lady, to leathers obviously made for a warrior. Mara glanced at the armor, noting how beautifully crafted it looked. It took all her might to drag her eyes away, willing her mind to fall silent.

She settled on a pair of brown leather pants and a bell-sleeved green shirt made of the softest fabric she had ever felt. They hugged her body as if they had been made for her. There was a handheld mirror on the writing desk by the door, and she grabbed it hesitantly.

Mara frowned at her reflection. Her face was much thinner than it had been a month ago; dark purple circles lined her eyes. The sallowness to her usually plump cheeks made her look sickly. Her hair was shorter than it had ever been, jaggedly short in the back and long about the face. She twirled one of the curls around her finger, feeling the slight fray of the burned tips. She remembered the way Cyfrin looked at Lingrain as he sliced through her captured locks. It was a look of murderous intent and pure wrath. Mara's stomach gave a flutter as she replayed the look in her mind, and she cleared her throat loudly to force the image away.

Displeased by her gaunt appearance, she placed the

mirror face down on the desk and sighed. There was a knock at the door. "Mara?" It was El's voice that drifted through as it cracked open. "I'm here to bring you to dinner. Are you ready?"

Mara closed her eyes, taking a deep breath. *I just have to get through dinner,* she thought. *If I can get well-fed and well-rested, I can figure a way out of here. Reinforcements or not, I can do this. I am strong.*

She stepped into the hall and El gave her a nervous smile. She had changed from the scale hide Mara had grown so used to seeing her in the past month. A beautiful, pale orange dress flowed about her cleanly scrubbed body, and she wasn't wearing any shoes. She looked like a noblewoman, a far cry from the battle-hardened warrior on their journey here. "I hope you've got an appetite!" El said, trying to lighten the tense mood as they started up the hallway. "Sounds like we're to have a feast in celebration of your…of our return."

Mara saw her throw a hesitant glance in her direction, and she did not respond. They walked in silence down the dark wood hallway. The walls were lined in paintings of fantastic beasts and faraway places, the multi-colored orb lights from outside dancing about overhead.

The wooden floors were mostly covered in plush rug runners, and the windows facing out towards the village had all been opened to let in the soft breeze. Mara stared about her as they walked, studying her surroundings. Though it had been their Queen's residence, this place looked nothing like her uncle's castle. Or truly any of the noblemen's estates across Delinval. It felt more like…more like a *home*. She bit her lip as she thought this. The warmth here was impossible to deny; everything, down to the arching wooden ceilings and soft furniture in every room they passed, was made to be welcoming.

I hate this. It stood in such stark contrast to the cold marble of her uncle's kingdom that it made her uncomfortable, out of place. She felt the same longing she had felt watching the four warriors interact so lovingly with one another.

The sound of booming voices reached them, growing louder as they moved. Mara recognized the boisterous tones of Kain and Drake, and the sound of clinking glasses.

The scent of baked sweets and succulent meats surrounded her. She inhaled deeply, and her stomach growled in desperation. El smiled as she heard it and Mara's frown turned into a scowl. They had reached two large oak doors. Carvings of what looked to be the crystal lake from yesterday rested upon its surface, and Mara marveled at the detail in the work. El pushed them wide and they entered in to a warm, domed room.

On one side, facing the babbling river and tree topped homesteads beyond, was a great open terrace. Lightning bugs mingled with the glowing orbs in the dying sunlight, and music from the village drifted in on the wind. There was a massive fireplace on the other end of the room. It held crystals in its hearth in place of wood, the flames reaching high as it gave heat to the entire room. A stunning mural stretched across the whole of the ceiling, depicting the Zenoth's creation of the world. Glowing, ethereal beings stood around a great ball of blue light, their hands held forth in an act of giving. Some were using magicks, some engaged in what looked like dance. It took Mara's breath away.

In the center of the room sat a large round table, like the one in Caerani's war tent. Soft-looking chairs with clawed feet circled it, and nearly every seat had already been filled. They all looked up as Mara and El entered.

Drake and Caerani sat nearest to her, Drake not stopping his conversation with Kain as he looked up at her with a wink. Caerani was pouring wine in to Cyfrin's goblet, both looking exhausted. Milios inclined their head in a small bow as they entered. Cyfrin was the only one that did not look up, his expression cloudy as he downed his entire glass of wine. The table was covered in food of all kinds, steaming and mouth-watering. Mara eyed the feast greedily. El grabbed her hand, and Mara allowed herself to be led to the table.

Mara sat beside Kain, El taking the seat on her other side. She filled Mara's goblet with wine as she began to shovel food onto her plate. Caerani was watching her over the top of her goblet as El joined the spirited conversation between Kain and Drake.

"Are you telling me," Kain was saying. "You've used metal forged directly by my father on the thing, and it *still* won't skin?"

Drake nodded, looking agitated. "The blasted scales are tougher than any other monster I've pulled from the ocean's pits. Not a blade in our arsenal has yet to withstand it."

"Another sea serpent?" El inquired, filling her plate to the brim with hearty scoops of mashed potatoes.

Drake raised his flask to her, winking. "Nearly triple the size of my last. Enough to feed the patrons at Milvana's tavern for a month, even with Kain as her regular."

They shared a hearty laugh, clinking their glasses together at the jest. Mara's eyes passed to Cyfrin, though she did not intend them to. *I'm so used to him hovering about around me,* she thought with a grimace, *I've practically trained myself to keep an eye on him.* He was looking at everywhere but Mara, and she couldn't help feeling that he was pointedly dodging her glances. *And why should I care if he's chosen to avoid me now?* She bit off a large chunk of her bread, furrowing her brow. *Perhaps I'll finally be saved the annoyance of his constant commentary.*

Mara spent most of the dinner staring at her plate as she stuffed herself full. The rest of them spoke light-heartedly about their adventures the last month as she ate with near reckless abandon. The wine was sultry sweet and tasted better than anything she had drank in Delinval. Mara, her mind racing, welcomed its invitation to numbing warmth.

"...took six whole vials of concentrated acid to bring it down," Eleanora was saying, referencing their encounter with the Chaos magick in the bogs above Ylastra. "It had split itself in near thirty parts by the time it burned away."

"Aye, but we're much too clever to be bested by such a beast!" Kain chortled, raising his glass to her. "Or, I should say, *you* are much too clever. I was content with smashing the bastards till there was nothing left to multiply from." El flushed at this, raising her tankard to drink and hide her face.

"We would have been long dead by now, had that been our approach," Milios chimed in; eyebrow raised. "Demiel had crafted it specifically to stretch into a thousand if the need arose. You would have seen us drowned under their force."

Drake scoffed. "You give Demiel too much credit, old friend. Were it not for the Chaos Beast dwelling within him, my brother would be nothing but a rat whose head I could add to my lucky collection." He shook his rat skull necklace for emphasis, winking at Milios.

Mara froze, the bite of meat she had been about to take poised inches from her open mouth. Her eyes flashed up from her plate for the first time that evening, coming to rest on the white, glowing tattoos across Drake's skin. Tattoos almost identical to the ones she had seen on Demiel's face. *Drake is Demiel's brother,* she thought with a gulp. *Does that mean he can change himself into a monster too?* She forced her eyes back to her plate, resting the fork on the edge as her appetite wavered.

El was refilling Mara's cup with more wine when Caerani cleared her throat and leaned forward. The room fell silent, even the fire stilling in the hearth. "I've been giving a great deal of thought on how to proceed," she said to Mara as the group straightened up to listen. "It's difficult, and I fear it will only grow more so. To start with, we thought you dead till three months ago."

The air in the room was growing heavy around Mara as she stared at Caerani, working to keep her face even. The general strummed her fingers against her goblet as she continued. "As I said before, I would have taken you for a simpleton, had you accepted our tale as truth upon your arrival. You were raised as Grathiel's ward and taught his side of history as truth. It would be a shame and dishonor if you didn't hold loyalties to him and Delinval."

The wrathful beast in Mara was raising its head, growling in her core. She felt her face growing hot from a mixture of that and the wine, her gaze sharpening. Caerani's eyes flashed in response to her expression of hatred. "I think it best, therefore, that we start from the very beginning. We could spend a lifetime, giving you every detail. But for now, I shall keep it brief. And perhaps by the end you will have grounds to question you unwavering loyalties."

El filled Mara's goblet once more, expression dark, as

the rest stared silently at Caerani. Mara took two giant gulps, willing her anger to be still. *Nothing good would come of an outburst,* she persuaded herself. And she was desperately curious now as to what they had to say.

Caerani cleared her throat once more before beginning. "Long ago, a few hundred years before you were even a glimmer in all that was, I was an Odelian warrior. One of many and chosen personally by the King to be part of his honor guard. Our warriors are matched in groups of ten or more, when they first begin training. We call these clusters 'War Parties', a term I'm sure you've heard used in your journey here. In some cases, there are magick users whose powers greatly outweigh that of the many. These elites are teamed in small groups and are the front line to all our military might. That was the case for these four here," she motioned to El, Kain, Milios and Cyfrin. "And for Drake and me. And for the King's only child, Alora. Our future Queen and your mother."

Mara bristled at this, skin crawling, but remained silent.

"The three of us were a mighty force, an unstoppable trio whose prowess in combat was told the world over." She paused, rubbing the knuckles on the back of her left hand. It was a motion repeated by Drake on his own hand. Mara glanced down to see the edges of what looked to be identical tattoos, drawn across this spot on their flesh. Try as she might, she couldn't discern what the images depicted from her spot across the table.

Catching Mara staring, Caerani dropped her hand to her lap, drinking from her goblet once more before continuing. "As honor guard to the King our duties extended beyond simple brute force, we were often called away for diplomatic missions at his side. This is why we traveled with your grandfather to Delinval nearly fifty years ago now.

"This was before the Great War, back when all people existed alongside one another. Many Odelians lived in the outer city of Delinval, creating a bustling hub of trade for all across Zenafrost. Your grandfather's goal was to strengthen relations with the Delinvalian court and help them to continue to flourish in any way we could. The King of Delinval had two sons, just on their way out of adolescence. Crown Prince Grathiel and his younger brother, Patro, both of them willful and stubborn in their own rights. Prince Patro was one of the first truly narrow-minded individuals I had ever met. He felt that magick was a burden, a curse rather than a gift, and that those untouched by it were somehow *purer* than all others. He was quite brazenly vocal about it, even during our visits to Delinval."

Mara's heart was thundering in her chest, and she could feel the heat in her face betraying her rage. *Narrow minded?* The jab spun circles around her head, fueling the angry fire with each pass it made. Her leg began to shake as the force of keeping quiet became nearly unbearable.

Caerani sighed, swirling her drink in her goblet. "I often wonder if it was this rippling hatred of his that sowed the seeds of destruction that followed. I feared what such coldness would bring, even then. But try as we might, Patro never did accept our offering of friendship."

"*I* never felt any desire to befriend that horrible ass," Drake grumbled, and Caerani elbowed him hard in the side.

Mara gripped the edges of her seat, fingernails digging into the cushion as Caerani continued. "This unfounded hatred harbored by Delinval's youngest prince did not extend to the rest of his family. Prince Grathiel was fascinated with magick, in awe of it just like his father before him. We became fast friends, after he assured us he did not share his brother's views. He asked endless questions about our powers, our peoples, our lands. He was particularly interested in Alora's abilities, and the two of them shared in a close friendship. Over the years, that friendship began to change for Grathiel. I had seen it happen to many before him. Alora was kind, and beautiful, and caring. How could one not be taken with her in an instant? But her heart had already chosen its mate in the great warrior of legend, Yvanar, who would later become king at her side. They had been betrothed long before our first journey to Delinval, and their love was a force beyond measure. In the summer of our seventh visit to the kingdom, Grathiel confessed his obvious feelings for Alora. He knew of her betrothal but was steadfast in his own resolve, blinded by his love for her. Alora, with all the grace of her character and station, declined his advances. But she valued him, valued the friendship they had made with one another and begged it not to change. She knew not the path this heartbreak would set him on."

Mara didn't believe a word of it—she refused to believe. She could feel a scowl rising on her face, the injustice of the lies pushing her to the breaking point. She bit her tongue to keep a level head as Caerani went on. "When we took our leave the following day, neither Grathiel nor Patro joined their father in seeing us off. Years passed. The king of Delinval moved on to the Great Beyond, and Grathiel took his place as bearer of the crown. Alora rose as Queen of the Odelians not long after, and we lived in quiet harmony for a time."

Her eyes grew dark. "But Grathiel had grown cold with the years, distancing himself from communications with our court. And while he ignored us as his allies, he sent many, many letters to Alora personally, begging her to reconsider what his heart so desired. I don't think he had ever been told 'no' in earnest before her, in all honesty. Alora responded in her gentle manner, declining with soft words, hoping to rekindle their once beautiful friendship. But Grathiel's love had changed to obsession, and that obsession soon became jealous hatred. Hidden behind his great, white walls, he amassed a terrifying army. Once powerful enough, he began to attack our settlements like a fitful child, taking over every inch of land he possibly could as he went."

Drake knocked once on the lid of the box still attached to his hip as Caerani paused for another drink. "Our western forces were falling in great droves, and when we finally realized why, it was too late. Grathiel had done the unthinkable in his resentful pursuit: he'd found a way to harness dark magick. He was imbuing his soldiers with it, corrupting their souls in exchange for the power to defeat us. Our warriors became infected by the blight he brought forth, and all who stood in our defense eventually succumbed to the effects of the darkness."

Mara had heard enough. Her chin tilted up. Her eyes, like fire, stared down at Caerani over the bridge of her nose. *"How dare you say such things!"* she hissed, her jaw clenched with fury.

Drake let out a laugh. "My, it's been ages since I've seen that look. You know, Alora's nose wrinkled the same way when she would get mad." Mara turned her burning gaze on him. He chuckled again, tears glittering in his eyes. "Yes, just like that. You should've seen her back in our early hundreds at the temple when Caerani and I—"

"Enough, Drake," Caerani cut him off. Drake silenced himself as he grabbed his glass of wine. Caerani rolled her eyes and continued, unfazed by Mara's enraged expression.

"With the help of whatever dark deal he had made, Grathiel's corrupted forces were overpowering us. King Yvanar had already fallen to Grathiel's troops by this point in the war, and Queen Alora had come to the last Odelian encampment to rally her people. To get them home safely, before we were wiped from the face of Zenafrost. But…"

She paused, and Mara saw her swallow hard. "But she was already well with child when she came. A child that she birthed in that war camp, surrounded by bloodshed and battle magick. I begged her to leave as soon as the babe took her first gasps of breath, but Alora refused to abandon her people. Grathiel heard of her arrival and sent word to our encampment within the forests outside Delinval. He said that if Alora were to deliver herself to him, he would cease the senseless slaughter. And let our people, or what was left of us, go free. Without her immediate surrender, he declared he would show no mercy in taking the lives of all Odelians left standing. I tried everything in my power to convince her otherwise. But your mother…"

Her eyes were misty as she stared out across the terrace and into the glowing night. The memory seemed to cause her great pain. Her voice was strangled as she next spoke. "Your mother loved her people and honored her duty as their Queen. She would do anything for them. For *you*." She slid her eyes to Mara's. "She commanded you be taken back here, to our village. That I gather a group of my best soldiers and run. She knew that by surrendering herself, it would at least buy us enough time to escape into the mountains and out of Grathiel's direct path of ruin. We'd be safe once past the borders of the Forgotten Wood, where his men could not enter. Without Alora's sacrifice, I am certain Grathiel would have ended us all that very day."

Cyfrin had finished the entire bottle of wine sitting

before him and was glaring down at his empty cup, as though willing it to fill itself. He reached across Milios and grabbed the bottle of unopened wine next to them, pulling the cork out with his teeth and rising from his seat. He crossed the room with the bottle to his lips, walking out to stand on the terrace. Mara watched the looks of concern pass among Kain, El, and Milios as they watched him drink.

Caerani took a steadying breath. "We took you that night and fled, hastening towards the mountains. But Grathiel's forces caught up with us much sooner than we expected. Much sooner than they would have been able to, without the help of the dark magicks. They trapped us within the pass, came at us from all sides. Battle ensued. I lost a great many of my finest warriors. There was no escape and you…you were taken."

The silence that filled the room following these words was all-encompassing. Caerani eyes did not leave Mara's. "We thought you had been killed. Were sure Grathiel would have made a show of ending your life as he ended your mother's. And for twenty years, we lived here with the shadow of that death looming over our village. Looming over us all."

Milios stood from the table. They crossed the room and walked out on the terrace to stand beside Cyfrin, whose head was drooped. The emotion in the air was palpable, so thick was their deep regret. And though she was desperately clinging to the idea, Mara had a hard time believing these feelings could be faked.

Her eyes returned to Caerani's as she went on. "And then three months ago, a travelling merchant crossed into the kingdom of Delinval. Our supplies in the village are limited, and often our traders will disguise themselves in order to enter Grathiel's borders and do business. This merchant said he walked through the streets amongst the common-folk and came upon a grand parade for their king. He stood in the crowd to watch as the court rode past on their steeds. And he was shocked to find that Grathiel's niece, the crown princess of Delinval, looked near indistinguishable to our late Queen. He returned here to the woods and told me of how he came across this doppelgänger. Of how curious he found it that the princess bore such close resemblance to our Alora. But I found it more than curious. And the more I sat and pondered it, pondered how vindictive and vengeful Grathiel had become in the end, the more convinced I became of what I now know to be true."

Caerani raised her glass towards Mara, expression serious. "You are the stolen princess. Raised by our enemy to loathe us, named after that which he felt you to be…a martyr. Grathiel spent twenty-one years feeding you lies, living off the knowledge that even though Alora was gone, her torment in the afterlife would be eternal. For what greater revenge could be had than stripping her legacy of all it was? And so, I gathered my best people—" She motioned around to El and Kain who looked bashful, and to Milios and Cyfrin who still stood with their backs to them on the terrace. "—to retrieve you from your gilded prison. I was the one who asked them to keep their true motives secret until you arrived here, until I could be certain of your identity. I thought it best you be told all of this from the place where it all began. I thought it might help you accept the truth."

Mara's mouth had been hanging open and she slammed it shut, trying to sort her thoughts before she spat back a retort. "And you expect me to just believe you?" Mara demanded, letting out an exasperated laugh that made Caerani raise an eyebrow. "You steal me from my home, drag me across mud and blood for a *month* to bring me to this place so you can, what? Convince me of this madcap fairytale you've spun?"

Caerani shrugged in response to Mara's anger which flared it ever hotter. "I expect nothing of you, Mara. But I hope you will at least take a moment to consider what I've said. I do not take you for a fool. Blinding yourself to the evidence, however, would make you such."

Mara, her mind reeling, dug through her slowly unraveling brain. Alarm bells sound inside her, warning of an imminent total explosion. She pulled her hair back and pointed at her rounded ears. "I look nothing like you people," she cried, motioning beside her to El's pointed ears.

Pure fury flashed across Caerani's pretty face as she considered them. "I can see from here that you have scarring all across those tips, girl. Pray tell us where you got them?"

Mara blinked. She reached up and drew her finger along the deep scarring on the top of both her ears. Her eyes went wide. She had never questioned it, never had reason to.

Until now.

Caerani was leaning in towards her, holding a bundle of yellowed parchment out for her to take. "I know your mind is telling you not to believe a word I've said to you, and that it's all too fantastic to even entertain. I would expect nothing less than iron will from the daughter of Alora. But my words are truth. And I think some part of you must know that, or else you would not still be sitting here."

Mara had taken the papers from her and was staring down at the top of them, feeling dazed. Her eyes glazed over the bundle, and she realized from the few words she read in her pass that these were love letters. Her stare fell on the signature at the bottom of the first page, and her heart sputtered. She felt the blood in her veins grow cold as she recognized the carefully scrolling handwriting, mouth falling open in horror.

There, written below the line *I await reply with a heart that is only yours, forever* was her uncle's signature.

CHAPTER 20
A LIFETIME OF LIES

Mara stared down at the letters, blinking furiously. The possessive tone inked across the paper made her skin crawl. It reminded her of the young lords back in the court, barking at her with lustful entitlement. There had to be some sort of explanation. Some sort of trick she was not seeing. But she recognized her uncle's handwriting—recognized his *voice* in the words.

Hands trembling, she threw the letters onto the table as if they'd burned her and pushed her chair back. "These are lies." But, in her heart, she knew they weren't.

Caerani gave her an appraising look.

Kain heaved a mighty sigh and patted her on the back. "Mara…" he began.

Mara launched to her feet. "You're all lying!"

She'd yelled it this time, her voice echoing around the dining hall and out into the night. Her world felt like it was crashing in around her. "It's— This cannot be! I will *not* believe it!" She clenched her hands into tight fists to keep from screaming. A strong hand reached out and touched her shoulder. Cyfrin was suddenly at her side.

Mara's eyes flew to his face. She saw her anger mirrored in his expression. With a flick of his wrist, he slammed something down onto the table. She turned to see her ornate dagger—the gift from her uncle—sticking up out of the polished wood beside her plate. Its black metal glinted in the dancing orb lights, and everyone in the room stared at it in shock.

Cyfrin locked eyes with her and gestured at the dagger. "That night in Grathiel's castle, you pulled that dagger on me. I wondered where I had seen it before. It looked so familiar, but I couldn't quite place it." His voice was rough. Mara could hear the danger lying just beneath the surface of his smooth tone. He looked across the table at Caerani. The general's attention was transfixed on the dagger. "I'd seen it so many times before," he continued. "I don't know how I didn't recognize it then and there."

Caerani rose from her chair and came around the table to stand beside them. She stared down at the dagger with misty eyes. Drake appeared at her shoulder, a similar look on his face. They both unsheathed something from their belts. Black metal flashed. Two thuds resounded. Now three daggers were driven, blade first, into the table.

Mara's heart skipped another beat.

The three daggers were virtually identical, save for the large gemstone in the center of each hilt. Caerani's gem was a fiery shade of red; Drake's a shade of purple that was very nearly black. The dagger that King Grathiel had given her bore a deep green gem that Mara had spent hours admiring the night she'd received it. Now standing at attention next to one another, the gemstones were pulsing in unison with energy.

Horrorstruck, Mara took a step back, her legs shaking with realization.

Caerani closed her eyes. A single tear dripped down her cheek. Drake was gazing at the blades with a distant look on his face. "The three of us crafted them hundreds of years ago," he said. "Our gift to ourselves for completing the trials to join the Odelian warriors. The stones were imbued with a drop of blood from each of us. The metal crafted by our own hands."

Caerani folded her arms and turned to stare out across the terrace. "That bastard," she growled.

El had lowered her head. There were tears sliding down her face. "He kept it as a bloody trophy."

Kain's expression was dark as he placed a calming hand on El's shoulder. "We should have killed him when we rescued Mara."

Milios had stepped back into the room. They frowned as they leaned against the wall, bringing a brisk, stormy wind with them.

Mara felt hollow. She had no words. She stared down at the steadily pulsing daggers and felt her world slipping away. *Everything I've ever known, every moment leading to this. Was it all a lie? If what they're saying is true, if it's all been a sick, cruel fabrication...*

The One Who Sees words floated through Mara's mind. *"And you, one who bears not their name."*

Mara's mouth went dry. Drake moved closer, brandishing a bottle of wine, and she took it without a word, drinking it in giant gulps. Warmth spread through her, but it wasn't enough to quell the icy nothingness welling within her.

The room had fallen silent. Then, El placed a comforting hand on Mara's shoulder.

Mara did not shrug her touch away. Instead, she

turned to look at her through the fog of pain. "Is it true?" she asked so quietly she almost didn't hear it herself. *Please*, she thought, *say it's all a trick. A desperate, evil trick.*

El squeezed her shoulder, her eyes filled with sorrow, and she gave a small nod in response.

A cry ripped from Mara's chest. "Everything I've ever known... My whole life... It's all been a *lie?!*" She was shaking, her knees weak. She felt faint. The dull numbness she had adapted from her life confined in Delinval began to overtake her. She took another long sip of the wine. Salty tears mingled with strong drink. "I wish to be taken back to my room."

El's hand slid from her shoulder and gripped her hand firmly as she nodded at Caerani with a steely expression.

"Please." It was Caerani who spoke, in a tone softer than any Mara had yet heard her use. "Rest. Take as much time as you need to process and soak in everything we've told you. There's so much more to say, and I'm sure you'll have many questions when your heart finally catches up." Mara looked at her dimly and was met with misty eyes. "This is your home. We're here when you're ready for us."

And with that, El led her out of the banquet room and into the moonlit hall.

THE NEXT SEVEN days went by in a blur. Time seemed meaningless. Mara had locked the door to the bedroom—though she doubted very much if it would stop any of the Odelians from entering—and only opened it when she heard the gentle knock that indicated food had been left outside. The once perfect bedroom now lay in utter chaos.

The first night, Mara had ripped open every drawer, torn every pillow from the bed, and thrown every painting onto the floor. Every painting, save for the portrait of the late Odelian King and Queen. She could not stand to look at it, pressing the balcony door against it to keep their faces out of view. She screamed into the night, howling like a wounded animal through her tears. But none of her violence had soothed the cold emptiness that had taken up residence in her heart.

She'd lain awake every night, going over all the formative moments between her and her uncle, every smile, gesture, and word that stood out. She'd always thought his general aloofness with her was due to his constant duties. He scarcely had time for himself, let alone the fleeting fancies of a young princess.

But now, every idle wave of his hand, every allowance he had given her to keep her preoccupied and away from him, gleamed like shining monuments to the lack of care he truly had. In fact, as she ran back through her childhood, it was not her uncle's face she saw at holiday, birthdays, and dinners; it was Lady Len's. Every gift she had been given came from Len, as was made obvious by the many tomes, texts and study resources she'd received. *Every gift but the dagger,* she thought. *He gave that one to me himself. He made sure of it.*

"You remind me so much of your mother." Playing back this moment and thinking on his words, Mara couldn't stomach it. She'd expelled the contents of her stomach at the memory and fallen further into despair.

She could remember every festival celebrating the end of the war and the beheading of the Odelian queen, the great, straw statue erected in the square being set ablaze to uproarious cheering. The knowledge of what it truly represented, and the realization that her uncle had made Mara sit beside him and watch knowing full-well who the queen was to her, made Mara physically ill.

By day three, she felt utterly empty. Her eyes were swollen, her body heaving with great dry sobs as her tears stopped falling. Who was she now? The home she had known her whole life had really been her prison, and she had been none the wiser. The numbness grew even heavier with this thought. She barely got out of the bed, staring out the open balcony doors from sunrise to sunset, refusing to close those doors and expose the portrait that lay behind. By day four, she had stopped eating entirely. The water pitcher by her bedside seemed to be refilling by common magick, and it took every ounce of energy Mara could muster to sit up and drink from it.

There had been a sword mounted on display above the writing desk when she had arrived. That sword now lay hidden under her pillow, always inches from her fingertips. Even in her diminished state, she felt driven by a need to protect herself; to never let down her guard. This final base instinct seemed the only thing she had left.

El knocked on her door at least once a day, trying to coax her into coming out or letting her in. The first few days Mara hadn't responded, but now she'd taken to barking, "Go away!" El's pity only made Mara draw further into herself. She could feel her body growing weaker with every passing sunrise, but she couldn't bring herself to care. Nothing had ever been real. Twenty-one years of life, and none of it even mattered.

By day seven, she didn't care if she fell asleep and never woke up. What was left to live for?

As the sun began to set on the seventh day, there came a sharp knock on the bedroom door. Mara grimaced, her eyelids fluttering open from the in-betweens of sleep. The knock came again, a little louder this time. She pulled the pillow over her head, growling like a feral animal. "Go away, Eleanora!" she called out, and the knock resounded again in response. "I said *go away*, damn you!"

There came a sound that Mara recognized instantly. The lock unlatched by magick from the inside, and she sat bolt upright in time to see the door swing wide.

Cyfrin stood in the doorway, hands clasped behind his back, staring in at her. He wore dark leather pants and a billowing white shirt tucked in at the waist that was thin enough to silhouette the many thick bands of muscle lying beneath.

Jaw clenched, Mara stood beside the bed on shaking legs and slipped her hand beneath the pillow to where the sword lay waiting. Whatever his plans, she would not allow him to involve her again.

He stepped into the dim room, surveying the chaos all over the floor with raised brows, and then looked at her, assessing her weakened state before he spoke. "You've stopped eating."

Mara bared her teeth at the statement but did not respond. He moved toward her. "So, your new plan is to starve yourself, is it? Or to simply let the depression eat away till there's nothing left of you?"

"I am not depressed," she growled at him.

His brows shot so high they disappeared under his mess of white hair. "I've spent a good many of the past years with the same look on my face that you're wearing right now. If you truly believe your words, you're cowering at the bottom of a hole and lying to yourself about it. Do you truly think *this* is handling things well?" He gestured to the room around him, to the destroyed pillows and clothes, to the upturned paintings and shredded papers.

Mara fumed, enraged at being compared to him, of all people, and gripped the hilt of the sword. Cyfrin's eyes flashed, as if he knew what she intended to do before she did it. The sword felt light in her grasp as sliced it through the air, coming to rest with the point firmly at his throat.

Cyfrin didn't so much as flinch, his hands still clasped behind his back as he stared down at the blade. His gaze drew slowly back to hers, eyes glinting through his lashes. When he next spoke, it was without the notes of sarcasm and mockery that so often seemed to lace his words. "If spilling my blood will help to mend your broken heart, then I happily give you my blessing to do so. But I can tell you from experience, it will not."

Mara's sword hand was quivering from days of starvation and unrest. He made no move to overpower her, though she knew it would be laughably effortless for him to do so. Instead, they stood in silence like this, his blue eyes holding her fiery stare.

His brow furrowed. "You are not a prisoner here."

"Then what am I?!" It was a weighted question, one that had been torturing her for days, and by the compassionate look that came over Cyfrin's face, Mara knew he understood its deeper meaning.

He angled his head to the side, still maintaining his connection with her gaze, and broke into a small, dimpled smile. "Perhaps you can start by being our friend."

Mara blinked up at him. *Friend?* The only friend she ever had was Adrian, and she wondered how he would feel knowing that she was the blood heir of their greatest enemies. Her arm, no longer able to hold up the sword, fell limp to her side. The sword clattered to the hardwood floor.

Mara saw a glimmer of concern in Cyfrin's eyes. "You really do know your way around a long blade. Not easy maintaining that steady of a hold. And then there was the way you attacked me in that tower." He flashed his wicked smirk. "Though, I did manage to disarm you in a matter of seconds."

Mara clenched her jaw and balled her fists. Her nails dug painfully into her palms. "I was taken off-guard, you prat," she spat at his smug expression. "And still drunk—*and* it was dark."

Cyfrin tutted at her. "Excuses, excuses. They're wholly unnecessary. I've been training with a blade for hundreds of years. Held one before I could even walk, in fact. It would have been a great dishonor to my people to lose to you." He leaned in slightly, his sweet honey scent dazing her. "But I do look forward to you trying it again."

Her eyes darted from his gaze to his full lips, watching the runes across his flesh suddenly begin to pulse with dim light. Mara opened her mouth to give an angry retort, but he stepped back and continued before she could.

"Kain and I were going to spend a few hours sparring in the practice fields while no one's around to bother us," he stated. "I had come to see if you'd like to join." He looked around the room again, throwing her a hesitant glance. "It isn't healthy to lock yourself away like this. It won't help anything to sit in the darkness and stew. That will only breed hatred, which does not become you. Besides, Kain's an excellent punching bag. I'm sure he'd let you get in a few practice blows to let off some of that explosive fury you're harboring."

Mara stared out across the balcony to the village far below, at the candlelit buildings bustling with the sounds of nightlife. She remembered the expressions of the Odelians that she had passed while Caerani led her to the Crystal Falls, the looks of shocked recognition as they stared at her face, nearly identical to their beloved late queen. A shiver ran down her spine at the thought of seeing that look on their faces again.

"I don't want to be seen." She hadn't meant to be so honest with him and regretted the words as soon as they left her lips. Her cheeks went hot in an instant. But Cyfrin's playful gaze had turned soft, and Mara saw no judgment in his eyes.

He turned from her to the pile of coats and cloaks she had ripped from their hangers and thrown in the corner. He stooped down low, digging through it for a moment before returning to her. He was holding a heavy blue cloak, draped across his massive forearms. He swung it high, the material billowing out around Mara and coming to rest upon her shoulders. He reached behind her back, and the scent of pine and honey filled her nose. He pulled the large hood up over her head. It shadowed her face, nearly dropping down over her eyes. Cyfrin stepped back to admire her.

"There," he said in a low, muted voice. "Now you've got no excuse." He turned from her and walked to the door, pulling it open and turning back to glance at her. "Come on then, princess. Back to the land of the living for you."

He winked at her, and Mara threw him a deadly look. He disappeared through the doorway. She bit her lip, heart fluttering with a nervous thrill. Her pulse fluttered faster and faster. She threw another anxious glance out across the balcony before rushing forward to follow Cyfrin into the hall.

CHAPTER 21
LEARNING TO LIVE

The Grand Halls during the daytime were dazzling, bathed in sunlit splendor. But the halls at night were an incredible sight to behold. Lit only by the many flickering orb lights floating in through the open windows, they cast a glow around like sunbeams through stained glass. Mara kept her hood pulled far over her face, hidden away in shadow beneath it.

Cyfrin led her in silence, his broad frame blocking her from view as they stepped out into the cool night air. The river babbled before them, flashing lightning bugs dancing across its surface in the moonlight. Cyfrin glanced over his shoulder at her, his pale eyes lit by the still soft glowing of his tattoos.

The doors to the buildings around her on the cobblestoned streets were all opened wide. People slipped in and out of the welcoming, warm interiors. Mara noted that everyone here knew each other, embraced one another like long-lost kin. The Odelians were a cheerful bunch. Not a single night had passed that there wasn't boisterous noise till the early hours of dawn. Before long, they came upon a group of people standing outside an overcrowded tavern.

Six of them were holding different colored wooden instruments and playing a tune that made Mara's heart skip along to its beat. She paused for a moment, unable to draw herself away from the sound. Cyfrin came to stand beside her, patient and still while she listened. The people around the six playing were cheering and dancing, laughing, and drinking. They all seemed so uproarious and joyful together, a constant celebration of life. Mara pulled her eyes from their merry-making and stared at the ground.

With everything that's happened, how am I to ever feel such happiness as this? She closed her eyes, waiting for Cyfrin to continue up the path.

Many people called out to him as they passed, offering food and drink in exchange for tale of his recent journey. They welcomed him back home with open arms, some commenting on how healthy he appeared to be. Mara looked up at Cyfrin's face at this, taking in the bashful glow as he thanked them. She wondered if he had been sick before his journey to Delinval. The villagers implied as much, loading his arms up with broths and savory pies they had baked fresh.

The hollowness in Mara grew somehow in the presence of it all. She grimaced. *How bitter can you be that their joy brings you such pain, you fool,* she scolded herself. She pulled the cloak tighter, a cold chill encircling her. They were off the cobblestone street now, back on the carefully beaten path through the woods toward the ocean, Cyfrin matching his longer stride to Mara's.

They emerged into the training fields on the cliffside. Drake's ship rocked gently on its lone patch of calm waters, and Mara could hear celebratory sounds from its deck as they stepped from the tree line. Lightning bugs lit the entirety of the field, and the moon shone across the ripping waters like sunshine. There was no one in the practice arenas, save for three faces that Mara recognized in an instant.

Kain, Milios and El were standing at the edge of one of the largest circles drawn in the ground, talking animatedly with one another. They all wore casual clothing, very similar in nature to Cyfrin's, though Kain was standing shirtless. He had muscles that Mara had never even known existed, rolling beneath stretches of dark hair across his body. As Cyfrin and Mara approached, they all looked around with broad smiles.

"Zenoths bless! You managed to get her out of her cave!" Mara shot Kain a blazing look that only redoubled his smile.

El was studying her sallow features, frowning. "How are you feeling? Are you hungry?" she asked.

Mara shook her head, lowering the hood of the cloak slowly. It wasn't a total lie. She had fought off her hunger pains for enough days now that she barely felt it anymore. The thought of eating still made her sick to her stomach.

"Well, I've brought bread and cheese with us," Milios said, also looking on with concern. "And some wine if you're willing. But not till you eat first."

They sat on the ground, and Kain grabbed his great sword from its spot propped beside Caerani's tent. Milios pulled a large loaf of fresh bread from their sack, setting it beside a bottle of unopened wine. Mara's stomach gave a violent growl despite her best efforts, and she walked forward to sit beside them. Her movements felt foreign, almost zombie-like with every motion. She grabbed the chunk of bread and cheese Milios cut for her and began to devour it.

Kain and Cyfrin stepped into the middle of the circle

to face one another, Kain with a threatening smile. Cyfrin returned it with the wicked smirk he loved to give Mara etched across his handsome face. She glanced down at Cyfrin's hands and raised an eyebrow. He carried no weapons, standing with open palms before Kain's hulking blade.

Mara swallowed her overlarge bite and turned to El. "Is Cyfrin to fight unarmed?"

El gave a little laugh. "Cyfrin's never unarmed," she said, nodding back towards the center of the ring.

Mara turned to see Cyfrin's eyes glowing their blazing shade of blue. His hands were engulfed in crackling lightning of the same color, the tattoos that sometimes pulsed with dim light now burning like sunshine on his skin. He stood in a battle stance as if wielding a sword. Mara's eyes went wide as she realized what was about to happen.

Kain let out a great roar and lunged at Cyfrin, his sword moving at the same speed with which Mara had seen it kill. She gasped, watching in horror. But Cyfrin's eyes flashed, the smirk widening to a laugh as he raised his arm high.

Mara cried out, her hand flying to her mouth. There was a metallic *clang*, sparks flying from the spot where blade met flesh. "Ha!" Kain drew the sword away, leaping back. Yet Mara saw no blood.

El grinned at the look of shock on Mara's face. Milios chuckled beside her, pouring three glasses of wine. Kain and Cyfrin were moving around each other in perfect step, the same sort of dance that she and Adrian moved to during their practices. Flawless, in sync, fluid.

"Kain's blade was made long ago by his father," El explained. "He placed an enchantment on it so that it could never do harm to Kain, if wielded against him. Cyfrin was really the only person that would train with

Kain, as the other Hopeful Warriors found him laughable."

"So, his father placed a secondary protection enchantment on the blade. It could never do harm to Cyfrin, in the same way it could never harm Kain. And that meant Cyfrin and Kain could practice to the full extent of their abilities without fear of harm."

Sparks flew high with every contact they made. Cyfrin's magick whipped up the blade. Lightning flashed in warning, but never extended past Kain's hilt.

El continued the story. "This village used to be quite empty, used solely for the royal court and the warriors. Cyfrin's father was the Odelian War Captain before Caerani, and so Cyfrin lived here with him. Kain stayed with his parents, who made a home here as the official weapons masters to the crown. It's so difficult for our kind to have children, you see. So, they were truly the only two here for years."

She was looking at Kain with a misty expression on her face. Her eyes passed over his exposed chest, lingering for a long moment before she flushed and looked away. "He has no magick, you know. He wasn't kidding about that. His family have been blacksmiths, leather workers, tavern owners for centuries now. Their ancestors were not among those who chose to take the Zenoths' gift." She took a long drink of her wine before she went on. "But Kain…he's never let his lack of magick stop him. He went through the same training Cyfrin and I did, and no one believed he would even survive it. Even *I* tried to talk him out of it countless times. Passing the Trials to become a warrior is a nearly impossible feat, even for a magick user. Let alone someone just swinging around a broad sword."

Kain lunged towards Cyfrin, his step filled with all the unnatural grace of his training. But Cyfrin was too quick, spinning out of the way just in time. Committed to the attack, Kain moved to make another swing. He missed by inches, tumbling to the dirt.

Cyfrin let out a hearty laugh. "Through already, brother? And here I thought you fancied yourself the strongest of us."

With speed disproportional to his size, Kain shot up from the ground. He let out a roar, the sound quickly dissolving into his booming laughter. He lifted Cyfrin into the air, arms tight around his torso. Cyfrin let out a yelp of surprise, flailing. Kain slammed him to the dirt, a cloud of dust kicking around them. They began to wrestle, sword and magick forgotten.

El shook her head, eyes clouded in memory. "Those days were hard. Almost insurmountable at times. The three of us banded together to make it through the Trials, but we never once treated Kain as if he needed the help. He had to do the work, same as the rest of us. Cyfrin and him would train like this for hours, days on end sometimes to build his strength. Till their legs would give way and they'd lay in the ring on the edge of unconsciousness for me to come drag away."

Milios nodded, refilling Mara's cup. "Kain's got a power all his own. He is by far the most stubborn man I've ever encountered, and the most resilient. I doubt very much if he'd still be here with us, were he not."

Mara turned to look at their practice once more. Kain and Cyfrin had resumed their battle of blade and magick, laughing and repositioning themselves as they worked through their paces. They moved in formations Mara had never seen, with an inhuman swiftness that made her mind boggle. It was mesmerizing to witness.

They had finished two entire bottles of wine and the loaf of bread between the three of them before Cyfrin and

Kain paused for a break. They were both panting, but with happy expressions on their sweaty faces. They drank down great gulps of wine in between their labored breaths. Kain was berating Cyfrin about how dulled his fighting skills had become over the last few years.

"Not that I'm surprised," he said with an expression of mock innocence. "You spend twenty years drinking yourself in to an early grave, things tend to get a little rusty. I can't imagine what else of yours must have lost its talent during that time."

A bolt of blue lightning shot past Kain, grazing the top of his head. Mara saw a few strands of hair sizzle beneath its heat and Kain looked scandalized. "No need to be touchy, Cyf! You just need to get back into shape, is all! And that's where I come in! To whip you back into fighting form!"

Cyfrin glared at him, incredulous. With one arm, he pulled his shirt off over his head and tossed it aside. Mara couldn't stop her stare, nor the heat that rose rapidly to her cheeks. Kain's body was built like a mountain, but Cyfrin's looked carved out of moonstone. Her stomach flipped, taking in every indent and powerful curve. She might have drooled, had Cyfrin not turned to her with a satisfied smirk. His eyes lingered over her flushed cheeks, and something flashed behind his gaze. Mara scowled at him and turned away, taking another drink of wine.

The lack of shirt had revealed more of the rune tattoos that adorned his flesh. Mara couldn't help wondering what they symbolized. *If they cover his entire torso,* she pondered over the brim of her goblet, *do they cover every bit of him?* She glanced back to where Cyfrin and Kain now stood comparing bicep sizes. Her eyes trailed down his chest, across his stomach, stopping on the deep lines that created a V-shape dipping past his waistline. Her heart hammered in her throat and Mara shook her head to clear it.

Lacing underneath the scrolling runes, startlingly white against his tanned skin, were deeply set scars. Many overlapped one another, as if the attacks had been made repeatedly over time. Mara didn't allow herself to ponder on them too long, lest her terrible curiosity get the better of her tongue.

She felt so disconnected and out of place sitting here beside the four friends. They laughed and joked with one another so easily, like they were a family. Kain and Cyfrin continued their light-hearted sparring session, Milios continuing to fill her cup with every bite of food she took. Something was boiling deep within her stomach, one of the first emotions she had felt in days. It made her heart lurch every time she focused on it.

Her mind drifted aimlessly to Adrian as she watched the sparring men before her. Adrian, who had defied every remark from his friends and family when they told him to stay away from her as a child. Adrian, who would stand and practice with her for hours, just as Kain and Cyfrin did. But even then, her relationship with him was nothing like the closeness these four had.

I'm jealous, she thought. *They have such unquestioning loyalty and love for one another. And I am jealous.* Disgusted with herself, she grabbed the half empty bottle of wine from in front of El. Standing quickly, she stomped her way to the edge of the cliffside. She sat down in the dewy grass and stared out across the ocean. The unforgiving crashing of the waves mirrored the war waging within her. The ever-present bright lights of Delinval had all but blocked out the stars in the sky most nights of her life. But that was not the case here.

Thousands of dazzling, twinkling stars winked down at

her from above. The sky blended down into the dark waters, creating the illusion of an endless galaxy. The sound of a fiddle mixed with the roaring of laughter drifted up from Drake's ship to her and she took another gulp of wine. *I will never be that full of life. I will never be whole or joyful or happy. Never.*

Her body didn't feel like her own, and even her thoughts had become strained and foreign inside her head. She was overwhelmed with the sudden, wild urge to run down the remaining feet of earth and launch herself into the rocky waters below.

There was movement on either side of her. Cyfrin, Kain, El and Milios had joined her at the cliff's edge. They stared out across the ocean in respectful silence. Mara had grown so used to their presence over the last month that having them beside her in this darkest of hours was comforting.

They sat like this for a few long minutes, the sounds of waves, frogs, and softly chirping bugs chorusing through the silence. Mara was the one to break it, asking a question that had haunted her for days now. "Why did my uncle... Why did Grathiel send his men to retrieve me? If I am not of his blood, if he kept me merely as a prisoner or a *pet*, then why did he try so hard to get me back?"

The four exchanged dark looks. Anger flashed across Cyfrin's face before returning to his usual cool expression. "We're not sure," he replied, still gazing out across the waves into the horizon. "Caerani's guess is that he views you as his property. Property that we've stolen from him. Drake thinks it's just because he's a greedy bastard."

"My money's on that," Kain chimed in.

Mara felt the ghost of upset that they were speaking of her uncle in such a manner. She pinched her arm, wincing. *Not* your *uncle*, she thought. Her heart felt ready to break.

El cleared her throat, eyes brightening. "Cyf tells us you're a bit of a swordsman!" she said, changing the subject as Mara's mind floated close to the dark abyss she had lived in for days now.

She felt suddenly bashful, staring around her at the four warriors. She grimaced. "I trained every day. I had a friend back at the castle. He and I would practice together, under one of the knight captains. I was never actually allowed to train with the troops because…well, because I'm a woman."

Cyfrin laughed, but it was a humorless sound. "Because you're a woman?!" he replied, looking thunderstruck. "Zenoth's golden light, if Caerani heard you say that. Your prowess in battle has nothing to do with what's not between your legs."

Kain looked thoughtful for a moment, then held out a hand to her. "Come then, tiny assassin. Let's see what Delinval was able to teach you!"

Mara rose without taking his hand, and her head spun a little as she did so. The wine was gaining on her, and she welcomed the warm numbness. Kain did not pick up his great sword, instead grabbing two basic longswords from a rack on the edge of the arena. He handed one to Mara, who took it with hesitation.

She had never gone through any of her practices while drunk before. It would have been unacceptable back in Delinval. Mara felt sure she was about to make a fool of herself. But El and Milios were standing behind her, booing animatedly at Kain and shouting words of encouragement to Mara. Cyfrin was standing with his arms folded across his broad chest, a bemused smile on his face. Kain had his sword pointed towards her, beaming. His other hand motioned for her to attack.

Mara gripped the hilt of the sword in both hands,

lowering her head to glare up from under her brow. She twisted in the dirt, trying to center her gravity. She positioned her feet to lunge forward at him. Squinting towards his face, willing herself to sobriety, even though her vision had begun to blur. Her mind, hyper-focusing on the anger coursing steadily through her veins, warped the reality before her. Kain's features were growing fuzzy, almost as if she were dreaming.

Mara blinked, and suddenly it was King Grathiel she imagined standing before her. His smiling face was morphed with the evil she now knew lay just beneath his skin. It filled her with a renewed fire. She let out a mighty cry and lunged.

The wine had made her uncoordinated, wobbly like a newborn calf. Kain allowed her to close the distance between them before parrying the first blow with ease. He pivoted to the left, leading her tumbling past him. She planted her feet, narrowly avoiding crashing to the dirt. Mara spun back around, re-engaging him. She met his block with another great slash. Kain looked absolutely delighted. Mara moved slowly around him, trying to ignore the feeling that the earth was spinning.

Mara squinted at Kain's torso. She closed one eye, trying to focus in on her target before she lunged once more. He took one step to the side and Mara tumbled forward through the space he had occupied. Her knees hit the ground first, then her face. Dirt plumed about, blinding her as she lay winded. Kain was roaring with laughter above her, and she rolled on to her back, groaning. Everything was blurry, the dancing orb lights around them looking more like bright stars. The world rotated round.

Kain's face swam into view above her. He leaned forward, beaming. "Not bad! Especially not for someone three bottles deep on wood wine! You'll have a mean hangover in the morning, but you should join us for practice regardless!"

He extended his hand down to her, but she shook her head, still groaning. She wasn't sure her legs would hold her anymore, let alone her stomach holding in its contents. The warm numbness still flowed through her, not allowing for any of the deeply intrusive, destructive thoughts of the past weeks to penetrate. Mara shut her eyes tight. *The ground's not so bad,* she thought. *I've been sleeping in the dirt for a month now. What's the harm in one more night beneath the stars?*

But just as she felt she would pass into dreams…she was suddenly in the air. Warm, strong arms were wrapped around her, folding her against a bare chest. They were moving. She knew in an instant it was Cyfrin without even opening her eyes. His sweet, woodsy scent surrounded her every sense, an electrical pulse beating into her cheek from his chest. The gentle rocking motion his stride made filled her with unwavering drowsiness.

She could hear the bustle of the village nightlife winding down, and she wondered how long they must have been out in that field drinking and sparring. The sounds disappeared, replaced by gentle, flowing water. They had entered the Grand Hall, and Mara felt the deep rumble of Cyfrin's voice against her head. "You've no choice but to show up to training in the morning after that drunken display. I know you've got much more in you than that."

Mara grumbled, trying to lash out verbally, but unable to make the words. She slapped her hand against his chest, and she felt him let out a breathy laugh. She was being unfolded from against him, her body placed delicately on her soft bed. She cuddled into the pillows, her eyes much too heavy to open. She hadn't been this tired, this unable to even think, in over a month. She welcomed the silence inside her head, even if it was only the temporary effect of drink.

Mara felt the blankets being pulled up around her, and Cyfrin rested a hand against her forehead for just a moment. The spot where his hand touched still tingled for minutes after he pulled it away. She heard the door open and close almost soundlessly, the last thing she remembered before drifting off into a very deep sleep.

CHAPTER 22
THE WARRIOR'S PATH

The warm sun against Mara's face gently eased her from her slumber. She opened one eye, squinting against the morning light filling her room. The crystals on the ceiling were casting thousands of tiny rainbows around her and the soft bustle of morning life was starting from the village. She groaned. Her head gave a mighty throb, her mouth drier than sand. Clasping one hand to her eyes, she swung her legs over and slowly sat on the edge of the bed.

The smell of floral and citrus drifted through her nose, and she turned to look over at her bedside table. Beside a tall glass of water, there sat a cup of steaming hot tea. A berried scone lay on a plate close to where she had been sleeping. A note laid atop it.

Good morning! Cyfrin said you wanted to come to training today, but he always goes early to help Kain set up. Meet me in the entrance when you're up and dressed! It was signed with a scrolly *El*.

Training. She had forgotten that Kain had even suggested it in the first place. Mara frowned, staring down at her hands. The thought of being amongst so many warriors, warriors with magick who had hundreds of years' worth of training, was making her steadily more nauseous.

How can I possibly be expected to be a worthy opponent against one of them? Even in a training arena, my skills would be laughable, at best. She took a sip of the tea, shuddering at the thought. She had never been the type of person to wallow in self misery and doubt, having spent her life building walls against it. But that was before.

Perhaps the new her would simply vanish into the void, never to see, hear or feel this intolerable pain again. Or maybe the one thing that truly *was* her was the love she had for battle. The careful dance of sword fighting and the sweet intoxication of adventure. The joy it filled her with was *hers*, and no one could fabricate or change it. And this thought alone made the decision for her.

She scarfed down the scone, chugged the water, and leapt from the bed, more energized than she'd been in weeks. She arrived in the entrance hall several minutes later, hair pulled high on her head and wearing the set of newly cleaned black leather armor that had been laid out in her bedroom. She assumed they had been Alora's, by the near perfect fit.

Etched in tiny dark green stones all along the black leather were scrolling vines of ivy. It reminded Mara of the etching on Alora's dagger; intricate leaves painstakingly crafted across the design. El and Milios were already in the entrance hall waiting for her, beaming.

"Ah, the armor fits!" El clapped her hands together, walking around Mara in excited circles. "Caerani was hoping it would! Oh, this is going to be a tremendous day!"

Milios put a hand on El's shoulder. "We should get going. Cyfrin will be merciless if we're late. He'll tell us we're bad influences for letting her sleep off last night's drink." Milios winked at Mara.

El grimaced. "I'll not have his annoying remarks ruin my fantastic mood." She looped her arm through Mara's and walked them out into the sunlight.

Without her hood to hide her face, the Odelians were freely staring in wonder. Some gasped, some spun round to stare after her, a few people even bowed. She blushed heavily and El pulled her onward a little faster. Mara noticed that, though most of the villagers seemed tearfully joyous to have her here, some gave her dark and incredulous looks as they passed. They trailed whispers behind them, and Mara worked to keep her heart steady. She set her face into a mask of cool calm, refusing to allow the unwanted attention to get the better of her. "What kind of training will we be doing?"

"Swords, hand-to-hand combat, some people will be paired up for magick practice. Most of the warriors present today are still just Hopefuls, though there's always a few that have graduated that attend in order to teach. Like me, Cyfrin and Kain." El motioned to Milios. "Milios doesn't usually join us, but Caerani's asked they assist with magick practices today."

They were walking on the beaten path towards the training fields, and Mara could hear metal clashing, the crackling of magick on magick in the air. Loud voices carried to them through the wood, and she felt her palms growing sweaty with anxiety. Panic welled up inside her. *What am I doing? I have no place amongst these people, these joyous, mighty, resilient people. What am I doin?! What am I doing?!*

She had been so safe back in her bed the last week. Maybe not healthy, definitely not happy, but safe. She cursed Cyfrin in her head. *It's his bloody fault I'm out here. His stupid, nagging quips and the way they make me feel.* She gulped as they stepped out from the trees and into the sprawling field. Mara's eyes went wide. The sun was hanging high above them in a cloudless blue sky. It shone down on to the waters of the Brisenbane, sparkling against its surface like a million tiny crystals. Drake's ship, swaying in its supernaturally calm port, looked like something out of storybook. The scene of its sails framed by the perfect dark waters left Mara momentarily breathless.

The training fields were packed with people. Most of them were men, but Mara could see the faces of some resolute looking women in the crowd as well. All turned to watch El and Milios lead Mara to the circle from last night. Whispers filled the air.

Do not show them weakness, she thought. Her face grew hot from the attention. Cyfrin and Kain were standing in the circle, both with large groups of trainees around them. They were each leading a different strike progression, yelling over one another as the warriors around them followed suit. The sharp, deliberate motions were so clean, they looked unreal.

El squeezed her arm, pulling Mara's eyes from Cyfrin. "I'm teaching the newest trainees this morning. Pick a weapon and join me?" She pointed over to a large rack of weapons to their right, surrounded by chatting Odelian warriors in various forms of armor and weaponry.

Mara whimpered, but El just turned away, walking over to her slowly forming group. Milios had left them to join a crowd on the edge of the field, sparks and flashes of light coming from its center sporadically. Mara fidgeted, eyeing the crowded weapons rack with apprehension. Her stomach thrashed with nerves. But she needed to feel the familiar weighted swing of a sword in her hands, to the point where it was almost unbearable. She pushed all her discomfort aside, moving towards the rack with deliberate stride.

She did her best to make herself small and unnoticeable as she stepped through the crowd, but it was no use. The Hopefuls closest to her stopped talking at once, all eyes fixing on her. She kept her back to the crowd, studying all the blades, axes and war hammers hanging before her. They were all in different states of use, looking to have been passed down from one generation to the next. The sharp hiss of whispers grew behind her, and her heart hammered in her head.

"Well. I can't believe they actually did it."

Mara turned around slowly. The man who had spoken was smirking down at her, his hazel eyes glinting with malice. Mara grimaced. *Is there not a single Odelian who is not near perfection?* His hair looked like beams of sunlight carefully plaited down his back in a long rope. He was leaning against a giant battle hammer resting in the ground. Mara took note of the dozen or so men that surrounded him, like sheep to their shepherd.

He sneered down his angular nose at her, and she worked to not flinch away from his uncompromising glare. "Our long-lost princess, back from the dead. You tremble like a scared rabbit, your highness. Is that what they taught you in Delinval?"

The men around him laughed. Mara blinked up at him. The disgust in his tone was something she remembered well from the courtiers in Delinval, and it was almost laughable how little it affected her. Hatred held no expectation, no reverence or responsibility. Nothing like the bowing villagers from earlier.

He leaned forward to level himself with her eyes. "Oh no," he said, his voice thick with mock concern. "Are you dumb as well, princess? Or simply deaf? Zenoth's blood, what else did I expect from someone raised by the ungifted. I asked you a question. Tell us what they taught you back in your traitorous kingdom. Tell us what—" He stopped short, his eyes filling with dread as he stared behind her. He was suddenly standing alone, the men surrounding him vanishing practically into thin air. Mara felt an ominous presence looming behind her and she looked back.

Cyfrin was standing over her shoulder, glowering down at the blond Odelian man with such fire that she felt he might evaporate on the spot. Cyfrin cocked his head, a hunter locking on his prey.

The blond man diminished under his glare, stammering up at his imposing form. "Cyfrin, I—" the blond started.

Cyfrin stopped him with one look. His jaw was clenching and unclenching. Mara could see the veins and tendons in his hands flexed at his sides, and tiny sparks emitted from his fingertips. "Tell me, Filigro," Cyfrin growled. The man named Filigro flinched back as if struck. "Did you wake for practice this morning wishing to be short a limb by sundown?"

Filigro shook his head, eyes wide with fear.

Cyfrin sneered at him, stare still blazing. "And what about your testicles, Filigro. Do you enjoy them as they are? Attached to your body?"

The blond nodded now, sweat beading on his brow.

"Interesting. That's certainly not the impression you're giving me by the way you're addressing your future Queen." Cyfrin stepped around Mara, walking forward till he was toe to toe with the terrified Filigro. "I'd suggest you join Kain's group, and make yourself very, very small. Wouldn't want to draw my attention again, peck."

Filigro stood at attention before spinning on his heel and hurrying away with fright still etched across his face.

There was a moment where Mara did not dare move.

Then, Cyfrin let out a chuckle. When he turned to face

Mara, his eyes were no longer wrathful, his expression calm and mischievous. "I hate to admit it, but I really do enjoy scaring the cocky bastards. The ones who deserve it, anyway." His eyes trailed across Mara's new armor, and she felt stripped bare beneath the intensity. "You'll have to regale Kain with that little encounter. Pretty sure Filigro pissed himself, the great sod."

He was studying Mara's face now, his eyes tracing over her heated cheeks. "Whatever that prick said to you, don't listen. He comes from a long line of magick users, and his family have made many bids for the throne and crown over the years. Caerani would never let it happen, but your arrival certainly set that in stone. It'll take some people time to adjust to your presence here." He shook his head, smiling at her. "But nothing they could say or do will ever change the fact that this is your home. And we will protect you, and *it*, till the end of all."

Mara blinked at him, dazed by his stunning grin. The last seven days had been spent in such despair over the loss of her home in Delinval that she had given almost no thought as to what this place could or would mean to her.

Your home.

His words whispered through every corner of her mind, and she felt some of the darkness in her loosen its grip on her heart. Cyfrin stepped forward, placing his hand on her back. Even through the leathers, she could feel the electricity flowing through him. He grabbed two swords from the rack, handing one to her before leading her forward.

The place where his hand sat tingled with renewed vigor. Mara imagined tiny lightning bolts zapping into her body from his. From the corner of her eye, she could see the runes on his skin begin to pulse white. The other Hopefuls gave them a wide birth, Cyfrin directing the way towards an empty circle near where Kain stood teaching.

"Am I not to train with Eleanora?" Mara asked, anxious when they passed the last row of students.

Cyfrin glanced down at her, smirking. "No, princess. You'll not be getting off that easily. Your training here will start with me."

Her heart skipped a beat, not only from the thought of sparring with him but also the low possessive tone in his voice. It sent an irresistible thrill through her body. They were standing in the empty circle now, Cyfrin letting go of her back and stepping into the center. Mara remembered every moment she had seen Cyfrin in combat. He had defeated monsters, beasts, some of Grathiel's best men. His form was perfect, and she hadn't seen him falter once in his attacks. Her stomach clenched, and her legs gave a nervous wobble.

Cyfrin offered her a reassuring smile that set her heart racing. "We'll just be working through some footwork today. No need to panic," he said, winking at her.

Mara glared at him, annoyed by how understanding he was being. She positioned herself before him, raising her sword the way Kain had taught her the previous night.

Cyfrin chuckled, pointing his sword down at her feet and shaking his head. "You'll be knocked on your ass in an instant like that," he said, tapping the flat part of his blade against the inside of her calf.

Mara opened her stance wider in response, and he slid his foot in between hers. Her pulse echoed high in her ears. *Pull yourself together, dammit,* she chastised. *What has gotten into you?!*

Cyfrin was standing close enough to electrify the air once more. "You need to keep yourself angled out, to present a smaller target, to start with. And put your feet further apart, or you're going to trip over yourself. Don't give me that look; you know I've seen you do it before."

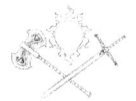

Cyfrin spent the next two hours correcting and tweaking every motion, every movement, every step. Mara was flabbergasted that so much of her training seemed to pale in comparison to the Odelian warrior's basics.

She was growing heated and annoyed with Cyfrin. He nit-picked every little detail of what she did. Mara got the distinct impression that he was doing so on purpose, noting the glint in his eye at her mounting fury. She had intentionally stepped on his foot a few moments earlier, earning her a hard tap on the shin with the broad side of his blade.

Cyfrin stepped back to stand across the circle from her, slashing his sword through the air. He bowed low. "Right then. Let's see if you've got that down, shall we?"

"We've only been at it for a few hours!" Mara replied. She glanced around at the many eyes that had kept staring at them as she worked. "Can't you show it to me once more?" She stuck out her bottom lip for emphasis, her palms already clammy at the thought of such a performance.

Cyfrin's eyes flashed. His gaze flicked from her eyes to her pouting lip and back again, so quick that Mara questioned if she had imagined it. He shook his head, his mouth twisting up into his dimpled, wicked smirk. "I will show you once more…by demonstrating the way through the steps with you. I have faith in your ability to complete this progression. It's one of the simplest. We teach it to literal children, dear."

Mara's eyes narrowed at his cocky expression, heat building in her chest. She raised her sword high and stepped forward to meet him.

If her sword practice with Adrian had been a dance, then this was a symphony of epic proportion. She weaved her way through the step progression he had taught her, their blades making contact in great, silver flashes. Cyfrin was beaming, his eyes filled with pride. Everyone who had been standing watching grew still, as if enchanted by their hypnotic gliding. They moved faster, faster, round and round. The fields became a blur of grass and sky, but Mara kept her eyes fixed on Cyfrin.

His sword looked weightless in his hands, his feet practically floating him across the dirt below. Mara felt herself pulled along somehow by him, her body refusing to fall out of sync. This was her element. No matter how disconnected and lost she felt about every other aspect of herself now, this was something that would never change. The darkness grasping her heart weakened a little more, and she felt like she could breathe a fraction easier.

With every careful connection of the blades, Mara felt more anger ebb away. They finished the final steps of their movement and stopped, the fields around them quiet. Cyfrin was stunning, glowing in the sunlight. He gave her a broad smile. A long moment passed before the sounds of training picked up around them once more.

"And you were afraid you couldn't do it," Cyfrin said, rolling his eyes.

Mara was breathing heavily, her arms sore from the work they had put in already. But she was finally feeling something besides the cold angry sadness that had built its home within her. Before she could catch herself, she was smiling back at Cyfrin.

His face fell a little, something strange rippling through

his eyes. The runes on his skin glowed bright white, mimicking the blinding sun. But then the moment had passed. His tattoos dimmed; he raised his sword once more, his expression determined. "Again."

THEY WERE at it for hours, till the sun was hanging low in the sky and the Hopefuls had started dispersing back towards the village for the evening. Mara's legs were jelly, her arms two heavy weights at her side. It was a struggle to pull the sword back to the rack, but she felt almost pleased with herself. Peaceful, at least. The painful soreness was normal for her after years of training, and it made her feel calm. El, Milios, Kain and Cyfrin were standing beside Mara at the racks, discussing the day.

"You'd swear we were monsters, the way they look at us," El was saying. She frowned, folding her arms across her chest. "They have no idea how much worse it could be. Can you imagine if they had to train under Caerani like we did?" She cringed, Kain and Cyfrin shuddering in unison with her.

"She'd have them fighting down in the wave pools," Milios said. They glanced down at the waves crashing against the rock face. "And strap them to Drake's ship if they got taken by the tide."

"Half of my group from today won't even *make* it to train with Drake." Kain shook his head. "And where they stand now, he wouldn't even let the second half on his ship for the month at sea."

"The month at sea?" Mara asked, confused.

Kain nodded at her, pointing towards the ship in the

dock. "Hopefuls go through all sorts of nightmarish Trials to be granted the honor of being an Odelian warrior. But the final and most difficult challenge is the trial aboard Drake's ship, the *Red Froth*. The strongest Hopefuls board with him, and they depart on the Brisenbane for an entire month away." He grimaced, all four of them gazing across the water with strained expressions. "Some don't make it back alive. The ones who do, Zenoths rest our aching hearts, get to join Caerani's ranks."

Mara stared at them all. The Brisenbane Ocean was harsh and unforgiving, surrounding the entire continent. She had never even seen a ship like Drake's before, as no one dared sail on her depths. There were stories of legendary monsters that lived in the fathoms below, and Mara shivered at the thought of facing something terrible emerging from within.

"So, the four of you have…?" She motioned out at the ocean.

Cyfrin nodded. "Aye. All of us but Milios." He gave Milios a look of mock disapproval.

Milios smiled bashfully. "I don't do large bodies of water," they said simply.

Kain let out a bark of a laugh. "Thousands of years old. Faced every manner of beasty you can imagine. But Zenoths forbid if you got a little wet." The wind behind Kain whipped up, slapping the back of his head with enough force to knock it forward. Kain gave Milios a look of feigned outrage, readjusting his now windswept ponytail.

"We were going to dine at the Grand Halls tonight and take a break from our usual tavern," El said to Mara, eyeing her with apprehension. "Would you like to join us, Mara?"

They were all staring at her now, hesitation on their

faces. Mara looked down at the ground. She couldn't help remembering the discomfort, the earth-shattering revelations of last dinner. But the thought of going back to her room, left alone for her thoughts to creep back in…it was a far worse option in her eyes. She nodded in response, still looking down.

El made a happy little squeak and Mara glanced up to see them all smiling at her. Cyfrin had his hands behind his head, looking up at the picturesque sky. But Mara could see the dimples on his cheeks, marking his grin.

"Good! And we can talk all about how great your footwork was today!" El looped her arm through Mara's.

"Well, she did have a great teacher," Cyfrin said. He gave an animated twirl of his hand, giving El a mock bow. Kain slapped him on the back, and he stumbled forward. Milios reached down to muss his hair as they chuckled and El threw him a dirty look. They gathered up their gear and weapons and, together, began to march back up the path towards the village.

CHAPTER 23
BOUND TOGETHER

A fire crackled away in the hearth of the great hall, where Kain, Milios, El, and Cyfrin, already changed into casual clothing, sat around a table loaded with bountiful food. Kain was pouring wine in a new goblet at an empty seat, and Mara took it without the others so much as glancing up from their conversation. Their faces were drawn and serious.

"It's unprecedented," Milios was saying, shaking their head. "There's a reason that the Odelian trainings takes so many years, a reason unbalanced magick users shouldn't become warriors this quickly. We've cut training time by more than half already. If we were to try and bring those fools into battle right now…"

"If you've a better alternative, Mil, we are all ears," Cyfrin replied, his tone sarcastic. He raised his glass to Milios before downing its contents.

El was pushing food around her plate, frowning. "There's no use arguing about it. We've got to be ready, and Cyfrin's right. There is no good alternative here." Her voice was gloomy.

Mara swallowed the overlarge bite she had taken of her chicken. "Why must their training be halved?"

The four of them turned as one to look at her. Cyfrin cleared his throat and spoke. "I take it you noticed the state of the land on our journey here. You were taught by Grathiel that dark magick from the war is what corrupted Zenafrost. I suppose that wasn't entirely false—only about who wielded the power." A cold chill passed through the room. "There's only one way Grathiel could have obtained the sort of power he used against us all in the war. Magick like that comes from making a deal with evil. Evil on the most high." The light in his eyes vanished when he said it. "The King of Delinval struck a deal with Mezilmoth, in exchange for the might he needed to win. For what price, we do not know."

His words cut through Mara, another dagger in her heart. She pushed her plate away, all appetite gone. Her whole life, she had been taught that the Odelians had thrown the first stone in the Great War. That their evil, corrupted magicks had made the whole of Zenafrost sick, save for the small oasis they had fought so hard to protect in Delinval. *The man I once called uncle.* Her heart couldn't possibly break any further. Not even the steady thrum of warmth from the fireplace was enough to cut through the icy grip holding tight to her heart.

She continued to stare down at her plate as Milios spoke. "The corruption gets worse with every passing day, every passing moment. We've done everything in our power to slow it but putting a bandage on a hemorrhage does very little. The damage has been done."

Mara forced herself to stop the train of dark thoughts filling her mind and looked up. Cyfrin was staring at her with a strained expression.

Kain banged his empty goblet on to the table so loudly

that El and Mara both startled. He looked furious. "I say we take the fight straight to him," he growled. "Grathiel, Mezilmoth, the both of them. I don't care. What good are we sitting around here, trying to power-drive years of training into those Hopefuls? For Zenoth's sake, we were in the heart of Delinval, and we didn't even *try* to take him out. We had the element of surprise!"

"We weren't there for a bloodbath," Cyfrin's voice rumbled through the room, silencing Kain. "No matter how satisfying it may have been to gut him, the four of us were there for far more important matters."

Mara felt herself flush, eyes dropping once more to her abandoned dinner. She hadn't given much thought to the fact that these four risked life and limb to come and save her from Grathiel's game. They had no idea if she really was Alora's daughter at the time, working purely off rumor and the mere whispers of hope. She had spent the entire month on the road throwing every form of verbal abuse at them she could think of. She had *wanted* to inflict pain. And still, each of them had held steadfast, protected her from the dangers they faced. Save for Cyfrin's snide, mocking remarks to her, they had shown her nothing but welcoming kindness.

Kain looked ashamed. "I know that," he replied. He gave Mara a meaningful look and refilled her glass. "But my point still stands. What good comes from us sitting on our asses here?"

Cyfrin cocked his head at Kain. "What do you propose then? We walk on up to the Dark Gate, knock, and tell Mezilmoth we've come to snuff out his infernal light? Sounds like a great idea, Kain. When shall we set off?"

Kain shot him a nasty look, which Cyfrin returned in kind.

"Enough!" El snapped at them. "You're such children

sometimes, I swear." She shook her head, bringing her goblet to her lips before continuing. "We have to train them as best and as quickly as we can. It's their only hope for surviving the battle to come—and it *will* come. We're poised on the very brink of war from every front. There's no sense trying to ignore that fact."

Mara wasn't sure which she'd rather face, the Deceiver or her false uncle. *I can scarcely see the difference in the two from where I'm standing,* she thought. But for the first time in a week, she was feeling something other than sadness; she was feeling rage—pure unfiltered rage at the lies, the malice, and the injustice. Grathiel had used her like a puppet, kept her locked away from the world *he* had destroyed. *All in the name of a broken heart,* she thought, furious. *He kept me like some sort of pet to exact blind vengeance on the woman who would never be his. The woman he killed in cold blood. My mother.*

Mara stood suddenly, unable to stop her legs from shooting her upright. They all stared up at her in surprise. She worked to steady her heart, her knuckles turning white from her grip on the table's edge. *Something... I must do something.* She could no longer sit and listen and dwell on the past. Could no longer bear to try and sort out the shattered remnants of who she thought she was and what she could have been. A burning heat was rising in her chest.

"Please," she began. "Please, I want to help. I will do anything, just…just tell me how I can help."

They were silent, all staring at her with a mix of shock and awe. Mara bit her lip, cheeks growing hotter, but continued. "I-I feel this guilt inside of me. This angry, unforgiving, ugly thing." A lump filled her throat, but she forced her voice past it. "I've lived my whole life with such *hatred* in my heart for your kind, for your people— *my* people. And now I'm here and you're all so damned kind and forgiving and warm and...and I just can't stand it anymore. Please. Please, let me atone by helping you." Tears beaded in her eyes, and she bowed her head low to them all in respect.

El reached out and grasped Mara's hand, squeezing it reassuringly.

Cyfrin was staring at her, his eyes dark. "You have nothing to atone for. It is us who owe you dearly. We allowed you to be taken. To be raised all these years in that place, with *him*." His voice was so soft and filled with such deep regret, that Mara felt her heart might break from the sound.

She wiped the tears from her eyes and stood a little taller. "I want to help you. I *will* help you. I have only one thing left that is truly mine, and that is my prowess with the blade. I can train every day, from dawn till dusk. I can make myself useful so that I may stand alongside you in the battle that is to come. I am at your disposal. If you'll have me."

Kain and Milios were staring up at her with huge grins on their faces, but it was Cyfrin that Mara could not look away from.

His eyes were still filled with such sadness, but a faint smile was pulling at his full lips. He bowed his head at her, raising his goblet. "If that is your desire, princess. I am duty bound to ensure you have it."

"Caerani and Drake will be thrilled," Kain said, clinking his goblet with Cyfrin's.

Mara sat back in her seat feeling anxious but pleased. "Where are they? I haven't seen either of them since we last dined together."

"They've gone to speak with the Wise of the Woods," Milios answered. "They're the eldest of the Forest Dwellers and are more in touch with Zenafrost than practically anyone. Caerani and Drake have gone to discuss whatever's to come. They'll be back in a few nights time."

"Fat bit of good that'll do," Kain said. His voice was muffled around the bread he was chewing on. "We all know Milios here is the only Forest Dweller who can stomach bloodshed."

Milios sighed, shaking their head. "I wish that weren't so true. But perhaps this time will be different. Caerani has quite a way with the elder Rivalion. Maybe her words will cause a change of heart."

El gave a dark chuckle. "Let's hope so. You know how, erm...*outspoken* Drake can get at those meetings. Very little patience, that man."

"Outspoken," Cyfrin repeated. He raised an eyebrow, smirking. "That's one way of saying 'loud, crude bastard,' I suppose."

"I'd like to speak with them, when they return," Mara requested. She remembered Caerani's parting words at their last meeting, about all the questions she was sure to have. *I have a thousand questions,* she thought. *An entire lifetime of them, threatening to consume me if I don't get answers soon.*

Milios nodded to Mara. "Yes, Caerani had thought you might."

They sat without speaking for a long moment, the fire crackling away behind. The music from the village drifted in through the terrace. Mara felt an odd calm washing over her, as if having this renewed sense of purpose was shining light on the shadows squeezing her soul. She looked around at them all. At Kain who was opening yet another bottle of wine. At Milios who was spinning their fork idly in midair. At Eleanora who was filling Mara's cup from the pitcher of water, and at Cyfrin who sat staring into the flames in the hearth.

These people were decimated by Grathiel's legions, forced into hiding here within the forest. Yet, they live in such light, with such joy at simply being alive. Mara felt an overwhelming sense of shame, shame that she had spent so many years believing the Odelians were monsters. Calling them Dreads, the way Grathiel had intended.

You remind me so much of your mother. Grathiel had said that to her mere hours before her twenty-first birthday, over the dagger he had pulled from her mother's corpse-- right before they set the symbolic dead queen of the Odelians ablaze. *A monster,* she thought. *I was raised by a monster.* She felt disgusted, like there was some invisible layer of grime on her body. She feared no manner of scrubbing could remove its foul touch.

Mara cleared her throat, breaking the silence. "I never got the chance to thank you all. For rescuing me. I said such terrible things before I knew. I spent countless nights plotting your downfalls. And you still granted me patience, kindness, and safety. Still welcomed me into your home with more than open arms. I owe you four my life."

Cyfrin was on his feet before she had fully finished speaking. He wasn't looking at her, but his fists and jaw were both clenched. "Your gratitude is unwanted." His voice was so low, Mara barely heard the words as he spoke. He turned and stormed out of the room, leaving a trail of cold energy behind him.

Kain sighed, staring after him. "Do we let him wallow?"

El slammed the remainder of her wine, already standing. "It'll be our hides if he launches himself into the Brisenbane or finally finds the limit to the alcohol he can consume. Come on." She squeezed Mara's shoulder, Kain and her following out behind Cyfrin.

Milios remained with Mara, who stared thunderstruck at the door they had left through. "He was there that day, you know. The day you were stolen from us." Mara turned to face Milios as they spoke, eyes wide. Milios was looking into the distance, as if seeing the memories playing in front of them. "You were born a month early, brought into the world at the heart of our last war camp. Not long after your first breaths, Grathiel sent word demanding Alora's immediate surrender."

The silence in the room was pressing all around them, Mara's rushing pulse drowning out all else but Milios' voice as they went on. "Queen Alora had entrusted you to a group of her best, strongest soldiers. She knew that her sacrifice would only buy us time before Grathiel resumed the attack. But she prayed it would be enough. Caerani was still just a captain, and Cyfrin was one of the elites under her command. Kain, El and I had orders to escort the remaining Odelians to safety here in the woods. Caerani and Cyfrin, along with a group of our most powerful warriors, took off with you in the night. Just as Alora marched forth to her death."

The wind swept past them, caressing Mara's cheek and rustling through Milios' hair as they continued. "They made it all the way to the mountains with you before they were attacked. Surrounded in an instant. At the exit to Bardro's Gash, to be exact. Enemies descended on them at the front from the Outer Plains. Grathiel's forces wielded dark magicks from their rear. Soul-corrupting and tainted, but deathly efficient. Caerani fought them in droves at the front line, even as her comrades fell around her. It was a mighty battle, scorching the surrounding mountains with its power."

Mara remembered how the entrance to the mountain pass had looked. As if the sky on the darkest night had laid itself to rest there amongst the rocks. The piles of bones swept across the stones flashed in her mind's eye, and the crater laid deep in the ground amidst it all.

"But Grathiel's men were mad with their mission, driven to succeed or die trying. Caerani exhausted her magick, and the fires she wielded turned on her. Flame magick is incredibly hard to control, and extremely temperamental even if you can. It should have killed her. They must have thought it had or I have no doubt they would have finished the job." Milios' grey eyes looked like they were swirling with threatening storm clouds. "Only one person remained standing to guard you: Cyfrin. He fought with everything he had, breaking himself as he used his body to protect yours. But it wasn't enough to hold off hundreds. They bested him, grabbed you. Took you back to Delinval that very night. They left Cyfrin alive, barely breathing, to serve as a final message."

They looked back at Mara, whose eyes were swimming with tears. "One of Grathiel's generals gave him that scar on his face. I'm told he dragged the blade through the bodies of the fallen Odelians first, dousing the tip in their blood before inflicting the wound to Cyfrin. Cyfrin fought even then, struggling so hard that he cracked the earth in two. The enemies tortured him to the breaking point, leaving him unconscious amongst the dead when they were finished. They stole you away, back to the kingdom where we thought they would surely kill you as they did Alora."

They dropped their gaze, shame shadowing their perfect face. "Cyfrin arrived in the forest over two weeks later, carrying Caerani's charred body. He collapsed as soon as he set foot out of the woods. Didn't wake up for six days. When he came to, he was a different man than the one I knew before. He never forgave himself for your loss. Spent the last twenty years trying to drown himself in drink, and almost succeeded. Not a single one of us was able to reach into the depths of his grief and pull him out." They looked thoughtful. "I don't think he wanted to be saved from it, though, if I'm being honest. He placed the full weight of the blame on himself. And when Caerani told us you might still be alive, that the princess of our greatest enemies could very well be *our* princess… Her sending us on that mission to rescue you was the first time I've seen the spark back in his eyes since before the Great War."

Mara was speechless, the tears flowing freely down her cheeks. Milios smiled at her, reaching out to brush them from her face. A breeze rushed off their hand and rustled gently through Mara's curls, breathing softly across her skin.

"Why?" she whispered, her voice breaking. "Why did you all risk so much to come for me?" It made no sense. They were safe within the forests borders, Grathiel unable to touch them and their thriving little village.

The wind caressed her cheek once more and Milios gave a soft chuckle. "Because you, even the *rumors* of you, were worth the risk. You are our kin, and the blood heir to the Odelian throne. And we felt it not only our duty, but our utmost honor to be the ones to bring you home."

CHAPTER 24
TALKS OF IMMORTALITY

Mara spent the next week training in the fields from dawn till dusk. She stopped only to eat when El forced her or to collapse into her bed at the day's end, exhausted. The intense exercising left her drained, giving her brain no time to spin between rage and deep shameful sadness. Cyfrin had handed her training off to Kain, careful to avoid Mara after their last dinner together.

She found herself trying to catch his eye multiple times a day, with little to no success. She wasn't sure what she wanted to say to him, but she felt pained at the grief he still harbored. *It's not fair that he shoulders that weight,* she thought. *I'm alive and well, which is shocking given the circumstance. Surely, this should have relieved him of his burden of guilt.*

They had moved on from the basics of Odelian sword fighting and progressed to hand-to-hand combat. Mara had never fought with her fists a day in her life and standing here now before the smiling Kain did not seem the best time to start. He had been overjoyed at being entrusted with Mara's training, working her to the bone every single day as if he knew the relief it brought her. Today was no different.

The trainees had been paired off in groups of two, standing around the fields and sparring with one another. Kain had chosen a begrudging Mara to partner with him and had shown her no mercy. He had her throwing punches at his bare hands, correcting the way she balled her fists, and remarking on how she "threw the hit" instead of driving it forward. He was standing in a fighting stance, facing Mara with absolute glee in his eyes. "Let's try an advance, shall we?" he said, bobbing backwards and forwards on the balls of his feet. "Position yourself like you would with a sword. Then come at me with all you've got."

Mara hesitated, staring at the size of Kain's raised fists compared to her own. But he nodded at her, the picture of encouragement, and she gave a resigned sigh. She brought her hands high in front of her face, advancing towards Kain as he had taught her to do the last few days. She extended her arm with what she thought was enough speed to hit him, but Kain was too quick. In an instant, he had grabbed her, launching her backwards through the air and on to the ground.

Mara yelped. She landed with a dull thud, knocking the wind out of her, and jarring her brain. Gasping, she looked up to see Kain's smiling face.

"Shall I tell you what you did wrong before or after you get up off your ass?" he asked.

Mara swung her leg up and kicked him in the thigh. She yelped again; it was like striking solid rock. Kain laughed, reached out a hand, and pulled her to her feet. She was brushing the dirt off herself, grumbling curses under her breath, when El came running towards them.

Eyes bright, El gave Mara a once over and threw a disapproving look at Kain. "They're back!" she said, excitement in every word. "Drake and Caerani! They've just returned from the deep wood!"

Mara's heart skipped a beat. She had been awaiting their return to the village every waking hour, a thousand anxious questions whizzing through her head. Drake and Caerani had served as Alora's right and left hands. While they'd eaten, El had told Mara many stories of the times before the Great War, of the prosperity brought by the joint leadership of General Caerani, Captain Drake and Queen Alora. They had been her best friends, and Caerani had been the last person to speak to Alora alive before she surrendered herself to Grathiel.

There was so much she wanted—no *needed*—to know. It was overwhelming, filling her every night with restless tossing. She had vivid dreams of standing alongside her parents in that portrait that hung on the wall in her bedroom. Dreams of donning a crown of sunlight, and racing to battle alongside El and Kain and Milios. Alongside Cyfrin, whose face was always clearest of all. *His icy stare and dimpled cheeks and his lips curling up into that smile.* Mara shook her head, exasperated at her own drifting thoughts.

They ended their training early, the five of them rushing back to the Grand Hall to wash and change before dinner. Mara had come to the realization days ago that the four of them also stayed in the Grand Hall, in rooms just down the hall from Mara's. It brought her comfort to know that she was never fully alone when the nightmares would shake her awake in the dark of her room.

She changed into a pair of leather pants and a dark blue satin blouse, choosing to forgo shoes all together. It was a habit she had picked up from the other four, who seldom wore any themselves. The feeling of the sun-warmed wood against her feet helped to soothe the soreness from her hours of training. The dining hall sat as it always did, warmed by the dancing fire in the crystal hearth, lit by the unreal sunset beyond the terrace and treetops, filled with the smell of great food and the distant sound of lively music.

Mara entered to find the table almost full. El and Kain sat beside each other, flanked on either side by Milios and Cyfrin. Caerani and Drake looked up as she entered, both of their faces exhausted but offering her warm smiles none the less.

Mara ground her teeth. The only seat available was beside Cyfrin, something he looked aware of as well based on his wary expression. She swallowed the feeling of tense panic rising in her throat, stirring flutters in her stomach. She sat down beside him, and the air around his body seemed to be even more electrified than usual. Her leg brushed against his as she adjusted herself, and she felt him stiffen beside her. She twisted in her seat to avoid the contact happening again, grimacing at his pointed reaction.

Drake had his head in his hands propped atop the table, smiling at Mara with a dreamy expression. "I hear you've started training with these fools," he said, nodding around to the four of them. "I hope you haven't been too hard on them."

Mara stifled a laugh. "I think Kain has made it a personal goal to bruise every bone in my body," she replied, and her light-hearted tone had both Caerani and Drake blinking in surprise.

"Hardly," Kain scoffed through a mouth full of food. "Be grateful it's not Cyfrin you're doing hand-to-hand with. The man's completely mad. Has no sense of when to stop himself. Zero self-control. Notice how I haven't *broken* your bones! Not even a one." He looked proud of himself.

Milios turned to Caerani as Mara filled her own goblet, trying to figure out where to begin with her line of questioning. "Tell us what happened with the Wise of the Woods," Milios said.

Drake grumbled something that sounded like "Dirty tree people," under his breath.

Caerani rolled her eyes at him, leaning back in her chair and sighing. "Well, they've agreed with our very obvious sentiments that something big is coming, and at a much more alarming rate than expected. But they've once again stated that they will not take a side. They'd rather *let the land decide the fate*, or something wishy-washy like that." She clicked her tongue, strumming her fingers against the wooden tabletop. "You'd think they'd be more willing to assist us, considering that it's the land that suffers, and it's the land they serve. But, you know them. They're devoted to their old ways."

"Blathering idiots," Drake said, throwing back his goblet of wine and refilling it in the same motion. "You should have heard them speaking to Caerani." He sat up straight, making a face of mock superiority and placing his hands neatly on his lap. "General Caerani, we cannot aid in the coming war. We're much too busy preening ourselves and admiring the newly grown mushrooms!" He grimaced. "What a load of shit. Neutrality is a farce. We'll see how steadfast they still are when their whole bloody forest is ablaze and overrun by the darkness." He threw Milios a sudden apologetic look. "Meaning no offense to you, that is."

Milios chuckled. "I have long since accepted that I am not of the same cloth as my kin. A fact they made quite clear when they, erm…*politely* asked me not to return to the deep wood."

Caerani patted Drake once on the leg and he kept

silent, though Mara could only imagine the thoughts behind those dark eyes.

Milios was frowning, staring out into the darkening sky. "Still. Their apathy is disappointing. I was truly hopeful they'd be of help this time round. But I suppose it was wishful thinking." They turned their attention back to Caerani who was swirling her drink in her crystal glass. "There are still some Forest Dwellers who will take up arms beside us when the time comes, regardless."

Caerani gave them a nod, her eyes passing to Mara now. She gave her a crooked smile, her gaze softening as it darted over her face. "You're looking better than when we last saw you." she said. "More alive…the training field suits you."

Mara returned her smile. "I was hoping you'd allow me the honor of training in earnest. I want to join your fight. *Our* fight. I want to help in any way I can, and I think this will be the best way for me to do it."

Drake looked surprised, but Caerani's face flashed with pride. "I would expect nothing less. Battle is in your blood, there's no denying that."

"And I…I've been thinking a lot. About everything. *Really* everything." Mara nodded towards the four sitting beside her. "I've gotten bits of information during training, about your histories and such. I still know very little, I fear. And I was hoping you could help me fill in the blanks." The words tumbled out before she had a chance to give them proper shape.

There was silence in the room, Caerani and Drake exchanging a knowing look before turning their full attention to Mara, waiting. She hesitated, unsure where to even begin. Every question whizzed by her at once, her mind grasping on to the most pressing ones as they passed. She bit her lip.

"My mother and father... They both were magick users. Is that correct?" This felt like the best place to start, one of the more burning questions that kept popping into her head.

Drake let out a bark of a laugh. "Your mother could craft sunbeams into whips. Could meld starlight into arrows. She was one of the most magnificent magick users I've ever met. Not as magnificent as Caerani, of course. But magnificent, none the less."

Caerani ignored Drake's wink, addressing Mara. "You come from some of the most powerful magick users there ever were. Your bloodline can harness the powers of the sun, the moon, and stars. They wielded an art called celestial magick, something unheard of beyond your family. The core that resides within you is said to have come from the very first Zenoth, the same being that strove so desperately to create our world. Your ancestors were given the name Dawnbringer by the Zenoths that once roamed these lands for this reason."

"Dawnbringer," Mara repeated the name, testing how it felt on her tongue. *My family's name. An ancient line of magick users. Something I, alone, belong to.*

Caerani was speaking again, pulling Mara from her pondering. "Your father, King Yvonar, was one of the greatest warriors to ever arise from the Hidden Village. He was the only outsider to ever be granted courtship amongst the Druids of legend, and he was a stalwart champion for a moon God they were said to worship. He wielded an axe that possessed immense cosmic energy. Melded his magick with the blade and was nye unstoppable in battle."

Mara didn't understand what "melded his magick" meant, but she didn't care now. This was the first information she had learned about her father. King Yvonar, Champion of the Moon. Mara knew nothing of the Druids, save for a cautionary tale sung by the bards in Grathiel's court. The song depicted beings from another world, whose magicks were not governed by the laws of Zenafrost. They were primal, beast-like men, rivaling the might of even the Zenoths. Or so the legend said. The painting of the smiling King in Mara's room felt more familiar now. More powerful. This feeling of power spurred forth the next question.

"If they both possessed magick, does that mean that I... Could I possibly wield it as well?" Mara had wondered this for days now, trying to remember even a moment of her life where something *could* have been magick. But there were none.

Caerani blinked, confusion on her face. "You think you have no magick?" she asked.

Even Cyfrin looked up from his goblet to stare at Mara. She felt her face flush with color. "Well, I...yes."

Drake chuckled and Caerani smirked at her. "Darling girl. Magick is merely a muscle. One that you've never been taught to use. I'm sure there is a wealth of ability lying dormant within you. It'll just take a bit of practice to get it to wake up."

Mara's mouth fell open, slumping back in her chair. *Magick. I'll be able to do magick.* She felt scared and excited at the same time, the prospect of magick training making her heart race. But another question was now at the forefront of her mind, sitting her bolt upright and setting her face in to a serious expression.

"If I am an Odelian, then does that mean... Does that mean my age..."

Caerani knew what she was asking before she could properly form the words. She nodded at her slowly, deliberately. "Yes. It means you have been blessed with immortality. Or cursed, depending on who you ask."

Mara slumped back once more, her mind reeling. She stared into the fireplace beside her, watching the flames lick the crystals below it. She had never thought much about death, or dying, or growing old. It's just something that simply *was*, for all things ended, and there had been no sense dwelling on it. But now, faced with the prospect of *forever*... It was too much for her mind to begin to comprehend.

She shook her head, trying to rid the feeling of infinity from her being. Cyfrin had silently refilled her goblet while she spiraled, and she took a drink from it. There would be time to panic later. Mara cleared her throat before speaking again. "Our goal is to stop the corruption and bring life back to Zenafrost, is that right? How exactly are we to do that?"

The atmosphere in the room changed, the temperature seeming to drop ten degrees as Cyfrin straightened up beside her.

Caerani looked thoughtful. "I'm not sure we have an *exactly* quite yet. We have an end game, but the getting there is still fuzzy." Drake rapped his knuckles hard against the lid of the box on his hip, and Caerani shot it a look before proceeding. "Dark magick is eating away at the wards left by the Zenoths. It seeps through the shield and condemns all it touches. The only way to save Zenafrost is by sealing the Dark Gate for good. By blocking off any contact Mezilmoth has with this plane of existence."

Mara gaped at her. "The Dark Gate is weakening and your plan is to go poking around looking for a lock?"

Caerani raised an eyebrow, but Drake laughed. "Aye, that's about the gist of it," he said, raising his goblet. Kain and Cyfrin followed suit. Mara was still staring at Caerani, incredulous.

Caerani looked grim. "Think of what you walked

through to get here. All the death and sickness and corruption. The darkness is winning. It *will* win if we do not act and cut it off at the source. Any other action we could attempt would merely be—"

"Putting a bandage on a hemorrhage," Mara interjected, repeating Milios' words from the week before.

Caerani nodded gravely, leaning back in her chair.

Mara felt like she was dreaming. *Magick, immortality, a great and terrible threat...* If it wasn't all so painfully real, she would think she'd gone mad. She closed her eyes, thinking. Caerani wasn't wrong: Zenafrost was dying. She'd have to be a fool to not see it, to not *feel* it. Every night, she was haunted by nightmares of Reflector Beasts, Necromancers and Darklings. Sometimes, she was back in the dank corridors of Ylastra, awaiting her fate at the hands of the chaos wielders. But always, she was surrounded by that dark, oppressive feeling that hung over them all on their journey here.

Mara's eyes opened, fire blazing in her core. "Right then. How quickly can we get me trained up?"

CHAPTER 25
A QUICK STUDY

Their dinner went on for four hours, over much discussion on Mara's training. It had been decided that she would begin working on magick the very next day, doubling her workload as she was still expected to continue her usual core trainings.

Caerani was sitting across from Mara, half her face in moonlight, the other glowing by the fire's light. She was looking out at the stars above the village as she spoke. "In three weeks, the recruits in training now will be asked to begin their trials. It will be months before the next one, so I would encourage you to start with the rest of the group."

Milios looked aghast. "You want her to undergo the trials that soon?"

El shifted in her seat, looking uneasy. "She's only just started her hand-to-hand basics."

Cyfrin set his goblet down, hard enough to draw all eyes to him. "I have no doubts about Mara's ability to do so. She'll have to work twice as hard as her fellows, but she's been doing that from moment one."

Mara barely heard the exchange, wide eyes fixed on

Caerani. "Three weeks?" she asked, her voice squeaking. "I'm to learn magick in *three weeks*?"

Caerani flashed her crooked grin. "At least some magick, yes. From what I hear, you're quite the quick study. And with the blood that courses through your veins, I doubt very much that you'll have any issue getting started." She gave a mighty stretch, stifling a yawn.

Mara bit her lip, not wanting to keep her any longer but unable to suppress her following question. "Am I allowed to know what these Trials consist of?"

Drake looked aglow with sudden excitement. "The Trials are what every Odelian Hopeful goes through on their road to becoming a warrior," he said, the fire in the hearth dancing in his eyes. "Ends be damned, it *is* the road to becoming a warrior. All of us, save for dear Milios—" He nodded at Milios, who inclined their head in a slight bow to him. "—have undergone the Trials and survived to tell the tale. Some of us by the mere skin of our teeth, but alive none the less. You'll be asked to undergo four challenges, designed to test all aspects of yourself." He waved his hand, as if the concept of the specifics bored him. "And if you're weighed worthy, you'll get the great honor of joining our merry ranks!"

He raised his tankard, but his eyes grew dark. His expression clouded as he stared at her from under his brow. "But it's not for the faint of heart, or weary of soul. The Trials are made to weed out those who lack the will and power to fight what's to come. If you enter them, you must do so without a doubt in your mind."

The room was still and quiet. Mara shivered despite the warmth from the fireplace. "And what are the challenges?" she asked into the stillness of the air.

Drake's eyes came back in to focus, filled with their excitement as if nothing had happened. "Well first, we hold a great big celebration to send the Hopefuls off on their journey. A little tradition of my own creation, you can thank me for it later. We do it the night before they leave on their first challenge. It's quite the fantastic sight to behold, watching a bunch of poor, hungover sods disappear into those woods." His smile gleamed, red eyes dancing. "The first challenge, you're paired up with a partner and sent off into the Forgotten Woods for a month to survive alone off the land. If you manage to make it to the end, with or without your partner, one of us will come in to retrieve you." He motioned between El and Cyfrin. "These two were partnered during their Trials way back when. And just look at them now!"

El stuck her tongue out at Cyfrin, who narrowed his eyes to glare at her. Their sibling-like annoyance with one another seemed the worst possible combination, in a survival situation. Mara couldn't believe they had made it an entire month together, alone. The thought of teaming up with one of the Odelian Hopefuls on her own Trial, of being an anchor to them…it made her mouth run dry with nerves.

Drake chuckled and continued. "The second challenge is that you must retrieve a crystal from the falls past the temple. Remove it from the earth and present it before Caerani and myself. Sounds easy enough, I know. But the second trial eliminates more Hopefuls than any other." He took a drink from his goblet before proceeding. "The third challenge involves the catacombs beneath the Temple of Old." He winked at her. "Not much I'm allowed to tell you about that one. You'll be told what you need to know, if and when you pass your second trial. And besides, it's the fourth and final challenge that *really* matters. You, me, and the remaining Hopefuls will board my ship with my crew and sail off into the Brisenbane to an island called Hope.

There, you'll spend three weeks fighting for your life, your limbs, sometimes your immortal soul." He turned thoughtful. "You never know what you'll get there. The creatures that inhabit the island come through a rift located on its shores. All sorts of things slip through that damned rift. Change the very fabric of the island itself. And it's all kept trapped there by ancient wards and magicks. So, you can imagine how, erm, *irritable* said creatures are by the time we reach them."

He smiled once more, slamming a fist on to the tabletop. "And if you return, you'll take your oath to protect all of Zenafrost, all of its creations, all of your peoples. And you'll be a Warrior at last." He leaned back with a sigh, closing his eyes with the smile still on his face.

If you return. If. If. IF. The chosen word sent waves of fresh fear through Mara. Her mind felt filled to bursting with everything she had learned that night, let alone this word. It was like every bit of information was screaming to be heard all at once. *If you return. IF you return.*

Caerani yawned once more, patting Drake's knee as she rose from her chair. "That's enough history for one evening, I think," she said, giving Mara a soft smile as if she could hear the war raging in her head. "Tomorrow is a big day. We should all get as much rest as possible."

Drake stood as well, bowing his head at them as he followed Caerani from the dining hall.

Mara stared after them, her eyes starting to feel heavy from the day and drink. Kain and El were standing shoulder to shoulder at the fireplace, their bodies swaying as they spoke in hushed tones. Kain was staring at El with such longing as she spoke, that Mara felt as if she was intruding on something deeply personal. She looked away at once.

Milios was using what Mara assumed was their wind

magick to manipulate the flames on the candles before them. They danced high off their wicks, whipping around in a careful tornado of fire as Milios studied it through narrowed eyes.

Cyfrin, who had left the table halfway through dinner, now stood at the terrace railing, looking out on the woods and orb-lit village beyond. Mara bit her lip, shuffling her feet underneath her chair and staring down at her plate without really seeing it.

Caerani and Cyfrin had laid down their lives, fully knowing the likelihood of death, to save her as a child. And while Caerani seemed more than relieved by her return, Cyfrin still seemed in agony. And she couldn't understand why. A dark voice in the back of her mind told her that he was unhappy with her presence here, and she shoved it forcefully aside. She stood from her chair, walking by Milios who she could have sworn smiled as she passed.

The gentle breeze on the terrace brought the smell of sea air and pine trees, and she came to stand beside Cyfrin. He did not acknowledge her, but his fingers began to rhythmically thrum against the dark wood railing. They stood in silence for a long moment, listening to the music, laughter, and voices from the village over the babble of the moonlit river. Mara glanced up at Cyfrin through her lashes. His eyes were glued somewhere above the treetops, but his eyebrow raised as she stared at him.

"Is there a reason you're boring a hole in the side of my face, Mara?"

Her name sounded like music from his lips, and Mara pinched herself to stop the flutter in her stomach. She cleared her throat, standing fully upright as she turned to face him. He turned as well, his eyes finally meeting hers for the first time in days. They were dimmer than usual, the pale blue looking almost dead against the dark purple circles beneath them.

Mara frowned up at him "I need to say something. And I don't want you to interrupt or make some snide remark or quip in the process. Got it?" She had said it with more force than she intended, but her stance did not waver.

He blinked down at her, eyebrows raised and looking vaguely amused, but nodded once.

She took in a deep breath, steadying herself. She studied the darkening beneath his eyes, losing track of her purpose for a moment. "You've not been sleeping."

Cyfrin cocked his head, smirking. "You've come to stand at attention before me and discuss my nightmares?" He breathed a laugh.

Mara grimaced, fighting off the urge to retort. "I wanted you to know... I need you to know that I do not blame you for Grathiel's men taking me." His eyes widened slightly, the air growing still, but he did not speak. So, Mara continued. "Milios told me what happened all those years ago in Bardro's Gash. How you, Caerani and your troop were overrun, and how badly you were hurt in the aftermath." She didn't have the heart to elaborate on this.

Cyfrin growled, barring his teeth, and dropping his gaze from hers. "It was not Milios' place to tell you that." His voice was low and quiet, but Mara felt it echo deep within her. Cyfrin shot a dark look into the dining hall, no doubt aiming for the place where Milios still sat.

Mara folded her arms across her chest, her eyebrows furrowing. "Wasn't it you who told me that wallowing was unhealthy, Lightcleaver?"

Cyfrin looked startled that she had used his surname, his eyes flashing with the wicked mischief Mara had grown so used to. Her gaze softened, and she relaxed her arms to her sides, letting out a little sigh. "I shouldn't need to say it, but I forgive you for what happened. One man cannot best an army, most especially not one the size of Grathiel's army. It is a burden you no longer need bear."

Anger rippled across Cyfrin's face, and he turned to stare back out at the village. He let out a breathy laugh that was void of all humor. "You forgive me. And what if I cannot forgive myself? What then, Dawnbringer?"

Mara blinked up at him. It was the first time anyone had used her family's name in reference to her. And even though he had done it in retaliation for her use of his own surname, she couldn't help feeling a warmth beating steadily in her heart.

He spun to face her, stepping forward and leaning down slightly to look into her eyes. This close, it looked like there were literal constellations in the depths of his irises. His face was pulled into a mask of cool calm, but she could still see the shadow of agony laced across it. "You're right. When you were taken from us, it did destroy me. I felt such pain in the knowledge that your life had been ended, that I didn't feel worthy to live my own. How could I? You were taken from my hands—*ripped* from me." His eyes flickered with the memory. "I drank myself into nothingness, I shoved away everyone I've ever cared about, I hurt anyone who tried to help. I wasn't deserving of any of them."

His eyes dropped to the ground between them, and Mara remembered his words from before. *Your gratitude is unwanted*. Not unwanted, *undeserved*. In Cyfrin's mind, he was as guilty as Grathiel, and Mara felt a great sadness rip through her.

He brought his eyes back up to meet hers, still brimmed in that same deep agony. "And when we were told there was a chance—no matter how small—that you were alive, living this whole time in a prison of Grathiel's design…" His head tilted back, exposing his sculpted neck as he stared up into the starry sky. He let out another humorless laugh. "That was almost worse than thinking you dead. Knowing you had been raised to loathe us, knowing you were being lied to, *toyed* with, imprisoned, and Zenoths only know what else."

Darkness shadowed his face, his fists clenching as lightning flickered between his fingers. The runes on his skin, already lit with a faint white glow, blazed with sudden blinding ferocity. Mara saw him take a steadying breath, watched as the lighting dissipated with the glow of his tattoos. His voice was soft and nearly a whisper as he spoke again. "How am I to forgive *myself* for twenty-one years of lies? Twenty-one years of a life lost, *your* life lost. It is unspeakable."

Mara felt close to tears. Her entire life, Cyfrin had spent running from this. From his deepest shame, his darkest regret. He wasn't unhappy that she was here; he was distraught that she hadn't been saved sooner. She swallowed hard, refusing to let the tears flow under his pained stare. She didn't know the words to say, wasn't sure any could mend such a gaping wound. And before she truly knew what she was doing, her feet were leading her forward. She closed the distance between them and wrapped Cyfrin in a tight embrace. Her ear rested against his hard chest, and she heard his heart skip a beat before continuing at a hummingbird pace. His body had stiffened as she grabbed him, and she could tell he had stopped breathing.

"Perhaps," she murmured into the side of his thick bicep. "Perhaps it is not our darkness that define who we are, but how we choose to rise from the ashes of our wreckage." As she spoke the words, she found herself breathless. The truth of them echoed in her heart, speaking to her own pain as she spoke to Cyfrin's. The dark claws gripping at her soul loosened even further, and she felt a glimmer of hope dawning deep within her.

She felt Cyfrin's muscles tighten, and she was wrapped in his arms. The size of him muffled all other sound, narrowing her world to their heartbeats. He squeezed her gently to him, his chin resting on top of her head as he gave a small sigh. His breath rustled the top of her head. "Perhaps," was all he said, before giving a final squeeze and releasing her.

He stepped away, and Mara could see a flicker of light in his stunning eyes. The runes on his skin pulsed white, seeming to keep pace with Mara's own pulse. Cyfrin gave her a small smile, bowing his head before turning and leaving her alone on the terrace feeling breathless and enveloped in a fog of pine and honey.

Mara awoke the next morning filled with renewed vigor. She had a *purpose*, a direction to aim the fiery bolts of rage burning within her. And as she walked beside El to the training fields through the cobblestone streets, she felt more at peace than she ever had before.

There wasn't a single day that had gone by in Delinval where she hadn't felt out of place, a stranger in her own kingdom. And now she understood why. She *was* a stranger there, in a place that was never really hers to call home. The thought was strangely soothing to her.

They entered the training fields, and Mara saw far fewer Hopefuls then she had the past weeks. She looked at El with confusion as they moved towards their usual circles.

El nodded. "Only the trainees that are to take part in

the Trials will be here in the coming month," she said, motioning around at the thirty or so people sparring around them. "Everyone else is to do private studies till they begin. The lot you see here are the ones who will be undertaking them with you."

They were walking towards Kain and Milios who stood on the edge of Mara's usual practice circle. Mara looked at Milios as they approached, nervous and excited. She was bouncing on the balls of her feet, unable to contain her excitement "So! How do we begin teaching me magick?"

Kain laughed, continuing to stretch as Milios smiled at her. "Ah, you won't be starting your magick training with me," they said, eyes glinting with amusement.

As if in response, Cyfrin stepped out of the tent behind them. Mara blinked, taken aback. He was positively glowing, his eyes brighter than she had ever seen them before. The runes on his skin were shining a steady shade of white, unfaltering in their light. He was standing to his fullest height, shoulders squared and hands on his hips as he beamed around at them all, his face full of wicked humor.

It was far from the gloom of the last week, and it suited him in a way that left Mara's stomach feeling weightless. She was still gawking at how perfect he looked when his ice blue eyes settled on her. They flashed, and Mara wondered if her admiration of his face had shown on hers. She felt heat rising in her cheeks, betraying her.

Cyfrin cocked his head, smirking. "It's impolite to stare," he said, and Mara glowered at him in response.

Their three companions turned and walked to their respective training groups, sensing Mara's displeasure.

"Why can't Milios train me?" she demanded, glaring at Cyfrin's cocky expression. She almost preferred his brooding to the steady electrical pulse now emanating from his body. It left her feeling energized, but wild. Verging on uncontrolled.

But her burning stare seemed to only deepen the smirk on his face. "Because believe it or not, Dawnbringer, I know a thing or two about magick." He wiggled his fingers before her for emphasis. Tiny bolts of lightning crackled from their tips and the ground below Mara's feet shifted.

She looked down to see a thick green stalk rising below her, leaves unfurling as it reached towards the sky. It stopped growing when it was level with her eyes, a large bulb at its crown. As Mara watched, the bulb opened wide, growing before her. The head of a beautiful sunflower now stood at attention, swaying softly in the ocean breeze. Mara looked up at Cyfrin who was still smiling down at her, looking pleased. Another wave of his hand and the sunflower burst with a mighty *pop*, showering them in yellow petals.

Mara glared at him, refusing to look impressed. "So, you're to teach me to grow pretty flowers for the coming war, then?" she asked, her voice rich with sarcasm.

Cyfrin raised an eyebrow, eyes flashing at her tone and looking amused. "You could only be so lucky. Creating life, whether it be earthen or otherwise, is no easy feat." He turned to lead her to their training circle. "I doubt you'd be able to grow as much as a blade of grass right now."

Mara shot him a dirty look but followed behind to their circle. They stood in the furthest one, completely opposite of the others training in the field. This was clearly a safety measure, though she felt very sure it was unnecessary. *What are we keeping the others safe from,* she thought with dismay, *my immense embarrassment when it turns out I cannot do magick?* This thought had kept her up much of the night, tossing and turning as she imagined the other Hopefuls watching her. Mocking her.

Cyfrin's expression was serious now, bending to unlace his boots. "You'll want to be barefoot for this," he said, pulling off the first boot. "Makes it much easier to feel the magicks in the earth your first few times."

Mara obeyed, kicking her boots off, and throwing them to the side along Cyfrin's. He stretched his arms, his neck, and Mara copied his motions. His eyes locked with hers and she did not flinch away from the steady gaze.

"Close your eyes." The command in his voice made her stomach flutter, something warm sparking in her core. His eyes narrowed as he watched the expression on her face change, and she bit the corner of her cheek. She did as she was told, slowing her breath as she met the darkness behind her eyelids.

"Good. Keep your breathing even and focus on the feeling of your feet against the ground. On the sound of my voice in your head."

Mara wiggled her toes, digging them in to the cool, soft dirt underneath her. She let all sounds drift away. The steady crashing of the waves against the hillside, the drone of the sparring Hopefuls across the field and whimsical whistles of the birds filling the trees.

There was only her, the dirt and Cyfrin.

When he spoke this time, the sound seemed to come from inside Mara's head instead of from his mouth. "Imagine the sunlight. See it in your mind's eye now."

There was a golden glow starting to form around the outer darkness of Mara's vision. Like the sun had wiggled its way through. She had no time to wonder if she was only imagining it, before Cyfrin went on.

"Now see yourself reaching out and grasping that light. Pulling it into yourself like you would…like you would swallow wine. You're quite good at that."

His joking remark nearly broke her focus, but she

clenched her teeth and held on. She saw her arms reaching out before her, hugging the dim glow into herself, and latching it to her body. It felt silly, but she could have sworn she felt warmth building from somewhere deep within her as she did so.

Cyfrin's voice echoed through her once again. "See the light within you, imagine it like the waves below us, ripping and thrashing. Then calm those waves to your command. Become one with them. Focus them down your arms, into your palms."

Mara screwed up her face in concentration. With Cyfrin's words, the well of warmth inside her had sprung to life. She could feel it banging around in her core, like a desperate animal fighting to be released. She felt hot, too hot, the fire blazing through her face and down through her chest. Then slowly, almost painfully, she focused it on her arms, willing it to do as she asked. The light was fighting tooth and nail, a roar rising within her that blocked out even Cyfrin's voice as she used every ounce of will to contain it. There was another roaring sound, and she realized it was coming from her open mouth. The fire was moving down her biceps, through her forearms. She could feel the heat in her palms, stretching out through her fingertips. She heard Cyfrin's husky, almost breathless laugh in her head, and her eyes flew open.

There, dimly glowing between her two outstretched hands, was what looked like a miniature sun.

It pulsed, trying to glow into life. Mara gasped, and it vanished in an instant. She stumbled back, staring at her hands as her feet nearly came out from underneath her.

Cyfrin's hand was wrapped around her wrist, steadying her. Mara's eyes flew to his, still in shock. They were sparkling with the many constellation-like spots throughout his irises, his mouth twisted up into a wide smile. He was looking at her with so much pride that she felt she might crumble beneath its beauty.

There was commotion behind them. Mara turned to see Kain, El, and Milios sprinting towards them, cheering, and waving their arms.

"You did it!!" El was crying out, bouncing with joy as she collided with Mara. She hugged her tight, squeezing the breath out of Mara before releasing her. "*I can't believe it*! Your first time and you *really did it*!"

Kain clapped Cyfrin on the back, both looking triumphant. "I guess you haven't lost your touch quite yet, Cyf!" he jeered, and Cyfrin zapped the hand on his back with a bolt of blue lightning. Kain yelped, though his smile did not falter.

Mara blinked around at them all as they celebrated this smallest of victories. The glow had barely been there, fighting for life between her palms. But she couldn't help herself from joining in their joyful cheers of triumph. Because this was the very first moment in her whole life that Mara finally felt *right*.

CHAPTER 26
SUNBEAMS AND SOLDIERS

To say Mara's first victory in magick training had been short lived would be a massive understatement. As the week dragged on, her every waking hour devoted to training with Cyfrin, her first successful attempt was beginning to feel more and more like a fluke. Her frustrated roars of outrage at every failure had become commonplace on the training grounds, the other Hopefuls long past their flinching at the sound.

Cyfrin had taken to forcing her to pause between her attempts, having her hit his palms with precision at fifty strikes each. "To loosen some of that clouded wrath," he would say each time. She hadn't thought it possible to be any more annoyed by Cyfrin, but with every smirking comment, every bit of "helpful" advice he offered, she felt her agitation spark anew.

"I've been thinking…" Cyfrin was saying to her on the eve of their 8th day. Mara was casting a barrage of punches into Cyfrin's calloused palms, beads of sweat dripping from her face. He hesitated before continuing. "We're wasting time trying to force the magick out of you. It'll come when it wishes, regardless of our best efforts. We should re-double our focus on your weapon skills."

Mara stopped throwing her punches, looking hurt. "Oh, just say it. I'm *hopeless*," she groaned, covering her eyes, and shaking her head. She had been so thrilled that first day, so sure that this was some innate talent she'd just excel at. She felt like a failure, not only to herself, but to the memory of her parents. She groaned again, her hands sliding down her face in grief.

Cyfrin rolled his eyes, smirking. "Ah, the dramatics of a princess!" He threw his hand to his forehead, pretending to feel faint.

Her grimace twisting into a snarl, Mara grabbed one of Cyfrin's boots from the ground and hurled it at him. It struck him in the chest, splattering grass and mud over the front of his faded linen shirt. "You, being the resident *expert* on dramatics, Lightcleaver!" she snarled at him. "With your immense, oh-so-sensitive ego!"

Laughing at her, Cyfrin brushed himself off. "Yes, so rest assured I know what I'm talking about when I say *you* are being dramatic. Mastery of magick isn't something that just comes overnight, Dawnbringer."

There it is again, she thought, her stomach fluttering, *that damned feeling every time he speaks my name.*

He tilted his head, his blue eyes softening. The runes on his skin glowed a shade brighter. "These things take patience. Everyone here has had hundreds of years to understand and harness their gifts. And not one of them can do the things you will be able to do. Not even me."

She frowned at him. "And what if I'm not? Powerful, I mean," she asked, dropping her gaze and nudging the ground with her foot. This was something that had worried her for days now. Beyond days, it had worried her in one way or another her entire life. And now it was growing heavier with each individual failure.

Cyfrin laughed, drawing Mara's eyes back to his face. "Is that what you're so worried about? Darling, you conjured your own sunspot your first try. Do you really think that's subpar? Below average? No, you are powerful just as you are."

But Mara had frozen. *Darling*. The word drifted around her head, her eyes widening with her hitching pulse. *Be still*, she willed her heart. *If he hears, I'll never know the end of it.*

Cyfrin looked unfazed as he turned from her to the weapons scattered about the edge of the field. He tossed her a long sword, taking his usual position across from her and giving a low, mocking bow. "Shall we continue our squabble, or would you prefer putting it to the blade?"

She gave him a nasty look, slashing her sword through the air before they began their careful dance. The sun had vanished from the sky by the time Mara's temper allowed them to stop. She had pushed herself to the limit for hours at that point, meeting Cyfrin blow-for-blow. He'd had very little comment or corrections for her during their sparring, and it gave her the smallest amount of gratification.

Cyfrin sat beside her in the dirt, sweaty and panting. His sleeves were rolled up to the elbows and he was pouring water on to his head as he tried to catch his breath. Mara would have been flustered by this, had she not been equally as winded. She lay on her back, staring up at the stars above her that twinkled against the ink black sky. Her heart was threatening to pound straight out of her chest, each breath ripping from her. Her arms felt like lead. Her legs felt like liquid. But she had almost chased off the feelings of inadequacy at her inability to produce any more magick.

"Sleeping on the job, I see?"

The voice had come out of nowhere, Cyfrin and Mara both jumping at the suddenness. There was a roar of laughter. Drake stood above them, Kain at his side as they cackled.

Cyfrin cursed, the lightning that had flared at his fingertips receding. "One of these days, I'm going to drop you both where you stand," he said, gripping his heart. He stood and helped Mara wobble to her feet.

Drake winked at him, but his eyes flashed. "I'd love to see you try, ya cocky bastard," he replied, much to Kain's enjoyment. Drake turned his attention to Mara, looking bemused as she tried to steady the tremor in her legs. "Training's going well, I take it?" He looked down at the sword at Mara's feet, frowning. "If she's struggled with pure magick, why didn't you have her try melding with the sword?"

Cyfrin rubbed the back of his neck, looking thoughtful. "I didn't think it prudent to try and teach her yet another technique when we barely have time for the basics."

Drake's eyes flashed again, their glint looking like moon backed rubies under the starlight. "Then you simply haven't tried the proper weapon."

He crossed to the edge of the pitch, stooping low over the discarded weapons. When he turned back to face them, he was holding a two-handed axe, its hilt nearly as long a staff. Its head was decorated by ornate scrolls that had been weathered down into the metal with time.

Drake approached her, holding it out and beaming. "While *pure* magick is difficult to focus, and even harder to control, *melding* is something nearly every magick user is capable of. Instead of focusing on creating magick from your core, you narrow your intent on to your weapon. The magick's not nearly as potent, but it's a good place to start. Different magicks prefer different forms of weaponry to be channeled through." He nodded towards Cyfrin. "Take Cyf for example. His magick prefers blades. Even forms itself into blades on his body when he fights. Caerani's magick prefers broad swords to most anything else. You follow me?"

He was still holding the war axe out towards her, but Mara shook her head. "No. No if that was the case, then I would have an affinity with blades. And Cyfrin said it himself, I haven't felt a single spark during our sword training."

Drake winked at her. "Mmm, I heard him. But I've got a great feeling about you and axes." He nodded encouragingly, looking borderline mad as he brandished the axe even closer to her.

Mara let out a feeble groan but took the axe without another word.

Drake stepped backwards, motioning Cyfrin and Kain to do the same. "Right!" he exclaimed, rubbing his hands together. "Let's see if I can walk you through this. It's been hundreds of years since my training days. No guarantees we won't blow up the whole damned field by mistake. Close your eyes now."

Mara, anything but reassured, glanced back at Cyfrin and Kain, who had taken several large steps away from her. She gave a reluctant sigh, shutting her eyes slowly.

"Now, focus on the hilt in your hands. Feel its weight in your arms."

It was impossible for Mara to not feel the weight; her arms were already weak from the day's training. She shifted her hands on the hilt, stacking one atop the other.

"Focus on nothing but my voice and that weight."

And just as it had with Cyfrin, all noise began to fade away. The sea silenced itself, the purring hum of bugs and frogs ceasing as Mara plunged into darkness.

"Perfect. Still with me then, dearest?" Drake's voice echoed through the black.

She felt herself nod once. It was disconnected, disjointed. She was trying not to get her hopes up, trying not to read into the gentle hum of energy vibrating in her core.

"Excellent. Now, Mara, this is very important... I want you to imagine that hilt as an extension of yourself. Like the axe and your arm are fusing. See it become you, and you it."

Mara could see her arms before her, and she willed the hilt and her to become one as they swam in her mind's eye. As they melded together, a strong golden glow began to pulse from the point where they joined.

"Hmm, that looks about right. Now give us a swing."

Mara's eyes flew open, swinging the axe high as if it was weighed nothing. She brought it down with all her might, colliding with the ground at full force.

Crack!

Like a seam stretching six feet before her, the earth cracked. Just enough to reveal bright, scalding beams of what looked like sunbeams etching in every direction. They shot into the sky, lighting the space around them so much that Mara had to squint.

The light vanished, leaving a deep scar in the ground that was emitting a faint crackling of energy. The sounds of the field came rushing back in. The axe was heavy once again, and it fell from her damp palms as she was lifted into the air.

Kain had her round the middle, roaring with triumph as squeezed her tight. "The tiny warrior finally shows herself again!"

Cyfrin was beaming, shaking his head. "Should have known you'd conquer the one thing we'd yet to try."

Mara was breathless, still overwhelmed by the feeling of magic coursing through her veins. Kain set her on the ground and she swayed unsteadily in place. "How did you know?" she asked. "How did you know I needed to use the axe? Swords have been my life since I started my training in Delinval."

Drake had a mysterious grin on his face, drumming his fingers against the lid of the box at his hip. "Your father's magick allowed him to wield one of the legendary weapons of the Druids. A war axe known as Moon Render. I knew you needed an axe because it is in your blood to use it." He inclined his head in a bow at her. Turning and waving behind him, he began to make his way towards the staircase to the dock.

Mara felt a tingle of electricity at her shoulder and turned to find Cyfrin inches from her. Their eyes both flicked downward, taking in the scarring beneath her discarded axe. Mara flushed, her pulse still racing.

Cyfrin smirked at her, his eyes returning to hers. "What was that you were saying about not being powerful, your highness?"

CHAPTER 27
FASCINATING MELODIES

Mara's training with the war axe had been even more intense than the sword, forcing her to learn an all-new fighting style in less than two weeks. Though she had been awkward at first, arms wobbling like a newborn calf, the hard work had finally begun to pay off. She was consistent with every blow, knocking deep scars into the earth around their training circle that would burst with sunlight. It was still nowhere near as dazzling as the other magicks she saw erupt around the field during their hours out there, but it was far better than nothing at all.

All in all, the three weeks had passed in an absolute blur of practice, pain, rest, repeat. Mara was grateful for the distraction, too exhausted for the creeping nightmares that threatened to plague her every night. She could feel the shift of energy in the training fields as the first trial approached. The heady, anxious murmur that flitted through them all between metal clashing and the crackle of magick. She took to hovering by Caerani's empty war tent during the sparse minutes of rest, staring absently at the strange symbols painted above the entrance.

"Ah, I see you've found the Bond of the Brethren." Cyfrin had approached in silence, sneaking in behind Mara like a shadow.

She jumped at the sudden nearness. The air was filled with his humming electricity, with the smell that rolled off his skin. Mara gulped, drawing her eyes back to the symbols above the tent. "The...sorry?"

Cyfrin chuckled, motioning up at them. "The Bond of the Brethren. It was a pact wrought of ancient magicks, taken by the warriors of old. Only the closest War Parties ever bound themselves to one another in such a way. It's said to amplify the magick of those who forge the tie."

"I've not heard of it. Why doesn't everyone enact such a thing?" Mara asked, though the look on Cyfrin's face made her regret it at once.

"It's unheard of now. The kind of soul-tethering magick the Bond invokes is power beyond our understanding, made by the first magick-users to walk Zenafrost. A warrior's life often leads to a warrior's death. The loss of one of your Brethren... The pain of that missing fragment was too dire to bear, for most. It goes past heartbreak. It's world shattering. These symbols...well, they belonged to your mother's War Party."

There was silence. Mara's eyes widened as she stared at the symbols with new understanding. Alora had been Bonded to Caerani and Drake. And she had been ripped from them, in ways that Mara could not possibly comprehend. She had to fight to swallow back her tears.

Cyfrin cleared his throat softly beside her. "That reminds me. I've brought you something." He was holding out a dagger, one Mara recognized at once as her mother's. It had been freshly cleaned, all dust and debris removed from its shimmering black surface. "The war axe won't do you any good in close quarters," he said, placing the hilt of the dagger gingerly in Mara's hand. "You'll need this in case anything gets the jump on you. Which, given how quickly I was just able to sneak up here, is not that difficult a feat."

His taunting words still filled Mara's head days later.

She was standing in her room that evening, staring at her reflection in the full-length mirror and wearing a deep grimace. Tomorrow morning, her group would be paired off and sent deep into the forests. Mara was so nervous she had awoken that morning only to vomit before she went to training. She had done everything she could to prepare herself for the challenges to come, but the thought of leaving the safety net of the training fields was daunting. And the prospect of being some hundred-year-old Hopeful's deadweight during the whole ordeal was even worse. She shuddered, studying her reflection.

She was wearing a dark green dress made from soft satin, its fabric draping across her broad shoulders and framing her body. She looked stronger than ever. Her curves were defined, her muscles stacked and sculpted. She was barefoot with a bell covered anklet that Milios had gifted to her encircling her ankle. It matched the jingling golden bracelets she had donned from Alora's desk. The sun was hanging low across the treetops, and the sound of celebration cascaded up from the village into Mara's room.

She had been dreading the farewell party, Drake's final "bit of fun" before the journey ahead. It meant smiling and bowing and being on what Grathiel always called "her most glimmering behavior." The sound of his voice in her head made her nauseous, shivering with a sudden cold chill. Her black curls bounced around her shoulders with the movement, two long strips framing her tanned face. There was a knock, and her bedroom door opened a crack.

El's face poked in, a crown of glowing flowers on her head. She was rosy and grinning from ear-to-ear. "End's gleaming gates, you look incredible!" She stepped fully into the room, a pale-yellow dress flowing about her on the breeze. She was holding another glowing flower crown in one hand, and a bottle of sparkling wine in the other.

Mara eyed the crown with apprehension. "You've already got me in the dress, El. Must we wear the tiaras too?"

"Oh, hush now," El replied, tossing the crown in a perfect arc onto Mara's head. "There!" she said, her eyes misty. "Not only a warrior, but our future Queen as well. I dare any man to resist us!"

Mara laughed, adjusting El's crown. "Men are the farthest thing from my mind at the moment, Eleanora."

"Oh?" El raised an eyebrow, looking wicked. "And is that *all* men? Or just the ones who lack the right *spark?*" She winked, leaning into the final word.

Mara felt heat rising in her face. *Is it that obvious, then?* She scolded herself, grabbing El's arm and pulling her forward from the room. El howled with laughter all the way down the hall. The Grand Halls were empty, as were the quiet grounds surrounding it. The two of them came over the bridge and into view of the cobblestone streets that lay just beyond. Mara gasped, stopping in her tracks.

Multicolored orb lights were whizzing past, making bright swathes of light in the air at random as they went. The glowing flowers atop El and Mara's heads had been used to decorate every open surface across the village. Strange flickers of white light popped about, sending sparkling dust across the crowds as they whistled through the air. Bells of all varieties dangled from the open doorways of buildings, creating melodies on the warm breeze.

A band was playing a lively tune somewhere down the street that had multiple people spinning around in jubilant song. Mara and El took their time walking through the village. They passed dancers, people offering them food from their taverns, people offering them drinks from their open casks. All with the same bright eyes and laughing voices. A village celebrating the last night with the Hopefuls at home in unbridled cheer. They entered the town square and the breath left Mara once more.

Caerani was in the center of the square, juggling six separate-colored balls of fire. Her eyes were glowing a bright shade of red, a smile on her beautiful face. Drake was standing beside her, tapping his foot and filling villagers' tankards full of wine from a massive barrel on the ground. The band was seated here, and the music was so loud that Mara could feel it beating straight through her. Her eyes found Cyfrin on the other side of the square through the crowd of wild, swirling people. She was shocked at how quickly she had located him, how naturally she had searched. He and Kain stood watching the Odelians flail and spin around the street in dance, each laughing at whatever the other was saying.

Milios was seated next to the band, their silver flute in hand as they trilled along with the jig. This was nothing like the parties in Delinval. This was comfort and familiarity, safety and peace. In the face of the coming darkness, it felt like a glimmering beacon of warm hope. Mara pushed the anxiety for the following day from her mind, determined to enjoy this last night here amongst the Odelians.

Drake had spotted them, making ushering motions with his hand to lead them to him. El and Mara squeezed their way through the crowd to his place beside the barrel.

There was a wicked glint flashing in his eyes and El stepped back, looking nervous.

"What is it?" she called over the sound of the band and roaring circle of fire Caerani had created with her juggling.

Drake beamed at her, pulling a large bottle of dark, swirling liquid from the inside of his cloak.

El's jaw dropped. "*Is that deep wine?!*" Her voice was almost shrill over the noise.

"Deep wine?!" As if summoned by the words, Kain appeared between El and Mara's shoulders. His eyes were taking in the bottle with a feral sort of need.

Drake uncorked the bottle, shoving it under Mara's nose. The wine smelled of cherries and chocolate, making her mouth water. Kain grabbed the bottle, taking a large swig before Drake could snatch it away from him.

Drake looked incredulous. "I don't recall offering any to *you*, ya smarmy bastard!"

"Whoop!" Kain threw both fists into the air before turning from them and disappearing into the fray.

Drake shook his head, holding the bottle out for Mara to take. "It's an Ylastrian specialty," he said. He put a finger to his mouth, nodding towards Caerani and hissing behind his hand. "Don't tell Caer that I've got it. *Someone* got it banned from the village fifty years past." He shot a dark look after Kain, scowling.

Mara took a hearty gulp from the bottle. It tasted exactly as it smelled and a warmth filled her every muscle. Her fingers and toes tingled, her vision shifting to view the world through a rosy, defined hue. A laugh bubbled from her chest. El giggled beside her and handed the bottle back to Drake. He slipped the bottle into his jacket and shooed them away from his barrel of wine before Caerani could stop her juggling.

El tugged at Mara's arm, her cheeks red with drink. "Dance with me!" she called over the upbeat tune now echoing around them in the night air.

Mara giggled, a small hiccup escaping her lips. She felt more energized than she had in her whole life. The world was beautiful; this place was beautiful; El was beautiful. Mara felt light, like she might sprout wings and soar into the sky. She was beaming at El, who returned her smile and took her hand. They fell into step with the crowd of people circling in tandem to the song. The Odelians laughed and sang, including Mara into the melodies even though her mouth struggled to form the words. It was as though she had been a part of this her whole life.

She was elated, her heart threatening to rocket clean from her chest with every step she took. They spun round and round the cobblestone street, fueled by the strange magick of the deep wine. Somewhere far in Mara's brain, she wondered what could have possibly been in the drink to make her feel this way.

The musicians paused for a moment, giving both them and the dancers a chance to refresh their drinks. The two girls emerged from the bouncing crowd and found themselves standing before Kain and Cyfrin. The men towered over them, smiling.

"I was just on my way to fill the tankards," Kain said, with eyes fixed only on El. "Take Mara's and we'll go fill them together?" He leaned in towards El, offering his hand.

El nodded, tearing Mara's tankard from her and taking Kain's arm. They stumbled away, El trailing giggles behind her.

Mara was left staring at Cyfrin, transfixed on him. In the dancing orb lights around them, the harsh scar across his face had softened. His tattoos were glowing like freckles of starlight across his exposed skin.

"You're staring again, Mara." His voice was soft and deep, the words passing across his cat-like smirk.

Mara blinked up at it, a flutter starting in her stomach. *Mara. Has my name ever sounded so beautiful?* Her pulse was singing in her ears, mixing in strange ways with the deep wine. She giggled at the feeling, and the giggle became a full-blown laugh.

Cyfrin's smirk fell from his face as he stared at her smile with an odd expression—something near hunger. The look energized Mara, the unnatural warmth and peace that the deep wine brought her fueling the fire. She reached up and took Cyfrin's face in her hands. His eyes grew wide.

"You really are funny, Cyfrin!" she said through her fit of giggles. "So full of sarcasm, always ready with your next witty remark." She squeezed his cheeks closer together, laughing as his lips puckered with the force. "So *intense* all the time. It's a wonder you don't combust!"

Cyfrin grabbed her hands, and Mara felt the familiar whiz of electricity. He pulled them slowly from his cheeks, keeping a loose grip on her wrists. He raised his eyebrow. "Drake let you two into the deep wine, didn't he? The bastard. Caerani will kill us all if she finds out. Kain got it banned from the village years ago."

Mara couldn't think around his touch. It was like a cloud she never wanted to lift. She pulled one of her hands from his and put her finger to her lips. "Shhh. We were sworn to secrecy by our captain. You mustn't ruin it, Cyfrin."

The music had started back up, kicking into a hypnotic melody that had Odelians paired up and spinning in dance and drink all around them. Mara watched the dancers with a misty expression.

Cyfrin chuckled. "Look at you, all bright-eyed and full of wonder. What happened to your sternness and temper, your highness?"

She sighed, her eyes still fixed on the beautiful dancers. "Must everything be so sarcastic with you, Lightcleaver? You're far too handsome to be this irritating." The words spilled from her drunken lips, unfiltered. Mara felt heat rise in her cheeks through her haze of intoxication. She didn't dare look at Cyfrin, afraid of what she might see in those crystal blue eyes.

"Come with me, Dawnbringer."

His low, husky voice made Mara's pulse speed along at an impossible pace. He was grabbing her hand and leading her into the fray of twirling bodies. Mara trailed behind him, unable to see his face from her angle. She looked around to find El and Kain by Drake's barrel of wine. Both looked shocked.

Cyfrin stopped pulling her. Mara gulped, Cyfrin spinning her about to face him. The moonlight made his hair look like stardust. His stern face was so stunning she could've wept before its beauty. *Surely, this is the effects of the deep wine,* she thought dimly. *Surely.*

Cyfrin's eyes were stormy, hooded. He bowed to her, never taking his gaze from hers. Mara felt breathless, her heart pounding in time with the music. She wondered if he heard it, from the satisfied little smile now playing across his face.

Trouble. This is trouble.

He pulled her in close to his body, and Mara felt the electrical current that seemed to live within him at the connection. But this was different than it typically was, a *purr* rather than a shock. Cyfrin began to move, and the world around them seemed to slow. He led her through the dance like they were back on the practice fields, blissfully in sync, his eyes holding her captive. She felt like she was floating as he twirled her about, lighter than air in his powerful arms.

She had danced before at the balls at Castle Delinval, but never like this. This was passion and heat, flying and falling and everything in between. Mara realized through the fog that was Cyfrin and wine that many of the Odelians had stepped off to the sides of the square. They stared on, though Mara was too fixed on Cyfrin's face to notice any of theirs. The searching intensity behind Cyfrin's stare made her feel stripped bare. In that moment, she felt she would've given him anything he asked. *Anything.* She could not look away—she didn't want to. When would she ever get the chance to be this close to something so beautiful ever again?

Before she knew it, the music was beginning to slow. Cyfrin spun her wide, pulling her back in with a single, smooth motion. He dipped her low, his hand sliding to her lower back to steady her. He was impossibly close, sharing breath with her now. His eyes flickered. Mara watched them dart from her wide gaze to her parted, panting lips and back again. But it happened so quickly, she passed it off as her mind playing tricks.

The square around them erupted in applause, yanking Mara back to earth. Cyfrin pulled her upright. He kept his hand on her lower back, leading her from the gathering crowd of dancers. A much faster tune was now circling from the band. Cyfrin grabbed her hand, leaning over and brushing his lips against it. Mara felt a zap of electricity pulse through her arm, but she did not pull away. Kain and El were elbowing their way through the crowd towards them, and Cyfrin was upright again before they drew level.

Kain was roaring with laughter. "My great beyonds, man!" he said, a massive hand slamming on to Cyfrin's back. "You were smooth as silk out there! When do I get to have a go with those twirling toes?"

Cyfrin's eyes narrowed. "Why, I had no idea you had such an interest in dance! You can have a go right now, Kain!" He grabbed Kain's hand tight in his own.

Kain stumbled forward as Cyfrin yanked him, both laughing, back into the dancing crowd.

El nudged Mara, smirking. "I think if you were any redder, we'd be able to hang you up beside the decorations," she said, elbowing Mara playfully.

Mara scoffed. "Oh, please! You've been bright as a berry since we got here. Tell me, El, whose got *your* blood boiling?"

It was well into the early morning hours before the five of them slogged their ways back towards the Grand Hall. Only Drake and a few stragglers who looked to be part of his crew remained in the square, singing drunken sea shanties into the night. Caerani was draped across his lap, eyes closed and conducting them with a lazy hand.

Mara's eyes felt too heavy to hold open, her feet dragging on the cobblestone. Discarded petals from the glowing flowers lit their path, deepening Mara's exhaustion with their dim pulse. There was suddenly an arm wrapped around her waist. Another wrapped around her from the opposite side, and she peeled her eyelids open. Cyfrin held her from the right, dragging his feet but holding her steady. Milios stood to her left side, with a sleepy smile on their face. El had her arms wrapped around both Milios and Kain, staring with one eye open at the path.

"There once was a gal," El was singing off-key around hurried hiccups. "They called her Sweet Sal. And she was who...she was who..." She grumbled, frustrated. "Dammit, who was she?"

"They called her Sweet Sal!" Kain picked up the melody with gusto. "And she was who all the fair lads called their pal! For when they would meet, her dance was so sweet, they'd kiss her from breast to her sweet little cheeks!" Kain gave a hearty laugh. "And not the ones on her face, mind you."

"Ah," Milios said, chuckling. "If there's one thing our Captain Drake is renowned for, it's his colorful limericks."

Holding onto one another, the group traveled in a giggling line to the Halls. In what felt like the blink of an eye, Mara was standing outside the door to her bedroom. El, Kain, and Milios continued up the hallway to their rooms, but Cyfrin lingered.

He stood outside her doorway, smiling softly. "Straight to bed with you. You'll not be getting much rest at this point, and you'll need all the strength you can get in the morning."

Mara rolled her eyes in mock annoyance, smirking. "Commanding me, are you? And how do you plan on enforcing this order, Cyfrin?" She had meant it as a joke but felt the meaning behind her words as she said them. Her pulse quickened, watching his face.

His jaw tensed, his gaze flicking from her face to the dark room behind her and back again. The runes on his skin glowed so bright, they cast shadows across the walls around him. For a moment, it looked as though he was considering something. Then his muscles relaxed.

He breathed a laugh and turned from her doorway, waving his hand behind him. "Dream sweetly, Dawn-bringer," he called over his shoulder.

Mara was left standing in her doorway, hyper aware of the lack of electricity around her now. But the lingering smell of pine and honey was enough to send one last thrill to her heart. The butterflies in her stomach made her feel weightless, and she was still smiling as she settled into bed for her final hours of safe rest.

CHAPTER 28
INTO THE WOODS

Mara awoke with the sunrise, feeling as if she'd had no sleep at all. She sat up with a slow groan, cursing Drake and his damned *traditions*. She held her head, wondering which parts of her night were real, and which part vivid dream. They all seemed to blend together in a blur of wine and pine and musky honey. Her mind had been filled with Cyfrin's face, his burning expression leaning in closer and closer, his parted lips ending the distance as he breathed her name...

Mara shook her head rapidly, trying to ignore the throbbing as she stood and dressed in her leathers. She was moving slow, much slower than she'd need to in the forests. "So much for avoiding being dead weight," she grumbled to herself, dejected. She strapped her mother's dagger to her hip, securing her worn war axe to her back and examining herself in the mirror.

Realization set it. This was the last time she'd see herself, for an entire month. Her face was anxious, deep bags already brimming beneath her eyes. *If I survive this,* she thought, grim, *I'll never take another drink of deep wine again.* She gave a heavy sigh, dragging herself from the mirror and stepping into the sunlit hall. She pulled her hair into a band high on her head as she walked, admiring the beautiful lights cast through the open windows. Her four companions were already standing in the entryway as she approached.

El looked like Mara felt, her disheveled hair still pinned in the same braids as the night before. Kain, in contrast, looked just as jubilant as ever.

Cyfrin was already smirking at her, and Mara was careful to avoid direct eye contact. She wasn't sure what all she had said the night before, but from the gleam in Cyfrin's eye, she knew it had inflated his ego.

Milios was handing her a cup of steaming orange liquid. "Drink. It'll help the hangover."

Mara took a sip and almost spat it in Milios' face. It tasted like mud and soot, burning somewhat as it went down. She winced, gagging. "What in the fuck is that?"

Milios chuckled, shrugging. "I didn't say it would be *good*. I said only that it would help."

"Come on," Cyfrin urged, nodding back towards the double doors. "You can finish that on the way down. We're late."

The walk through the village to the forest's edge did nothing for Mara's nerves. Her four companions were taking turns rattling facts and tips to her about the woods. It had to have been the hundredth time in the last three days alone that they had done so, but Mara didn't care. She wasn't sure if it was helping her anxiety or fear but being overly prepared was certainly better than the alternative. Their voices clashed over one another as they spoke.

"Remember to avoid any caves you come across," El was saying, worry gripping her voice. "They might seem like safe shelters at the moment, but the creatures already living in them thought so first."

"Trust your instincts, not your eyes!" Kain added, cringing. "Always go with your gut. Just because something *looks* real doesn't always mean that it is."

"Don't give any information about yourself to *any*one," Milios said. "Ancient beings still wander those woods. Names hold power, Mara. And you never know who might be listening."

Mara shivered, remembering back to their encounter with The One Who Sees. She had a gift ready to present her, should the need arise. A braided leather bracelet El had given her their first week in training. But the thought of stumbling across her again, the thought of her swirling energy and all-knowing sight... It was a nightmare Mara was not eager to relive.

"That's enough," Cyfrin said. "She's as ready now as she possibly can be. No sense in scaring her further."

They had reached the edge of the village, now facing the gathered crowd. Mara could see the thirty other Hopeful gathering in the center. Her palms were clammy, cold sweat beading on the back of her neck. The same frightened voice from her first week in the village shot through her mind. *What am I doing? What am I doing?!*

El gave a small sob, throwing her arms around Mara's neck. She gagged as El squeezed. "We'll see you before you know it," she said, releasing Mara from the chokehold. "When the month is up, it'll be one of us that comes to retrieve you from the woods."

"And a month isn't even that long," Kain said, patting a hand onto Mara's shoulder and almost buckling her knees. "You'll do great. Just don't *die*! That's really all you have to do!" He yelped as El sent an elbow into his ribs.

Milios stepped forward. They smiled softly at Mara,

reaching out to give her arm a reassuring squeeze. "You've trained for this," they said, a gentle breeze dancing through their hair.

Mara was reminded irresistibly of standing before Adrian during the tournament saying those exact words. *"I've trained for this."* Her heart gave a shudder. She'd had no time to think on Adrian, no want to focus on that particular piece of pain. What would he say if he knew what she was about to do? *What would he say if he knew who I was?*

El grabbed Kain and Milios by the arms, dragging them into the crowd and giving a small wink to Mara.

Cyfrin stepped forward now, eyebrow raised, and looking serious. "Are you afraid?" he asked her.

This was the first time since arriving in the Hidden Village that someone had asked her this. Mara stared up at him, nodding once.

His smile softened. In one swift movement, he had her pulled against his chest, his arms wrapped around her body. He was warm, the sound of the crowd dimming as he surrounded her. She could feel his muscles tense, the electricity licking warmly against her skin. She closed her eyes, breathing in his scent. Memorizing it.

Then his lips were at her ear, a hand brushing her hair aside as he spoke. "You have nothing to fear, Mara. You are mighty. *It is the world that shall learn to fear you.*"

Mara's breath caught in her throat as he pulled away. His eyes flashed with proud satisfaction as he took in the look on her face. She opened her mouth to speak, but nothing came out. *Tell him*, she thought. *Tell him how you feel. This could be the last time you see him. Tell him how you feel.*

There was a hush falling over the crowd, and Cyfrin was pushing her forward towards the other Hopefuls. His hand left her back, taking with it the last pulses of electric energy. Caerani stood at the front of them all, her hands raised to silence the many voices. Drake stood to her left, still in his clothes from the night before, and a man stood to her right that Mara did not recognize. But she knew in an instant that he was a Forest Dweller.

He held the same sort of otherworldly beauty that Milios did, though his features were distinctly masculine. His dark blue hair had been pulled into a tight bun at the top of his head, a billowing green robe flowing about him. He was staring around at them all with cold appraisal.

This was it. The moment she had been driving towards since her arrival. Her mind was battling with itself, the core of her fighting against the useless voice telling her to give up and run *now*. She clenched her hands into fists, willing her heart to still.

Caerani spoke into the silence. "The Trials are an ancient rite. Challenges passed from many generations before to test our magicks, our wits, and our souls. You stand before us, on the ground where so many of our kin have stood, ready to face the unknown that lies before you. You stand here with hope in your hearts, and fire in your blood. The drive to protect has brought you here, and it is protection that I wish over you all as you proceed forth." She paused, letting her words sink into the silence.

There was an uneasiness rippling through the crowd, the Hopefuls shifting in place with nervous energy.

Caerani raised her hands high. There was a muffled thud at Mara's feet, echoed before the other Hopefuls around her. A small sack had appeared beneath each of them, no more than ten pounds in weight.

"In this bag, you will find two flares," Caerani said, the Hopefuls strapping their bags to their belts. "In the event that you are injured, or otherwise unfit to continue with your Trial, you may use one to denote your location. You will be rescued but barred from the remainder of the challenges. One month from this moment, those of you who have succeeded in this Trial will be located and retrieved from the woods in similar fashion."

Mara's panic reached a fever pitch. She thumbed the bag nervously, feeling the outline of the flares within.

Caerani's eyes settled on Mara and flashed. "I wish you all the best of luck. May your magick be strong and your blade stronger. And may the Zenoths protect you."

The man beside Caerani raised his hands out before him, his eyes glowing pure white as a beam of magick shot from his palms. And Mara was thrown into darkness.

She felt like she was being shot, very quickly, through a very narrow tunnel. The air was thin, making it impossible to breathe in the nothingness. If she could have screamed, she would have. Then, as quickly as it had started, Mara had slammed to a sudden halt.

She lay on her back in knee-high grass, winded, looking up at the sunlight beading through the canopy of trees. Mara groaned as the noises around her came into focus. She felt like the world was still spinning and she closed her eyes, listening to the sound of birds and bugs and the soft falling of leaves. There was a noise beside her, a groan that mirrored hers. Mara sat bolt upright, looking down through the grass to her right.

A woman was lying on her back beside her. Mara recognized her from the training fields, and as one of the barkeeps at a tavern in the village. Her armor was dark brown and fused with the thick hide of some mighty beast. Her long, dark blonde hair was plated in a braid down her back and her eyes were squeezed shut. She groaned once more.

"Are you alright?" Mara asked.

The woman startled, her eyes flying open. They were a shade of dark grey that reminded Mara of Milios. Like a storm above troubled water. She sat up, looking at Mara with her mouth agape.

"Erm…are you alright?" Mara repeated, looking for signs of hurt on the woman.

The woman gave a hurried answer. "Yes, I-I've just never been teleported before. I wasn't expecting…" She moved her hands in a zig-zag formation, shaking her head and adjusting the bow on her back. "Sorry, I'm being rude. I know who you are. Well, *everyone* knows who you are, really. And you have no idea who I am." She gave a nervous laugh.

Mara offered her an awkward grin. "It's alright. I don't bite, regardless of what Cyfrin may have told you." She grimaced, remembering that Cyfrin *had* in fact warned some of the Hopefuls that she was, quote, "a feral woman."

The woman's face relaxed, and they both got to their feet. She extended her hand to Mara, who shook it. Her palm was callused, her grip strong. She held Mara's eyes as she spoke. "My lady, I am Elise. Elise Darkmoor."

Mara laughed. It had been so long since someone had called her "my lady" in any sort of earnest, she had almost forgotten how it sounded. "Please, just Mara," she said, bashful. "I don't think there's much need for formalities where we're heading." She took in their surroundings, spinning slowly as she tried to get her bearings.

They were standing in a small clearing, the trees towering high above them shading the light before it hit the ground. The grass was up to her knees, oddly shaped flowers dispersed throughout the swaying blades. Mara could hear strange noises coming from every direction, and she frowned. *Definitely not the ideal place to set up camp.* Milios had told her their starting location was chosen at random, with some being better off than others. *Could be worse*, she reminded herself. *Could have dropped us right on top of the One Who Sees.*

She turned back to Elise. "Right. We need to find higher ground to set up our base camp. It should be our top priority. Are you ready to move?" Mara was shocked to hear the command in her tone, worried about how her new partner would respond.

But Elise nodded quickly, looking relieved that Mara had taken the reins. She unhooked the bow from her back, though Mara noted she did not seem to have any arrows. Mara unbuckled the war axe from her back, grasping the hilt in her hands.

"Keep close," Elise murmured, dropping her tone. "Not sure how much of a warning we'll have if something decides to test us in these reeds."

Mara set her eyes across the top of the tall grass, watching closely for any signs of movement beyond the breeze. Slowly, silently, they began their trek through the overgrown underbrush in search of higher ground.

CHAPTER 29
A TRIAL OF WOOD AND WHIMSY

It had been over two weeks since their arrival in the woods. Mara and Elise had found a hilly clearing the night they arrived, bordered on all sides by thick tree line. An ideal spot to hide themselves away while still keeping an eye out for attack. Mara was overjoyed to find that Elise was a skilled hunter and trapper—far more skilled than Mara had become in her brief training. She felt guilty, as she knew she would, about her comparative lack of skills.

Elise took it in stride, reassuring her every step of the way. She had Mara watch with the tasks she struggled in, learning on the go. Elise had set up careful traps all along the outside of their clearing, which served a two-fold purpose. These traps caught many of their meals, and they feasted on small forest creatures foolish enough to stumble upon them. Each trap was attached to a bell, alerting them should anything bigger decide to come investigate. They had already survived one encounter with a large, bear-like creature that charged at them from the tree line. It had made horrifying honking sounds, snapping the beak that served as its mouth and flailing sharp talons through their snare traps. Mara had bested him with one mighty swing of her axe, giving her momentary relief from her feelings of inadequacy.

Their shelter was small, just enough to keep them both covered when they slept in shifts. The night was more dangerous than the daytime, by far. The moonlight seemed to awaken a whole world of creatures. *Hungry* creatures. Mara could see many eyes watching her as she sat by her tiny fire pit, warming her hands by the smoldering ash. Her axe sat at the ready in her lap. Occasionally, she would hear something stepping vividly close to one of their trap lines, but nothing ever came near enough to trigger the bells. Mara felt somehow more disquieted at this fact.

They were sitting by the fire in the fast-dying sunlight, eating the meat of a fluorescent-colored tree creature that Elise had killed and had Mara skin the day before. Elise was filled with useful skills like how to remove, clean, and tan hide, what could and couldn't be eaten, and which plants could heal and which could kill. Of the many times she'd seen her working at the tavern, she would have never guessed the woman to be the endless trove of knowledge she was.

They did very little talking, afraid to pull the attention of some wandering monster to their haven by the sound. They knew shockingly little of one another, for a pair that had lived in such unified harmony the last weeks. It was strange to Mara that someone like Elise would join the Trials at all. She seemed so timid at times, outrightly screaming just the other day when a bird had launched from a tree just a shade too near them.

Mara set down the bones from her dinner, which she had picked clean, looking at Elise with curiosity. "You've never told me what brought you here. What made you decide to do this, of all things?" She motioned around at the forest, towards the eyes already winking to life in the shadows of the trees.

Elise stopped moving, swallowing hard. Her eyes were staring deep in the fire, lost in faraway memory.

Mara knew that she had stepped over a line. "Please, don't feel like you have to tell me. I'm sorry. You don't have to explain yourself to anyone, let alone me."

Elise raised her eyes from the fire, the ghost of a smile on her face. "No, no, it's fine. I never really get the chance to talk about it, is all. But it's important, I think. To still remember." She was quiet for a moment, the sounds of the beasts in the woods around them the only respite. "Before the Great War, there were many Odelian villages and settlements across Zenafrost. Our people lived at peace with all, only resorting to battle when it was a threat to the whole of Zenafrost." Her face grew clouded. "When Grathiel declared war against us, it was not with written word or spoken decree. He sent his forces to the nearest Odelian city, not far from the borders of Delinval. And they laid waste to its people."

"The Marred Lands," Mara said, her voice sounding far away.

A tear shimmered on Elise's cheek. She dashed it away. "My family lived in a town beyond the Krakenbär mountains, but my brother was a Warrior stationed in the city by Delinval. No one survived that first attack. Not men, women, or children. So few did in the war, with the dark magick on Grathiel's side. They burned the city to the ground. It was a massacre—" Her voice cracked with emotion.

Mara's fists clenched. The injustice of it all was unbearable. The more she learned the truth of what happened in The Great War, the more enraged she became. So many had died on both sides in a pointless tantrum by a lying King. It killed her knowing that all the people in Delinval still believed the Odelians to be the villain of that story, especially as she sat there across from the tear-streaked face of her Trials partner.

Elise cleared her throat, wiping her eyes. "My mother and father were devastated by the loss of my brother. We all were. We named the tavern in the village after him, actually. *The Grismond.* My sisters and I thought that a little normalcy would help my parents through their grief. Not sure if it ever really did. And I...I never could shake the anger." Her eyes grew dark. "I thought the sadness at his loss would be the worst part. But I was wrong. The true agony was in the rage. Rage at Grathiel, rage at the dark magicks that took my brother's life, rage that he had let them best him. I know that must sound so childish. What's a man, against a whole army? But that's the truth. And I had nowhere to direct it. We were a broken people. We went from hundreds of thousands of us, to the few hundred some-odd of us in the village. And when the war was finally over, everyone just went on their merry way rebuilding. As if nothing had happened. As if we had lost *nothing*."

Her hands were balled into fists on her lap, an eerie white mist circling them. "But I couldn't do it. I couldn't bring myself past it all. The war never ended for me. And it was Caerani that brought me to my first training. She saw the pain in me, gave me a place to channel it." She gave Mara a smile, the mists around her hands vanishing slowly. "And that's my burden. We all have them, I suppose. Can't think of many people who'd go through these Trials without that sort of weight pushing them." Her head tilted to the side. "Tell me yours. I've heard only rumors in the taverns, and Cyfrin's War Party isn't the most forthcoming with information. I can only imagine what your life must have been like."

Mara flinched. She had done such an excellent job shoving all her thoughts on the past down deep. The constant, exhausting training had forced her to focus elsewhere, and she had much preferred it that way. The pain of facing the truth seemed far too great. But sitting here now across from Elise's sincere face, surrounded by nothing but the trees and beasts hidden within in... *She trusted me enough to tell her story,* Mara thought. *She deserves the same faith.*

Mara took a steadying breath. "I knew nothing of this life. After I was taken, Grathiel raised me as his own. He has built his entire kingdom upon his gilded lies. He told us all that I was the daughter of his brother, the crown prince, and his wife who died during childbirth. Seems as though that child died with its mother, though, and I...I was put in its place." She thought back to the portraits of the prince and his wife hung in her room at Castle Delinval. At the hours she had spent dreaming of what they must have been like. "I spent my life thinking that I was to be the next ruler of Delinval, their protector from all. I trained so hard with the sword because I knew that one day we might be attacked again, that I might get my chance to avenge our fallen. It was drilled into me, that hatred for magick and those who used it. For twenty-one years."

Mara felt a lump rising in her throat but forced past it. "I always thought that my feeling of not belonging came from the way Grathiel's court treated me, the way none of them wanted anything to do with me." She let out a cold laugh. "It's funny. I'm fairly sure none of them knew who I truly was, but it was like they could all sense I wasn't one of them." She brushed her hair behind her ear, her fingers dragging across the scarring at its tips. Flashes of memory danced in her mind. Lady Lenorei, handing her a carefully wrapped present. It had been a journal, meant for her studies but used by Mara for her doodles. Lady Len had scolded her for it, but a framed piece of art from that journal had hung on the study wall behind her desk as far back as Mara could remember. It was the most warmth Mara ever gotten from any adult.

She imagined Adrian next, with his warm eyes set on hers. She thought of how she might tell him all of this, of where she would possibly begin. The image became distorted, his face twisting into disgust in her mind.

Mara shook her head to clear it, shrugging. "I suppose we're both here to channel our fury into something productive. I fear it would've destroyed me if I didn't have the training to keep me sane. The Trials gave me direction. Gave me a purpose again."

They sat together in contemplative silence.

That was the first time Mara had spoken of her past, to anyone. The pain of it sat heavy in her chest, the wounds still fresh as the day she arrived. She wondered if maybe someday, she'd be free of its hold entirely. She remembered Cyfrin, his arms wrapped around her as he whispered into her hair.

"Perhaps."

Her stomach flipped at the memory of his voice, and the feeling of him against her. She leapt to her feet, faster than she had intended. *This isn't the time for distractions*, she reminded herself. "I'll take first watch," Mara said in a hurry, before Elise had the chance to question her frantic energy.

RISE OF THE DAWNBRINGER

Mara sat in complete darkness. The fire from their last meal had been extinguished, and she stared out into the tree line. Elise was breathing slowly, asleep under their makeshift shelter behind her. The moonlight glowed through the thick canopy above, casting dancing shadows all about their clearing. It was making Mara's paranoid imagination run wild.

Every night out here had been this way. The noises around them were constant, but they had both grown accustomed to the howling, growling sounds from unseen beasts in the trees. Mara did her best to focus only on the chirping of bugs and steady whistle of the wind. She had been braiding three long pieces of grass together in her boredom, when she realized that the noises around them had suddenly ceased. And she knew from her travel across Zenafrost that the silence was far more deadly than the sound.

She reached back and shook Elise, who shot upright, eyes glassy. Mara stood with her war axe ready in her hands. She strained her eyes around them, trying with little avail to see beyond the shadowed tree line. She could feel in her bones that there was something, or some*one*, standing just beyond her vision. The unshakable, uneasy feeling was enough to make her skin crawl. Elise was on her feet, back against Mara's and bow cocked. They spun slowly together, watching all angles in the impossible silence. But no bell sounded, no trap sprung.

"Can you see anything?" Mara murmured over her shoulder.

"Nothing," Elise breathed back. "I can feel something though. *Watching* us."

Even after the sounds began to return around them, neither slept the remainder of the night. They didn't even sit down till the early morning light of dawn poured down upon them.

Exhausted, eyes heavy, Mara looked to Elise. "We need food," Mara said, her voice rough. She stretched her aching legs, wincing. "We're easy prey, sitting here with no energy. We need protein."

Elise nodded, yawning. "I set a few traps further out into the wood yesterday. We can go check them. Who knows? Maybe we'll have caught ourselves a decent breakfast."

HAD their situation been less dire, Mara would have enjoyed the mystique of the Forgotten Woods. Save for the imminent threat of attack, it truly was a place of great beauty. The trees grew in different dark hues: reds, greens, blues. No two had bark in the same shade, made even more brilliant by the multicolored orb lights that floated aimlessly through their leaves.

She couldn't even begin to catalog the different species of vine, mushroom, and flowers they had encountered. Some glowed, some sang haunting melodies, some expelled puffs of whimsical-looking clouds, which Elise warned her heavily against, calling them the nightmare seed. There were vines made of what looked like raindrops, held together by the magick that imbued the land. And Mara would swear that she saw a tree become a woman, who danced off into the wood in a flash of leaf and root.

They were standing by a similar tree now, Elise cutting the small woodland rat she had caught out of her trap. She grumbled scornfully. "Rat again. One would think with all the tracks we've gotten out here, we would have caught something bigger by now."

"Look on the bright side," Mara said, resetting the trap behind Elise. "I think I've really acquired a taste for them now. I hardly notice how, erm…*chewy* it is."

"Well, that makes one of us." Elise dropped the rat into her pouch. "What I wouldn't give for a nice, hot pint of—" She was cut short by the sound of a twig snapping, followed by another.

Footsteps.

They heard it at the same time, taking their positions back-to-back. Beasts were one thing, and after the massive killer bird-bear they had encountered nearly a week before, Mara was hardly afraid of anything they had since encountered. But these footfalls were distinct, made by a creature walking on two legs. She remembered back to her training drills, Cyfrin and El running her through anything she could encounter while in the forest. And Milios' voice echoed through her head.

"*There are ancient things in these woods.*"

Figures were looming closer out of the darkness of the trees, and Mara raised her war axe. She felt Elise pull her bow taut behind her, elbow locked in place. Out from the shadows around them stepped three men. Mara recognized the one nearest them.

"Filigro," she said, keeping her weapon raised.

"What the hell is this?" Elise snarled.

All three of the men had their weapons drawn, Filigro dragging his massive hammer behind him through the underbrush. He smiled at Mara, but it was not a kind look. "You remembered my name! I'm pleased to hear I left such a lasting impression." His voice was ice; his stare was calculating. This was not playful banter.

This was a threat.

"We're not supposed to interact with other pairings during the trials," Elise said. "Lower your weapons and leave. Now."

Filigro cackled. He screwed up his face, like a bully mocking a child. "*Lower your weapons now!* Mind your place, bar rat. This isn't about you."

"What do you want with us?" Mara spat, watching the two men flanking Filigro raise their swords.

Filigro cocked his head. "Well, your highness, we've been doing a lot of thinking these last few weeks. Thinking and talking to many, many of the Odelian people. *My* people. We've been discussing how beautiful our Hidden Village has been these past, oh...twenty-one years?" His eyes flashed with malice. "As a whole, your Ladyship, we've decided that the last thing we need is another Dawnbringer *brat* on the throne. Your whole damn bloodline has done nothing but besmirch the throne. Your grandfather was a drunkard, your father was a Champion for our enemies, and your mother, ha! Your mother was nothing but a cosmic *failure*. Their inability to use their power to rule over these lands led us to our ruin. It's time for a new era to rise." He gave her a mock pout. "And that just can't be done with your pretty face traipsing about, now can it? You came so close to foiling all my plans. Everything I've worked so hard for since before you were even born. And Zenoths bless me, when you entered the trials?!" He let out a laugh and its sinister sound echoed around them. "You practically presented yourself to me on a silver platter! How could I pass up on the opportunity to end my suffering? To end *your* suffering. And I'm sure you must suffer greatly, with all that's happened to you." His smile was unhinged.

Elise's heart was pounding so hard that Mara could feel it in her back, slamming against her from the place their bodies met. "Traitorous bastards!" Elise roared at him. "How dare you?!"

Mara glowered at Filigro, disgusted. Her wrath, ever present just beneath the surface, bubbled forth. "And you think by killing me, Caerani will simply just let you take the throne? *My* throne?" She stood up straighter, squaring her shoulders to present her full and powerful figure. Filigro's smile faltered. "You know why you never succeeded in any of your tries for the crown, Filigro? It isn't due to any birthright I may have. It is because you are *weak*. You are weak and they can see it written all over your face." She scoffed. "I could *smell* it on you the day we first met. Worse than that, you're arrogant in your weakness. You're so pigheadedly cocky that you have the balls to stand here, three versus two, and brag about your plan to murder us. As if we would be taken so easily!" She raised her axe high.

Elise followed her lead, springing to action. Thick, white mist erupted from her, engulfing them all in the space of a heartbeat. Mara felt her cocking the bow, a ripple of energy building behind her back.

The two men accompanying Filigro cried out, but Filigro roared. He charged forward, swinging his great hammer in the space where Mara and Elise had just stood.

But they were already on the move. Mara spun about, watching the purple magick glowing from Filigro's hammer a few feet away. Elise had vanished, but Mara could hear the steady "*thwack*" of her magick-made arrows flying around her.

Filigro was spinning around in the mist. Mara could see his eyes glowing with the same hissing purple magick that engulfed his weapon. Her axe would be no good in this confined space, especially with no way to aim with certainty. The possibility of hitting Elise with her blinding, earth-splitting powers was too heavy a risk. Mara threw it aside, grabbing her mother's dagger from its place on her hip. The sound of her axe hitting the ground was muffled by the scream of one of the men.

But Filigro's keen eyes had spotted the movement—even through the cloud of Elise's magick. He charged forward with startling speed, swinging his hammer high. Mara dove, the hammer missing her by inches. As the magick winged past her cheek, she felt a sharp pain followed by wet warmth. She touched her face, pulling her hand away to find it covered in blood.

Filigro was laughing behind her. Mara spun round to face him. His eyes lit up as he lunged forward again, but he this time it was not towards Mara. Instead, he was charging forward into the mists, directly to the space where Elise stood. Her back was to him, carefully aiming a bolt in the opposite direction towards one of Filigro's men.

There was no way to catch Filigro as he sprinted towards Elise. No way to stop what was about to happen. "*Elise!*" Mara cried, raising the dagger high. And time seemed to slow.

Elise loosed a bolt of magic. She half-turned, eyes wide as Filigro charged.

An intense heat reared up inside Mara. It shot through her like a mighty wave, crashing higher and higher till it begged to swallow her whole. Everything glowed with a bright, golden light, illuminating the mists around them so that Mara saw everything with crystal clarity. She threw the dagger, in a last feeble attempt to save her friend. It shined with the same golden light her war axe did when she melded, the same as the mists glowing around them. There was a wet *thud*, and Filigro stopped inches from Elise.

The dagger quivered, lodged deep in his back.

His hammer, still raised high above him to strike, fell to the ground. There was a ringing like a thousand bells overtaking the woods around them. Mara clasped her hands over her ears, Elise mirroring the motion. Cracks began to explode across Filigro's body like stone. Light gleamed out of each new wound, the chiming reaching an ear-splitting volume. Mara hunkered down against the noise, dropping her head low and gritting her teeth. After what felt like an eternity, the sound ceased. Mara lifted her head slowly.

There was no longer a man standing before her, but a giant pile of sparkling, golden dust. Alora's dagger sat still quivering in the ground at its center, dripping red with blood. The wind began to carry the dust away over the fallen battle hammer.

Filigro was no more.

CHAPTER 30
A PROPHECY OF UNDONE

The mists around them began to disperse, and Elise was the first to break the silence. "What in the End of All was *that?!*" she cried. She motioned helplessly at the vanishing golden dust pile between them.

Filigro's two companions lay dead on both sides of them. They were riddled with holes from arrows that had vanished with the mists.

Mara shook her head, eyes wide. "I have no idea! I… I've never done that before!"

Elise had bent down, rubbing some of the glimmering dust between her fingers. "I've never seen a person reduced to ash. Can't say he didn't deserve it, I suppose."

Mara continued to watch the golden ash being swept away by the breeze. She had been overwhelmed by emotion when Filigro took off towards Elise, so filled with righteous fury and fear. The dagger was her only means of attack. But the magick had felt the same, the same as when she'd used her axe, the same as that day in the fields with Cyfrin. Though this time had been tinged in pure, untamed power.

Elise stooped, pulling the dagger from the ground, and handing it to Mara. "Was that your first kill?"

Mara gulped. "First human one. Yes."

Elise reached out and gave her shoulder a squeeze. "I won't lie to you; It never gets easier. And if it does, you should start worrying." She shot a nasty look at the two corpses, at the burnt circle of ground where Filigro had once been. "These three were pigs, Mara. It's not as if this was unprovoked. You were only protecting us. Protecting me."

"I know," Mara replied in a soft voice, but she couldn't stop staring at the bodies of the men.

El patted the sack with the wood rat, breathing a heavy sigh. "Come on. Nothing like a good breakfast to clear your mind."

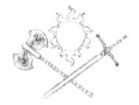

"Bastards!" Elise threw the sack with the rat to the ground in exasperation. It was the first time she had cursed in their entire time here. "I *knew* we were being fucking watched last night!"

They had arrived in their hilly clearing only to find their campsite ransacked. Their makeshift shelter had been torn to the ground and set ablaze, its cinders still smoking in the dirt. All the furs Elise and Mara had skinned to keep them warm in the night were smoldering at the top of the pile. Their packs had been turned upright; their contents scattered through the grass. Mara suddenly felt a lot less guilty that she had just incinerated the man who she knew did this.

Elise groaned, dragging her hands down her face.

"They probably took some of our gear too. Zenoths curse us, it'll take *ages* to find their bloody campsite to loot it back!" Elise marched around, gathering the remaining supplies into their sacks and mumbling profanities under her breathe as she went.

Mara stared around the razed site. The men had watched them, studied them, waiting for the right time to strike. The thought of them staring, just out of sight, made her stomach churn. Something on the ground shimmered in the sparse sunlight. She knelt to get a closer look. At this angle, Mara could clearly make out a path through the grass, leading to a mangled deer carcass a few feet towards the hills edge. *They'd already destroyed our camp. Why take the time to defile it in such a way.* And then it hit her. A week prior, Mara had stood watching Elise bait one of the traps deeper in the woods. "Hopefully this will bring us a bigger meal," she had said.

Filigro was not the fool Mara took him to be. He had thought three steps ahead, planning for the worst. In the event Mara and Elise escaped and returned here, he had turned their campsite into a trap. And they were live bait.

Mara leapt to her feet, startling Elise. "We have to leave. *Now,*" she hissed, pointing at the entrails behind her.

The color drained from Elise's face. Mara's brain scrambled to form a plan, and fast. This much blood in such a concentrated space was sure to attract something big. As if in response to this thought, the trees behind them began to shake. They whirled around, and Elise let out a whimper of panic.

At the base of their tiny hill stood a massive figure, crouched on all fours. It had the shape of a dog, but violently green leaves stood in the place of fur. Thorns stuck out from its heavily muscled limbs. It was snarling at them, sharp rows of teeth dripping in dark green liquid jutting forth from its maw. Its eyes were a brilliant shade of purple, and what looked to be a third eye was opening in the middle of its skull.

"Is it dangerous?" Mara breathed, unable to tell if the beast was snarling in threat or defense.

Elise was reaching with deliberate slowness towards the bow on her back. "Deadly," was all she replied.

Mara grimaced. "Of course it is." She reached up with the same care as Elise, trying her best to unlatch her axe without startling the beast.

Its head tilted, stopping at an unnatural angle. It snapped its mighty jaws in the air, digging at the ground with thick claws. And without warning, it leapt at them.

It took the hill in two leaps, colliding with Mara before the axe was in her grip. Elise's bow was already in her hand, and a bright bolt of magick collided with the monster's head. Mara and the beast tumbled backwards together through the grass, tipping her world on end. Mara's head slammed on the ground and her ears rang with the impact.

She was lying on her back now, staring up at the canopy swirling high above. The beast lay a few feet away, eyes void of all life. Mara could see misty arrows vanishing from its hide, leaving gaping holes deep in the muscle.

Elise was pulling her to a sitting position, the world continuing to spin. "*You have to move!*" she heard Elise saying through the ringing in her ears. Elise looked around frantically, her bow still in hand as she yanked Mara to her feet. They scrambled down the hillside and into the trees, leaving their once-perfect haven behind as they ran.

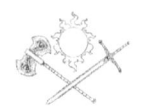

They didn't stop moving till the sun was long gone from the sky. They had walked for miles, with nothing to show for it. They hadn't found a single place like their high ground hidden in the trees. The two had settled for the evening into a thick gathering of bushes, pressed against the dense wood. The foliage surrounded them completely, a lone red tree standing in the circle with them. They sat on the cool, hard ground with their backs to the tree, forgoing fire and dinner all together.

Elise had drifted off to sleep, her bow still held tight against her chest. Mara didn't mind staying up to watch over her. She wasn't sure she could sleep even if she wanted to. There was a stabbing pain in her side that she had avoided mentioning to Elise, for fear it would slow them down. But sitting there alone, she looked to examine the spot in question.

Mara adjusted her axe, moving gingerly. There was a clear gash through the side of her leathers from where the thorns of that beast had struck her. She reached down, fingers grazing the cut. It was wet and sticky, no doubt with blood. She whispered a curse into the night air, furious that such a small wound was causing her so much discomfort. Pulling the sack of salvaged supplies towards her, she removed a dusty cloth bandage from its depths and pressed it hard into the cut.

While Mara sat wincing, trying not to make a sound, a pulsing light began to filter through the leaves of the dense bush before her. She froze, her ears perking up for any sign of movement. A ball of flittering white light, much bigger than the small orbs that floated the forest beyond, appeared above her head. Mara had the strange, distinct impression that it was looking at her somehow.

She stared up at it, gripping the hilt of the dagger at her hip. Her eyes narrowed in distrust. The light was making sound, like the whistle of the wind or a whisper on the breeze. Mara sat up straighter, trying to make it out.

"*Yvaine.*"

Mara fell back against the tree, shocked as the whispers began to form her true name. The orb hummed with renewed intensity, rotating above her as it whispered a chant in what sounded like many voices at once.

"*Dawnbringer. Dawnbringer. Dawnbringer.*" It whizzed backwards out of Mara's sight, taking the soft whispers of her name with it.

Mara glanced at Elise, still sound asleep against the tree. Her curiosity was crying out, urging her to stand, to follow. She knew it was an idiotic idea, knew what Cyfrin would say if he knew she had even thought it. But the light had spoken her name, without her giving it. *Stay put, Mara.* She heard Cyfrin's berating voice in her head. *Stay put and stay safe.* Mara bit her lip, glancing back at Elise. Then she stood from their hiding place and took off silently after the orb.

The light was bouncing along a few feet away, waiting for Mara to emerge. She fell in step behind it. "You're smarter than this, Mara," she mumbled to herself, but her resolute walk behind the orb was proving this to be false.

She walked in silence behind the whispering light, her name dancing back to her on the breeze. It led Mara into a small clearing ten minutes past where Elise slept, glowing flowers lighting their surroundings with dim color. As she entered the space, the orb vanished into thin air.

The sounds of the woods around Mara stopped with unnatural quickness. A terrifying energy had sprung to life behind her.

"Ah, Dawnbringer. *There* you are."

The drawling voice was all too familiar, having haunted many of Mara's nightmares. She squeezed her eyes shut, dread bottoming out in her stomach. She had felt no motion but knew that it was standing mere inches from her back. Mara could've kicked herself, cursed by her own stupidity. What would Cyfrin, El, Kain and Milios say when they found her body strewn from the trees above? Would they curse her? Would Cyfrin return to drinking himself into oblivion? Would they even bother to pick up her scattered pieces?

Mara squeezed the hilt of her dagger so tightly that it hurt. "Oh, great One Who Sees All." She bowed her head, her eyes still clasped shut. She felt the presence circle to the front of her.

The One Who Sees chuckled, the sound like chimes on the wind. "I have waited since the beginning of all to see your face, child of light. Many came before, but none were you." The One Who Sees stepped closer. "I see you have found your name. You have taken up your rightful mantle. The path beckons you. But I sense there is still much you do not know." A pause, the silence around them deafening. "Tell me, child. Have you brought me a gift?"

Mara froze. The bracelet El had crafted for her. It had been burned in the pyre Filigro and his men made of their campsite, or else lost in the escape from it. She swallowed hard, her mind racing. There was only one thing that could be done, and the idea alone was heartbreaking. Hands trembling, Mara unsheathed her dagger and held it before her. "I bring only my mother's blade with me, great and terrible one. It is all I have to give."

The air around Mara was vibrating with the power rippling through the clearing. The dagger had been taken from her hands, a pang echoing in her heart as it had lifted. "I knew your mother. And your mother's mother. And all the mothers before that." The One Who Sees let out a soft hum. "Each a part, but not the whole. Their souls ring true here, even now. I can see them all within you."

Silence again. Mara didn't dare open her eyes, remembering the deathly warnings she had been given about this entity before.

"Have you accepted your destiny, Dawnbringer? Will you take up the fate that was handed to you by the cosmos? Before every and earth became one?"

Mara frowned. The One Who Sees seemed to enjoy talking in riddles, and this was one she did not understand. Laughter once more. "*Ah*. I see. You have not been told of the prophecy."

Mara nearly looked up, catching herself at the last second. "What prophecy?" A shiver ran through her body.

The One Who Sees was leaning into her, their faces only a few inches apart—she could smell and feel sickly-sweet breath wafting across her face. "The Prophecy of Undone."

The wind whipped up around them, throwing glowing petals and leaves about Mara's feet. "I don't understand. What is that?"

"*Your destiny*." The voice had come from behind Mara, drifting to her on the dying breeze. "The oldest in the land. Set down by the first seer in the midst of battle and bloodshed. It has been called, and you must answer. There is no other way. I look forward to your release, Dawnbringer."

And then the creature was gone. The noise of the forest came back as suddenly as it had left, a symphony of sound crashing around Mara. She stood motionless in the flower-lit clearing, her mind reeling. She stared down at the ground where the One Who Sees had stood.

Lying amongst the flowers, flashing in their glow, was her mother's dagger.

CHAPTER 31
THE POISONED PRINCESS

They spent the following few days searching high and low for a place to make a stable shelter. Mara had not spoken with Elise about her encounter with the One Who Sees, but her brooding had not gone unnoticed. Elise asked multiple times a day if she was all right, to which Mara would reply with a small nod and a forced smile. She could tell Elise didn't believe her, but she never pressed the matter further.

It was driving Mara mad to know that she had been lied to once again. She grimaced at the word. Not exactly *lied* to but certainly kept in the dark. Which was nearly as bad in her eyes. She had flipped the One Who Sees' words over in her mind again and again. *A Prophecy of Undone*. It haunted her every moment, keeping her awake through the night during her turns to sleep.

The fact that they had yet to find a place to reset their shelter was doing nothing for the women's moral. Mara had elected to keep the cut on her side from Elise, refusing to make her worry any further when they were so close to the end. But that morning, stripped bare and bathing in a small creek they had found, Mara had finally gotten a truly good look at her wound.

The cut wasn't very big, all things considered. But that was the least of her worries. Fluorescent green tendrils were veining out from the gash, thick and painful to the touch. Mara remembered the green ooze that had dripped from the thorned beast's mouth, and she cursed. The pain and exhaustion that doubled in Mara every day both pointed to one thing, poison. She had pulled her leathers back on carefully, padding the wound with the last of their cloth bandages. *Nothing that can be done for it now*, she thought. *We've just got to make it a little while longer. Then the healer can fix it right up.* A nagging voice prodded back. *And what if they can't?*

They were walking through a beaten path hours later. Deep claw marks had been gouged into some of the trees, but it was nothing they hadn't seen before. Mara's stomach had been growling for the past hour, their food supplies scarce as they were forced to remain on the move.

Elise eyed her with concern. "Are you really not going to tell me what's wrong?" she asked, for what felt to Mara like the hundredth time that day.

Mara let out a heavy sigh, head dropping back as she closed her eyes. "There's nothing to tell, Elise," she replied, her voice thick with exhaustion. "I'm tired, I'm hungry and my feet are sore. Same as you."

But Elise looked unconvinced, eyes narrowing on Mara's sweat strewn face. "You can tell me, you know. Whatever it is, I'm here. Maybe I can help—"

"I don't need help." Mara hadn't meant for her tone to come out with such bite, and she saw Elise flinch a little. Mara softened her expression, both stopping to face one another. "I'm sorry. I'm sorry, I didn't mean that. I just meant that there's nothing to help with."

Elise's brow furrowed. "You just seem…different, somehow. And you've been like this for days. I'm worried about you."

Mara gave her a small smile, touched that she was so invested in her well-being. She waved her hand, turning to continue up the path. "I'm just ready to be out of here, and in a nice hot bath. Aren't you?"

Elise chuckled. "You have no idea. I *dream* of sudsy water and a good, hot meal. Maybe a warm pie and a pint while I'm at it. It shouldn't be long now before we —*ARGH!*"

Mara spun around as Elise screamed. Her heart stopped.

Elise was being held off the ground by her neck, a terrifying creature lifting her high. It stood seven, eight feet tall, clawed hooves at the bottom of its powerful legs. It was vibrating in place so quickly that its black, scaly body was all but a blur. Its face was comprised of two beady orange eyes and a giant, gaping mouth. A long, snake-like tongue lolled out the side of it. Sharp horns jutted out from its head, twisting around the skull like a dark halo. Its long fingers, which reminded Mara of the Necromancer in Bardro's Gash, were wrapped completely around Elise's neck.

The fury that rose in Mara drowned out every ounce of fear fighting to surface. Her axe was in her hand in a flash, raising high as she rushed forward. *"Let her go!"* she roared, bringing her axe down upon it. But it made no contact, slamming through thin air and colliding hard with the ground. The earth cracked, glowing bright as magick shot forth from the place of impact. Mara whirled around.

The creature had teleported feet away, still holding the flailing Elise aloft. It stared at Mara with head angled. Elise's face was turning purple. She was sputtering and trying to kick the beast.

Mara swung her axe again, and this time the creature reacted. It threw Elise hard through the air, slamming her body into a nearby tree. There was sickening *crack* as she hit, and Elise crumpled to the ground.

The creature grabbed the head of Mara's axe. Her magick glowed blindingly bright against his long, scaley hand, the creature tilting his head ever further at her. Her axe was vibrating at the same impossible speed as the monster, his hand squeezing tighter as he held the weapon captive. And then the blade shattered.

Light blasted out from the tip of the hilt where the axe's head once stood, the metal crashing to the forest floor like it had been made of glass. The force of the magick shooting out the end threw the monster back several yards, crashing through the trees and underbrush. Mara tossed the useless hilt to the ground, rushing to the spot where Elise lay motionless.

There was a trickle of blood slowly falling down Elise's face from a deep gash on her head, her neck already bruising around the spot she had been held. Her right leg was jutting out at an awkward angle, clearly broken. Mara put her head against Elise's chest, listening, hoping.

Her heartbeat was desperately faint, but it was there.

Mara let out a sigh of relief, though the moment was short-lived. The creature had appeared without a sound once again, floating towards them as it vibrated violently. Mara bared her teeth like a feral beast, staring it down as she raised her hands high in defense. She cried out as the monster lunged for them.

Mara's hands were hot, so hot that she felt they must surely be aflame. Her heart was slamming against her ribs, and she was suddenly blinded by brilliant golden light. It exploded from her palms and shot straight through the monster, its force slamming her back into the tree Elise had fallen against. The creature was shrieking, the sound like ripping flesh. *Boom!* The forest shook around them; the monster exploded. Golden ash blasted through the air, marking where the beast had been. Mara was thrown into crisp silence, mouth agape.

The dust floated softly down around them. But Mara had no time to celebrate her self-made magick, no time to marvel at what she had done for the second time. Elise was groaning, and Mara dropped to a knee at her side.

She took Elise's hand, staring horrorstruck at partner's mangled body. "Elise, I have to send out the flare," Mara said gently.

Elise's eyes fluttered open. She cried out, looking down at her leg in agony.

Mara forced her voice to be calm. "I know. I know. It's going to be okay. I'm going to call for help." It didn't matter that it would end the Trials for her, didn't matter that Mara would have to continue alone. She dug through the pack of their belongings Elise had been carrying, frantic. Cursing, she dumped the contents of the bag onto the forest floor.

But the flares were nowhere to be found. Elise had slipped back into unconsciousness, her face still screwed up in pain.

Mara's mind was whirring. Filigro and his men had ransacked their camp. Why hadn't she thought to check this detail before? Sitting here now, staring in desperation around at the trees as if something was magically going to appear at her aid, she realized they had taken their only means of escape. One final "fuck you" from the man who meant to usurp her. Mara wanted to cry. She screamed into the sky, overwhelmed, and birds shot from the treetops above. Her eyes fell back on Elise's crumpled form. And Mara made her decision.

She tossed the empty pack of supplies to the side, leaning down to wrap Elise's arms around her shoulders. Mara dragged her partner's body across the back of her neck, hoisting her onto the place where her axe once sat. The woman's dead weight was heavier than anything Mara was used to, but she locked her knees and forced herself to stand. She roared as the pain ripped through her, her legs wobbling with dangerous threat. But Mara was on her feet, Elise draped haphazardly over her shoulders. She was careful to avoid squeezing her broken leg, latching on to her good one to keep her steady.

Mara had no idea how many days were left in their month out here. No idea how long they could possibly last this way. But she could not, *would* not, sit here waiting for another horrible thing to come sniff them out. The first few steps were the hardest; her legs screamed under the weight. She pushed forward, gritting her teeth, and leaning to disperse the ache more evenly through her body.

And Mara began to walk them back up the trail.

THE FOLLOWING days and nights passed seamlessly, an unending stream of agony on Mara's end and tears from Elise during her few moments of consciousness. Mara tried to keep her awake during their excruciating trek through the woods, fearful there would come a time when she would not wake back up. Mara talked to her about her life in Delinval and the journey Cyfrin and the others had taken her on to get to the Hidden Village. But it seemed Elise's head had been more damaged from the blow than Mara had realized. Her moments of lucidity were becoming fewer and further between.

They never stopped for very long when they did take breaks. Mara was afraid they had entered a spot of the forest teeming with monsters like the one they had just faced, so haunting were the noises that came from the trees around them. She was past the point of exhaustion, running on berries she had foraged from the bushes on the path. She was feverish, cold sweat now a constant on her clammy skin and the gash on her side sending sharp, shooting pain all the way up to her head with every step she took. She wasn't sure how long they had been at this, or how much longer they had left. Time seemed endless, maybe even hopeless, and Mara wondered in her feverish fog if anyone was going to come for them at all.

She was trudging through the trees and overgrowth, Elise slung across her back. The sun beating down from above was her only indication that a new day had begun. Mara was stumbling every few feet, her body feeling strange and disconnected. The colors all around her were blending, bleeding into one another. She watched a few flowers sprout feet and dance around them up the path.

Mara paused at this, a small voice in her head speaking. *Completely bloody mad. You've gone completely bloody mad, Mara.* The wind was sweeping past her, bringing with it a faint voice. Or perhaps this too was her imagination. Paranoia had taken hold, and she could swear there were figures in the trees just beyond them. Waiting to pounce. The wind was speaking to her. *"Sit in the soft grass,"* it murmured through her tangled curls. *"Sit and wait awhile."*

"No, I can't," Mara spoke to the breeze, only dimly aware that the fever was causing her to hallucinate. "I can't stop. I haven't the time." Her foot caught a root and she stumbled, nearly toppling over with Elise on her back. She caught herself, righting her feet as she forced her eyes to remain open. But the world was starting to spin, her vision fogging over. Her pulse echoed in her head, faster than it should have been. Sleep was all she wanted, all she *needed* to keep going.

"No," she repeated, her mouth bone dry. "No, I can't stop. I have to keep going." The weight on her shoulders seemed to be lifting. But this was not her mind playing tricks on her.

Someone was taking Elise.

Mara fumbled for the dagger at her hip, spinning around to face whoever was there. Heat rose to her palms as she slashed through the air, sending out a violent wave of magick in an arc from her hand. The blurry light flew into the trees, striking a trunk a few yards away with a dull *thud*. Mara swayed, her legs failing with the release of Elise's weight. They gave way beneath her, and she fell back. Mara closed her eyes, ready to accept whatever was to come if it meant she could finally rest.

But she didn't hit ground, instead tumbling into something equally solid just behind her. She was being lifted into the air, brought against a warm chest as strong arms cradled her. Mara knew this scent, the musky sweetness of pine and honey.

"Cyfrin," she sighed his name, giving her eyes permission to close at last.

"I've got you," she heard his husky voice say, rough and low. But it sounded impossibly far away. There were noises, though Mara could not place where they came from. It sounded like a battle, the distinct clang of metal on magick clear even now. But Mara didn't care. She had done it. She had finished her first Trial, despite everything stacked against her. And as the chaos of battle became more distant, Mara drifted into the sweet abyss of unconsciousness.

Fin

*Join our intrepid band of heroes in the second book of the series,
Bornbane: A Prophecy of Undone*

BONUS CHAPTER

Cyfrin

It had been twenty years since Cyfrin had left the borders of the Forgotten Woods. The last he had seen of the lush landscapes of Zenafrost had been at the end of the Great War, though he had only blurred memories of half-dragging, half-carrying Caerani's charred body back to the Hidden Village to serve as reminder of those times. In the month it had taken he and his war party to cross the continent, his unwavering fury against Grathiel had only tripled.

The king of Delinval had begun that damned war, started the age of reckoning and darkness that had overtaken Zenafrost in the years since. It was unforgiveable, the festering wound that bore the poisoned fruits of all their demise. And it was only the knowledge, this smallest glimmer of hope, that kept him from taking off to burn their white kingdom to the ground. Perhaps his greatest failure could be redeemed. But he tried not to think it, for there was none more undeserving of redemption than he.

BONUS CHAPTER

They had arrived in the Marred Lands, the abandoned outer city of Delinval that once laid host to Delinvalians and Odelians alike before Grathiel's sudden betrayal.

Before he slaughtered not only Cyfrin's people, but also his own.

The once-great city stood in ruin around them, starving the air of any semblance of happiness they had held till now. There were noises coming from behind the towering white stone walls of Delinval. Boisterous, loud with laughter, music, and cheer. Clearly a celebration. Cyfrin's jaw clenched at the sounds, sparks lightning his fingertips as he stretched his hands in attempted calm.

"What do you suppose all the fuss is about?" El asked, her tone dark as she too stared towards the kingdom with vengeful eyes.

Milios looked grim as they replied. "I can fly up there for a moment if you'd truly like to know. Peek over the wall."

El shook her head, dropping her gaze to the ground and looking strained. "Not worth the risk. Our plan depends on stealth."

Beside her, Kain slowly polished/sharpened his great sword, his usual air of humor gone. His face mirrored Cyfrin's, both wanting nothing more than blood to atone for the war. Blood, and Grathiel's head on a spit.

Kain paused, cloth halfway up the blade as he stared thoughtfully at the sky. "Suppose it is just a rumor. Suppose the merchant who saw the princess was mistaken, and this is all for nothing? What are we to do then?"

Cyfrin kept his steady glare on the kingdom walls as he replied, "Simple. We blow the place to the End of All and deliver their souls to the damnation they so crave."

El rolled her eyes, scoffing. "Oh, spare me, Cyfrin.

Even if we were to launch an attack, you are woefully out of practice. Spending twenty-one years drowning yourself in a tavern isn't exactly training to take down an empire, is it?"

Cyfrin felt his anger mount as she said this, but it was stifled instantly by his overwhelming guilt. After the loss of the baby Dawnbringer, he had spiraled into despair. They had pried her from his bloodied, beaten body, not even had the decency to kill him; To spare him the agony. It was more than he had ever been forced to bear, in all his hundreds of years.

He lost count of the taverns, the barrels of wood wine, the bottles of deep wine Drake thought were so well hidden aboard the Red Froth…All to stem the waves of disgust he felt every time he looked at himself. Every time he stopped to think.

Caerani was more than generous, allowing him to take the lead on this mission. Cyfrin was no fool. He knew it was her way of trying to pull him back to the land of the living. He had spent days sobering up, letting his body expel the poison he had ingested for twenty-one years. Kain and Milios, first to forgive, had held him together throughout the darkest hours of this. But Eleanora's tone still held an edge, and one Cyfrin far from blamed her for. El, determined to save him from himself, had spearheaded an attempt to rescue him in those early years. He had spit on his friends' offers, had done his damnedest to burn every bridge between them. It would take him hundreds of years more to fix the things he had so carefully broken.

Cyfrin's tone softened, eyes apologetic as he replied. "You're right. Bursting in and blowing them to pieces is the wrong move, no matter how appealing it may sound. I'm sorry. Give us the plan again then, El."

BONUS CHAPTER

El looked surprised at his apology, blinking as she granted him a nod of understanding. "Right. Well, I think it best we let them finish their unearned revelry. No sense in charging in when the whole kingdom and royal army are gathered."

Kain scoffed. "Not much of a fair fight, besting a bunch of drunkards. No honor or reward in that."

El threw him a cold look. "The point is to not fight at all, you insufferable bastard. We're here for the princess. Not to judge whether we think she's Queen Alora's babe. Not to kill those who have wronged us. Just the princess. Is that understood?"

Her words held an authoritative tone that Cyfrin had never heard before. She continued to glower at Kain and Cyfrin, both men grimacing beneath her newfound ferocity. "My plan is simple: subdue the guards at the gate to the castle, slip inside, locate the princess and escape with her before they know what hit them. It grants us the most time to get headway before Grathiel lets loose his military might."

Cyfrin's muscles tensed in longing at the thought of driving his blades deep into knight after knight, his magick bursting the hearts of every man unfortunate enough to come across him. Grathiel's soldiers had been young men during the war, had probably begun their own families by now. His magick pressed hard against his warded flesh at the injustice in this; how could these people live their happy little lives when so many of Cyfrin's people had perished twenty years ago? Zenoths be, how he yearned to feel the warm rush of blood down his arms as he flayed flesh from bone.

"There won't be many lucid guards left after their party, by the sound of it," Cyfrin said, ripping his deathly glare from the castle and biting his tongue to keep his anger in check. "We'll be quiet as a dormouse, El. In and out in no time."

"I can lift us over the back wall fairly easily," Milios said, scratching their chin thoughtfully. "If Cyfrin stuns the soldiers standing at the gates, I can use the winds to lead us straight to the princess."

"So, then what? We just wait here?" Kain groaned, looking put-upon as he stared fondly at his newly cleaned blade.

"Yes, Kain," El sighed, pinching the bridge of her nose in frustration. "We wait."

It was well into the early hours of the dawn before the sun had even begun to rise, when the last of the partygoers seemed to disperse. The War Party gathered their weapons in silence, marching as one to the back wall of Delinval. Cyfrin's heart was hammering in his chest, face set in resolute determination as they moved in silence.

This was the moment he had been waiting for. Either they entered the castle to find the princess had been mistakenly identified or they would come face-to-face with the last Dawnbringer, hidden behind enemy lines. His heart leapt at the possibility, then his thoughts turned grim. I'll throw myself in the Zenoths-forsaken Brisenbane if this has all been some wild hunt.

It was the first light he had seen in twenty years, the only thing that stopped his pointed path of self-ruination. But a cold chill creeped in around the hopeful feeling, squeezing in threat of snuffing it out. If it was her, Caerani

BONUS CHAPTER

had made one thing perfectly clear: she will have been raised knowing nothing.

Nothing but the Odelians as her enemy.

In some respects, this was worse than thinking her dead as her mother. How do you tell someone they've been locked away in a gilded prison their whole lives? That the man who raised them is a monster; that everything they've ever known has been a lie?

Cyfrin shook his head free of his dark musings as they approached the outer wall, holding the strangling feeling around his heart at bay. Milios held up a hand, silently stopping the group in their tracks.

They were staring ahead with a mild admiration. "Huh. They've warded their borders."

"What?!" El hissed, eyes widening at this unforeseen development. Kain hissed and Cyfrin clenched his teeth, but Milios waved a hand absently.

"Oh, they haven't it done it well. It'll be easy enough to tear a hole right through here. But it's fascinating to me that Grathiel had the foresight to at least try..."

"Can you sense who made them?" Cyfrin asked in a muted tone, now very aware of the dim scratching of dark energy now caressing his skin.

"Something quite dark," Milios replied, hands moving expertly through the air as he worked to dispel the wards. "This sort of magick isn't made by tainted mortal hands. No...no, I suspect Mezilmoth will have sent a Darkling to hoist these up. Just a few more seconds and...there."

Many things happened at once.

There was a shimmering ripple that passed through the air before them, the faint constriction of dark magick dissipating in an instant as Milios gave a final wave. As it did, something tore through Cyfrin like a tidal wave. It ripped from him every ounce of what he thought he was, chased away all thought, all feeling from every recess of his brain.

It was like a tether, sudden and unwavering, pulling him irresistibly forward. Something was stirring deep in his core, far beneath the wards that his father had burned into his flesh long ago. For the first time in over five hundred years, Cyfrin's control wavered. He took a sharp intake of breath in his surprise, and a smell washed over him. Rosemary and honeysuckle, faint but somehow still overwhelming to his senses. It smelled like home, intwining with the persistent pulling at his heart.

Need overtook him in that instant. He barely noticed Milios' oddly knowing stare, or Kain's sudden boisterous smile as he saw the expression change on his face.

Cyfrin dove under El's arm. She, too, saw the change and tried to stop him in his tracks. But she was too slow. Whatever had spun to life within him had fully dusted off the cobwebs brought by those years of drink and darkness.

Cyfrin shot forward like a lightning strike, a blur of blue and white as he slammed a hole right through the wall of Delinval. The stone blasted around him, crashing to the ground. With startling speed, he made his way across the only green earth he had seen since leaving the Forgotten Woods. Grathiel had been successful in his plan to separate Delinval from the sickness he brought upon Zenafrost. And this success only served to flare Cyfrin's fury even further.

He reached the castle gate in seconds. Just as they had suspected, the guards by the entrance were slouched in relaxation, yawning and making small talk with one another in their ease. It took Cyfrin no time to disable them, flinging lightning from his outstretched hands like a whip as he passed. The tendrils struck the guards, each crying out for only a moment before falling in convulsing heaps to the marble floor. The strangled screams alerted

BONUS CHAPTER

the guards on the inside, the lot of them drawing their weapons as Cyfrin rushed the entry hall. The largest knight, the one with the cleanest and most decorated armor, stepped to the forefront.

He held his sword high, pointing it forward with a look of cold fury as he addressed Cyfrin. "You have made a grave error here today, peck. Lay down your weapons, and perhaps we will grant you mercy."

Cyfrin paused, cocking his head to the side. The scent of honeysuckle and rosemary was much heavier here, intoxicating as it prodded the newly awakened beast inside him. There were thirty men at arms before him, maybe more. His eyes passed over them, over their swords and spears and veiled fear. A smile broke across his face, despite his best efforts.

The soldiers barely had time to scream. Cyfrin fired off a bolt of electricity into the first guard. It struck him through the chest, shooting out the other side and into the guard beside him. A chain of lightning momentarily linked them all as they stood suspended in a blue glow. Thirty castle guards dropped with one fell swoop. He had held himself back from unleashing completely lest the marble hall become rubble around them, leaving all thirty soldiers frothing and foaming on the entryway floor.

They should feel lucky to still draw breath, he thought. But all prior hope of a bloodbath had been washed from his brain with the unrelenting pull inside of him.

Cyfrin felt frantic as he raced through the castle, felling knights, and throwing open chamber doors as he went. He left screaming lords and ladies in his wake, each convinced he was there to kill them. The smell was everywhere, building as the feeling in his core pulled him up, up, up. Floor after floor he went, waking the whole of the castle from the drunken slumbers as he searched desperately.

BONUS CHAPTER

Where is she? Where is she? Where is she?! His thoughts had become wild, his need to find the princess all-encompassing.

This was different than it had been the last month. Unlike the drive he had to save the Dawnbringer and redeem himself, this was a feral need. It had stripped him of caution, of common sense, leaving him with only the mind-numbing roar in his core.

Cyfrin had reached a narrow staircase, twisting up to the highest tower of the castle. He could hear knights gathering in the floors below over the screams of the nobles. The scent was drifting in swirls of beckoning warmth from the floor above.

There, he thought as he shot forward onto the stairwell. *She's there.*

He reached the top to find a short hallway, only four doors lining the wall to his right. And at the very end of the hall, like a beacon to their prize, were a gathering of palace knights. They had begun to yell, brandishing their weapons towards him, and closing ranks about the door beside them.

Cyfrin scoffed, rolling his eyes. Fools. They've exposed the very thing they were trying to keep hidden.

One of the knights loosed a spear in tandem with several arrows fired at this head. He stopped them with a wave of his hand, disintegrating the wood and steel with a crack of lightning that shook the narrow hall. He watched their fear reach a fever-pitch, saw their panic as he descended upon them with a grin. Their screams mingled with his lightning's mighty crack, the fight over before it had really begun. In a matter of seconds, the final line of defense for the princess fell at his feet.

Cyfrin stood looking down at them all, amused by their frothing, slightly convulsing bodies. Then the scent took

BONUS CHAPTER

over his senses once more, and the beast within him raised its head in wait. He turned to face the heavy oaken door beside him, surveying its exterior.

Dried flowers had been tacked by the door frame, what looked to be tumbled river rocks mounted haphazardly just above it. He glanced down at the floor, noting the flecks of paint that looked to have been dragged out by the hem of a skirt. His heart was fluttering in his chest, making his breathing hitched.

He shook his head, brow furrowing. *What in the End's great gate is wrong with you, Cyfrin? Get ahold of yourself,* he scolded internally, reaching for the doorknob with clammy hands.

It was locked. He smirked, breathing a laugh. Such a small, meaningless act of defense. But at least she had tried.

The sound of forces gathering on the floors below was growing in volume, yet Cyfrin hesitated. He couldn't imagine the fear this poor female must be feeling. It would only be made worse the second he set foot in her room, the second she saw him for who he was: Her would-be enemy. He frowned, lifting the hood of his cloak up to shield his face.

There was nothing for it, no better way to proceed with the situation. This was their best and only chance, regardless of how the princess might feel in the process. He sighed and waved his hand, electricity flashing. The satisfying *click* of the tumblers within indicated that it had unlocked, and he pushed the door wide as he stepped silently into the room.

It was dark, the only light coming from the moon hanging low in the distance. Hand-drawn pictures and bits of paint scattered the floor, hung from every inch of wall around him. There were collected rocks of various sizes,

BONUS CHAPTER

dried plants and herbs placed haphazardly across the small room. His gaze hovered over a discarded set of armor and his eyebrows raised, curious as to its purpose in the room of a princess.

The window was open wide, reminding Cyfrin of his own room in the Grand Halls. The wind swept in past him, circling his face before leaving in an unnatural gust to report to Milios. The bed was disheveled but empty, an empty bottle of mead by the abandoned pillow and a tiara thrown nearly onto the floor at the foot. As Cyfrin stared at it, he sensed movement from behind him. He barely had time to unsheathe the knives from his belt and spin about to block the assault.

He stopped a dagger mere inches from his chest, his attacker disconnecting from him as he guarded himself. His eyes flew to the shadowed face, and time stood still.

Immediately, all doubt about the princess's identity left his mind. She was Alora reincarnate, though the green eyes staring murderously up at him were that of the late King Yvonar. Her jet-black curls were tangled about her shoulders, the imprint of her pillow still shadowed on her face.

Zenoths be, what a perfect face it is.

Cyfrin had never seen something so absolute in its beauty. Even through the clear danger in her icy glare, she was art in motion, a song of love brought to life before him. The indescribable feeling that had pulled him here was throwing its head back, roaring in triumph and demand—demand to embrace her. He felt his power grow suddenly white-hot, pushing against his skin and agitating the wards that held it in. From the bottom of his vision, he saw the runes tattooed across his face begin to dimly glow. He had only a second to wonder why, when he wasn't using his powers, they had begun to alight.

BONUS CHAPTER

In this moment of distraction, the princess pulled back and took her opening. She lunged once more, Cyfrin raising his blades to block hers. But she was quick, much quicker than he had given her credit for. The hilt of her dagger flashed as it drew upwards, slamming into the bottom of his jaw. He grunted in pain and surprise, his head snapping back and the hood falling clear of his face.

He had to stifle the bark of a laugh that rose in his chest as he adjusted his throbbing jaw. So much for the *helpless princess*. Her attacks were clean and calculated, even in the face of would-be danger. She had training, that much was certain. He drew his gaze back to hers.

She has frozen in place, staring up at him with mouth slightly agape. Something flashed in her eyes as they trailed across his scarred face, something like dawning recognition. She took a step back, and Cyfrin was able to see her body in its entirety. Rolling, full curves placed upon a figure that could have been pulled from the tapestries of the Zenoths back home. A gossamer purple dress clung to her, and Cyfrin felt his heart skip a beat as his eyes lingered a moment too long.

He could hear noise coming from the floor below, the full force of Grathiel's army beginning to awaken. It was painfully clear to him that there would be no reasoning with her, just as Caerani said. And with the fight she had just displayed, simply carrying her away would be out of the question. There was no other way. He gave another glance towards the clothes he was forcing her to leave in, grimacing at himself for diverting from El's plan. She was right, it would have been better to sneak in. But he had completely lost control of himself in that moment, overwhelmed by whatever had blazed to life within him.

Feeling regretful at the first impression he was about to set, he raised a hand and mumbled "Veevanesca". Magick

BONUS CHAPTER

vines materialized below the princess, twisting up her legs and binding her where she stood. Cyfrin watched pure, terrified panic wash over her face, feeling slightly ashamed as she opened her mouth to scream. The vines rose to gag her as she did so, the dagger she held falling from her hands as she struggled. He swept low, catching it by the hilt before it hit the cold marble floor. His eyes passed over the blade, clearly made at the Gofannon forge in the Hidden Village.

What is this doing here? How did she get this? It looked so familiar, but there was no time to study it further. Footsteps, shouts, and cries were echoing towards them from the spiraling staircase that led to their hall. Cyfrin cursed, slipping the dagger into the pouch at his belt and returning his attention to the princess.

The terror had left her, replaced once more by murderous intent and unbridled rage. She struggled against the bonds, her shouts muffling against her gag. Her fight was impressive, reminding Cyfrin of a beautiful, wild beast who had been snared in a trap. He grabbed her by the arm, pulling her to the still-open window and looking down towards the ground. Far below, staring up at them with expressions ranging from humor to wrath, were his friends. His heart thundered in his chest as he swept the princess up into his arms.

Once again, the beast within him roared, and the runes on his skin heated as if he was exerting a great amount of magick. The woman grew still against him as he held her, and he felt a strange warmth reverberate through his being. The door to her bedroom burst open, and guards rushed in. Feeling alive for the first time in twenty years, Cyfrin found it impossible to stop himself from throwing one final smile at them over his shoulder.

He launched from the window frame, holding the

BONUS CHAPTER

trembling princess to his chest. Cyfrin had never set much stock in fate. But in the weightlessness of their fall, it was impossible to ignore the feeling inside of him. The feeling that destiny was grabbing him by the hand and throwing him forth. That the cosmos were awakening to set the world in motion.

AUTHOR'S NOTE

Dearest friends,

This page was originally to be a place for "correct pronunciations". However, I have found that the "correct" way, in many cases, is what feels best for *you*. We have had an incredible artist render sketch of our characters, which can be found on our website, alongside the original pronunciations for the words in the world. But these are guidelines. I encourage you to paint the world as you see fit.

Zenafrost has been my life's work, truly. The people on these pages are my family, breathing soul into the words I've written. And I am so happy that you've chosen to take this journey with them. You have my heart. Thank you.

With a love that extends far past the Beyonds,

Beau

Long live the Dawnbringer

Printed in Great Britain
by Amazon